The Wish Maker

ALI SETHI

PENGUIN BOOKS

PENGUIN BOOKS

THE WISH MAKER

'Written in astoundingly assured prose that belies the author's youth . . .
a steadily absorbing read. Leaves you wishing for much more from Sethi,
whose buzzing talent is unmistakable' *Time*

'Sethi's is a measured, often witty voice that shows admirable control
over the history his protagonist has inherited . . . the wish maker's
world enthralls' *India Today*

'Sethi writes with real feeling . . . *The Wish Maker* is a product of love, both
for the craft of fiction and for what it lets us remember and store for ever'
Chicago Sun-Times

'First-rate . . . Sethi's prose evokes the comic mislocutions of Jonathan
Safran Foer and the vertiginous mania of Zadie Smith'
The New York Times Book Review

'A brilliant example of the new global novel and a sad but
sometimes funny song about the way we live now'
Gary Shteyngart, author of *Absurdistan*

'Debut novelist Ali Sethi creates a dizzying context to growing up in
nineties Pakistan' *Verve* (India)

'A confident and personal debut. Ali Sethi's is a fresh voice from a new
generation of Pakistani novelists'
Mohsin Hamid, author of *The Reluctant Fundamentalist*

'Much as Khaled Hosseini's *The Kite Runner* did for Afghanistan, this timely
first novel, told through the eyes of a boy grappling with adolescence,
brings to life the tumult of Pakistan . . . Individual vignettes are powerful
and vivid, providing insight into a country that is increasingly pivotal on
the world stage' *People Magazine* (US)

'Soars with Sethi's delicate prose and his ability to capture and convey nuances and complexities of human relationships' *Asian Age* (India)

'A bittersweet coming-of-age tale' *USA Today*

'Sethi has promise, style and confidence . . . [He] writes with humour and with a sharp eye' *Outlook* (India)

ABOUT THE AUTHOR

Ali Sethi was born in Lahore, Pakistan, in 1984 and grew up there. In 2002 he left to attend college in the United States and graduated in 2006. He has since written reviews and articles for several publications, local and international, and has co-produced and narrated a documentary on student politics in Pakistan. He lived in New York City for a year and now lives in Lahore, where he is making music.

For Dadi Apa

The difficult task of knowing another soul is not for young gentlemen whose consciousness is chiefly made up of their own wishes.

– George Eliot, *Middlemarch*

ONE

I

The clouds approached from below and went upwards and onwards until they had left behind the view; and it was of the turf, grey turning to green and brown, a mosaic that now grew zones and roads and began to show the specks, expanding into vehicles, that were moving and heading in the pale morning light to destinations of their own.

Naseem was at the airport. She stood near the railing with her small, stout form pressed ahead into the bars. Her feet were placed solidly apart; she was trying to thwart the pushing crowds, trying to dominate the commotion with the square cardboard sign that was held above her head. It said my name (MISTER ZAKI SHIRAZI) in my mother's assertive handwriting.

I waved.

Naseem saw. She lowered the cardboard and grinned.

'Salaam, Naseem.'

She embraced me and tried to take my suitcase.

'Don't worry, Naseem –'

'No, no.'

'Naseem –'

'No.'

'But –'

'No, no.'

I followed her outside, where the air was moist and cold. The new airport had a beige exterior (the old one was white) and was planted with advertisements in the car park: we went past a sign for a restaurant chain, then a live screen that was showing an ad for a new brand of toothpaste. The ad was soundless; it ended with a splash of colour and started up again.

'It's not that cold,' I said.

'You're right,' said Naseem. 'It's not.'

The car was in the last row. A man was waiting inside, a young and relaxed-looking man with his knees drawn up to the steering wheel, his wrists crossed in stylish repose behind his head. He saw us and sprang up; he smiled and nodded vigorously and shook my hand and hurried to take the suitcase from Naseem, who didn't introduce him and instead monitored his movements with a tolerating look, the assessing, unsmiling stringency of delegated authority. She stood behind him and watched as he lifted the suitcase with a moan and hauled it into the boot. The impact sent up the smell of new carpeting.

'Had it serviced,' said Naseem.

She sat next to the driver and gave him unnecessary directions out of the car park. At the toll-booth she gave him ten rupees, which he gave to the warden beyond his window.

'Receipt,' said Naseem and secured it notingly.

The driver rolled up his window and began the drive away from the car park, away from the airport and out onto the road. His hands gripped the steering wheel. He was frowning in concentration and licking his lips.

'New driver,' said Naseem.

'I see,' I said.

'Yes,' she said.

We drove along a curve in the road and the car tilted, and Naseem reached for the strap above her window. Then the road was straight again. A part of it was cordoned off and still being paved; the labourers were absent and had left behind some of their implements as a promise of return. The road led into the bazaar and became cracked and dusty and crowded. Naseem was still holding on to the strap, and switched on the radio with her free hand; it interfered with the noise, the bumping and the shuddering, which lasted for some minutes. After that the bazaar was gone and the road was smooth again: we were in Cantt now, among large residential walls overgrown with bougainvillea and ivy, and among old trees and parks and military compounds that grew behind unproclaiming gates. The road was mostly empty. The driver became emboldened and skipped a traffic light, then another.

Naseem didn't stop him. She was absorbed in the radio: a female voice was lecturing its audience in a soft American accent on the perils and advantages of love. The voice laughed from time to time and Naseem laughed with it, and brazenly, for she was laughing at the audacity and outrageousness of the concept. She slapped her thigh and shook.

'Radio,' she said with a fond nod towards the thing.

'Ah, yes,' I said. 'Radio . . .'

We drove for some minutes in a radio-expecting silence.

'So, then,' she said, 'how is America?'

'America is well,' I said, as though formerly it wasn't. I wanted to say more but the question was vast.

'Good,' said Naseem. 'And how are your studies?'

'My studies are very well.'

'Very good.' She paused, holding on to her strap, her smile one of accepting and continuing goodwill. 'You know there is no place like Saudia.'

She had been recently to perform the Hajj in Saudi Arabia.

'Really?'

'No place like it in the world,' she said, and gave her head a slow and solemn shake. 'Everything they have: KFC, McDonald's, anything at all, you name it and they have it.'

'Really.'

'Oh yes. And the house of God – it opens up your eyes. Everyone is there: black, white, this, that, everyone from everywhere. Over here I am a servant, but over there no one is a servant. It has such a feeling of peace that your heart fills up with tears. I kissed the Black Stone with my own lips.'

'How does it feel?'

She blinked, trying to recall the experience. It took her a moment. 'Like a stone,' she said eventually with a note of surprise.

We passed a hoarding on the bridge. It was advertising a new deal for mobile phones. The model was a local girl and had her shiny shoulders up in a shrug; one hand held her pelvic bone; the other pressed a phone to her ear. Her head was tilted and her enlarged eyes were startled.

'Where is everyone?' I asked.

'Here and there,' said Naseem. 'No rest in this time. But weddings will do that. Always, always, it is madness. You will see when you get home. No one is the same.'

*

The house was on its way. The paint was fresh and drying quickly on the outside walls; the wrought-iron gate was sharp with varnish; the driveway, once lined with cracks, was smooth now and still shining wetly in places with newly laid asphalt. And the lawn was mown. A dense row of marigolds on its fringes gave it the feel of a real garden, rather than just a plot of grass, while at night it became a rich, golden place, a revealed world of glowing depths and shadows, of dimensions and mysteries created by the positioning of hidden lights.

'The bride can't come right now,' said my mother. It was morning and she was talking on the telephone to the tailor, who was altering the blouse and wanted to have another round of measurements. 'This is no way. We have trusted you, and this is what you are doing. We could have gone to many other places, but we came to you. And this is what you are doing. This is no way.'

Eventually my mother granted a time for the fitting but insisted that the tailor should come to the house with the outfit. The bride was resting and would see him briefly, and then he would go back and stitch up the blouse and deliver it on the promised date. After settling with the tailor she spoke to the beautician, again on the phone in the veranda, where she was sitting in a white wicker chair and leaning forward and rocking slightly with apprehension: the beautician was a detached Chinese woman who first wouldn't come to the phone, and who then gave a weak and suspicious-sounding answer, an 'Okay' or a 'Maybe' that confirmed only the possibility of an appointment. And then there was a quarrel with the caterers, who had not included Diet Coke and Diet 7UP in the revised order: my mother threatened to cancel the order; they insisted it was right; she threatened to expose them in the magazine she owned;

and they backed off slowly, coming round to the need for an apology, which she accepted in the end.

'I don't know why I'm doing this,' she said. She meant organizing the wedding, and organizing it single-handedly, for though the funds and the resources had come in from all quarters of the family, there was a feeling, aired more and more now, that the toil had been left disproportionately to my mother. 'I resent it,' she said, and gave a short curt nod. 'I do.'

Then she sighed and sank back into the chair and covered her eyes with her hands, as if to say that she was overworked and undervalued and thus allowed to say unreasonable things from time to time. And when later in the day the wedding cards arrived in a mound from the printer's and were found to be satisfactory, she did say, 'One does it for the children,' in a way that affirmed her organizing role, her skills and her patience, as well as the vague parental function she was serving, and recast the whole thing in a positive light.

'Look at this,' she said, and trailed a proud finger along the first line of the invitation card:

You are cordially invited to the wedding of Samar.

'What do you think?'

I said it was nice.

And it was more than that: it was valid and it was true, the granting of a wish-made send-off to Samar Api, who was my first cousin, once removed, and for whom, after years of separation, I had now come back to do the rites.

*

I had returned to Lahore for the first time since leaving for university. And it was of university that I was still thinking. Over there, in Massachusetts, it was winter break now, the end of the autumn term, and that life – of snow and wind, of blocked, frozen streets and the retreat into heated buildings, the snow continuing to descend outside – that life went on as an imagined progression of familiar feelings: taking the shuttle on time to class in the morning, then from class to the dining halls and back in time for class. And at night: the sofa before the fire in the common room, a place that became noisy and rushed on the weekend with music and dancing and a crowded slippery bar area, and then the culminating solace of a bedroom. That was my memory of it, newly formed. And with it I was filling up the present, knowing too that the halls were locked, the fire dead, the campus emptied and shut down.

That was there, and I was here now, at home.

But home too was changed. The airport was new, and the roads were new; the hoardings and buildings on the way from the airport, many had come up in these last two years alone and pointed again and again to the ongoing nature of things. There was an added estrangement from the known: the drive home was too short, the bridge too small, the trees not high enough on the canal, while in the house there was an odd shrunken aspect to things that made them less than what they once had been: the bed in my room was just a bed, narrow and hard, and the pillow was incongruously large, the room itself just a room with patching walls that would curl with moisture in the summer. The veranda was no longer an avenue, and all day the kitchen had a smell.

'What smell?' said my mother.

The smell of frying oil and onions.

'Drink lots of water,' said my mother.

It had a taste.

'There is no taste in water.'

'There is.'

'Then get your own. Go to the market and get your own. Put your own things in the fridge. Make your own food.'

I got my things from the market and took them to the fridge. And it was full: the raw vegetables were in the bottom compartment, the saalan dishes and the chutneys and condiments on the upper shelves, the preferences of different people stacked precariously and collectively for now to make room for the bride's requirements, which were on the final shelf: a small jug of freshly squeezed orange juice and a few cans of Slim-Fast, and some empty space for other things.

8

'Grilled things,' said my mother. 'Dieting things. But sometimes she wants sweet things. You never know.'

*

My mother was staying indoors. The books and magazines and newspapers in her room, once stacked on the floor and left to accumulate, had been organized and placed on shelves on the walls. There were lamps on all the tables now and no overhead lights: she had read about the adverse effects of bare lightbulbs, and said that she had always felt it as an influence on her temperament but had never had the sense to sit down and identify the problem. She believed in identification: she spent the last few hours of every night researching health-related topics on the Internet. And in the morning she was slow to rise and shift to the sitting area, where she lay again on the sofa and read newspapers, not one by one in quick succession, the way she had before rushing to work, but slowly, and with genuine involvement, lingering over things that had once been irrelevant. Over the course of the morning she drank down the tea in the teapot and sent it many times to be reheated. And she kept the TV alive. She watched it for the news but also for the cooking shows, the talk shows, for Indian shows in which young people stood on stages and sang old film songs with live orchestras behind them, and were then judged by panellists. My mother had favourites whose progress she followed until the end: she noted their singing skills but also their expressions, their dressing habits, their postures and physiques. She knew about physical fitness and sat through the late-morning exercise shows with the fast-paced music in the background. Sometimes she tried to repeat the moves, and the curtains were drawn. Then she showered and went to the office in her new car with the new driver, and Naseem came in to clean the room and afterwards sat on the sofa and watched the TV channels. In the evening my mother returned with Zarmina and Rubab, two new girls who were working with her on the magazine, which had expanded, and required a division between the management of content and revenue: Zarmina commissioned the pieces and subbed the English and sent the files on a CD to the Urdu department, which translated everything for the Urdu version of the magazine; and Rubab sat in a rotating chair at a desk and spoke on the phone to advertisers, making statements about sales and target audience and about the quality of the product, which was made with the 'bouquet' approach and offered a wide range of things to read and things to look at. The last issue of *Women's Journal* had reports on rape and domestic violence, and an interview with the victim of an acid attack who was now seeking treatment in Europe; a long piece on literacy among the women of Pakistan, with pictures of peasant women squatting outside schools in the Sindh Desert, their arms stacked with bangles, and with accompanying pie charts in desert colours that gave percentages and years and the comparative costs of primary education in the four provinces; and a four-page spread on the global community of Muslim women who had in their own ways resisted the recent American invasion of Iraq, a piece written in an admiring and accessible tone by a Pakistani student at the University of Birmingham, UK. The last quarter of the magazine was devoted to Society, to photos of people at tea parties and dinner parties, weddings and milaads, the pictures brightened on a computer and accompanied by the names of the subjects, many of whom called in afterwards to thank the *Women's Journal* team and to give information about upcoming events, the corporate balls and fashion shows that had begun to occur frantically among the people who, in one of the earlier articles in the 'Issues' section, had been described as 'the new crop of disconnected elites that has come up in Karachi and Lahore'.

'Well, it's true,' said my mother, and went on talking despondently on the phone to a woman, an NGO-worker friend of hers who had sold her property just before the boom.

So there had been a boom. And there was talk inside the boom, talk in magazines and on the radio and talk on the TV channels, which had multiplied and were being watched by more and more people. In the morning, while cleaning the rooms, Naseem switched on the TV and saw politicians cut ribbons and make speeches for seated audiences. She heard the speeches and learned about violence, extremism and enlightened moderation. She saw the news when it broke: a programme interrupted, the flashing red silence and the newsreader's announcement; then sirens, policemen, the ongoing chaos at the site of the attack – the bombers had come in from both sides and blown up the cavalcade; the president had escaped but his guards were dead; then the shift of scene to the well-lit studio, where analysts sat behind a long, continuing desk and were questioned by a journalist, who frowned and appeared to take notes. There was talk of the establishment, talk of America and its allies, its interests and its changing relations with the Pakistani military. There was talk of 9/11 and the Jews. And there was talk of Islam, a religion of peace that was being misunderstood. Some channels were devoted exclusively to Islam, to its history and doctrinal particularities, to questions about the hereafter and to questions about the here and now as well – the correct Islamic expressions for meeting and departing, the right amount of head-covering and the issue of make-up, whether things such as nail varnish were haram or halal. And there were channels where these things were taken for granted, channels where women appeared in half-sleeves and sat on sofas with their legs crossed and chatted with other women who held degrees in subjects such as child psychology. The women conversed and then took questions from callers. A housewife from Rawalpindi was worried because her eight-year-old daughter had seen one of the films her father kept in his night-time cabinet. The caller said she wasn't worried about her husband, who was unstoppable; she was worried about her daughter, whose young mind must now be rushing with things the caller couldn't bring herself to articulate, let alone explain in some way to a child. The housewife wanted to know of a way to undo those things and take them back out of the child's mind. The host nodded understandingly and deferred with her palms to the expert, who said that the question was a good one, the issue here was trauma, the child had been exposed at an early age, but there was no way of undoing the exposure; in fact it wasn't even necessary. It was parents who had to accept that children were intelligent and had motives of their own and were always going to break out of sheltered environments. Later in life they became adults and had children of their own and created those very same shelters; and again the children broke past. 'But that is the fact of life,' said the expert and smiled colludingly at the host. 'It is always going and going in circles.'

'Going and going in circles,' said Naseem. She was chopping salad vegetables on the stone worktop in the kitchen. She chopped briskly and transferred the choppings into a bowl, then returned to the act of chopping. 'We are also going in circles.' She said it comically, with a self-disparaging laugh, but also with a philosophical intention, a need to draw connections between ideas and things as they were in the real world, a need she had developed during her time in Saudi Arabia. There she had seen the people of the world brought together in one mission: they wore the same cloth and prayed to the same God and went round and round the same monument. It had alerted her to the presence of a single underlying system.

'The house of God,' she had said. 'It opens up your eyes.'

Now she sought that larger logic in the everyday and came up repeatedly against herself. Last week she had been made the recipient of some money, ten thousand rupees that Daadi, my grandmother, had passed on to her as an offering, a kind of alms given out to mark the approach of a wedding. At once Naseem was planning what to do with it, seeking counsel and discussing possibilities. My mother advised her to invest in a sewing machine and to start a part-time stitching business from her quarter at the back of the house. It was a start, said my mother, and offered to print a black-and-white ad for Naseem in the magazine. Naseem was persuaded. She made the calculations and found that she would have some money left after buying the sewing machine, and she set aside a part of it for a well-known lottery. Then she announced that she was going to buy the bride a wedding gift.

'No, no,' said my mother, who was refusing on behalf of the bride.

'But I must,' said Naseem.

'Why must you?'

'I must.'

'No, but why?'

'*Buss.*'

'But why?'

'She is my child.'

'She is everyone's child, Naseem. We are all doing what we can. And you have done a lot; you have done just as much as the others. You don't have to buy a gift. You must do no such thing.'

Naseem went on swaying where she stood, blushing and looking down at her feet, made emotional by her own offer, which was not that of a servant because it exceeded the means of a servant.

'Save your money,' said my mother. 'Start your sewing business.'

And Naseem smiled and said that she would.

Then the weekend arrived, and she heard that her husband had appeared outside the gate. He was not supposed to be seeing her because he was unemployed after quitting his job at a factory near the village, and was known in these periods to exploit her. Naseem went outside the gate to see. He was there. They spoke. Naseem brought him inside, fed him in the kitchen and allowed him to stay the night. And in the morning, after he had gone, she was filled with remorse, having parted with most of her money and exposed herself again as a weaver of wishes, a person who habitually amounted to nothing.

'You deserve nothing,' said Daadi from her bed. She was in her seventies now and shrivelled; she no longer spent time on the sofa in her room and merely sat on it occasionally with her back hunched, her palms placed for stability on her knees.

Naseem stood where she stood and said nothing, her fists clenched and her toes curling.

'Ten thousand rupees,' said Daadi. Her eyes were narrowed in cold amazement and her eyebrows were up.

Naseem was swaying.

'How much is left?'

Naseem said, 'Two thousand.'

'Two thousand!' said Daadi.

'She can buy a pair of shoes with it,' said Suri and laughed lightly. She was the elder of Daadi's two daughters. She was considered active for her age and lay on the other side of the bed with her back propped up against pillows.

'Or you can give even that to him,' said Hukmi, Daadi's other daughter, who was younger than Suri by three and a half years. She made her comment and looked around to see if the others saw that this was exactly where those two thousand rupees were going to go.

'It was my fault,' said Daadi. 'It was my fault. I shouldn't have given her the money. I should have gone and thrown it in a well.' And this was rhetorical, since there were no wells nearby.

'Oh no,' said Suri calmly. 'You won't throw it in a well. You'll give it to her again. You'll *keep* on giving it to her.'

And Hukmi said, 'And she'll *keep* on giving it to him.'

Naseem, smiling, drawing strength from her own abasement, looked up from the carpet and said, 'Round and round.'

Hukmi looked at her blankly, then looked excitedly at Suri and said, 'Village mentality!'

And Naseem went on smiling, not knowing what that was, not caring at the moment that she didn't; the lift out of the scolding and into the present comicality had enabled her retreat, which was what she wanted.

But the talk in the room was of money even after Naseem had gone; it was of money for the rest of the afternoon, since it was money and not love that made the biggest difference, money that in the end made marriages and families and enabled understandings between people and money that made the world go round and round.

The sisters were inside the boom. Suri's husband was now working out of an office at home and using phones and a computer to trade on the stock market. And Hukmi's husband was running his own showroom of used and reassembled cars near Kalma Chowk on Ferozepur Road. They were living in the same area still but had restyled their homes: the driveways of both houses sloped gently outwards past steel gates, and the names of the owners and the house numbers were inscribed on separate brass plaques that were nailed to the outside walls. Inside too there had been changes: the upstairs bathrooms were fitted with jacuzzis and modern showers; there was wallpaper on the walls; there were split-level air-conditioners with remote controls in the living-dining area and also in the bedrooms; and there was wall-to-wall carpeting downstairs, for which the removal of shoes was required. One of the homes, Suri's, had been used in an ad for a telephone service-providing company, and the experience was continually recalled with surprise and merriment: the names of the executives and the professionalism they had shown from start to finish, and the antics of the cast and crew, and the things they had said, on screen and then off screen, about the house and its contents.

'The sofas they all loved,' said Suri. She was not one to boast but this was a fact.

'And the loveseat,' said Hukmi. 'The actress wouldn't come off it. She said no, no, leave me here, leave me here.' She closed her eyes and swooned.

'*Taubah!*' said Daadi, and clapped her hands excitedly. '*Taubah!*'

To Suri and Hukmi she had surrendered her dependence. They took Daadi in the morning to the market, to the bank and to the tailor's and to the fruit and vegetable stalls outside Pioneer Store, where they haggled for her with the vendors, since it was they who now managed her money. They took her to the doctor's when she felt unwell but only when their own attempts to locate the problem had failed: they measured her temperature with a thermometer, took readings on the blood-pressure pump, stroked her back and monitored her posture on the bed. They were followers of physio-therapy and had replaced her mattress and had made her buy a new foam pillow that kept her neck straight at night. They regulated the items on her mantelpiece, the medicines she could need at any time and also the things she needed generally, the Swaleen pills and the packets of Johar Joshanda, which she drank every morning to kill the colds that developed suddenly in winter. The doctor had said that at her age it was necessary to take precautions. And for this reason the windows were kept shut, the heater was kept alive until night, and the tub of Vicks nose rub was always kept on the bedside table, between a tall cylinder of Tender Rose air-freshener and a framed photograph, old and spotted now, of Flying Officer Sami Shirazi, Daadi's son and my father, who had been dead for more than twenty years.

'I can't sleep,' said Daadi. She was sitting up in bed. Her hair was spoiled. She had been changing the position of her head on the pillow but the noise outside had gone on.

'You'll never say anything,' said Suri unhelpfully. She meant that Daadi was unwilling to go outside and stop the labourers who were setting up the marquee on the lawn. 'You won't say a word.' She lifted a hand and ran it unhurriedly through her hair. 'You won't say or do a thing.'

Daadi said, 'What can I say?'

'You can say you will not have people in this house after two o'clock. You can say that, can't you? This is your house too. You too have given for this wedding.'

'We have all given,' said Hukmi grandly.

Daadi frowned for a while, then said, 'Does anyone listen? Does anyone care what I say?'

Suri said, 'And how will they care if you keep sitting here and saying things? How will they care, when they have been *allowed* to think that they own everything?'

Hukmi said, 'They *don't* own everything.'

Daadi continued to frown, her annoyance brought out in this way and made binding by the involvement of her daughters. 'I am telling her,' she said decidedly. 'I am telling her to wrap it up. There will be no hammering here. There will be no tent and no wedding. She can think what she likes; she can write it in her magazine.'

She meant to say these things to my mother, her daughter-in-law, who lived in the same house and ran a magazine and was organizing the wedding and was felt to have acted as if she owned everything.

'There will be no wedding,' said Daadi. 'We are not responsible for any wedding.'

She had gone too far.

'There is no need,' said Suri philosophically, 'for anyone to do anything for anyone else.'

'And still people do things,' said Hukmi.

'They do,' said Suri.

'From their hearts,' said Hukmi.

'From their hearts.'

'And we are doing whatever we can from our hearts.'

'Because we feel,' said Suri and placed a hand on hers, 'that the girl is *our* child, that this wedding is *our* duty. We are not doing it for ourselves.'

And Hukmi said, 'There is no doubt in it. There is not a doubt.'

It had come up earlier in the week. They had gone to Saleem Fabrics to buy outfits for the groom's mother and sisters. It was an important marital tradition – the women of one family gifting embroidered cloth to the women of the other, so they all went: Daadi, Suri, Hukmi, my mother. And inside, amid the unfurling fabrics and the busy mewl of bargainers, they had managed somehow to agree: they consulted one another on colours and patterns, pressed their fingers to the material, made faces and asked for rates. Within the hour they had formed a pile of possibilities that was then reduced to eight final pieces, two from each of them. They monitored the measurements and oversaw the folding and wrapping. And at the counter their resolve collapsed: they were short of money, this was typical, who was short of money, and why should *we* give when *you* haven't, and from there the accusations flew: I have done so much for this wedding while *you* have done nothing, *well*, well, what? Well, *we* are not responsible. Then who is? Who is?

The cashier pressed his palms together. Who was the mother of the bride?

They looked at one another and looked away.

Hands went into handbags. I'll pay, no I'll pay, no let me, no please . . .

And they left the shop and returned to the house in the car with the gift-wrapped bundles clutched to their laps.

*

I had been asked to distribute the invites. It was distressing. I didn't recognize most of the names and addresses that now appeared in embossed golden script on the envelopes. But weddings, like funerals, required staging to an audience, and the final list of names had come to one hundred and seventy-three. I now had to make perhaps as many trips to unknown houses in the city and was grateful when Isa and Moosa, my cousins, offered their help.

They had changed. Isa, Suri's son, had settled into adulthood (he was twenty-three this year) with an airtight, burp-coming chest and a toughened but tolerant look. He wore full-sleeved shirts with the sleeves rolled up to his elbows and with his thumbs tucked into the pockets of his jeans, which were fitted along the thighs and bulged provocatively at the back with his wallet. (He had joined one of the new international banks on Main Boulevard.) When we met he posed many quick questions about life in America and then answered them for himself. He asked about housing, rent, taxes, interest rates, and then disregarded my answers and delivered an unprompted omen on the boom. 'Too much too soon,' he said in English, shaking his head gloomily, and I heard him repeat it later at night, so that it appeared to have been picked up from one of the new business channels on TV.

And Moosa had changed too, but not in the same way as Isa, who had come to inhabit his personality with an air of confirmation. Moosa, Hukmi's son, was twenty-one this year, only two years younger than Isa (and older than me) but somehow elderly already, as though he had learned a humbling lesson that had left him subdued and even grateful; he wore sweatshirts and baseball caps and walked around the house with a slouch. And he hadn't shaved in weeks, and responded to related inquiries with a smile.

'Mullah!' I had cried in greeting.

'Naw, man,' he said, shaking his head in the new disarmed way, 'bro's a hippie now. No more drama, man. No more of that stuff.'

It wasn't clear what he was referring to – he was aggressive once but that was long ago, a thing from childhood.

'Smoking?' I said.

Again he shook his head, this time in defeat. 'Old habits, man . . .' And again he smiled, incorporating the habit into his new, pleasant take on life.

Their car was now a red Honda City that Isa had acquired with a loan from the bank. It was a strong, stout car, inexpensive but efficient; Isa gave me a proud external tour of the thing, tapping the shiny bonnet and praising the tough tyres that he claimed could handle a mountain. 'Get in gear,' he said, soaring his hand like an aeroplane, 'and that's it. Take off.'

'Frickin' awesome,' said Moosa, who was standing nearby and nodding.

I thought of the old Suzuki with its one functional headlight, its dark, furry boot and slackened dashboard. The memory was attached to the faults, things we had then wished away.

'Solid,' I said, and knocked on the bonnet to confirm it. 'Yup. Looks good. Take it for a ride?'

'Sir,' said Isa obligingly and held open the shiny door.

Most of the houses were in Defence, and these were easy to find – the division into sectors was surprisingly reliable. In two trips we had delivered more than half the cards. But areas like Gulberg and Garden Town were difficult: the houses had retreated from the roads, which had succumbed to boutiques and restaurants and shopping plazas, many still bare with cement and guarded by smart neon screens that came alive at night and painted promising pictures of standards surpassed and goals achieved. The houses were hidden behind these hasty conjurings, lost in a confusion of unnamed lanes that often died abruptly in empty plots. And other parts were stranger: the one time we went to Mughalpura our car got stuck in an alley. There were no boutiques here and no plazas, only small, unshuttered shops on the sides and rubbish heaped on the streets. Our car was stranded between a bus and a donkey cart, and attracted a pack of children, who were thrilled by our misfortune and banged their fists on the bonnet and dragged their squeaky palms across the windows.

Isa lowered his window and shouted, *'Maaderchod!'*

The laughing boy darted into the recessed shade of a house and made a shoving gesture with his fist.

'Frickin' *wild*,' said Moosa, who was sitting in the front and wearing sunglasses.

The children stared and kept walking, past the car and then along the sides of the bus, dragging their palms with slow sureness across its shut doors.

Moosa said, 'They're like *monkeys.*' He lit a cigarette and lowered his window a little.

And Isa said, 'Education,' and stared defiantly at the children outside, without saying whether he thought this was the problem or the solution.

Morning was spent locating caterers and light-wallahs in obscure, grimy corners of Ichhra, then ordering the flowers in bulk from stalls in Liberty and stopping at the roundabout to negotiate with the dhol-wallahs, who wore starched silver turbans and yellow clothes and sat on the footpath with their drums. They took down the address and promised to be there on the night of the wedding. But there was more to do the next day, as the chores were renewed and led again into the afternoon, which was long and touched with sunshine and then a little cold, the large low sun hanging red behind the rising dust. In the evening we were asked to collect Aasia and Maheen, sisters to Isa and Moosa respectively, from their tuition centres in Muslim Town. They were in secondary school now and were preparing for their end-of-term exams but had nothing to say on the subject; they sat at the back of the car with their mobile phones, and played with the buttons and watched the luminous screens for results. They were girly in their habits but physically complete: their shalwar kameezes were tight around the waist and accentuated the bust and the pelvis, the sleeves short and modern. Aasia was older and had stocky upper arms that she stroked from time to time as if to soothe a rash. She had thin eyebrows and stylish black glasses with thick rims, and wore her hair in a ponytail that rose and fell in a fluffy *S*. Maheen was pale and lanky, also ponytailed, and wore no make-up other than a striking smudge of black around the eyes. Both carried handbags. They were at that place where, after years of conflict, they were discovering a quiet understanding with their mothers, who now appeared sympathetic and weirdly familiar.

At night I went with Isa and Moosa to see the new places of leisure. There was a mini-golf course near Centre Point with gently sloping islands and fountains that coughed colourful water; a karaoke bar in Defence Market that played songs too new for nostalgia and not new enough to stir up the excitements of the present; and once a dim sheesha bar in Gaddafi Stadium, where two waiters in waistcoats sat idly at a table, surrounded by the dark décor and a ghostly absence of customers. They were surprised to see us, and talked and motioned erratically as they led us up a winding wrought-iron staircase into the smoking section. We settled into a sofa by the window and I saw that our arrival had stopped the advancements of a date: they were sitting in a corner, the boy now looking sourly in our direction, the girl speaking rigidly to the table as though someone had just switched on the lights after promising not to. An abandoned hookah sat between them like undestroyed evidence. They ordered the bill and paid it quickly, and left maintaining a careful physical distance.

And that was it. There was nothing more to do. There were still no bars or nightclubs in Lahore or in the rest of the country, where alcohol was banned. Isa said it was unnecessary since people went on doing what they had always done. He gave the example of Dubai, where they had achieved some kind of regulation by allowing alcohol only in the clubs; you couldn't buy a bottle and take it home with you. That system was better because it allowed things in small amounts and saved people from excess in the end.

'Over here,' he said, 'everything goes on underground. Everyone does everything.' He meant the people in the Society pages, from whose world he was excluded. He went on to list their vices in a burning whisper: 'Parties-sharties, coke-shoke, anything and every-thing, E *bhenchod*, speed and heroin.' He recovered his voice and said, 'What the fuck is booze, man? It's nothing.'

'Orgies,' said Moosa with a smile of depravity, a guilty smile that suggested complicity of intent if not in the act itself. 'Swapping partners. There's a club in Karachi where you swap your car keys first.' He laughed mordantly, as if at a hard but distant memory of the thing. 'And gays. So many gays.' He said it with a sigh of amazement, a yearning for a time when it was still an occasional occurrence and not a pervasive phenomenon, a thing that happened but didn't yet demand a reckoning by showing up so obviously around him.

'And bombs?' I asked.

'And bombs,' said Moosa, who hadn't thought of it like that. 'And bombs.'

'Basically it's all changing,' said Isa, whose vision of it had suddenly expanded and gone beyond the horizon; he saw it all at once and it compelled him to bring up his hand and rock it to either side like a raft in water. 'It's all up for grabs,' he said. 'It's all up for grabs.'

The alcohol still came from bootleggers. And their names were the same: Samuel, Emanuel, Joseph, Ilyas, Christians with purchasing licences. The imported bottles were sent from the warehouses of embassies in Islamabad, and in Lahore they were always more expensive. One evening we set out in the car to acquire our stock for the wedding. We were following directions delivered by the man, who was gruff and edgy on the phone and spoke only in codes ('the stuff' was ready, he said, five 'browns' and five 'whites'). The place was in Cantt, which was surprising, since only rich people and retired generals lived in Cantt. We got lost trying to find it. It was late already; the maghrib azaan had sounded and the sun had vanished behind the thick, dark trees of a park. Night would soon descend, and the policemen would surface at the kerbs, waiting to stop cars like ours (too rich to be poor, too poor to be rich) so they could search the seats and boots with torches.

'Dogs,' said Moosa, 'bribe-eaters.'

'No worries,' said Isa, who had tried this sort of thing and succeeded.

We found it in a dusty lane behind the polo grounds. It was a large grey house guarded by a tall gate of thick blue iron. The owner's name was inscribed on a white plastic plaque outside. It was not the name of the bootlegger, who went only by Ashfaaq.

Moosa offered to ring the bell.

'No,' said Isa and dialled a number into his mobile phone.

Moosa began to gallop his fingers on the dashboard.

'Don't,' said Isa.

Moosa didn't.

'Ji!' said Isa to the phone, suddenly buoyant. 'We are outside. Yes, right outside. Okay, no problem, no problem.' He held up the phone to check that it was the same number, then tossed it into the dashboard.

'Coming?' said Moosa.

Isa nodded. He was watching the gate beyond, which opened at last with a whine and a clang: a man emerged with his shoulders thrown back as if to further project the bulge of his stomach. A duffel bag was carried on his palms. He paused at the gate and looked quickly to either side.

'Boss,' said Isa through his window. He brought two fingers to his forehead in a casual salute.

'Boss,' said the man in response, with a wide but withholding smile that took in the seats, the open dashboard, our clothes and faces.

'Stuff ready?' said Isa.

The man passed him the bag, and Isa settled it in his lap and searched it with his hand, rattling the glass inside. 'Set,' he said and brought out the cash. He counted it carefully to ensure it was the right amount, licking his forefinger every few notes.

The man watched without altering his expression.

Isa stacked the notes on his knee and handed them over in a drooping wad. 'Otherwise? All well?'

'God's grace,' said the man with a hand on his heart.

Isa held on to a look of contentment and reversed the car. He kept his speed in the lane, then outside the lane, on the streets, avoiding the checkposts and waiting until the danger had passed. And now came the rise of Sherpao Bridge, the wind and the lights in the sweep of transit: it was a memory and then a feeling, sitting in another car with Samar Api, her face turned to the window and waiting for a thrill that by then had always passed.

I looked now and found that there was no horizon, only the lights of distant houses coming on in the dark.

*

The days leading up to the wedding were marked by the bride's absence. She was to be unveiled on the last night, after the two families had established themselves in a series of marital procedures that began with a milaad. It was held at our house on a weeknight. The veranda was covered in white bedsheets, which were spread out in overlapping squares and spotted with maroon velvet cushions rented from a shop in Canal Park. It was a ladies-only event; they left their shoes at the entrance and sat in solemn rows on the floor, their heads covered and swaying to sad songs in praise of the Prophet. Then we attended a dholki at the groom's house. Our party went in two cars, the men in starched white cotton and the women in fabrics of varying intensities, led by Daadi, who wore cream silk and a collaring of pearls, and approached the house with a frail arm in the nook of Naseem's elbow. We were showered with rose petals at the entrance. Hands were held and cheeks were kissed. A photographer knelt and took pictures. We were shown onto the enclosed lawn and were asked to take the front row of chairs, Daadi in the centre, Naseem at her feet on the carpet. Instantly she began plying Daadi with tissue paper to show that she was cared for in unfamiliar environments; twice Suri and Hukmi stopped a bearer to demand a glass of water for Daadi, and my mother leaned in repeatedly to name the guests and to locate them within the forming family network. Daadi listened with a steady unsurprised expression as though the accruing information only validated opinions that had been aired earlier.

The dances began. First the groom's aunts performed the *luddi* in slow, restrained circles. Their dupattas were tied like sashes across their torsos and slipped when they bent to clap. Then the young men of the clan performed a rowdy bhangra. They wore matching black kurtas and yellow scarves in siphons around their necks, and kicked the air and jabbed their forefingers at the ceiling. Now a hush fell upon the room, and someone cried, 'Auntie! It's Auntie's turn!' There was whistling and hooting as a well-preserved woman emerged from the seated crowd and took confident, youthful steps into the centre of the room. Her golden sari held its shine in brassy dents. She began to tap her foot to the gathering beat, her eyes closed, a hand massaging the chunky pendant at her throat. She was warming up. And now, her feet moving, she began to dance, but slowly, using only the features of her face, her mouth and her eyes and her eyebrows, and occasional twirls of her hand for expression. Daadi watched the dance with her own hands folded in her lap. She watched when Auntie closed her eyes and smiled, watched when Auntie began to dance in circles and stumbled and scowled and resisted with her fists the attempts of a concerned relative who was trying to take her away.

Later it was agreed that the event was mediocre at best, the groom's relatives brash and uncouth and overly affectionate and oddly endearing in their lack of refinement. It was a way of measuring the first defeat, theirs, against the success that was expected to be ours.

But the next event was a dholki organized by Aasia and Maheen, and it fell into the hands of their friends, girls as well as boys, many of whom were newly befriended and took their time to arrive. They began to appear on the lawn after dinner had been served, the girls in long, flowing skirts and short blouses, the boys in dark blazers and shawls that were worn over plain shalwar kameezes. Their arrival caused excitement among the guests: there was talk now of dancing and speculation about the possible pairings. In a corner the girls and boys were being organized into dancing positions by their leader, a thin, rosy girl called Bushra who had come from Dubai and wore her hair in a pile and was instructing her subordinates with swift slashing movements of her arm. A rumour began to circulate, instigated by a male fashion designer in a declarative mood, about the girl's temper at a photo shoot; she was a model or had been a model in the past; it was a shoot she had done for a magazine or a newspaper; the story travelled to the veranda, which had been converted with a screen into a place for men to stand with drinks and chat. Isa's colleagues from the bank were there, and Moosa was trying unsuccessfully to enter their conversation. He was nodding a little too much, his loud laughs were incongruous, and he was drinking against this growing failure as a form of resistance, a refusal to submit; soon he was lost in an expression of bitter recall and staring with a drunk's disdain at the extended folly of sobriety. He was seen wagging his finger at someone, then smiling slyly and saying something about loans. After that he attached himself to the idea of Bushra, who was about to start her dance. He announced it many times, in each instance with fresh excitement, and it began to have an effect on the gathering, which dispersed and reformed into a crowd of clapping onlookers. Bushra danced alone in a clearing to a fast-paced song about a veil the singer wanted her lover to touch: she was dancing back and forth with her own veil held taut between her hands, plunging forward and coming up and plunging and coming back up. Among the watching women there were expressions of admiration, shock, enchantment and developing interest, as well as boredom and mild contempt. And the men's expressions on the whole were serious and preoccupied. Then Bushra was gone; she had sat down abruptly, and in her place a boy was dancing to the rest of the song, which was the lover's audacious response to the part about the veil. The boy too was fair-skinned and danced with slow movements of his shoulders, and it was instantly sexual, it was sexy in the extreme, and in the men's gathering to the side this was expressed as encouragement, acknowledged with small smiles and nods of recognition, while among the women it caused a contagion of chortling and hand-holding shyness. The song ended and another began; another dance was danced; the choreography went on as before and began to lose its grip on the audience, which was increasingly restless. There came a moment when the clearing in the centre was empty and the music continued unattended. A clapping uncle made the first incursion into this emptiness. And then the night belonged to all the guests, a democracy of dance that went on for almost an hour, and at last began to fade through small desertions, through partings and departures and through strange, sorrowful glances that seemed to acknowledge an unchanging truth that was always there towards the end.

So the day arrived. Almond-shaped lights appeared on the outside walls, on the frangipani tree at the edge of the lawn and around the pillars in the porch. A brass band was installed at the gate and told to perform the main tune only when the groom and his entourage arrived. To pass the time the band played patriotic tunes, and they drew the attention of mirasis: they appeared at the gate in their tattered clothes and stood behind their leader, who held a tambourine in one hand and held out the other hand and recited a long, musical benediction that was dependent for completion on implied acts of charity. When no one came they struck their tambourines and sang traditional wedding songs. The manager of the brass band came outside and told the mirasis to go away; the mirasis stopped singing and stared reproachfully. The manager went inside and complained, and after a while the mirasis were paid and left, and the brass band was able to go on playing patriotic tunes.

In the driveway the caterers had set up long tables and lined them with steel dishes. For now the dishes were empty and the lids were raised; the forks and spoons and knives were spread out underneath in adjoining rows, and every table had its own ostentatious display of salads and chutneys, desi as well as Continental. Bearers in white uniforms hurried out of the kitchen with trays of stainless steel on their palms and carried them into the bloated white marquee covering the lawn, where guests were sitting in chairs and standing around charcoal braziers, and were turning again and again to look at the elevated stage where a sofa had been placed before a screen of hanging garlands. The sofa was empty, and was waiting for the bride and groom, who were going to appear after dinner, but first the marquee had to fill up. At last dinner was announced, and the guests gathered in lines by the tables in the driveway and returned with their plates and drinks to the lawn, where the chatter was suddenly loud and hectic and the sounds from the brass band outside had reached a pitch.

Inside, removed from the music and laughter, the bride was complaining.

'This is too tight,' said Samar Api and snarled. 'I can't even breathe.'

'Try to sit up,' I suggested.

She was sitting cross-legged on her bed, slouching and making dejected faces at the ceiling. Her eyebrows, arched and sharpened during a frantic, seven-hour session at the beauty salon, had acquired strange new angles at the edges, and gave her face a cunning and almost comical look. Cracks appeared in the layer of foundation on her forehead when she frowned; it had been applied clumsily; her sleeves lifted when she sighed and showed the unpainted ochre skin underneath. She tugged at her blouse in agitation. Stars fell to the carpet.

'Stop it,' said my mother. She had entered the room and was holding a sheaf of envelopes. She dropped them into Samar Api's lap and began to count on her fingers: 'Five thousand from Mrs Khokhar, ten from Mrs Zaidi and a crystal decanter from the Shahs. That's fifteen plus a gift. Write it down.'

'My blouse is too tight,' said Samar Api.

'O God,' said my mother.

'And the foundation is coming off.'

'I knew this would happen.'

'I can't go outside like this.'

'Typical.'

'I can't.'

My mother was still. She shot me a wounded look and marched out of the room. I watched her from the window as she returned to the lawn, pulling her mouth into a smile for the guests.

'Did you bring it?'

'Here,' I said, and produced a flask from my pocket.

Samar Api held it, looked at it, then threw back her head and drank from it. The taste was stronger than she expected; she made

28

a gagging, fishlike face and fumbled under the bed for her cigarettes.

'Take it easy,' I said.

'Don't tell me that.'

'I'm just saying . . .'

'Don't.' She paused to light a Marlboro, squinting against the smoke. She drank from the flask again, prepared for the tatse, her eyes closed in advance. 'Do you think she's angry?'

'Come on,' I said, and took the flask from her hand. 'You know what she's like.'

'I know but still –'

'No –'

'No, I know –'

We were quiet. The room became vacant and was taken up by the sounds from outside.

'Is he here yet?' she asked.

'Any minute,' I said, watching the window. 'Any minute now.'

2

We had grown up together in the house. She was really my father's first cousin: her mother, Chhoti, was Daadi's younger sister and lived with her husband in Barampur, a small village that she disliked and considered unsuitable for the raising of her only child. So at the age of two Samar Api came to live with Daadi in Lahore. Two years later I was born, and though in moments of hostility she claimed to be my aunt, entitled by the nature of that position to deferential treatment, we were raised from the start to consider ourselves part of the same litter.

We weren't alone. Suri and Hukmi often went away in the afternoons and left their children with Daadi in the house. Aasia and Maheen stayed inside, played with toys and fought; and Isa and Moosa played squash against the wall of the veranda and cricket on the lawn with the boys of the neighbourhood. Occasionally they allowed me to play with them: they made me wait in the driveway, then let me field the ball or stand behind the wickets; and then they withdrew, sometimes citing a lack of skill as the cause, and sometimes nothing at all. It was made clear to me from the start that I wasn't one of *them*, since *they* had fathers, one each, whereas mine had left me for the skies.

My father, Sami Shirazi, had been a flying officer in the Pakistan Air Force. I had never met him. He died when I was minus two months old; my mother was heavily pregnant when news of his death reached our house. He was flying a new kind of aeroplane above the Sonmiani Hills when a fault occurred in the control column, causing it to lock, and the plane spun out of control.

I wasn't told the rest. It was withheld from me, for instance, that after taking the squadron leader's call my mother had abandoned the telephone and wandered with a hand on her belly out onto the lawn, where she had tried ambitiously to vomit. It was also withheld from me that the incident was quietly mourned – accidents in the armed forces were not to be played up – and a fussy funeral was not observed. In any case nothing had survived the crash, nothing but a few resilient components from inside the aircraft that were taken away at once for an inquiry. Daadi didn't take the news. She fumbled for her sleeping pills and took mental leave. Suri and Hukmi sat by her side and stroked her back, soothed her with words when she awoke, made her drink glasses of water, had her pace the room and encouraged her to go back to sleep. It went on like this until my mother walked in one afternoon with a baby in her arms, and Daadi sat up to receive the baby, reviewed its features and saw that they were hers. Only two words came out of her quivering mouth: 'My grandson.' Then she burst into howls. Suri and Hukmi began to stroke her back, and my mother recovered the baby from her arms and clasped it to her own chest, trying very hard not to cry.

And so I came to learn that I had been given to Daadi as compensation for the death of her son. 'Remember,' she would say, pointing a forefinger to the ceiling, 'with one hand Allah takes and with the other He gives. You were given to us.'

She taught me to recognize my father in the pictures on her mantelpiece. First he was a boy of six, posing with his cricket bat. His hair had been combed into two tidy flaps and his scalp was a stream. His face was guilty: the eyes were frightened and staring, a bit of tongue was showing – he had done something exciting and adventurous that had later turned regrettable, and he was trying now to hide it. Suri and Hukmi stood behind him. They were nine and seven respectively, wore matching white frocks, and stood with their fists clenched and their chins raised, their eyes aware of the photographer's presence and looking on mistrustfully.

At seventeen my father enrolled in the Air Force Academy and went away to live in Risalpur. He was a young man in this next photo, a cadet like the rest of his teammates, who had just partici-pated in a hockey match. He wore a vest and stood with his chest out; he had scored the last goal and his side had won the match, and his heart was still beating from the exertion. The boy beside him was starting to smile. My father had cracked a joke about the cameraman, and his friend was trying not to laugh. The other boys wore morose expressions to please the coach, who sat in the central chair in a tracksuit and was a middle-aged man with a dark, jowly, no-nonsense face, his hair dyed and combed back and his fists positioned demandingly on his knees. The names were listed under the picture on yellowing cardboard. *Second Row, L to R (standing): M. Khalil, B. Jabbar, S. Shirazi . . .*

But he outgrew the prankster and graduated from the academy, and passed the various tests and conversion courses, until he was posing for a picture with the first jet he was going to fly. He wore his g-suit here and was frowning in the sun, preparing himself for the flight, though he couldn't yet imagine the feeling. The new, unworn helmet was raised to his heart. *To my mother*, it said at the bottom in a swift, looping hand, *with all my love, Sami.*

'Look,' said Daadi, singling it out from among the other pictures on her mantelpiece. 'Your father was such a dashing young man.'

My father was a dashing young man in Daadi's room. But in my mother's room he was someone else, a scattered man who lived in many things. The few books he had owned were kept separate from my mother's in the last drawer of her bedside table, which had once belonged to him: they were books on aviation, *The Pilot's Encyclopedia of Aeronautical Knowledge* and *Episodes from the History of Pakistan Air Force: An Insider's Account*, and a book called *Poems by Faiz*, in which there was Urdu as well as English writing. The pages of this last book were crisp and deliberately yellowed, and the writing was black and rich. Some of the pages had folded corners.

'He memorized the ones he liked,' said my mother. 'And he recited them to me sometimes.'

I told Daadi.

She raised her chin and folded her hands in her lap, and said, 'I don't know about that. All I know is that he was a very serious young man.'

But there were pictures that my mother had and they testified to his whims. One morning he was stark and unshaven and went out to row a boat in a lake, or a river – only a stretch of water was visible behind him – and his hair was dirty and uncombed, his eyes almost shut against the glare. My mother said he looked like that because he had drunk a lot of alcohol at night.

'Nonsense,' said Daadi in her room. 'Who tells you these things? He never touched it. Others may have, but he didn't. He always refused it.'

I told my mother.

She said, 'It's wishful thinking.'

'Why does she do it?'

'Because she's his mother. She's had to keep him alive. People need things to believe in.'

She was lying in bed and trying to read a book.

I said, 'Even if the things aren't true?'

She lowered the book, thought about it and said, 'Well. It's hard to say what's true sometimes. One person might have one way of looking at things. And another person might have another way. You can hold your own beliefs as long as they allow other people to live their lives. You can't tell me that your beliefs are better than mine. I wouldn't like that. And neither would you, if you put yourself in my position.'

But Daadi had said, 'The truth is always there, whether you believe it or not.'

So I tried to believe in what remained of my father, and looked at his pictures and read his books:

The Indian Army had responded vigorously to Pakistani infiltration of irregular forces into Kashmir. With a double pincer on Badori Bulge, the Indians had captured the strategic Haji Pir Pass. Core areas in Azad Kashmir, including the towns of Muzaffarabad and Mirpur, lay threatened. The only way out of this critical situation was to launch a diversionary manoeuvre.

The shiny g-suit hung in the wardrobe and was ready for wearing.

Operation 'Grand Slam' was thus launched in the early hours of 1 September 1965. Audacious as the plan was, it took the Indians by complete surprise.

He stood beside the jet, his helmet raised to his heart. He was going to fly it alone for the first time.

A Pak Army force consisting of an infantry division and two armoured regiments, along with extensive artillery support, started the attack on Indian positions.

He was trying to move the control column but it was stuck in his hands.

Outnumbered and outgunned, Brig. Man Mohan Singh, Commander 191 Infantry Brigade, was faced with a critical situation.

The plane was shuddering.

He frantically called for air support.

But the plane went down. And he died all over again.

'Goodnight,' said my mother. She had finished reading her book; she returned it to the bedside table and reached out a hand to extinguish the lamp.

And the thoughts stayed on in the dark and changed their shapes and became wishes that were made silently to a dead father, who was always somewhere, even after he had died, even after it was known that he would never respond – he was alive and he was listening.

*

In the morning my mother shook me awake for school.

'I don't *want* to!'

'Well, you have to.'

And she forced me to bathe.

'What will they say? That Zaki smells? You want them to say that?'

'I do want that! I do!'

'Be quiet. You'll wake everyone.'

But Daadi was up already. She awoke at dawn to say the fajr prayer and was reading the newspapers when we went into her room. Naseem brought tea and rusks on a tray and sat herself on the carpet.

My mother said, 'This milk is bad.' She was standing above the tray with the small jug of milk in her hand, and was holding her

34

briefcase in the other hand. She took it every morning to the office of the English-language daily for which she worked, and returned with it in the evening; and by then all items for the running of the household had been bought.

Daadi looked up, saw the milk, saw the briefcase, wanted to say something, decided against it, and raised her newspaper instead and read out the headlines.

My mother stood above the tray and appeared to hear the headlines, while Naseem responded to the English with expressions of growing alarm, although it was not a language she spoke or even understood. Afterwards she went into the next room and woke Samar Api, whose schoolday started an hour after mine.

My school was dull. It had twenty classrooms and a canteen, a play area with a small sandpit for the kindergarten, and a barren sports field for the older classes. Every big wall carried a picture of Allama Iqbal, the national poet, who always wore a shawl and struck the same pensive pose in profile, and a plaque that bore the school motto, which was *Cogito, ergo sum*. It was never translated for our benefit but was always among the questions we were made to answer when a special visitor came to the school.

'What is the moto of our school?'

'The moto of our school is cogitoergosum.'

'What is an object?'

'An object is a non-living thing.'

'What is an organism?'

'An organism is a living thing.'

'What is a valley?'

'A valley is a low land between two mountains.'

In the first year we were made to read an essay on Aziz Bhatti Shaheed. It was the first essay in a book called *English for Class One Students*, authored by Brig. (Retd) Arif Ahsan. The cover showed a group of children playing under a banyan tree. The banyan tree was large and spreading; the children were fair-skinned and wore shalwar kameezes and not the uniforms that we had to wear, and were smiling and laughing and running around in the shade of the tree as if in a state of unsurpassable satisfaction. The first page of the book was blank but for a dedication. Brig. (Retd) Arif Ahsan had written: *This book is dedicated to the memory of my late father, Syed Ahsanullah, who instilled in me the very love of English that has culminated in the publication of this book.*

It should have been 'the very lovely love of English' or 'the very nice love of English', and not 'the very love of English'. Brig. (Retd) Arif Ahsan had left out an adjective on the first page of a book called *English for Class One Students*.

But there was going to be a test on the essay. It said:

Aziz Bhatti Shaheed was a major in the Pakistan Army. In the 1965 war against India he gave the supreme sacrifice of his life when an AP shell from the enemy tank struck him on the shoulder, killing him instantaneously.

I underlined 'instantaneously'. It was a long word, and was made up of small parts that were easier to say alone.

'Miss!' someone shouted. 'Zaki Shirazi's father was in the air force!'

'Yes, Miss!' cried someone else. 'Miss, he died in a plane crash, Miss!'

Now Miss, who was long and sharp and sheathed today in pink, looked up from the book on her desk and said, 'Zaki Shirazi, stand up.'

The legs of the chair made a scraping sound.

'Which war did your father die in?'

'No war, Miss. Accident.'

'Oh,' said Miss, disappointed. 'Zaki Shirazi, sit down.'

And I sat down and began to murmur the words in a desperate chant:

Killing him instantaneously. Killing him instantaneously. Killing him instantaneously . . .

At two o'clock the bell rang, sounding release, and the corridors became filled with commotion. The parents of children and their drivers were standing beyond the gate; there had been kidnappings at other schools and demands for ransom, and in response the school administration had decided to restrict the flow of movement:

the children and their claimants were separated by the thick iron bars of the gate, and the waves and shouts of identification were verified by an old, white-haired man who sat on a stool inside and kept his hand on the bolt. He heard a shout, pointed to the shouter, pointed to the child, considered their connection, then unbolted the gate and held it open and shut it again. I went with Naseem past the ice-lolly man, past the man roasting channa in a pit of sand on a cart, and then along the row of parked cars and motorcycles. Daadi sat at the back of her Suzuki with her window down for ventilation, a handkerchief pressed to her nose and mouth for protection against the fumes, and Samar Api sat beside her in the chequered school uniform, which was creased and dusty now, and stained permanently at the hem and near the sleeves with small spots of ink.

'Samar Api, give the masala please.'

She was eating a chhali and had kept the packet of masala with the lime and the other chhalis in her lap.

'Say please.'

'I already said it.'

'So say it again.'

'Please.'

'Say thank you.'

'Thank you.'

'Say "Samar Api, you're my favourite cousin."'

'Samar Api, you're my favourite cousin.'

She hesitated.

'Samar Api.'

'Wait!' She dipped a halved lime into the dusty red powder, stroked it lengthwise along her corn cob, licked the lime, shut her eyes and smacked her lips, and stroked it again along the corn.

'Daadi!'

Daadi saw.

'So he should take it himself,' said Samar Api and lifted the things from her lap and thrust them aside, and then looked away, implying with her manner that it had been a game or a joke and had earned a disproportionate response.

'Sorry,' I said.

But she wasn't in the mood.

We went onto the canal, where the traffic had collected in bundles. The small spaces that opened up continually on the dusty side-track were negotiable but required daring. Our driver then was Barkat, a shy old man who kept his skull in a damp coil of cotton in the heat as well as in the cold. He disliked confrontations and allowed other vehicles to get out of the way.

'He is careful,' said Daadi.

But his caution created a feeling of restlessness in Naseem, who knew the traffic laws and admired the audacity of those who broke them.

'You are not driving a donkey cart,' she said.

The light ahead was green, and a space had opened up behind a decorated wagon.

Barkat was driving and said nothing.

'Go,' said Naseem.

Barkat said nothing.

'Go on,' said Naseem and made pushing movements with her palms.

Barkat looked in the rear-view mirror.

'O Naseem!' said Daadi from the back.

Naseem pointed at the stopping cars ahead and said that we had missed our chance.

Daadi said, 'He is the driver. He will drive.'

Naseem said it was regrettable.

'Don't give answers to me,' said Daadi.

Naseem laughed.

'Don't answer!' cried Daadi.

And Naseem grunted and gave a shorter laugh, and said that it was regrettable and then withdrew with a casual chewing motion of her jaws.

The one TV in the house was kept in Daadi's room. It had a bloated screen and stood on odd thin legs, and was capable of being dragged on its small, whining wheels into the other rooms. To switch it on

38

we had to first connect the wires at the back, which Daadi had disconnected to prevent excessive electrical consumption. (She believed in physical isolation, in full severance of physical contact between things.) The TV was old and lacked a remote control; it had to be approached for adjustments, for the colour and the sound and even for the channel. In those days there were two channels, Doordarshan and PTV, and we called them India and Pakistan.

'My India is not coming!' Daadi cried in the evening.

She had said her maghrib prayer and then gone across the room to switch on the TV, and instead of the channels she had found a grey gushing, which showed flashes of colour when she changed the settings, and caught snatches of music from a programme called *Chitrahar*, which was presently showing the new Indian love songs she had intended to watch; but the settings had failed and the gushing had gone on.

'O Naseem!' she cried. 'My India is not coming!'

And Naseem was sent in a hurry to adjust the aerial on the roof.

We stood downstairs in the doorway and relayed messages from room to roof until the link was struck, colour showed on the screen, and the position of the aerial had been found and was held. Then the Indian songs were watched, and the Indian news, and then the Pakistani news; and after the news came the televised songs of Madam Noor Jehan, who wore colourful saris and stood in shiny settings with her hands clasped at her navel and moved her mouth around to the words of her own songs, which Daadi said had been recorded many years ago in the studios, where real, face-distorting expressions were allowed.

Friday was then the weekly holiday in Pakistan. On Thursday night we went in the car to Main Market, to a shop called Tom Boy's that rented out pirated videos of Indian films. It was a small, damp shop: the walls were stacked with titles that began with *Abhimaan* near the entrance, went around the room in a *U* and culminated in *Zanjeer* on the opposite wall, a world that began and ended with Amitabh Bachchan, who was the male lead in both films and was said to be the most famous actor in the world.

There was a story about his fame. It was about the time he was fighting the villain in *Coolie* and got punched by a real punch. It burst his intestine and he fell into a faint; an ambulance arrived; its doors opened and closed. For days the people of India sat in temples and prayed, and the doctors in the hospitals removed their glasses and shook their heads. The people prayed and prayed, but Amitabh stayed fainted, and the people prayed more, and the doctors said they were sorry but the people still prayed. They went into temples, struck bells and lit fires, sat on the floor and prayed with their eyes shut, their palms pressed together and their bodies swaying. One morning they opened their eyes and were told that Amitabh too had opened his, and the news spread quickly and the temples emptied and there was singing and dancing in the streets.

But Amitabh was ordinary, not fair or quick or clever like the other heroes of Indian films. He was a tall man, dark-skinned, with drooping, bloodshot eyes, hairy on his arms and on his chest, the hair densely swirled behind his shirt buttons, which he opened, one after the other, in slow, deliberate movements, when he committed to a fight. Even then his temperament was unaffected: he preferred to lean against barrels and sacks and walls and fought with resisting thrusts of his long legs. And afterwards, wounded, he staggered on his legs, but disguised the pain with humour, which was dark and sour and tended to attract the shadow of tragedy.

There was nothing remarkable about him.

'You can't see it,' said Samar Api.

'What is it?'

'I won't tell you.' She was lying in bed and writing inside a school notebook, turning her head from side to side.

'Why?'

'Because you're a kid and you'll go and tell people.'

I was wounded.

'Will you tell people?'

'I already said I won't.'

'So say it again.'

'I won't tell people.'

'Say "Godpromise".'

40

'Godpromise.'

She went on writing in her notebook.

'Godpromise!'

'Fine,' she said, and came forward and whispered it in my ear: 'His Vee Oh I See Eee.'

She was madly in love with him. The picture frame on her bedside table was made of two small hearts that touched when they folded, uniting her with Amitabh. And the walls were swarming with posters and stills from his films, including images from the very early years, culled from cracking magazines that were bought in second-hand bookshops and continued to fill the darkness beneath her bed. Every month she returned from the market with fresh supplies of *Stardust* and *Filmfare* and *Cine Blitz* and *Movie Magic* and flung them lavishly on the bed. The magazines contained lively articles with titles such as 'The Old and the Beautiful', and used a recurring stock of terms to report on the Indian film industry, of which 'vixen' and 'half-baked' were Samar Api's favourites. 'Oh, please,' she would say to the mirror, 'you're nothing but a half-baked vixen.'

On film nights we extracted the VCR from Daadi's cupboard and set it up with the TV in Samar Api's room. Our places were on the floor, before the TV, on cushions taken from beds and sofas. And the films were often familiar and contained songs and dances and dialogues we already knew by heart. But we watched them with a peculiar excitement, anticipating and also inhabiting the culminations, which we re-enacted afterwards: I lay on the floor and held an empty 7UP bottle and waved it about like an inebriated Amitabh. And she gasped with surprise and shrugged her shoulders like Parveen Babi in *Namak Halaal*, then wrapped herself in a bedsheet and stood on the bed and wept, the lonely Jaya Bhaduri of *Abhimaan*, her hands repeatedly drawing the veil over her head. She was suffering then, a woman in pain; she settled in a chair before the mirror and began to touch her face, her neck, recovering from her sadness. And then she was running down a staircase and the lights in the ballroom were coming alive and the guests were all turning now to look, and she was Jayaprada in *Sharaabi*, her dress billowing in the wind, and she was arriving at last to end the long wait of the night:

> *O mere sajna*
> *Mein aagayi!*

She danced and she danced.

And she danced and she danced.

Until she fell to the floor in a tangle of exhausted limbs, sweating and out of breath.

'One day,' she pledged to the ceiling between breaths, 'my Amitabh will come.'

'How do you know?'

'I know it.'

'You never know where life will take you.' It was something my mother had said.

But she was adamant. 'You'll see,' she said, seeing it in the ceiling, in the stars beyond, 'I'll find him.'

*

Samar Api's parents lived in the village of Barampur. Her mother, my great-aunt Chhoti, was married to a man called Fazal. Uncle Fazal was very serious. It was Daadi's description of him. And it was a compliment, because seriousness was a trait Daadi associated with virtue. But in Uncle Fazal that seriousness was a barrier to communication, a way of establishing his indifference to children. There was no cheek-pulling or coochie-coo with him, none of the appreciations that usually came from elderly relatives. His visits to the house were rare; he came only when he had business in Lahore. And even then he was distant, forbiddingly impressive, a fair-skinned man with a rounded, puffy face and thick eyebrows that merged in a frown, creating an expression of persistent regret. He declined sweets and drinks and watched them closely when he did accept, never finishing his portions and considering them with his fingers like a man attuned to the subtleties of poisoning. In his

42

presence this abstinence was fussed over but was later explained as the habit of an important man, a man who had served on zila- and tehsil-level councils and had twice won an election to the Provincial Assembly; in the village Uncle Fazal was seen frequently in his jeep with his subordinates, driving on dusty roads and dismounting near the banks of canals and ditches, walking with his hands behind his back, and stopping to ask questions about the water that was going into the fields. He was seen at the offices of councillors and magistrates, sometimes at police stations, where he went to get people released or to file the reports that got them arrested. It was explained as the nature of his work; it was what men like him were expected to do in the village. And it brought people to his house in the mornings, people who waited on chairs in his courtyard with their requests and their complaints.

My mother said he was a feudal.

'What's feudal?'

'Feudalism,' she said, 'is one of the oldest systems in the world. It's when a small group of people own a lot of land and make other people work on that land but eat up all the revenues.'

'What's revenues?'

'Money made from doing work.'

'Is Uncle Fazal a bad man?'

'Not *bad*,' said my mother. 'He just follows a very old system. Most of our country is rural. All rural areas are run by feudals. For them everything is property: land, labour, women. They have a lot of power. You have to see it to believe it.'

'Is Uncle Fazal a rich man?'

My mother thought about it and said, 'He's not *that* rich. He's got a few hundred acres of land.'

Daadi laughed and said, 'It's more than some other people have.'

My mother said Daadi was materialistic.

'What's that?'

'It's when people go after money. It's a historical concept as well. You should read about it when you're older.'

'Why can't you tell me now?'

'I've told you: it's when people go after money, when they want money above all else.'

I said, 'What happens in the village?'

She said, 'Agriculture. And exploitation.'

And I didn't ask for the meanings.

Samar Api's descriptions of life in the village were imaginable. She said she wasn't allowed to sit with her male cousins, she wasn't allowed to speak until she was spoken to, she wasn't allowed to step out of the house, not even to go into the garden unless she went with a servant. 'We have to wear chaadars when we go out,' she said. 'Even when we're sitting in the car. And I can't even see through it. And it's so bloody hot in Barampur, like a bloody oven. There are goats and cows everywhere. Sometimes, when our car goes through the town, strange women come out on the balconies and stare at us.'

Chhoti didn't complain about the village when her husband was present. But afterwards, alone, she expanded on opinions she hadn't expressed earlier, and gave reasons for things that had only been mentioned, things that had appeared to be of no importance until she had talked about them many times and revealed their enduring significance. My mother said people behaved like that when they became self-conscious. 'It's a feeling,' she said. 'It comes to people who feel like they don't belong somewhere.'

But Chhoti did belong to the village and described the things that happened there with an insider's tormented involvement. She talked about the wives of her husband's relations, women who, like her, lived in big houses in small, poor places and were known to one another because of their seclusion – a requirement for the women of landed families. It was a life, Chhoti said, of waiting in cars and houses, of waiting for occasions that required the playing of roles: the women went to weddings, funerals, milaads, sometimes to watch the ashura ceremonies that were hosted by Shiia families in neighbouring villages. They heard stories and told stories that led to new understandings, to engagements and marriages that could break and cause feuds. There was a tendency for things to get distorted that resulted from people's unavoidable reliance on

44

one another; there were only so many good families of so many good castes, and it was impossible to break out of some affiliations without imperilling others. Chhoti was grave when she described the things that happened to transgressors: their cattle were stolen, their fields were burned in daylight, their homes were broken into, and their women were abducted and paraded in the streets. She said such things were common in the villages, where customs were old and went largely untouched by the new ways that developed continually in the cities.

Daadi heard the stories but said afterwards that Chhoti was suffering from the very ailments she had set out to diagnose. (Chhoti suffered already from the medical problem of diabetes, which was described as a problem of the blood, a matter of highs and lows, and was monitored every few months in the blood tests she came to have conducted in Lahore, the results reflected in the changing colours of her face and in the dramatic expressions of her eyes and mouth.) Even while Daadi listened to the stories and appeared to be involved she withheld the hum of sympathy, which she said came too easily to those who hadn't lost things of consequence.

Daadi was of the opinion that Samar Api should live with her mother and father in Barampur. She said it was important for the girl to grow up around her parents and acquire a sense of proportion.

But Chhoti said, 'No. I will not allow it. You don't know what they are like.'

'They' were Uncle Fazal's three sisters, who had families of their own and lived in different parts of the district. They had each approached Chhoti for her daughter's hand in marriage for one of their sons, and had later tried to portray her refusal as a provocation.

'They are vultures,' Chhoti said. 'They are waiting for me to die. Then they will take everything.' Her eyes were wide and twitching with tears.

My mother said, 'It's a good thing you've kept your daughter away from that repressed environment.'

Chhoti was grateful.

But Daadi affected indifference, and said, 'Very well. Keep her here. Let her breathe this air. Let it get inside her lungs. What ideas she comes to possess here are of no importance.'

Daadi told the story of Chhoti's life one afternoon when it was hot and still outside, a dry, dusty day in late spring. The curtains in Daadi's room were drawn. She was in a mood; she had brought out the oval box of photographs she kept in a locked compartment of her cupboard and was contemplating the days of her youth, moments from the past that were quarantined in black and white and bounded by sharp grey borders. Various relatives appeared, old now and young then, rival truths that were hard to reconcile: a photograph testified to the freshness they had once possessed, their erect postures and their stark, unlined faces. But it didn't sharpen their gruff voices, and didn't make them pace the room in youthful demonstration. They remained immiscibly old-and-young, virile bodies with aged souls.

'Look,' said Daadi, 'so pretty we were then.'

It was a picture of two girls in a curtained room, both dressed in saris, both rigidly beautiful; the eyes were averted modestly and the smiles were subtle, barely smiles. Daadi stood in the front with her hands clasped at her waist. And Chhoti stood behind her with a hand on Daadi's shoulder, leaning forward with her lips parted as if about to make a suggestion. The effect was momentous, an artist's rendering of an interaction between two celebrated mythical beings.

Daadi cooed humorously at the picture and shook her head. 'You see it?' she said, pointing to a black dot above Chhoti's mouth. 'She made it with a pencil. Some days on her lip. Other days on her cheek. Above her eye, below her eye – she was very involved with the fashions.' Here she raised the picture and brought it near her face. 'But,' she said, squinting, 'it didn't do her any good.' She lowered the picture into her lap and sighed.

'Did it do her any bad?'

Daadi tossed the picture into the box. She said the bad wasn't a thing as such, it wasn't an event or an occurrence. It was a way of living in the world, a way of seeing things that did not exist and of not seeing those that did. She raised the oval lid from the table and placed it firmly on the box.

'There are things,' she said, whirling a finger in the air, 'things in the atmosphere that start to have an affect on the raw mind.'

Chhoti was only sixteen years old when she came home and made the announcement. It was the Malik boy, the brother of her classmate. They were a merchant family who lived in one of the newly built houses on the canal. Chhoti had been to their house, had seen the boy and had liked him. And she had reason to believe that he liked her too.

'He wants to marry me,' she said.

Chhoti's parents were alarmed but also bound by convention to consider that a family known to them was involved. And they could do nothing when they heard that the boy's family was preparing to send a proposal of marriage. Chhoti was confident of her selection; he was studying to be a philosopher, she said, he was going to write books and he was serious and accomplished.

The boy's family came to the house. The boy wore a blazer, a scarf and trousers, and sat with his knees wide apart. He shook his foot when he talked, and thick folds appeared around his mouth when he smiled. The family had a shoe shop in Anarkali but the boy wanted to publish books. There were ideas, he said, that were sweeping the world and would transform the way of man, and he wanted to prepare the minds of the youth, whose role in the future was going to be important. He became excited and produced a tin of cigarettes from his blazer pocket, opened it and offered the cigarettes to Chhoti's father, who declined, then extracted and lit one for himself with a match. He said he wanted to send Chhoti to the department of Oriental Languages at the university, where she would learn to read Arabic and Farsi. Then she could translate manuscripts for his publishing company.

He puffed at his cigarette and smiled at the curling smoke.

His parents said they were encouraging his ideas but also hoped that he could be persuaded to join their line of work.

And he said, 'Shoes. They want me to make shoes,' and tapped his foot on the floor and laughed, the folds around his mouth not forming.

His family proposed on his behalf. But he said he wanted to set a date for the end of the year because he wanted to obtain his degree first, a master's in philosophy that was going to take a few more months to complete.

In the afternoons Chhoti went out. She had befriended a European woman who had arrived to make paintings of the countryside but had then met a poet in the city and stayed on. They were living at that time in a rented apartment behind the Dyal Singh Mansion, and living, it was said, without the proper documents to show for their arrangement. Chhoti went to their apartment, went with them to the bookshops in Anarkali and to the coffee houses that lay in the shadows behind Mall Road. She came home in the evening and named other friends, and said that she had gone to the bazaar and looked at clothes and shoes and beauty potions. She laughed in those days without a hand to cover her mouth, and in their neighbourhood, where sounds were rarely heard outside the rooms of houses, it was a thing to keep in mind and report to others.

On a dull winter's day the news was delivered to their house. The boy's father himself had come to say it, and was led into the baithak room. He drew the curtains, sat on the floor, held his head and said that he was ruined.

His son was suffering and had always suffered, but it was now beyond their control. The boy wasn't right in the head; they had nothing to say for themselves; they were ordinary people, and their luck was bad; they could offer an apology but that would amount to an insult.

The engagement was off. No announcement was made; it was already known to the people of their neighbourhood, and none of them could claim to have been surprised. Only Chhoti was impossible to persuade and went to stand by the gate and said that she was going to his house. They had to hold her back, had to take her into her room and keep her there. Her mother went in with things to eat but Chhoti threw them aside. Her mother brought a rag, knelt to clean up the mess, then beat Chhoti with the heel of her shoe. Chhoti howled in her room and broke things. But they didn't let her out.

She passed her matriculation exams in the summer but refused to enrol at the university. Daadi had graduated from university, was married and had a child, and she knew that a bachelor's degree, while it was a thing for a girl to have, was not a requirement. It was enough that she was young, that she could read and write and had a family behind her and nothing significant or unusual in her past to explain. That was what they told the matchmaker, who came on a horse-drawn taanga from Begumpura, saw the house, appraised the things in it, and said that she had some families in mind. But she wanted to see the girl. And they were relieved when Chhoti came into the room and sat on a silken, cylindrical cushion on the floor and didn't say or do an untoward thing. The matchmaker went away with what they thought was a good impression, and reported back to them within the month and said that she had found a Khatri family of jewellers: they had a well-known shop in the city and a son who was working with his father and uncles.

The women of the Khatri family came to their house in a car, and it was grand, like wheels attached to a polished desk; the children of the neighbouring houses came outside and touched it, and were scolded by the matchmaker, who was escorting the family and wore earrings and held a purse. She lifted curtains and opened doors and led the women into the house, made introductions and asked for tea, then went herself into the kitchen. There she encountered Daadi and told her that she had a very good feeling. And Daadi said, 'Allah-willing, Allah-willing.'

At first Chhoti's silence was assumed to be a shyness, natural and becoming in a girl. The chatter around her continued, and she didn't contribute to it and didn't look up. Her silence became conspicuous, then odd and unnerving. The boy's mother asked her with a laugh if she was the kind of girl who stayed in rooms and read books. Chhoti said she wasn't. Then her own mother asked her to fetch the platter of sweets, and Chhoti got up and went into the kitchen, and returned with the platter, and took it from person to person like a child being made to carry out the particulars of a punishment.

The women sat with them for more than an hour. And then the wait came to an end: the boy's mother rose, the girl's mother rose, the boy's mother smiled at the girl's mother and was led outside by the matchmaker, who walked ahead of the Khatri family and said that she was going in their car. At the gate she looked at Daadi and said, 'Allah will help you.'

And Daadi said, 'He will,' and watched them get inside their car, one after the other, until they were all inside and the doors were shut, and the car was roused and went away and she was able to shut the gate and bolt it from inside.

The matchmaker came back to collect her fee. And after that she wasn't summoned. In the house a feeling of defeat had settled, and they had decided and said to one another that it was best to give the girl some time.

In spring Daadi had her third child, a son, and was able to move out of the home she shared with her husband's family – a cramped and unpainted house in Mughalpura, a house in which seven people lived out of three thinly partitioned rooms – and was able to move into a house that she had built for herself on a bigger plot of land, in an area where dark mango trees had once ranged, and where now, in the clearings, more and more houses were getting built. She brought Chhoti to this house and took her from there to the bazaars: they went to the sabzi mandi and bought fruits and vegetables from stalls, to the meat market on Mondays and to Anarkali and the Tota Bazaar on good days, when the weather and the mood matched. Sometimes they went into shops and bought things for the children, and Chhoti made suggestions and showed her tastes and inclinations. It was at her urging that they went to the Regal Cinema and saw a film called *Qaidi* with Shamim Ara in the main role; afterwards Chhoti sang the song with her chin raised, her voice quavering, her hand held out like a professional singer's and turning at the turns. *There is more to life*, she sang, *than romance, and there are pleasures other than those of love. So, my love, don't ask me to give you that first kind of love.*

She sang it well. And that made her more tragic, more painful to behold. She was showing a spirit and a willingness that was ultimately addressed to no one, and was settling into spinsterhood, a life of futility and dependence.

Daadi had a friend in those days, a girl called Seema who had been with her at university. It was Seema who told Daadi about a landowning family from a small village in the Okara district. Seema said that the boy, or man, considering his age, had divorced his first wife, who had borne him no children and with whom there had been a property dispute; the wife had been his cousin and that had complicated the divorce. But it was done now and they were looking for a girl, and were willing to consider a girl from the city as long as she was ready to live in the village and observe purdah. Seema said they were old in their ways, and their holdings, though they seemed unremarkable when compared to those of other landowning families, had been gradually acquired and were safe.

Daadi encouraged Seema, and Seema arranged a meeting between the women of the two families. And it was decided then that Chhoti would wed Uncle Fazal in a small nikah ceremony, with just the families and the qari present, and would go away to live with him and his family in the village.

'Then what happened?'

Daadi said, 'Then *buss*. She went to live in the village and is living there still.' She had placed the lid on the oval box of photographs and was holding it in her lap.

I said, 'The End?' It was the sign that appeared in large white letters on the TV screen when the story had run out and the last action or gesture of the actors was held in a trembling stillness.

Daadi thought about it and said, 'Yes.'

I said, 'Happy ever after?'

And Daadi said, 'That was our intention. But who knows what tomorrow will bring? Good things happen and they go bad from neglect, and bad things happen, and sometimes they lead to good things. There is no ever after in these things. One can only do one's work. And one can pray. One must always pray.'

I told my mother.

She said, 'Who told you?'

'No one.'

'Tell me, Zaki.'

I gave no answer.

'You are seven years old,' she said. 'You will behave like a seven-year-old. I will not have you snooping around.'

'Sorry.'

'And she has no business,' said my mother, 'putting these things in your head, because she is an old woman and you are a child. There is a difference. And she bloody well ought to know it.'

When Chhoti next came to the house she was taken to my mother's room and engaged in tones of cheery indignation. In the course of their meeting Chhoti's language grew coarse and her jokes became bestial, and the laughs these drew from my mother were appalled and also joyful, since for her a sharp tongue in an older woman of that background was a sure sign of victory. They stayed in these roles until Chhoti began to speak of her daughter. She said that she worried because hers was an only child, a girl, and was being raised so far away from her. It was necessary to keep her away from the village but no less troubling.

'There is no need,' said my mother, 'for you to worry. We are here. And you have done the right thing by sending her to the city. She goes to a good school, she has exposure, and these are good things. You are opening up her future. You must look at it like that.'

It was an afternoon in October. My mother was sitting cross-legged on her bed and was writing on typed sheets of paper that were piled in her lap. She was editing: the articles were due at the office before the end of the week, which had almost ended, and the notes she was making now were hurried and illegible.

'Do your work,' she said.

I was writing *My Name is Zaki Shirazi* along parallel dotted lines in the school notebook.

'I don't want to any more.'

'You have to.'

The windows in the room were open, and the smell of burning rot from somewhere in the neighbourhood was sweet and distinct.

'I want to go outside.'

She frowned at a long sentence in her lap and crossed it out, and made a note beside it. She said, 'You can't.'

'Why?'

She didn't answer.

Then she said, 'What's happened?'

Samar Api was standing before her with her arms stiff by her sides.

'What's happened?' said my mother and put away the papers.

Samar Api said, 'I went to the bathroom.' She closed her mouth and looked at me.

My mother said, 'What happened?'

'There was blood.'

'Come with me.'

They went into the bathroom.

And they returned.

'It's nothing,' said my mother. 'It's normal.'

Samar Api stood near the bathroom door and kept her hand on the doorknob.

'It's not normal,' I said. 'I've never had blood in the bathroom.'

Samar Api was crying.

'Zaki!' said my mother.

Samar Api sat on the edge of the bed and cried now with her face in her hands.

My mother said, 'It's normal for women!' She went across the bed to Samar Api and stroked her scalp. Samar Api's crying became emotional, an act of release. My mother hugged her and swayed her and made a steady shushing sound. Samar Api sniffed, snorted, pulled away from my mother and rubbed her eyes, then ran the back of her hand across her cheeks.

Her eyes were swollen but the tears had stopped. She looked up and sighed. And then she stood up and began to move away from the bed.

'You're an idiot,' she said, going away. 'It's normal for *women*.'

Soon after that she had her first waxing, which happened at the end of every month and was performed by a woman called Parveen, a Christian who lived in the small employees' colony behind FC College and came to the house on the back of her husband's motorcycle. Her implements were contained in a shiny brown bag, and were taken out after doors had been locked and the curtains of windows drawn. Parveen talked while she performed the waxing, describing the bodies of her other clients, the singers and actresses and wives and mistresses she claimed to know intimately, outlining their proportions with her hands and divulging the locations of their moles. Sometimes, while she talked, there were other sounds from the room, the sound of tearing cloth and screams of pain. But Parveen went on talking, and talked afterwards in the kitchen as well, where she smoked a single Gold Leaf cigarette and was given food and drink on a special plastic plate and in a steel glass that were kept separate from the others, even from the already separated utensils used by Barkat and Naseem, who said they had to maintain the separation because Parveen was a Christian and had a flat nose and very dark skin, which made her an untouchable. So later, when Parveen had gone, the plate and the glass were taken outside and washed under the tap that was used for washing clothes, and were then carried back into the kitchen and placed in an isolated corner on the shelf above the stove.

Samar Api's first waxing was anticipated for days; on the day itself her door was locked. There were sounds: Parveen talking, Parveen waxing, then a rip and a scream, and Parveen saying it would hurt less the next time. The waxing was slow and took up the afternoon. And, when the door opened in the evening, it revealed a room that had been cleared of evidence: Samar Api was sitting on her bed in a long cotton T-shirt and short shorts, and the legs were long and smooth and drawn up like hills.

'Look,' she said, and trailed a fingertip along a calf. 'It's soft and smooth.'

She began to exercise and stood on Friday mornings behind my mother, who had set up the TV and the VCR in her room. They wore tracksuits and stood in poses of attention, waiting for the woman to appear on the TV screen.

'Come on, everybody,' said Jane Fonda, and bent. 'Can you feel it?'

'Feel it,' said my mother.

'Feel it,' said Samar Api.

And she began to walk, and went to Race Course Park with my mother in the evenings. The broad dusty track went around a hill and a lake, where people went boating, and was lined with old trees that gave gnawed shadows at dusk, shadows that deepened as the walk progressed.

'Tell a story,' said Samar Api.

'Which one?' said my mother.

'A love story.'

It is a memory of walking under trees in the dark, of hearing the names of lovers whose love was doomed from the beginning; and of watching a girl, a shadow, walking with a woman's shadow, and repeating after her the words 'true love'.

3

My mother was friendly with unusual women. Most drove their own cars and went to offices, and dressed in ways that were not conducive to improvement, since there had been no initial attempt at decoration: the fabrics were often frayed and threadbare, the colours faded, the shoes plain and heel-less. The sandals were of an inexpensive local variety and were everywhere displayed on wooden racks outside shoe shops and kept separate from the items in the window. And the jewellery was sooty and dull, and irregularly shaped, like the jewellery worn by primitives, and clanked clumsily when a head was turned or an arm lifted and waved. Most of them worked for non-profit organizations and institutes, entities with names such as APNA and SAPNA and SURAT and SUCH, and went to conferences and seminars and presented papers and made proposals for the increased funding of their projects. Others were lawyers and journalists and were not invited to conferences, and maintained a friendly rivalry with the researchers, whose work they praised for its complexity and fineness. The women shouted when they agreed and shouted when they disagreed and came to the house in droves or not at all: they required situations and discussions, and they came to the house when these were available. Then the driveway filled quickly with cars and the veranda resounded with noises, women talking and walking and shouting and pulling chairs, sandals squinging and the door repeatedly opening and banging.

'I am not paying,' said Daadi, 'for the repair of that door with my money.' She was lying in bed with her feet crossed at the ankles and her arms crossed over her chest.

Suri stared at the carpet and said nothing.

'It's too much,' said Hukmi, and held her temples.

Daadi said, 'There is a limit.'

Suri shook her head and smiled faintly.

'Too much,' repeated Hukmi, and widened her eyes in wonderment. 'It is just too much.'

In another part of the house the noise was crowding, the voices all speaking at once and the glasses clinking with the ashtrays and the air souring with smoke, the sour joviality that had descended now on the gathering. Someone was listening to someone else who was making points on her fingers and saying, 'There are three strategies for getting out of the provincial quagmire . . .'

It was on a day in the summer holidays that the cars began to arrive. I was sitting with Barkat on the bench outside the gate and playing cards with his friends. They often gathered in the afternoons to play game after game of *Chaar-Chaar*, a variant of *Bluff* that gave quick results and had the added thrill of gambling. But there was no money to bet; the players were gardeners and drivers and chowkidars, men who worked in the houses of the neighbourhood and earned small salaries, and were free to make outlandish claims – cars they didn't own, wives they didn't love – that brought extreme consequences: there were cries of jubilation and excited handshakes and silent slides into depression when the results were declared. And there was magnanimity in a winner's voluntary surrender of his acquisitions, as well as a perverse joy in losing, which came when a player's wealth of possessions had been exhausted. The present game had progressed to the sixth round, and the stakes, though imagined, were rising.

The first honk came from afar. It was a black Toyota Corolla that displayed a large, bolt-shaped dent on its bonnet and was known to belong to a lawyer friend of my mother's.

Barkat went to stand by the gate.

The lawyer laboured with her window, which was jammed and lowered haltingly, and asked to know if my mother was home.

Barkat said she was home.

And had the others arrived?

There were no others.

The lawyer was surprised and disappointed.

Barkat opened the gate and the car went in.

Soon there were two more cars, a broad Lancer in the old model and an Alto behind it, and again questions were asked and answered and the gate was opened and the cars went in. Barkat returned to the bench to revive the game. 'The ladies are coming,' he said.

'Oh yes,' said Rifakat the gardener with a wobbling movement of the head. 'They are ladies. These are ladies.'

A short silence was allowed to pass.

Barkat sighed and caressed my head, and said that it wasn't fair to the child, and Rifakat the gardener looked away and said of course it wasn't, and then Pheeru the sweeper put up a palm and embarked on the sayings of the Prophet regarding mothers and their virtues, and with the other hand he took the hookah even though it wasn't his turn.

And now another sound came, and it was another car carrying ladies who weren't ladies, and Barkat got up to open the gate and indicated with a nod that the game was finished. The men began to gather their things: the cards were stacked and secured with a rubber band, then packed into a cracked plastic case, and the hookah was tilted and emptied. A crow came and settled hopefully on the bench, and was paid no attention, and hopped about, and finally fled as the zuhr azaan sounded from beyond the trees.

The veranda was in turmoil. Women were standing about and talking rapidly at one another with emphasizing hand gestures and expressions, as if involved in a veranda-wide dispute. But it wasn't a dispute, only the heat of fervid agreement; the lawyer, a short woman with shorn white hair, wearing a lawyer's black coat over a white shalwar kameez, was standing in a circle of listeners with her forefinger raised pointedly and was saying that the date for the election had been set for October but was likely to be postponed. 'You will see,' she was saying, 'they will cancel on the last minute. They will do it. The misdeeds they have cited are criminal, not civil.'

There were nods and murmurs.

'*Mala fide*,' said one woman who had been listening attentively, and was holding her chin in her hand. '*Prima facie mala fide*.'

Another woman furrowed her brow and looked around sarcastically and said, 'Which of us is surprised?'

'I just can't believe it,' said the woman with her chin in her hand, and directed her gaze at Naseem, who had come in to empty the ashtrays.

'Just imagine,' said the woman.

Naseem looked at the woman's face, looked at her feet, then sighed and began to lift the ashtrays from the tables and stacked them one atop the other on her palm.

'I just can't,' said the woman. 'I can't do it.'

Naseem went away with the ashtrays.

'Zaki,' said my mother, 'you're coming with us.'

I said, 'Where?'

'To the streets,' said the lawyer, and this was met with a fresh round of murmurs. 'We are taking to the streets because it is the only language they'll understand.'

I went to Samar Api's room. She was lying in bed on her stomach and reading a magazine.

'We're going to the streets.'

She looked fatigued. 'Who all?'

'Everyone.'

She closed the magazine, sighed, pushed herself off the bed and stood up. 'Wait for me,' she said, and went into the dressing room. 'I have to find my shoes.'

Outside, in the driveway, car engines were starting and car doors were slamming shut. We were going in my mother's van: one of the women had lent us her driver, who would be useful in finding parking on Mall Road, which was going to be a challenge in the crowds we were expecting.

'What's happened?' I said.

My mother said Benazir had been dismissed.

'Illegally,' added the lawyer, who was sitting with us in the large hollow box that made up the back of the van. 'We do not accept this constitution.'

'Why was she dismissed?' I asked.

A voice said, 'Because she is a woman.'

Another said, 'That is not the only reason. She has also made mistakes.'

The lawyer looked around and smiled peacefully and said, 'You can't look at it like that. You can't reduce it to a few mistakes. There is a larger *issue* here.' And she tried to show its contours with her hands.

The rebuffed woman persisted with her point: 'I'm just saying she shouldn't have made so many mistakes. It is not a sin to say that. We don't have to defend her to the *hilt* . . .'

'Tell me,' said the lawyer. 'Are you perfect?'

The woman blinked and opened her mouth.

But the lawyer said, 'Who is perfect? Who hasn't made mistakes here? And what are these people, the ones who have just dismissed an elected government?'

'Chauvinists,' said Samar Api.

'Even children know this,' said the lawyer, and looked around concludingly, then leaned back in her seat and gazed at Samar Api with admiration and gratitude.

The van went along the canal and the drooping willows on its banks went by in the window. The world outside consisted of the streets, blue and grey in the afternoon. Inside the van it was hot and damp. My mother looked at the window and said, 'The streets are not empty. People will come.' And she nodded at the faces inside the van.

My mother was a supporter of Benazir and had gone out to vote for her in the last election.

'There is no need,' Daadi had said.

But my mother had gone to the voting booths on the FC College grounds, and had stayed up that night before the TV with a pen and a notepad. In the morning it was announced that Benazir had won, and my mother had called up her friends to share the news and had then gone to the back of the house to wake Naseem.

'*Vekho ji*,' said Naseem, and shook her head expressively, '*dhee da kamal*.'

It was a popular version of the story, a version in which a young daughter returned from afar to avenge the murder of her father. My mother said Naseem had those views because she was a member of the avaam, the largest group of people in the country. The avaam was made up of those who didn't have schools to attend, or hospitals to visit when they fell ill, or food to eat at mealtimes, and had lacked the ability to express their wishes until Benazir's father had gone around the country and raised his famous slogan of 'Food, Clothing and Shelter'. He told the avaam that they were oppressed by a small group of factory owners and landlords, a group whose members were contained within twenty-two families alone. Benazir's father condemned those families and pledged to restore their wealth to the avaam; his government, when it came, seized schools and hospitals, banks and factories, and snatched the land of prosperous farmers and gave it away to peasants. But that era came to an end when the generals of the army declared martial law, arrested Benazir's father, threw him into jail and hanged him. That was when, according to my mother, Benazir first stood up and said that she was going to fight on behalf of the avaam; and for saying it she was kept in jails and sent out of the country and apprehended when she returned. She continued to fight: she fought from jails in the desert, from marches that she led on the streets, standing on the roof of a slow-moving truck and waving at the crowds who came out to cheer for her and dance for her; and sometimes she fought from the confines of her house in Karachi, which was surrounded by policemen and where she was kept for long periods without visitors. Then news came one day of a plane crash in which the generals died, and the army announced that it was returning to its headquarters. Martial law came to an end; a fresh election was announced and held, and Benazir won it.

My mother said it was historic.

And Naseem said, '*Vekho ji, dhee da kamal.*'

But Daadi said it was just another story, a story that had been made up to fool people like Naseem and to make people like my mother feel better about themselves. She said Benazir's father hadn't won that first election, much to his surprise, that it was another politician from another part of the country, which had then conspired with India and seceded. And she said that Benazir's father had done some terrible things to his opponents in his time, things only caesars and pharaohs had done to their enemies to set examples. He was like a king who has lost his mind, she said, a king who takes what he likes and spares what he likes.

'Dacoits,' said Suri, whose in-laws had suffered in the nationalization scheme.

'The whole family,' said Hukmi, whose in-laws weren't rich enough to have suffered in that scheme.

My mother said Daadi was an old-fashioned conservative whose negative thinking was untouched by the thoughts of other people. 'You should ask the poor,' said my mother, 'who don't have concrete homes, who don't have cars to take them every morning to the market. Ask them for their views and see what you get.'

Barkat said, 'The poor man is poor and the rich man is rich. That is all there is.'

And at school there were other views. One day a boy in my class called Atif Ali Khan went up to the blackboard and drew a long, flat stick, attached a pair of circles to it, drew criss-crossing lines inside the circles, then made a handlebar at one end of the stick and a triangular seat at the other end. It was a bicycle, the symbol of the opposition party. The boy sitting on the triangular seat was shedding large, curvaceous tears.

Atif Ali Khan pointed to the boy he had drawn and cried, 'Zaki Shirazi!'

And the class roared.

'You tell him,' said my mother, 'tell him that your arrow will puncture the tyres of his cycle.'

The arrow was the symbol of Benazir.

Atif Ali Khan screwed up one eye and said that a cycle could easily trample an arrow.

I drew the arrow on the blackboard and wrote his name under it.

He told the teacher, who struck my hand with a ruler and sent me to stand outside the classroom. And at lunch break he found me near the bushes behind the canteen and punched me in the stomach and on the face, and said that I couldn't do anything except draw arrows because my father was dead.

'You can't let it get to you,' said my mother. 'Look at Benazir. She was so young when her father died. But she learned. You have to learn. It isn't easy for anyone.'

Now she led the van contingent in a well-formed line along the service lane. We walked past the vehicles on the main road, which were waiting for the signal to change, past cars and motorcycles and rickshas, whirring and trembling in the enforced stillness, the passengers in the buses looking portentously out of the high windows, their faces gleaming with sweat; and then past shops on the other side of the street, shops for toys and electronics and shops for sporting goods with stalls set up outside, the merchandise hanging from strings and swirling and unswirling in an endless mime of bereavement. The men in the shops followed our movements with their eyes, and the old men sitting under trees on the footpath with colourful powders and bottles spread out on sheets before them turned their heads and stared.

We kept walking.

'It's over here,' said my mother, and led us towards a small gathering of people who were holding flags and posters of Benazir. They were standing on the footpath and facing the road, the men and women in shalwar kameezes and the children in jeans and trousers and brightly coloured shirts and T-shirts, some wearing perforated rubber sandals that displayed the caked dust on their feet. They were receiving instructions in Punjabi from a large, loose-limbed woman whose swinging gestures repeatedly caused the dupatta to fall off her head.

'The jiyalas are here,' said the lawyer, and nodded comically.

There were smiles and glances of recognition in our contingent.

My mother said, 'You can't compete with the jiyalas.'

'Oh no,' said the lawyer, and put up a palm of unventuring good sense. 'Not with them. *Bhai*, they are diehards. What they have seen and suffered you and I can't even begin to imagine.'

This led to sighs of astonishment. Someone lit a cigarette and was requested to pass around the lighter. Bags and briefcases were opening now, and scrolls and banners were emerging. The writing on the cloth was in English and Urdu, the letters painted in black and shaded with red and green dimensions. The woman who was instructing the jiyalas came by and spoke to the lawyer. 'Is this any way?' she was saying. 'Do they think they can end it all just like that? Who will let them? Will we let them?' Her knuckles were pressed into the flesh on her hips and her tone was loudly belligerent.

More people were arriving. They were dressed like us and spoke in a mixture of Urdu and English, the men commending the women for coming and the women pointing repeatedly across the footpath to the jiyalas, who were still waving their flags and posters at the traffic on the main road.

'This way!' cried the jiyalan. The crowd followed her across the footpath. She began to march and waved at a small, smiling boy, who stopped smiling at once, contorted his features, plunged a fist into the air and shouted, 'Ya Allah! Ya Rasul!'

And the jiyalan pressed her palms into her ears and cried, 'Benazir Beqasur!'

> *Ya Allah! Ya Rasul!*
> *Benazir Beqasur!*
> O God! O Prophet!
> Benazir is innocent!

The jiyalas waved their flags and shouted. And their followers shouted behind them: '*Pakistan ki Zanjeer! Benazir Benazir!*'

> The chain that binds Pakistan!
> Is Benazir Benazir!

On the main road the traffic continued. The lights of cars and shops had come alive in the gloom, and the streetlamps flickered and then came on all at once. The roads, just blue, were revealed in electric colours, in black, yellow, red and white. The shopkeepers came out and stood on their steps to see.

Girti Hui Deewaron Ko
Ek Dhakka Aur Do!
To these falling walls
Give one final push!

Policemen and policewomen were now moving silently ahead of the procession, escorting it past the shops, then across the street to where the cinema hoarding was, and down to the steps of the Provincial Assembly building. There the procession came to a halt: the jiyalas stood on the steps of the building and shouted some more slogans, and the jiyalan went down to the last step and gave a violent ultimatum to the president, who wasn't there and couldn't respond, and then named and thanked various other people who had worked for the Benazir government and had extended their support in different ways to the jiyalan and her neighbours, who were here today to represent the residents of Bhaati Gate. The jiyalan made these announcements and was joined on the last step by the jiyalas, who had folded their flags and now departed, leaving their inspired followers, the men in suits and ties and the women with the Urdu and English banners, to stand on the broad steps of the building with their statements stretched visibly in the borrowed glow of the night.

A man went down the steps, turned around, stood facing the men and women who remained, and waved his hands and arms in a downwards direction.

The bodies sank. The voices settled into a hum and then into silence.

The man raised a loudspeaker to his mouth and said, 'Brothers and sisters . . .'

The loudspeaker shrieked. He held it away and looked inquiringly into its wide, circular mouth. He was a tall, thin man with hunched shoulders, a man who wore his forty-odd years like a dying youth.

'My friends,' he said.

The loudspeaker didn't shriek.

'First of all I would like to thank you.

'For coming here tonight.

'And for showing your support.'

His voice was low and dim.

'For a leader we have elected.

'And a leader we will *not* see.

'Dismissed.

'By this puppet president.

'And this interfering army.'

There was applause from the seated audience. The police were standing near the doors of the building and gave no sign of stimulation.

The man was strengthened, and said, 'We have come here to say that we will *not* be intimidated,' and at once the applause returned.

From the road a passing car beeped encouragement.

The speaker smiled at the car and raised his loudspeaker like a mug of beer and said, 'Thank you, thank you!'

A boy stuck his head out of the front window and cried, 'Long life to you, my friend!'

The speaker nodded and said, 'Thank you.'

'Long life!'

'And to you!'

'*One two ka four!*'

The speaker was amused.

'*Four two ka one!*'

The speaker was nodding.

'O Mister Gentle Man!'

'That's enough,' said the speaker.

'O egghead!'

'That's enough!'

'Your mama loves it!'

'You have no shame?'

'*Khotay da lun!*'

The speaker was enraged. But the car, having roused his rage, had gone. And he was left with the loudspeaker still in his hand, the audience waiting for him to resume, the night vast and indifferent and surrounding.

He raised the loudspeaker to his mouth and began to speak with delayed passion: he spoke of the week's various connected occurrences and exposed them as part of an old conspiracy; and from there he went into the past, to the birth of the nation and beyond into the War of Independence. The seated audience was listening. The policemen and policewomen were standing on the steps and listening. But the speaker was sinking further and further into the past, and its depths were growing, and he had now lost control of the sequence and was repeating his words. A murmur caught and grew among the listeners. A few policemen came down the steps and stood with their batons. But the speaker was still speaking, and was trying now to revive the slogans, whose vitality gave no sign of returning. A policeman went up to him and touched him on the shoulder. But the speaker was trapped in his passion and spat at the recoiling policeman, who touched the spittle on his cheek, smelled it, rubbed it on his thigh, then swung his baton and struck the speaker's back, his arms, his hands, and struck them until the loudspeaker had dropped and the people in the audience were running up and down the steps. There were screams. Two police vans had pulled up to the building and were opening.

My mother came down the steps and was grabbed by waiting policewomen.

'My children!' she cried.

They tugged at her clothes and at her hair, and held her down.

'Where are my children!'

'Inside,' said the overseeing policewoman, who was waiting inside the women's van.

At the police station we were made to form a queue that led into the office of the SHO, a large man who sat under a framed portrait of the Quaid-e-Azam, the founder of the nation, and spoke from under a short moustache in a steady, unhurried tone: he asked the men for their names and occupations, asked the women for the names and occupations of their husbands, and wrote this information in the carefully partitioned columns of his ledger. Then the registered detainee was led out of the office, which was lit by a single lightbulb hanging tentatively from a long, nibbled wire, and down the corridor into another room, one of two separate rooms for men and women. A door was opened and shut, a bolt clanged, and the SHO went on writing in his ledger.

The light in the office went off.

He shouted.

Feet went down the outside steps, down into the courtyard and then past the gate of the police station, where queries were shouted and more men were sent out to investigate, while upstairs, in the small, hot office, crowded with bodies and breathing, the waiting in the dark became oddly loaded.

Someone coughed.

The SHO, invisible in the dark, said nothing.

A man's voice was talking.

The SHO slapped his hand on the desk and the voice was silenced.

The silence stayed.

The light returned.

The SHO picked up his pen and began to write inside his ledger. Above him the lightbulb flickered but went on burning. The ceiling fan groaned and caught, and then sped up, and the room was filled with stirring.

On the desk was a mug that said I LOVE MY COUNTRY and a family of pens was trying to escape from it, each leaning hopefully over the rim.

It was my mother's turn.

The SHO asked for her husband's name.

She gave her editor's name.

The SHO smiled and looked up at her face. The corners of his moustache were unaffected by the smile, and his eyes were searching and then disparaging; he tapped his pen on the open page, looked at the women behind her, at the men behind the women, and saw them all at once, the thoughts they had in their heads and the words that were waiting on their tongues. His own mind was made up, and he wrote neatly in the ledger: the name, the occupation and the punishment awarded.

'Next,' he said.

My mother was led out of the office and down the corridor towards a large, dim room where the registered women were being sent.

A policewoman stopped us outside.

My mother said, 'Why?'

The policewoman said the room was for ladies only.

'He is a child,' said my mother.

The policewoman looked at me, blinked wearily and looked away.

We went inside. The room had only wicker cots that were arranged in rows and gave it the appearance of a ward. Two naked lightbulbs hung from wires and burned, and the only window looked out onto a brick wall. The walls were patching.

My mother sat in a cot with Auntie Nargis, a tall, slim journalist whose son was at school with me.

'So?' said my mother.

Auntie Nargis raised both her eyebrows and attempted to sigh. But the sigh became a laugh that died before it was formed. She said, 'I don't know,' and looked around the room.

'Sit,' said my mother, and patted a place by her side on the cot. It sent up a puff of dust.

'No, thanks,' I said.

'No, thanks,' said Samar Api.

Women kept coming into the room, and the cots became filled. The hum was loud and echoed from the walls. The women were now speculating about their prospects: someone was saying that it was best to bribe a sympathetic policewoman and find out if the SHO had made any calls. But another woman advised against it, and said that her husband, a businessman, had been alerted and was going to send someone soon. The suggestions were accumulating but there was no way of knowing whether someone would come or not, or whether they were going to serve food in the cell before morning: a woman made a face and said that she was hungry; another criticized her for saying it; an argument began between the two and quickly spread and grew loud and heated in the small, hollow room. After a while it tired itself out: there was still no news. A woman started humming and was joined by two others, a slow, mournful tune that grew into a song. The others lay on their cots and heard the song, and later sang in the same sad style, securing the mood of resignation. Then another sound started: a man was shouting, was crying out repeatedly from somewhere; his cries came at a steady, unrelenting pace and then faded into yelps. An attempt at identifying the voice quickly failed; it was coming from one of the cells downstairs, which were reserved for ordinary criminals, people who came into the police station for things like murder and theft. The women, enclosed by the walls of the room, listened to the unknown man's cries in silence, and were soon unable to speak, knowing that for them there was only the wait.

The door had opened. A policewoman was calling out a name. The surprised woman stood up and was quietly led out of the room. After some minutes she returned: she had come to fetch her bag; her husband had arrived and she was leaving; the SHO was receiving people in his office and they were all going to be released. The speculation started up again; someone lit a cigarette and was made to pass around the packet, and the growing excitement was physical and a song was started to contain it, an anthem of deliverance with fiery, prophesying lyrics. The women sang it together, and at the end clapped their hands loudly and hooted, and the suddenness of their enthusiasm frightened a gecko and caused it to scurry across the ceiling.

'Samar Api,' I said, and pointed to the lizard.

'O God,' said Samar Api.

It was late at night when my mother's name was called. The room had almost emptied; the two other women were asleep on their cots. We were escorted out of the room by a policewoman and led back into the SHO's office, where the editor of my mother's newspaper was filling out a form. The editor wore a suit and a tie but looked tired and defeated; the SHO sat across from him with his feet up on the desk. His hands were behind his head and his eyes were shut.

'Thank you,' said the editor, and stood up.

The SHO opened his eyes.

The editor was holding out the form.

The SHO received the form and dropped it under his desk.

'Thank you very much,' said the editor again.

The SHO closed his eyes.

We followed the editor out of the office, down the stairs and into the courtyard, which was empty, the shadows yearning in the moonlight. The recessed cells in the corridors were black. A policeman was asleep in a chair with a long, slim rifle propped vertically between his legs. His head was turned to one side and his mouth was open. There was a movement, the dart of a cat behind a bin, and the tin it toppled was tantalizing until it came to rest. The policeman grunted. There was a pause. And slumber was restored.

On the gravel path the footsteps scraped and scraped.

'Where is your car?' said the editor. He had led us outside the police station, and was standing beside his car in the darkness, the road empty and receding.

My mother said it was parked in a service lane.

'I'll drive you there,' said the editor, and jangled his keys.

'We can walk,' said my mother.

The shadows separated.

'Don't come back to work!' the editor shouted.

My mother kept walking.

At home Barkat was waiting. He came outside, squinted into the headlights, identified the van and opened the gate.

The van went in. My mother parked it and said, 'Go to your rooms.'

Daadi was standing in the driveway.

'Go now,' said my mother.

We stopped in the veranda to listen.

Daadi said, 'I know where you went.' She was standing on the steps outside her room with a tasbih in her hand, working its beads through her fingers. Her head was covered.

My mother said, 'I don't have to tell you.'

'No,' said Daadi, and her voice was calm. 'You don't. I already know. You don't have to tell me anything.'

From the lawn came the sound of crickets shrieking in the darkness. It rang in the driveway, and bounced off the walls of the house, a rendering in the dark.

Daadi said, 'How dare you?'

And my mother said, 'How dare you talk to me like that?' Her voice was low and quick, her breathing heavy and rushed.

Daadi said, 'I know what you think. You think that you can do what you like. But you still live in my house. You live off *my* money.'

My mother didn't speak. The shrieking of crickets went on occupying the silence.

'I want you to leave,' said Daadi. 'I want you to pack your things and get out of my house. There is no room for you here and there never was. I should have known it in the beginning. And I should have sent you back to where you came from.'

4

Zakia Hussein had come from Karachi, and grew up there with her younger sister in the white-walled surroundings of the Beach Fantasy Hotel. Her father, Papu, was the general manager of the hotel, and her mother, Mabi, was the hostess at the Chinese restaurant with the revolving doors on the sixth floor.

Hotels did good business in those days. Karachi was a busy port city, a place for entering the rest of the East, and the passengers of vessels and airliners were likely to dismount and go into the city centre: the streets were broad, the buildings variously styled, the churches and halls, built by British administrators, sharply steepled or domed in the Italian way. There were things to do in the daytime, markets to see and walks to take on the beach; and at night there were dance halls and cabarets where the dancers were Egyptian and Lebanese but also Czech and Russian. It was said then that Karachi was the future of the East, a dream in the making, and needed only more of what it already had to eliminate the margins and have that vision of its successes become its totality.

Among the leading hotels was the Palace, stout and high-domed, and the Imperial, where the cabaret dancers were known for removing their tops and came by later at the tables. The Metropole was located near the offices of newspapers and was frequented by journalists in the evening. Duke Ellington had performed there with his jazz band, and had discovered, during one of his rehearsals, the astounding skills of a local saxophonist, with whom he then played in a freewheeling jam session that brought the house down.

Removed from the sights and sounds of that world was the Beach Fantasy Hotel. Drivers heading out from the city centre were required to navigate; and on the way the road began to crack and the buildings deteriorated. This was a greater Karachi area of plain, ugly buildings, with black windows that shone in the sun and stayed lightless at night, and where many people appeared not to live in buildings but instead on the streets. There were tents now in sight, and suddenly more people, women talking and walking and children playing barefoot on the pavements and old men who stared at the cars that went past, as if seeing in those rushed visions a reminder of things they had known and lost, or were promised and had yet to receive. The Beach Fantasy Hotel was located a little beyond this world in an area secluded by the high walls of buildings on one side and open on the other side to the sea. At once the breeze, warm and tinged with salt, brought on the memory, formed sometimes without experience, of a romance in the tropics; and the hotel, with its low white walls and its rose garden at the front and the line of turbaned bearers standing near the entrance, seemed to welcome and extend this impression past the doors and into the lobby, where a man sat playing old, familiar tunes on a piano. The general manager, a small, well-dressed man who spoke a kind of theatre English, was there to receive his foreign guests and snapped his fingers at the bearers, who wore their extraordinary costumes everywhere. The manager said that tips were allowed but not encouraged; the staff at the Beach Fantasy were better paid than the staff at other hotels and became spoiled by fluctuating expectations. It was one of those things he said, personal as well as professional, that revealed his reliability to his guests, who came to know him and his wife, Mabi, and their two girls in the course of the visit, and later sent postcards and thank-you notes that were displayed on a small, square table in the reception area for new guests to see when they arrived. Again Papu was standing in the lobby, his hair combed above his small, fine face and gleaming with wet, and his manner was sure and readying, that of a man who seemed to reside permanently in morning.

But he hardly slept. It was his habit, after he returned from work in the evening, to take his book and go out into the slender balcony that was attached to their three-bedroom suite. There he sat in a chair and read under a single bright light, and later ate his dinner; and he stayed there in the breeze with the sound of the waves behind him because it soothed his mind. He dreaded the night because that was when most sounds stopped. He went inside, brushed his teeth, changed into his night suit and went to lie down next to Mabi on their bed. But he turned from side to side. Mabi didn't notice it and slept with her arm thrown over her face. She didn't groan when Papu turned, didn't open her eyes or ask questions when he got up and went outside. Her sleep was a form of protest, a refusal to share in his miseries, which she said he had brought upon himself.

In the morning, when his daughters saw him on their way to school, his eyes were swollen as if from excessive crying. But they knew he never cried, and knew that he would go now for his run along the beach, running with his fists drawn up like a boxer's, after which his face was properly exhausted and needed only a cold shower to look refreshed.

'Discipline,' said Papu. 'It's all a man has.' He said it without pride.

Mabi said, 'It's all you'll ever have.'

She had told the girls that their father was a refugee, which was a person without a home.

Zakia said, 'We live in a home.'

But Mabi said that a small suite in a Parsi-owned hotel did not amount to a home. 'Forget houses,' she said. 'We don't even live in a country of our own.'

Zakia appeared to understand but didn't. At school she learned every day about the country they called their own, the country with the sea and the desert and with the mountains in the north, where the second-highest peak in the world was; the country that contained so many languages and ways of dressing in clothes, where Sindhis wore ajraks and the Baloch wore turbans, where Pathans herded mountain goats and wore hats that looked like pies placed on their heads, and where Punjabis, most memorably, carried pots on their hips and moved swayingly through mustard fields. She was sure this country existed. She just didn't see herself in it, or her father in his suit, her mother in her cotton sari, or even, for that matter, Sister Andrews, who taught them English at school and wore a cross and a wimple, and the girl called Edna who was darker than the other girls and lived in the Goan colony, and the sharp-nosed Parsi lady who owned the hotel and wore large, amphibian glasses and came by every Sunday afternoon with her friends and sat beside the pool and played cards. Then there was the other half of the country, the half that lay on the other side of India, the part where people ate rice and where, she knew, there was presently a tension.

'They want their own country,' Mabi had said after reading the newspaper. 'They are asking for it.'

Papu said, 'They won't get it.'

Mabi said, 'It's ridiculous.'

And it was one of those moments when, by belittling the desires of other people, they had happened to agree with each other.

Otherwise they themselves were those people, the ones with the desires, the ones who felt belittled and ridiculous. It was almost physical, that feeling, when Papu spoke of the things he had left behind in Kanpur, his home, which was now a part of India. He said he had lived in the best house in the best lane of a mohalla, a neighbourhood, with his father and mother and brothers, and had studied at the best university. But his father had died, and his mother had announced that they were going to move to Pakistan. She wanted to send Papu first, and Papu, being the eldest and the only married son, had felt it his duty to abide by her wishes. He left most of his things, his books and medals, his best clothes and shawls, his gold and silver tilla-worked shoes, in his room in a tin trunk. His gold-plated watch he left with his mother, who promised to keep it until he returned. He always thought he would return. It was inconceivable then that he wouldn't.

He took trains. They took him from Kanpur to Agra, Agra to Jodhpur, and from Jodhpur into Sindh. The train compartments became crowded. He looked past his window and saw desert turn to desert, and his mind filled with foreboding. He had a little money, and his clothes and his diploma were in his suitcase. He kept the suitcase between his legs. He closed his eyes and tried to think of

76

the city that awaited him, a city he had never seen but had to envision in that moment for his own sake.

'Brother,' said a voice.

It was the old man sitting across from him. He had asked Papu earlier to consider some items, some things he had with him in a cloth bundle.

Papu said he wanted nothing from the man.

'Oh,' said the man, as if hearing it for the first time. 'Oh, I see.'

The train went on shuddering on its tracks. Papu closed his eyes again. And again the man disturbed him, until Papu, unable in that crowded train to change his seat, had to sit with his eyes wide open, his face turned resolutely to the window and his ears unresponsive to the man's increasingly maudlin appeals.

Zakia said, 'Did it get any better?'

And Mabi said, 'It didn't.' She knew because she had been with Papu on those trains. She said that in Karachi they had had to sleep in camps that were set up in public places, camps that lacked water in the dry season and were flooded in the rainy season. When people protested they were beaten with batons and tear-gassed. Mabi said it was ironic, and told Zakia, when she asked for its meaning, to look it up in the dictionary.

ironic *adj.* (also ironical) 1. using or displaying irony.
2. in the nature of irony.

Then she had to look up 'irony', and the word had three meanings, of which the third Zakia recognized at once: irony was 'a literary technique in which the audience can perceive hidden meanings unknown to the characters.' It was like the time when she had wanted to build a sand castle and had told Papu and Papu had said, 'I don't think you have the initiative,' and it was like a pin going into a bubble. Many people were ironic, and Zakia decided that she hated it when they were.

'I hate it when you're ironic,' she told her friend Nargis at school.

They were standing outside the canteen. Nargis had just seen a film in which the woman took off her shirt and was describing it as if it didn't even matter.

Nargis said, 'You're oversensitive.' And then she said, 'It's just a film.'

And it was implied that Nargis, whose family was rich, was used to such things, whereas Zakia had yet to make the acquaintance of those kinds of pursuits.

Zakia said, 'I know it's a film. I've seen many films.' She said it calmly. She was good at doing to Nargis what Nargis did to her – an inverted challenge in which the seeker pretended to possess the knowledge that was eluding her.

And Nargis retreated, and became coy and merry and said, 'I know, I know.'

They were together in school. Then the time came for university, and Nargis was enrolled in a well-known women's college in America.

'I'm going to the East Coast,' she said in an exaggerated American accent. She wasn't excited and was listlessly packing her things into a suitcase. Zakia had come by to help, to sit around and stand around.

'I'm not sad or anything,' said Nargis.

Zakia saw that Nargis was preparing. She said, 'Of course not. Why should you be sad? You're lucky.'

Nargis said, 'I know,' but with too much meaning and feeling, so that it exposed her own conception of luck as being reliant on the lack of it in other lives.

Zakia said, 'Home is home.' And her composure, though it upheld her dignity, could do nothing about her own sense of failure, which on this occasion led not to resignation or disengagement but to a clear new feeling of deprivation.

'You'll have fun,' she said.

And Nargis said, 'No, I won't,' and sat down on the bed and began to cry.

Zakia stayed in Karachi. She went to her university in the morning and came back in the evening. Hostel life, which seemed to provide many thrills, was not hers, and studying beyond the memorization of passages and the making of notes and the planting of those same notes in the end-of-term exams was not appealing. It was a time of slowness, of slow-passing hours and slow-passing days, in which the search for new meanings was not encouraged and led to nothing, until repetition itself became a way of living, of waking in the morning and taking the bus to university and eating in the canteen with interchangeable people who had interchangeable preoccupations and concerns, and of walking back alone in the afternoons and witnessing sometimes a scene of excitement, students gathered outside the campus to protest the election results, students rioting and clashing with police, the screams and the violence, which she never saw directly but acknowledged like everyone else who read the newspapers.

'It's changed so much,' said Nargis when she arrived for the summer holidays. Her hair was short; she was reading a book called *The Second Sex*.

Zakia said, 'I know what you mean.' But she didn't. There had been a military takeover, the prime minister was in jail, and it had all happened in some other place. Her own life went on.

Nargis said she was shocked to see a decent-looking man being interrogated at the airport by uniformed officials for carrying a bottle of whisky in his suitcase.

Zakia said, 'It's banned now.'

Nargis said, 'I *know* it's banned. It's just not something you *perceive* until you *see* it with your own eyes.' This way of speaking she had brought with her from America, where everything was expressively recounted with eyes and mouth and hands.

Zakia said, 'It's not that bad.' And she meant only that the changes hadn't yet entered the consciousness of people like herself, who didn't require bottles of whisky and didn't walk around in airports with suitcases.

Nargis said, 'No, no, you're right. We shouldn't get worked up like that. I mean there's so much *more* that's happened, it's not just alcohol, you just have to look *around* here . . .'

Later she told Zakia about her friend Alice, who was black and a lesbian and was in the habit of settling Nargis's head in her lap and playing with her hair. 'She calls me her doll,' said Nargis.

Zakia didn't ask any questions.

'You're shocked.'

Zakia said, 'Not really.' She didn't know about those things.

Nargis said, 'But that's not who I'm having an affair with.' And she then told Zakia about Moeen, who was some years ahead of her and studied at MIT, and lived in a place called Kendall. 'He's from Lahore,' said Nargis and explained that they had met at the home of a family friend, a boy who went to Tufts and lived in an apartment on Beacon Street. 'There are all these people there,' she said, and it was tempting and dismaying at the same time, 'all these people you either know from before or have friends in common with. You meet them everywhere you go. It's like here. It's a small world.'

Nargis went back to America in August. And the next time she returned she was in love with Moeen, and in Karachi things were the same: the military was postponing elections and the prime minister was still in jail.

'I don't know,' said Nargis, 'if I could live here now. I don't know how you can.'

She came back in March. Her hair had grown back to its old length. And she was angry. Her parents didn't want her to marry Moeen, who was not a Bora and whose parents owned only a carpet shop in Lahore. But Nargis had arrived at her own conclusions and had decided to do what she had always wanted to do. 'Which is to change things. Take things into our own hands. We have to. The personal is political.'

She was planning a trip to the mountains and wanted Zakia to go with her. They would stay with Nargis's aunt, a widow who lived in a large, empty house in Nathiagali. Moeen would be there. He was going with his friends. But Nargis was telling her parents only that she was going to get some air.

They took the morning flight to Islamabad. Nargis had stayed up the previous night because she was talking to Moeen on the phone, and was now fully asleep. Zakia sat beside her in the window seat. She had brought *Middlemarch*, a book she had just begun to read. It was written by a woman who had assumed the name of a man, and in a high rambling way that at first was difficult to follow; but Zakia had stayed with it, going in and out, and was settling now into the ever-expanding world it described. The light from outside was bright and flooded the pages in her lap. She saw the texture of the pages, the minutely hewn paper on which every letter stood out like its own little act of creation. It was an aspect that had been there all along but one she had noticed only now, in the light. She stared at the pages and saw only textures, and then had to unremember them in order to go back to the meanings, which required absorption.

The plane landed in Islamabad. A car was waiting for them at the airport. There was a Pathan driver, an old man in a shawl with a tough, fair face and henna-red hair, and an elderly maidservant who smiled a lot and said that she recalled Nargis as a child. They drove from the airport to the hills, and then directly into the hills, which were small and rocky and shrubbed, and then became greener and grander as the winding road ascended into the mountains. Nargis, awake after her nap, was sitting at the back with her legs folded beneath her on the seat, and was smoking a cigarette and talking to the maidservant about her daughters and their children and the state of public hospitals in the villages. The driver was driving. And Zakia was looking out of her window and following the depths of the valley, which plunged just past the railing and suggested only violence, as though in some ancient era God Himself had pounded a fist into the earth. A flood came to mind. It would fill the valley and transform it into an ocean. And then she saw that that was what the ocean already was: height filled with water. So height and depth were the same, depending on where you stood. But here the thought became mundane. The world had expanded and then contracted and made Zakia its witness.

They reached the house at night. The gate was open and was flanked by fortune-teller lamps that glowed with hazy light. The car went in along the meandering driveway, and Zakia got out and was shocked by the chill, and then by the smell, which was like grass but greener, more distinct, the smell of pine trees roused by rain.

They went inside the house, Zakia following Nargis, who pointed out the china on the shelves and the old books in the cabinets and the paintings on the walls, which were done by the same artist in the same style, and showed shepherds and shepherdesses in traditional Punjabi clothes standing under trees and below clouds that bulged like ice cream. It was a famous style, Zakia knew, and she saw its appeal too, which was that of meritless indulgence and escape.

'Come, come!' cried the aunt from her chair. She was different from what Zakia had imagined. She was older; she was frail; her eyes were wide now with excitement, and the effort had stretched her face and brought out the veins in her neck.

Nargis went and sat before the woman on the carpet. And Zakia saw now that the woman, beneath the blanket that was covering her chest and knees, was sitting inside a wheelchair.

'This is Zakia,' said Nargis.

Zakia smiled.

The woman saw her and smiled faintly, and gave a nod of agreement, as though she had seen many girls in her time and recognized the one that stood before her as a pleasant type. 'Sit,' she said, almost scoldingly.

Zakia sat in a chair. Then Nargis described the ongoing dispute with her parents over Moeen; and the aunt listened and made tragic sounds and gave periodic shakes of the head. '*Just do it*,' she said at last, and put up a palm.

'How can I?' said Nargis. It came out in a sob.

'*Hai*,' said the woman and looked away.

'Who will let me?'

'I will,' said the woman, and it was apparent from her tone of sadness that this was unlikely.

'What do you think?'

The woman had asked Zakia.

'Oh,' said Zakia. 'Oh, I think she should. I think she should do what she wants.' It came easily.

And the woman said, 'Yes, yes, I think you are right. I think she should. I think you are all very right and should do what you want.'

★

There was a party that night at the house of a painter. Nargis wanted to go there to meet Moeen, who had arrived from Lahore and had telephoned from his friend's house earlier in the evening.

Zakia said she wanted to stay in and read.

'Come on,' said Nargis. 'You'll meet all these people.'

And that was a part of it: she didn't want to go unprepared.

'I don't know any of them,' she said.

'They're not extraordinary or anything,' said Nargis, who knew them from before. 'They're not like characters from your book. Stop worrying.'

Zakia said, 'I'm not worrying.'

'You are worrying.'

She ignored it.

'Come on,' said Nargis.

And she said, 'Fine!' and was surprised to see that the anger had led her to defy herself.

Nargis went upstairs to change, and came down with her hair puffed out and curved fantastically to one side. Her lashes were long; her mouth was red. She was wrapped in a dark shawl that over-suggested a desire for physical closeness. She asked Zakia if she wanted to use her toiletries. Zakia said she didn't. Then they went to say goodnight to the aunt in her room, and the woman was lying in her bed and swooned when she saw Nargis.

'We'll be back,' said Nargis without giving a time. 'Don't lock the front door from inside.'

The painter's house was a short walk away from the aunt's house. It was located on an incline, in an upward-sloping street of similarly built houses, which were distinct in their façades but had the same tin roofs and the same broad gravel driveways. Only one of the houses was lit from inside, and it gave off an intermittent trembling, which was enough to identify it as the house with the party and also indicated that the residents of the other houses had gone there tonight. A small group was gathered in the dim veranda. Nargis went past them stylishly, without looking or speaking and with a deliberate tottering of the heels, which was endangering and empowering at the same time.

'This way,' she said, as though Zakia needed to hear it, and went in through the front door.

But it was dark in the place where all the people were dancing, and the music was loud and dashed and tore. Zakia went between the dancers and was trying to follow Nargis, who walked ahead at her own pace.

'Nargis, wait!' she cried.

But Nargis had already gone across the room and was hugging a man, and they were swaying together in the embrace, and people looked but then looked away as well, as though that kind of exhibition was expected and only mildly interesting.

'Zakia,' said Nargis.

'Hello,' said Zakia.

'Hello,' said Moeen with an intent and unreleasing nod, and she saw that it was something he had to do a lot. 'I'm Moeen.'

Zakia nodded and said, 'Zakia,' though she was not used to it and hadn't been to America.

'I'm going to get a drink,' said Nargis.

Moeen didn't stop her.

They went towards the bar. The bartender was a boy of no more than sixteen or seventeen, and was wearing a shalwar kameez with the sleeves rolled up to his elbows. He was pulling out beer bottles from a bucket underneath and popping them open.

'*Ek* beer,' said Nargis and raised her finger.

'Only one?' said the boy in English.

Nargis looked at Zakia.

Zakia didn't want to.

'*Buss,* ek,' said Nargis, and waited.

The bottle was opened and given to her.

'*Shukriya,*' said Nargis.

'Welcome,' said the boy.

'My God!' cried a voice.

They turned to look. It had come from a man who was standing in the centre of the room with his hands now on his mouth, his back hunched with shock or pain, the posture of a comic in a black-and-white film of physical accidents and situations. He was wearing a bright shirt with the front few buttons undone. The people standing behind him were watching and smiling.

'My dear,' said Nargis, and went towards him with her beer bottle.

And he said, '*You* are late!' and pointed his finger at her face.

So he was the painter and he owned the house. He took them into a corner and sat with them, and began to chat with Nargis, touching her on the arm and on the knee, which she didn't seem to mind because it wasn't that kind of touching.

'I love your house,' said Nargis.

'I love it too,' said the painter, and withdrew as if into an alcove.

Nargis laughed. 'Tell me,' she said, 'what are you making these days?'

He said he was making sculptures with a special kind of wood that was found only here, in the mountains. He went back to Karachi to exhibit his work but his studio was at the back of the house. Zakia knew from the busy way in which his routines and plans were recounted that he took these things seriously, and it was strange but also heartening, since it was art he was talking about.

'I like your bartender,' said Nargis tartly.

'I like him too,' said the painter.

'You're bad.'

'I'm not.'

'He spoke to me in English just now.'

And the painter said, 'I know,' and smiled broadly, as though this was good of him but also very clever.

Nargis talked to the painter and then to someone else. And then she danced with Moeen, and they danced with the blundering intensity of new lovers. Zakia wasn't dancing. She was sitting in a chair in a darkened corner and listening first to a conversation between a man and a woman, who may or may not have been a couple, and then to the instructions that were delivered hurriedly in English by the painter to the trainee bartender, who heard them and nodded and went away. After that there was only the music, and it was the same. Zakia was tired beyond tiredness, experiencing a state of weightlessness in which the senses were remarkably active. The bartender came back with more bottles. She wanted to go home and sleep. Her thoughts went back to her own room at home, and then to her parents, and then she remembered that she had to call them.

She panicked.

She found the painter, and he said she could use the phone in his bedroom and pointed her to it; she went in and didn't switch on the light and sat down on the bed, which was hard, and dialled the code and then the number and waited.

She had nothing to say for herself.

'Hello?' It was Mabi.

'I've reached,' said Zakia.

'Hello, Zakia?'

'Yes, it's me, I'm here, I've reached.'

There was a pause. Then Mabi said, 'What time do you think it is now?'

And Zakia said, 'I don't know. Ten?'

'It's not ten,' said Mabi. 'It is eleven thirty at night. What kind of family do you think you're from?'

Zakia said, 'I wanted to call earlier . . .'

'*Don't* talk to me,' said Mabi and hung up the phone.

She held on to hers. The line was dead, the tone flat and mocking.

'Was that your mother?'

She turned.

'Was that your mother?'

And the second time he said it she saw his silhouette in the light of the doorway.

She didn't recognize the voice, didn't think it was right, and she switched on the lamp.

He was there. And he was still. His face was fair, his eyes small and black, his body slim and tall enough to touch the door frame. He was wearing a maroon chequed shirt with the front hanging out over his trousers. And he was holding a beer bottle in his hand.

'I don't know you,' she said, and began to get up to go.

A ghost had gone from the empty bed and had left her crying. And she had been crying from before, crying because she was alone, and the going-away was how it ended, in another departure. But it was not a dream, and she removed the covers and got up now and went into the bathroom. Nargis had gone in the morning. That was the thing she had seen – her bathrobed back going out of the room. She washed her face in the sink, gargled noisily, then spat out the water and wiped her mouth with a towel. The feeling was with her still. She went back into the room and flung aside the curtains, and in the light her thoughts were settling. The feeling wasn't real, she knew it was from the dream, and she remembered now that it had involved him, and in the kinds of circumstances that occur frequently in dreams. He had been himself but like someone she had always known. They had gone back to Karachi in the car and there her parents had rejected him. Then she was in her room and writing letters to him, and he was a dog in a cage and never responded to her letters. It should have made her laugh. It didn't. Instead she felt relief, sudden and overwhelming, to know that her dreams were hers and weren't being played out before other people while she was having them in all their pressing vividness.

She went to the wardrobe mirror and saw that the small sacks under her eyes were inflamed. She touched them cautiously, with her fingertips, and felt nothing.

She went to the bed and brought out her sandals from underneath, put them on, then tied her hair in one swift movement into a ponytail and went with her intentions out of the room.

The house was undergoing a slow revival. Sleep clung to corners doused in shadow, to the dim glass cabinets that gave no reflection on their own. But there was mayhem whenever she passed an open window and violently disturbed the golden dust particles suspended in slanting shafts of light. She stopped, became reverent and proceeded slowly. The sun was like a difficult god, present in the things it made visible: it was in the broad vertical gleam that lay on the washed bonnet of the car outside, in the sudden silver prongs that came now from the gardener's hose and fell on the daisies in their patch; and it was in the sky beyond, which was lost in clouds and had merged with the far tips of mountains.

The aunt was in the drawing room, and sat in the same wheelchair but without the blanket thrown across her knees. She was reading the newspaper, and her glasses were perched just above the tip of her nose, waiting to fall, though she had managed by some mastery of habit to keep them there. The eyes were alert, at once perturbed and seeking, and moved with the page when it turned.

She saw Zakia and said, 'Good!' She attempted to stack the newspaper on her knees, folded the pages and patted them subduingly into her lap. She said, 'Have breakfast.'

'I'm full, thank you,' said Zakia, and sat properly in a chair by the window, with her back arched and her legs crossed at the knees. She thought she was good at indulging the elderly.

'Nothing at all?' said the woman. Her face had creased with concern.

Zakia said, 'Nothing, thank you,' and gave a small smile of contentment.

'What do you think?' said the woman. 'Will they hang him?'

Zakia blinked. She appeared to ponder it, then made a serious face and said, 'I don't think so.'

The woman said, 'They say they will.' She picked up the newspaper and shook it open.

SUPREME COURT DISMISSES BHUTTO APPEAL.

'O God,' said Zakia.

'You see?' said the woman.

'Yes,' said Zakia. 'But I don't think they will. Because they can't. How can they?' And it was what she had heard others say.

The woman stayed grim. She said, 'It is all very frightening,' and shuddered. 'I don't know how they are keeping up. The wife, you know . . .'

'Yes,' said Zakia, because she did know that the wife of the deposed prime minister was presently fighting the case in court and had taken over his party. She was a slim, stylish woman, and was currently under surveillance.

'And his daughter,' said the woman, and her tone was awestruck and admiring.

'I know,' said Zakia, and smiled. It was the fashion, this attitude of affectionate concern for the girl, who was going around with the mother and trying to rouse people. They cheered for her. The general hadn't allowed the judges to acquit the accused because he knew it would end in his own elimination. It was infuriating but also understandable. And there was nothing anyone could do, certainly no one who wasn't a politician or an activist of some sort. It all led back to the larger scheme of things, in which there was no place for people like herself.

Zakia straightened the hem of her kameez and said, 'No, I don't think they'll hang him.' And as she said it she felt it grow into a conviction, or something like it, a temporary faith that was taken from the likelihood and made to console.

She went on talking now because she had to. She said, 'There's not enough evidence,' and saw that that line of reasoning had already been exhausted. Then she said, 'It's never happened before,' and knew at once that there was always the chance that it could. The more she talked the more she saw, with growing resentment, that she didn't know enough about a matter of national importance, which should already have engaged her to the degree that it was now doing.

The woman said, 'Eat something.'

But Zakia was overwhelmed by her own failure and said, 'No, no, thank you.'

'Why don't you go out?' said the woman, and put aside the newspaper. 'Go out and get some fresh air.'

In jail there was no fresh air for anyone.

'Take a walk.'

She didn't deserve it.

'I always recommend a walk to young people.'

And his daughter was only a few years older than her, and was going into jails. Zakia couldn't imagine going to see her own father like that because she couldn't think of what she would say.

She said, 'Do you think they'll hang him?'

And the woman said, 'No. I don't think they will. I don't think they can. I wouldn't worry about it if I were you.'

They played cards. It was a simple game called *Memory*, in which the cards were shuffled and then placed face down in rows. One had to lift a card, any card, and then lift another to see if it matched. One began to recall the cards and their particular places and to gather pairs that were then stacked in a corner. But she still made mistakes, and was unaccountably angry when she did.

'Don't worry,' said the woman. 'You are new. You will learn. Look at me. I learned. If I can do it, anyone can. That's how I look at things. Of course now there's another way, an opposite way, which is to think, *If others can do it, so can I.* That is the fashion now, is it not? Yes, yes. It is the fashion. Among some of the new girls.' And she enlarged and then narrowed her eyes, as if to grant the very reaction those girls were seeking before withdrawing it chasteningly.

They went on playing. The woman won the first round, the second round, and allowed Zakia to win the third. But the fourth the girl won on her own. It restored her. She asked the woman about the house and the things in it. The paintings, she was told, were made by Ustaad Allah Bux, whom the woman and her husband had known. 'We bought them when they were for nothing. Now they are worth more. Who knows how these things are decided? If a picture is pretty, I keep it. That is my approach. Don't you think that should be the approach?'

And they talked of Nargis, who had still not returned. The woman said she wasn't bothered. 'Not at all. It is love! I have al*ways* believed in love. Don't you?'

Zakia said she did, though her own experience was of nothing, and her real thoughts were embarrassingly unresolved.

'You know,' said the woman, 'I didn't have what they call a love marriage. It was not done like that in those days. Very few people. Some Hindus. And some Sikhs, because their women are like that.' She stuck out her elbows like a clucking chicken, though she was trying to imply physical robustness and independence of spirit. 'But among the Muslims it was not like that. No, no, we were very correct. Very. I met my husband on the day I married him. And I fell in love with him there and then. It is true. I have told my children and they don't believe me. But it was love at first sight.'

It had to be, Zakia thought.

'We had a happy marriage. He never looked at another woman. That was enough. It should be enough. Why should you make demands? You know' – she became stern – 'a wife must never make demands. You know why? Because it *spoils* the household. A wife should stay content. This is mine, she should say, and that is not. *Buss.* No more for me. I am happy with what I have.'

Zakia wanted to ask other questions but didn't think she could.

The woman said, 'He fell off a horse. That was how he went.' She picked up a card and it was the right one. 'Oh, look!' she cried.

'Oh!' said Zakia, and brought herself at once into that happy mode.

'Yes,' said the woman, smiling, and added the new cards carefully to her stack. 'Yes. He died. Just broke his neck and that was it.'

Zakia shook her head.

'Yes,' said the woman, and sighed. 'It was something. It was a shock. I grieved. Every widow grieves. But I was fine afterwards. You will be, you know. If you have your house and your children, you will learn to get on. In the beginning it is difficult. The things you are left with, they are like the noose, something you have never imagined. How can you? You cannot. But time waits for no one. That is a very famous saying. Did you know it?'

'Yes,' said Zakia, and saw that the maidservant had come into the room and was standing before them with a towel in her hands. She said the bathwater was ready.

The woman was alarmed, then dismayed and resigned. She held out her hands, which the maidservant clasped in hers, and Zakia went over to help her up and then stood by the chair and watched as the woman was led slowly out of the room.

She was alone once again. But her thoughts were with her. She went back to where she had sat and instead of sitting down in the chair she decided to stay standing, and stood above a shelf lined with small items of decoration. She subjected herself to the broad view in the window. It was late morning. The light was fierce. It would stay like this for a few more hours and then start to go. It was odd that there wasn't a single moment in the day when the sun began to set or began to rise, just as there was no way of catching the first hint of night. They were concepts of importance, sunrise and sunset and dusk and dawn, and were required by songs and poems. They were a convenience in that sense, things that people, even if they couldn't prove their existence, needed for a sense of sequence in their lives. And some lives were more ordered than others. She thought of Nargis, of her determination to have the things she wanted, which came from a sureness, a way of knowing where she came from and where she was going. She couldn't imagine Nargis ever having a conflicted thought and then keeping it like that in her mind; all her thoughts must be stalled and resolved. Which was not to suggest that Nargis was unflawed, or didn't have dilemmas of her own; Zakia knew that Nargis, like everyone else, was undisclosed and was in some ways capable of anything. But Nargis had a way with things, she was predictable, and Zakia knew now that she would return from her outing with tales of success, with news of annexations and expansions that would leave her tormented and filled with regret at her own inaction. That was the most predictable thing, inaction, a birthright, a void with which all people were born and had to fill with their own desires. But she knew herself, she knew her limitations and lived within them, and people everywhere had strengths and weaknesses. She raised a brassy urn from the shelf, brought it to her nose and took in the faintly sour smell. The gardener had watered his plants and left. Routine was life for most people. And if the novelty was bound to fade, if it was destined, like all living things, to move steadily towards an end, what was the point? (The point of wanting, not of marriage, which sat substantially in her hazy view of life.) She saw that she had strayed into irrelevance, and from there the punishing impulse quickly moved to snuff her out: it was best to forget the episode; in a matter of days she would be in Karachi, with her parents and her sister, and this glimpsed life would be in the past and at rest. She resolved to enjoy the scenery; she flung open the window and was startled by the fragrance, the same as yesterday's, a washed deep green. She closed and then opened her eyes, and watched with growing involvement as a pair of courting squirrels chased one another in an erratic spiral down the bark of a tree.

She was going outside to collect pine-cones.

The path led downhill. She had brought an umbrella, in case of rain, and had changed into a dark brown shalwar kameez and a black sweater so that the spatters wouldn't show. She started walking, hurriedly at first, then slowed down and developed a steady pace. She was going nowhere, a walk without a destination. She kept walking. The pine trees to either side of her shot far into the sky and had needles that didn't start to show until more than halfway up the bark. She even came across a white tree, white like ivory. It had been struck by lightning, and the thought held her: the sound, the shock, the sensation, then the lack of it, and then the way it would leave her looking, whitened and stiff and with her arms stretched out like a scarecrow's.

She screamed.

It was a monkey.

She calmed herself. Her heartbeat was audible. She began to walk again, but slowly, and with the umbrella in her hand, and the monkey didn't follow and went its own way, and she was able to go on walking. But the mind was astounding! It produced fear and also produced ways of ending that fear, was self-reproaching and self-correcting. Zakia thought of madness as she walked along that dusty track, the source of make-believe, the thing that enabled dreams and fantasies but also created hallucinations, delirium, hysteria; and of the mental asylum in a run-down part of the city, a vast concrete building that had no windows and from where, it was said, the most terrible sounds came until late in the night. She had seen those people in public places, the ones with the eyes and the unexplained laughing, the speakers of gibberish, those who had lost the ability to discriminate between illusion and reality. She detected a release in their madness, and an implied kinship in their communications with the sane, who were tongueless and confined, like caged animals, when confronted with the challenging nonsense.

She went on walking. She had nothing to fall back on. She had never known love, never known real hatred either, and was still a person of moods, a person with a temperament, a person who felt things with uncontestable intensity. It dismayed her to know that these things were imagined. But that didn't end the excitement, didn't make what she thought or felt any less compelling.

She saw that she had come too far. The path had ended, and the trees were thick here and deep, the light high up and out of reach, a twinkling between the tops. There was no one way now, just dusty improvised tracks that went in different directions and may or may not have been man-made. She thought of the time and recalled that it was early afternoon. But she could be delayed here until the light began to go, and then it would be impossible to get out. She took a few determined steps in one direction, became conflicted, stopped, turned to go in the other direction but was aware now of her indecision and had to stop altogether. She was surprised when she cried out for help and the sound came back, strangely disembodied and sinister, as though someone else had said it but in her voice, someone who knew things and now gave her this feeling of being watched. She cried out again, and the echo was louder this time; her eyes were shut and her fingers were gripping the handle of the umbrella, which had a blunt tip and which she knew she couldn't have used as a weapon.

A movement came from behind the trees. She heard the sound of nearing footsteps and became still.

'Do you need help?'

And she was overwhelmed with surprise and relief, because it was him.

'Are you lost?'

She saw that he was wearing the same shirt as the night before, and that it was crumpled, suggesting that he hadn't bathed. She forgave it. She saw the faint growing hair above his lip.

She said, 'I'm fine,' and tugged correctingly at her sweater. The umbrella was like a prop.

He was standing there.

She said, 'I lost my way. I didn't know how to get back.' The way she said it, with the attempted poise, implied that she now knew the way.

He said, 'I can show you.'

And she didn't allow herself to say anything to that.

The walk back to the street was surprisingly short (she wasn't lost – she had strayed only a few hundred yards from the main track), but the welcome twist of that encounter made the following few minutes pause and stretch with new significance. His explanation was credible: he had been browsing the woods for pine-cones and fallen branches to burn later that night in a bonfire – his friends were hosting a *Tambola* night at their hotel, a game like gambling – he said it was harmless and a lot of fun and pointed to the venue, a circular lawn enclosed by low white walls that emerged into the clearing of the street. So they weren't far from each other, and the proximity was almost poetic, but also pressing, since it immediately raised the question of what she should do next. She didn't want to appear too keen and decided to moderate her responses: she listened cautiously and then approvingly to the sound of her own voice as it hummed and provided agreement to the things he was saying. She was listening but barely: the fact of him was more engaging. His eyes were following his feet on the ground. She was trying not to look at him, and the effort made her rigid; even her small laughs were jagged, laughs of concession and not the casual collusion she was trying to suggest. She took the leap: she asked for his name. He said his name was Sami Shirazi. He said it like that, the full thing, and it was as if a schoolboy had stood up to say it for a teacher in a classroom. Then he told her that he was from Lahore but had lived for some years in Risalpur, which was a few hours' drive from here – he had been enrolled there in the Air Force Academy. And she thought it explained the steady, unthinking way he had of asking questions and then answering them; she made a funny face; he saw it and responded with a blink – an unexpectedly difficult moment in which they found themselves facing each other – and she looked away and repositioned the dupatta around her shoulders, still walking, and he began to provide a detailed review of the things his training had involved: he listed the various positions and titles in order of increasing importance – pilot officer, flying officer, then flight lieutenant, then squadron leader – and she heard in them a swishing speed, already out of reach, like the far-off peaks she could see on the horizon.

'What are your views on the army?'

He was surprised.

'This general and his chappies,' she said, growing into the role.

'Oh,' he said, 'they'll go away.' He said it lightly, with a short dismissing frown and a nod.

'You think so? I don't think so. He's been here for two years. And what have you done about it? Nothing. Have you seen his face? He lies through his teeth: elections today, no, tomorrow, no, no, the day after that . . .'

She was walking faster.

And he laughed in agreement, a laugh of surrender.

She said, 'Do you think they'll hang him?' And even as she listened and appeared to solemnly consider his answer, she was aware of the impulse that made her follow the movement of his mouth, the way his upper lip protruded slightly and the faint slanting hair above it; and she was ashamed because she wanted to kiss it, and was ashamed now for reasons that she couldn't identify and separate and then consider on their own, each with a different weight.

She said, 'I am so ashamed. I can't even think about it. I don't know why we don't do anything.'

They had slowed down. He was walking and looking at his shoes, frowning with the intensity that suggests an inner conflict.

'That's my house,' she said, and explained that it wasn't hers, she was only staying there for a few more days and then she would go back.

'Where?' he said.

'Karachi.'

'Oh,' he said.

They were standing outside the open gate.

His hands went into the pockets of his trousers. 'So come by,' he said, and gave a quick nod that sent his hair falling into his eyes, and then a toss that sent it back. 'Bring your friends, anyone you like, it's a family crowd. We're having a band and there'll be dancing.' He enacted a scurrying away with his fingers and smiled helplessly, as if to say that dancing, though unnecessary, was a not uninteresting pastime.

But she said nothing and went inside.

She told Nargis in the evening. They went into the bedroom and Zakia said, 'I have to tell you something.'

Nargis said, 'What?' and crossed her arms over her chest. She was smiling to show that she couldn't be surprised.

Zakia told the story. And it got reduced as she told it, became clear in new ways, and ended without a conclusion. She saw that nothing important had happened, that the consequentiality was a feeling and not real.

Nargis found in it a small reflection of her own dilemma and said, 'You should go. I don't see why you shouldn't. No one should be able to stop us from doing these kinds of things, you know.'

*

The lawn was bright with lights. They were strung around the trees in hoops, in jagged lines along the walls, and culminated in two towering lamps with bent necks that watched over the entrance like a pair of proud parents. The circular tables on the lawn were filling slowly with married couples who were now having to make conversation with one another, an imposition necessitated by the rigid fact of eight chairs to a table. The children were more direct about their feelings: those who got along flashed across the grass in squealing trains, and the outcasts returned to their parents with complaints.

Zakia was standing in the ballroom near a cavernous fireplace, in which there were logs but no fire. She was wearing an embroidered shawl over an outfit that belonged to Nargis, a silk shirt and a sweater and jeans, which she'd needed only a belt to wear, although the feeling was still one of heightened physicality. She was comforted by the shawl. It made her stand with her chin slightly raised, as though all embroidered-shawl-wearing women were cold and proud. Behind her the jaunty encouragements of the jazz band continued; there were some people in the ballroom but not enough to start the dancing. She had arrived on time, acting out of a new sense of duty, and had felt an early elation when she encountered him on her way inside.

'Hello!' she had said. She was smiling with her teeth.

'Oh hi!' he said, but had gone on running.

'Where are you going?' she had cried after him, and allowed herself the note of a whine; the distance between them had rapidly increased and was paradoxically liberating.

But he had shouted, 'Just setting up!' and had then disappeared behind a wall.

Now she stood beside the unlit fire and felt foolish.

'Zakia!'

It was Nargis. Moeen and the painter and another girl they had met at the party were with her. Zakia saw that they were smiling at her and waving, and she knew from this that Nargis had told them and brought them here for the show.

She kept smiling.

'Hi!'

'Hi!'

'Hi!'

'Oh hi!'

She was kissed with cheeks on cheeks. Nargis kissed her, the painter kissed her, the other girl kissed her and then Moeen shook her hand. It was quick and right.

'Where is he?' demanded the painter.

And Nargis was grinning.

Zakia said, 'O God,' and flickered her eyes and made a face but also kept the smile to show that she did not feel what they all thought she did.

They were waiting.

She said, 'He's outside.'

'Who's he with?' said the painter.

'No one,' she said.

'Oh, she wants him,' said the painter, and looked away as though the game was up.

'Stop it!' said Nargis to the painter, and smacked his arm.

They laughed.

Her smile became rigid.

Moeen said, 'Drinks?' to puncture the swelling silence, and at once they all agreed and were freed into chatter.

Moeen came back and said, 'They don't have it here.'

The painter said, 'What?'

And the other girl said, 'I don't *believe* this!' in a high, tremulous voice and with a delight in her disappointment.

'They don't have it here,' said Moeen again. He was surprised.

Zakia said, 'It's banned,' and wanted also to say that this was not the East Coast of America.

'That's the whole bloody problem!' said the small little thing with the high voice, and Zakia thought that she could tie her up and punish her and experience a new kind of pleasure.

'I'll go to your house and get it,' said Nargis practically.

And the painter said, 'Don't you touch my bartender.'

After that the people did come. And the dancing began. Nargis returned to a crowded ballroom and had to push and squeeze past the bodies. Zakia was standing with the others in a circle, which extracted a commitment but also gave protection. Nargis produced a small plastic bottle from her handbag; the liquid inside it was clear.

'Ooh,' said the painter, and rubbed his palms.

'Shall we?' said Nargis.

They opened the bottle and drank from it.

It came to Zakia.

'Come on,' said the painter.

Nargis said nothing.

And the other girl laughed and said, 'Don't force her,' and then looked away in a kind of dare.

Zakia took the bottle, held it, watched it, put it to her mouth and closed her eyes.

'She's doing it!' cried the painter, and clapped.

She scowled. The taste was vile but the heat inside was new.

Nargis said, 'Take it from her.'

The painter said, 'Give it here!'

And it became a joke in which she was newly acquainted with alcohol and they were all oldly acquainted, and they were trying to take the bottle from her and she wasn't letting go.

'Give it here!' cried Nargis, and laughed.

And Zakia drank more of it.

Then she was dancing with them in the circle, and then outside the circle, dancing first with Moeen, a friendly little dance, and then an extravagant dance with the painter, who held her and danced slowly and majestically, with exaggerated swaying movements, and the look on his face was a mock-serious one that she first found funny and then sad; and then she was laughing through her tears and they were laughing with her, and she knew she was separate from them but also had nowhere else to go, so that crying became the only way and swept over her and was fulfilling.

'Excuse me,' she said, and went past the bodies.

And they didn't stop her.

She cried until she was outside, beyond the warmth and back into the cold. She saw that he was sitting on a bench in the darkened patio, smoking a cigarette that he now threw away.

'I was waiting,' she said.

In the dark her tears were invisible.

'I came to find you,' he said. 'You were with your friends.' And then he said, 'I thought you might not like it . . .'

She walked over to the bench and lowered herself carefully into the place beside him. She sat very straight, with her back stiff and her hands folded for stability in her lap. The chairs in the garden were empty. The people had all gone, but the lights in the hoops around the trees and in the jagged lines along the walls were still on.

She spent five more days in the mountains. And on the seventh day, when they were returning in the same car, Zakia tried to explain to Nargis what it was like.

'It's this feeling,' she said, and found that she could say no more. She knew it well enough by now to recognize the things it did.

'It's love,' said Nargis.

That was sudden.

'Not yet,' said Zakia.

'I hope not,' said Nargis.

'Why?'

'Because,' said Nargis, and shifted around complicatedly in her seat, 'there's a price to pay for that kind of thing.' She was implying that she herself had paid that price.

'I'll pay it,' said Zakia.

And Nargis said, 'Good. I'm glad. That's the right approach. I'm really glad you're thinking like that.'

The car took them down to Islamabad, and from there a plane took them up in the air and south to Karachi. On the way Zakia thought about Sami, thought about meeting him again, then thought about her parents and decided that there was nothing to tell them yet.

At home her parents were waiting. Mabi was in the kitchenette, Papu was on the balcony. Her younger sister, Shazreh, was not at home. She was out with friends. But it was late. Zakia couldn't imagine Mabi letting Shazreh stay out that late. She wondered if they had changed in her absence.

She deposited her suitcase by the door and was struck by the smallness of the suite. Seven days in the mountains, in that large house, with open spaces everywhere, had shown this to be a confinement. She went to the balcony and parted the billowing curtains. Papu was sitting in his wrought-iron chair and reading a book under the burning light.

'I'm back,' she said.

'Yes,' he said, and looked up briefly from his book. 'Do sit down.'

She took the chair next to him. In the silence the breeze was an intimation.

Mabi came to the balcony and sat down on the third chair. They were all here now.

'Where's Shazreh?' she said.

'That's what we have to talk about,' said Papu, and tossed his book on the table. 'You tell her,' he said, meaning Mabi.

Zakia's first thought was of a hospital.

'Why should I tell her?' said Mabi. 'She's your daughter too.'

It wasn't a hospital.

'Fine,' he said, and cracked a knuckle. 'Your sister has run off.'

'Run off?' She looked from one parent to the other.

'Not run off,' said Mabi, who had prepared these words for the world, and did not have the ability to distinguish between that world and the members of her own family. 'She is with a man. A man who wants to marry her. It's been going on for quite some time, apparently.'

'Who is he?' asked Zakia. She was surprised because Shazreh hadn't given her the slightest indication.

'I don't know his name,' said Mabi, though it was unlikely that she didn't.

'His family is in Canada,' said Papu.

'Well,' said Zakia, 'that can't be bad . . .'

'Good or bad, I don't know,' said Mabi. And she sighed.

Zakia was tempted to leave. But here she only had her room. Her time with Sami was suddenly imperilled and she felt she had to tell someone.

'I say we get them married,' said Papu with an awkward movement of his fingers that seemed to enact the elopement as well as parental absolution.

'What are you talking about?' said Zakia. 'She's still at university. She has to finish her degree.'

'Degrees don't matter,' said Papu.

'Yes, they do,' said Zakia.

'Didn't do anything for *you*,' said Mabi.

She felt the wound and then the numbness. The life she had glimpsed was lost.

She got up from the chair and went inside, back into her room.

Nargis graduated in June and came back to Karachi. She was going to marry Moeen. Her parents tried to dissuade her, failed, and disowned her. She moved with some of her possessions to his house in Lahore.

Zakia went to stay with her.

'How are you?' she said.

'Oh, I'm fine,' said Nargis. She was living in the upstairs portion of a small house, in a room that had a large, square opening in one of its walls for an air-conditioner that was on its way. The leaves and bark of a tree outside were visible through the opening.

'Have you talked to them?' said Zakia. She meant Nargis's parents.

'No,' said Nargis, and it was difficult for her to say it but not as difficult as it would have once been. 'I haven't.'

Nargis had hardened. It made Zakia nervous.

'Will you?' She wanted to ask the right questions, the old soothing questions.

'No.'

They were quiet. It was afternoon, and the sounds from outside were of the birds in their nests.

Then Nargis said, 'It's not a free country.'

And Zakia sighed.

But Nargis said, 'It's not,' and went on to describe the new punishment for thieves: they would have their hands severed by special surgeons, who had to know the extent of the amputation and the location of the incision, whether it would go up to the wrist or not. Nargis said she had learned about it from a woman she knew, a lawyer who was trying to challenge the new laws in court. 'She's an NGO type,' said Nargis. 'They only talk about politics.'

Zakia said, 'You're making friends.'

Nargis put out her cigarette in the ashtray and said, 'I suppose I've made friends. I'm trying to make them. They're all Punjabis here.' And she smacked her forehead and delivered a line in a Punjabi accent, which was crude and comical. Then Nargis said, 'When are you going to meet him?'

And Zakia said, 'Tonight.'

'Are you going to his house?'

'No, no,' said Zakia. 'His mother is there.'

Nargis said, 'It's good like that. Stay away from the in-laws.' And she described some of her own encounters with her mother-in-law, who resented interference but also complained when Nargis didn't show an interest.

'You can't win,' said Nargis. 'That's my conclusion.'

Zakia's own view of Nargis's new life was tinged with fascination. She said, 'What should I wear?'

'Where are you going?'

'Some food place. He said it's outdoors. Please come with me.'

They went that night to a place called Paisa Akhbar. It was far away, far from Nargis's house, which was in a place called Gulberg, and far also from Sami's house, which was on the canal and which she hadn't seen. They went in Sami's car, a small car, but there were four of them in it and they fitted. They went to a stall that was surrounded by long metal tables and plastic chairs, and sat at one of the tables in the dark street, Nargis and Zakia on one side and Moeen and Sami on the other, and ate nihari with naans. The nihari came in small plastic bowls that had smears on their rims. It was a thick meat sauce; it slid repeatedly down her wrists.

'Eat like me,' said Sami.

The next day she said to him, 'What do you think of Moeen?'

'Good fellow,' he said.

'What do you think of Nargis?'

'She's nice,' he said. 'She's a good friend of yours.'

She thought it was an odd thing to say.

'Where are your friends?' she said.

He said they were in various places.

'When will I meet them?'

'When they're here.'

She accepted this nomadic life. He was serving in a government institution; it wasn't even a government institution, it was its own entity and had its own requirements. But her idea of Lahore was attached to her idea of him, and she needed him to make it come alive.

'What do you want to do?' he said.

They were driving in his car with their windows down. It had rained, and the water from puddles shot up and splashed beneath the tyres.

'I want to go to places,' she said. 'I want to see things.'

They went first to the shrine of Daata Saab, an eleventh-century Sufi who was believed to be the grantor of Lahore's many wishes. The courtyard was open. She left her shoes at the entrance and felt the stone under her feet, warmed at midday by the mild winter sun. A thousand years! She was expecting a ruin but had found a dwelling: there were people in the long corridors on the sides, huddled against walls and stretched out on straw mats, some asleep, others awake, still others in a median state. He led her through the courtyard to the grave, which was located within the shade of a marble enclave and was guarded by a brood of squatting pigeons. They seemed vaguely aware of intrusion. She raised her hands in prayer and tried not to look at the pigeons, then closed her eyes to show that she was lost.

And there were shrines that came alive only at night. One Thursday after sundown they went in Sami's car to the tomb of Shah Hussein, which lay behind many sodden lanes in a place called Baghbanpura. The saint, she knew, was buried next to his lover, a Hindu boy called Madho Lal. There was a graveyard before the tomb, with old, twisting trees that grew between the graves. A fire burned in a corner; a man was singing to the flames; another sat beside him and struck a drum from time to time. They went towards the grave but it was locked for the night; a shawl-wearing man, the custodian, led them in silence to another grave at the back of the compound, and it was the grave of the saint's sister, smaller but lit brightly with round electric lights that hung from strings on the walls. The custodian waited for them outside the chamber, was pleased to be paid, and told them to come back in a week's time for the saint's death anniversary. Then the courtyard was filled with noise and crowded with bodies; a woman was standing in a clearing with her hands on her knees and spinning her hair rapidly to a drummer's beat. Hanging on the air was the aroma of hashish, which was thick and sweet, and reminded Zakia of the other shrine smell, the compound stench of feet and roses and perspiration. She kept her head above the noise and kept looking at the things around her. Here too the colours and the sounds, brought out to commemorate the dead, were accompanied by the sight of useless limbs, of pustules and sores on the arms and legs of the living. But she could observe it only with an outsider's apprehension, an unease that came from an encompassing awareness of herself, the formality of her clothes, her shoes, the hair she had tied up in a pointless ponytail, the absurdity of being even slightly mindful in a place where others appeared not to care. She looked away and kept walking. And it fed the same experience, which was one of growing familiarity within a romance.

He showed her the fort and the dungeons underneath. They were dank and broken, littered with rubble. (She had envisioned complex chambers.) Other parts were suddenly grand: they sat cross-legged on the broad steps built for royal elephants and wandered into the royal gardens where queens and princesses had once frolicked, past their ghostly quarters to the narrow, octagonal pools where they had bathed. At the Shalimar Gardens she put her foot in a waterless pool and made a face.

'What's the matter?' he said.

'There's no water.'

He summoned a chowkidaar and paid him. The man was quick; he placed a hand on his heart and went to see about the water. And when it came she splashed her feet in the fountain frivolously, and didn't laugh or say that she was happy.

She bought a map. It was a jumble of locations and place-names. She decided she needed people to bring it alive.

But Sami's friends knew only one another. Even when they converged it was to sprint competitively in a park, or to gather around a table with beers and cards and talk of their days in Risalpur, the things they had done and said and the punishments they had been awarded. (There was a special kind of punishment that involved walking to the hostel with a parachute attached to the shoulders. It was intended, like the other punishments they had described, to humiliate.) They had nicknames that corresponded to their speeds: Scooter, Machhar, Cheetah, Fokker, Turtle. Around her they were gruff and uncommunicative. She felt like an obstacle.

'Where are we going?'

'Turtle's house. Some boys getting together.'

She appeared to think about it and said, 'Why do we always have to go to Turtle's house?' She had allowed her irritation to show.

'You don't like Turtle's house?'

She wanted to slap his face.

'That's not what I mean,' she said.

He said, 'Oh,' and sat down next to her, waiting for her to explain what she meant.

She complained to Nargis.

And Nargis offered to introduce her to her own friends.

Nargis's friends were the people who met in the evenings at the house of a woman called Hania Apa, a middle-aged woman of medium height who kept her hair in a mannish crop and didn't wear dupattas or shawls. Instead she wore the frayed handloom kurtas that Zakia associated with male politicians, and the sleeveless sadri jackets that were favoured by Punjabi ministers. She hadn't married, and lived alone in a two-bedroom flat with no help – she didn't believe in keeping servants – and drove her own car to the arts college, where she ran the Art History Department on a tight, unsubsidized budget. Her circular drawing room was like a museum, and had shelves on all the walls and hanging tapestries and oddly placed pots and metal artefacts that were deliberately left unpolished. The books on the shelves were about women and countries and diseases, and often had short confrontational titles that were easy to remember and repeat. Hania Apa enjoyed Nargis and watched her with amused interest. She wasn't warm or welcoming when Zakia first went to her house.

'This is my friend Zakia,' Nargis had said.

And Hania Apa had shaken her hand.

She was a chain smoker, and smoked so many cigarettes on that first night that the windows had to be opened and the fan switched on to relieve the asthmatic woman who was sitting on one of the colourful floor-cushions. There was drinking and talking, then eating and talking, then drinking and talking again.

'Did you like it?' said Nargis afterwards.

And Zakia said that it was interesting, which was what she had heard most people say that night about the things they were discussing.

She wanted to go again, and went.

'Not coming to Turtle's?' His voice was like a child's on the phone.

'No,' she said, the way Nargis would say it.

'I'll see you tomorrow,' he said.

'We'll see,' she said.

She hung up the phone and went into the drawing room to lay out the bottles and the glasses.

After nine o'clock the bell was ringing at expected intervals. Hania Apa was in her chair, her frank feet settled on a low ottoman, her hands clasped in brazen laxity behind her head. (Already there were blooms of sweat in the armpits, and Zakia switched on the fan.) Two women were sitting on the sofa and were listening appreciatively to Hania Apa's take on a law that was going to be passed within the month. A bald, slender man arrived, nodded at the seated women and bent over the table to pour whisky in a glass. The doorbell rang again; Zakia went to see but Nargis was already at the door, and it was Moeen, and Zakia had a view of herself in which she was here without Sami; she saw that the ice bucket was empty and went into the kitchen to get more, and on the way she had a quick mental argument with Sami about consideration for people's needs.

Dinner appeared: it was biryani that came in plastic bags from the market. Some guests stood around the dining table with plates, chewing and swallowing as they spoke, and others returned to sofas and chairs and to the cushions on the floor, large ones with tiny round mirrors embedded in the fabric. A large woman whose cleavage was emphasized by a low necklace was arguing with a small, enervated woman about the state of women's education in the country. The fat woman was saying that the private sector was the solution; the thin woman was shaking her head. Someone asked Zakia for the bathroom; she pointed it out; then a woman on the sofa looked her up and down, almost lewdly, and said, 'Pretty girl.'

Zakia blushed.

'Believe every word she says!' cried a neighbouring woman with wildly arching eyebrows. 'She's a first-class portraitist, you know?'

And the first-class portraitist continued to look admiringly at Zakia, as though she perfectly expected to hear such things said about herself and was glad to have Zakia hear them too.

It was almost midnight when the doorbell rang again. The guests looked at one another, looked at Hania Apa, who rose with excitement and went to the door. The pause was brief and expectant. And then Hania Apa reappeared, and was holding his hand.

The guests stood up.

He was younger in the pictures. Zakia recalled the headlines from the time when he was arrested for conspiring against the government, and again, when he was awarded a prize by the Russians (and not the Nobel Prize, which they didn't give to communists), and recently too, when the military had blocked him out, and he had had to leave the country. Still he was present in conversations, in songs penned by him and sung by others. They said he was the greatest Urdu poet of the century.

He settled with a halting effort into the chair.

'Something to eat?' said Hania Apa, who was stooping and held his hand in a devotional clasp.

The poet touched his belly and said that the doctor wasn't allowing him too much these days.

'Something to drink?'

He assented with a chuckle.

The conversation returned to its usual precincts. And at every turn now the poet was implored to supply a verse. The lines faltered in his phlegmy voice but were known, it seemed, to every person in the room; there was a mayhem of contributions when he paused or forgot. One poem in particular was summoned again and again. It was a love poem, but the love it described was strained and wearied. The opening verse was a supplication: my love, it said, do not ask me, it said, for that earlier, pristine love. From there it moved to memories of that first love, to the eyes of the beloved (a verse she particularly liked) and their unrivalled place in the world. But the gaze wanders, the gaze returns; and the eyes are not the same. It was this, the banishment, wilfully breaking the lull of innocence, that she found obscure and even a little contrived, a plunge into the abstract, a world that bore no relation to the real, which was the truth of the life she was living.

> This world knows other torments than of love,
> And other happiness than a fond embrace;
> Love, do not ask for my old love again.

She met Sami in the morning. He had come to fetch her from Nargis's house, where she was staying. They were going to Turtle's house now (she had agreed), and in the car she was avid and unrestrained. She recounted the details of other people's conversations with the fervour of a proud participant. The issues raised, the complex analyses, the verses from the poems, all of it had stayed on and acquired a new life in her retelling. She was outraged, she was saddened, she was lively and ironical when imitating the more farcical aspects of the evening, like the first-rate portraitist and her friend with the eyebrows. And then she was solemn and withdrawn, and she said that Moeen had been there too.

'You didn't invite me.'

'Still,' she said, 'you could've come.'

They were driving along the canal. Bigger cars went past and left them behind.

He said, 'I'll come tomorrow.'

'There's nothing there tomorrow,' she said. And then she said, 'They're not like your *boys*, they don't sit around and crack *jokes* all the time.'

His driving was unaffected by this, but she could tell that his mood had changed. She was glad that he could drive well.

She said, 'You should come with me the next time.'

'Go yourself.'

'I *will* go.'

'So go. Go.'

They went to Turtle's house. But she asked to be taken back to Nargis's, and Sami didn't look at her when she said it, and then Turtle summoned a driver and she went alone in the car and went back the next morning on the flight to Karachi.

He called her when he came to Karachi.

'You can't call my house,' she said.

Her mother came into the kitchenette and went past her to the fridge, didn't seem to notice, and went out again.

'You can't do this, Sam!'

'Sorry, sorry,' he said. But he was laughing.

'I'm putting down the phone.'

'Why!'

'Because you think it's *funny*. It's not the same for girls. Why can't you understand that?'

It was unmerited.

She said, 'Where do you want to meet?'

And he proposed a place.

They met at a dingy restaurant in Saddar. The place was empty. The tables had stained plastic tops that displayed a floral design.

There was a TV in one corner and it was showing the evening news, which was in Arabic, a new thing.

'Where do you want to go?' he said.

She tried to think of a place. She couldn't take him to a friend's house because her friends were girls; and she wasn't going to take him to a hotel.

He said, 'Are there any monuments?'

She tried to think of monuments. There were none. It came to her that Karachi had no history.

He said, 'What about a park?'

They couldn't go to a park. She knew of a girl who had gone to a park with a boy and was stopped there by a policeman, who had asked the couple for their marriage certificate, which was now required in public places, and had then taken the boy and the girl to a police station.

'No parks,' she said. 'Where are you going after this?'

He said there was an air base nearby.

There were air bases everywhere.

She said, 'No. Forget it. Let's stay here and eat.'

And they drank their Cokes and ate a lukewarm meal.

She went to Lahore again in the spring. She had timed her visit to coincide with his, and was staying again with Nargis. The night of her arrival there was a dinner party at Hania Apa's house.

'Can you come?' she said.

And he said he would.

She waited for him in that drawing room, surrounded by people who now knew her name and engaged her in ways that were still novel and exciting. But she was thinking of him. It was like a burden that was also a blessing. It coloured everything. She tried to imagine a life in which there wasn't this kind of waiting, this ever-present need for someone else, a need that was denied and then fulfilled and then denied again. She could no longer imagine such a life, even though she knew, in an abstract way, that she had once lived it.

The doorbell rang. And she saw that he had worn the right

clothes, a proper shirt and trousers, a slim brown belt, and black suede shoes on his feet. His hair was combed in a new way. A sadness came over her. She was surprised by the feeling and tried to banish it. She watched him watch himself. And then her view changed: it was of herself as an impostor. What did she want? She had never thought about it. He had met Hania Apa and shaken hands with her, and was sitting now on one of the cushions. But these conversations didn't require him. They would go on and on. She went across to the table and made a strong drink.

'You want?' she said.

And he said, 'Why not.'

The first-class portraitist was listening, and said, 'A supportive husband is a good one.'

'Oh no,' said Zakia. 'We're not married.'

It made her apprehensive.

The portraitist said, 'So get married!'

She looked at him.

'Why not.'

'Why not.'

They all laughed.

'Good!' cried the first-class portraitist and raised her glass grandly.

So for the rest of the night she was buoyant. She hugged Hania Apa, laughed at many jokes, nodded vehemently when someone made a passionate point about the status quo and said that it must be ruptured by a peasant revolt. Her glass was full. Then the poet arrived, and there were drunken salutations, and Zakia, her arms wide in greeting, leaped up from her cushion on the carpet and went towards the door to receive him. Later in the night the electricity went, and there were groans in the shadowy room, and abruptly it was back but with the sound of shattering glass. A bulb in one of the overhead lamps had burst.

Hania Apa sighed.

'I'll get it,' said Zakia.

'No, no,' said Hania Apa and flapped a lazy hand as if to dispel a fly.

'It'll take a minute!' Zakia cried from the kitchen.

She stood on a stool and slowly twirled the bulb into place. And beneath her the conversation continued: this army, they were saying, it would bring about the end of this country, there was nothing in the papers, just blank slots now and lines of print blackened out by markers.

'*Bataaein na phir!*' cried Zakia from the stool, and aimed her importunate look at the poet. '*Inqilaab kab aa raha hai?*'

So tell us: when is the revolution coming?

And the poet looked blankly at the faces around him, held up his glass and shook it contemplatingly, and motioned with an open palm towards the sprightly girl on the stool with the lightbulb in her hand and said, '*Bhai inqilaab tau tum lao gi.*'

It is you, my dear, who will bring the revolution.

He said, 'Let's get married!'

And it was not how she had wanted him to say it.

But she said, 'I'll think about it.'

They went to buy her an outfit. She was going to meet his mother and his sisters at his house, and he said it had to be right. They went to a shop in Liberty Market, and she was made to accept, after some pleading, a pink georgette shalwar kameez with short tassels on the shoulders. The next day they drove in his car to his house and it was strangely momentous. He got out of the car and opened the gate, which dragged noisily, then came back to the car and drove it towards the house. The driveway was cracked. The lawn was unmown and bordered by marigolds. And she saw the lone tree on its edge, with a dark, twisting bark and smooth, shining leaves. 'What's that?' she said.

'It's called something,' he said. 'Nice little flowers. Sweet-smelling. My mother planted it.'

They went through the veranda, which showed their blurred reflections on its floor.

The room was choked. The smell was frantic, recent, undecided between rose and varnish – she identified the cylinder of air-freshener on the mantelpiece, next to medicines and framed photographs and a telephone, the accoutrements of middle age.

The mother rose from her bed and came forward to formalize the introduction: she held Zakia's face, kissed her forehead and said, '*Mashallah.*' Then she led them to the sofa and the chairs, and Zakia noted that the dark wood was polished and the silk upholstery was opal.

Tea came with the maidservant, a woman called Naseem, who settled the tray on the long, slender table and sat herself on the carpet. She looked at Zakia from time to time.

Now the sisters, Suri and Hukmi – she knew them instantly; he had described them so well she wanted to laugh – came in from the adjacent room. They were married and had been waiting. She stood up for them, and they were pleased. Their glances were furtive, glances of confirmation. She could sense their anticipation.

Sami talked incessantly. She saw that they relied on him. The mother was nodding to the things he was saying and the sisters were proudly withdrawn. He was the man of the house now (his father had died two years before of a heart attack) and Zakia was going to be his wife.

She returned to Karachi with her impressions, and revived them daily for deliberation, nearing and nearing her decision, which was already made.

He proposed again.

'What about the aeroplanes?' She hadn't prepared the question.

'What about them?'

'You'll be away.'

He said he thought she had always known that.

'But it's going to be difficult for me.'

He said he would come home to see her whenever it was possible.

And it was enough. She said, 'Okay. I'll do it.'

*

She told Papu and Mabi. And they didn't resist. Shazreh had gone by then to live with her husband in Canada, and the general manager's suite on the fourth floor of the Beach Fantasy Hotel had about it the air of desertion. Papu asked about the boy's profession.

She said he was in the air force. Papu gave a grunt, as though it was both outlandish and predictable. Mabi said she didn't have the money or the patience to put up another wedding.

'You don't have to,' said Zakia.

But Sami's mother wanted to do it the proper way: she wanted to take a flight to Karachi and ask for their daughter's hand in marriage.

'It matters to her,' said Sami on the telephone, and she heard the indignation behind his pleading. 'Please. You must do something.'

She went into the lounge and made the announcement: the boy and his family were coming, and Papu and Mabi would host them. She didn't give them time to object.

The day arrived. She went downstairs to the lobby, alone but dogged in her singleness. She was parenting herself. It was gloomy and enjoyable. Her outfit was her own. Not having to buy a new one, not having anyone to fuss over the details, she was newly content with her appearance.

She saw them: Sami, his mother, his sisters, the maidservant, and another woman too, his aunt, his mother's younger sister. The greetings were practised, and the aunt's warmth was additional. She felt both encompassed and protected. They followed her into the lift. It was small. And abruptly she was seized by a panic: upstairs, her parents, the waiting awkwardness of the conversation.

But it happened. The guests were impressed with her parents, impressed to find the lounge and the kitchenette and the balcony above the sea, a life of containments. And Papu and Mabi were enabled to descend: Papu was casual and quizzing, and made Sami nervous, and Mabi in her sari was alive to her own novelty, which the women found fittingly unapproachable.

The wedding: a marquee on the golf course, the trickle of unknown guests, the gifts, mostly cash in envelopes. Mabi was counting. The bride and groom remained on a sofa on an elevated ramp, and the photographer's flash was incessant. But she had to smile, facing the future, which was bright.

*

She moved to Lahore and into the house. The things in her trousseau came down a few days later in a van. They were given two rooms: Sami's old bedroom and a sitting room, a part of the veranda that was now enclosed by walls and a panel of windows. Sami's bedroom was dusted and painted and made marital by the induction of a large, low bed. And the sitting room absorbed the rest of her trousseau: a Chinese screen that folded, a teak cabinet, a china set, another set of six large plates and six small plates and six bowls, a silver tea set (it went into the cabinet) and a set of silver knives and forks and spoons.

She bought a telephone and placed it on the bedside table.

She called Nargis, who was now a journalist and was busy with work.

She called Sami, who said it was inappropriate.

She called her mother, who was alarmed and suspicious, and said that it was an unnecessary expense.

'How are you?' said Zakia, meaning it.

And Mabi said, 'We're fine, we're fine.'

They were more responsive when she told them she was pregnant. Mabi took a flight and came to Lahore for the weekend. She brought herbs for nausea, and a book of advice for first-time mothers, authored by two Americans, a gynaecologist husband and artist wife who were pictured on the back, grinning and casual and confident of conversions. Mabi herself was metallic in her new surroundings. She slept in the sitting room, and was up at dawn, drawn by habit into the kitchen, which she said was disorganized and potentially harmful. There were too many people in this house, she said, too much noise with the coming and going of relatives. It must be difficult for Zakia, who was raised in peace and quiet.

It was true that the sounds were constant: Suri's son, Isa, was three years old, a perpetual presence in the veranda on his tricycle; and Hukmi's boy, Moosa, had just witnessed his first birthday, a confusion of balloons and people that happened without warning on the lawn and left it plundered. Naseem, the maidservant, was made to clear the mess, and complained in passing to Zakia, who was already aware of intrusion (Nargis had pointed it out) and added to these complaints her own. But they were relayed to Sami's mother, who took umbrage and complained to Sami.

He said he didn't want to get involved.

'It doesn't really matter,' said Zakia.

'It does,' he said.

So Zakia complained instead to Sami's aunt, Chhoti, who lived with her husband in Barampur and had sent her only child, a girl, to live with her sister in Lahore. The girl was three years old, and after fighting with her minders she fled always to Zakia's room, where she settled just as quickly into a new object of interest, the tears drying forgetfully on her face. Chhoti was appreciative. She sat with Zakia and talked to Zakia, made inquiries about the pregnancy and offered to find a nanny.

Zakia said there was no need. In the morning Sami's mother sent a glass of milk and food cooked in ghee. It was sickening. And the illustrations in the book were unhelpful: the section titled 'Watch Your Back!' continued to amuse with irrelevant diagnoses of pains and aches she didn't yet feel. Sami was away, and she was alone, surrounded and bored.

The food kept coming to her room.

'I don't want it,' she said.

Naseem took it away.

The next day there was no food.

Sami said, 'You shouldn't have done that.'

'What did I do?'

'You shouldn't have upset my mother like that.'

'But what did I do?'

'She sends you things only because she cares for you. You shouldn't have thrown it in her face like that.'

She said, 'You've gone mad.'

She wasn't going to apologize.

That week the money, which came from the rental of a property they owned in Anarkali, was difficult for Zakia to obtain. She was surprised. And then she saw the message in the refusal.

She called Nargis.

'So do something,' said Nargis.

'What can I bloody do? *She* has the money, and *she* doesn't want to give it to me. What can I do?'

Nargis said, 'A job.'

Zakia said, 'Nargis, I'm pregnant.'

'You'll get leave.'

'When?'

'When you're about to give birth.'

'What'll I do?'

And Nargis said there were still many things that a young and educated woman could do.

The meeting with the editor occurred. He sent her to the features desk for a test, which required her to condense a lengthy article about a flower show into three paragraphs. She was new to typing but she managed, using only the forefinger of each hand, and the result was awkward, a stunted piece that began languidly and came to a squatting end. They liked it. Her first assignment was a review. She went to an art gallery with her photographer, and interviewed a calligrapher, a distracted old man in a beret who claimed to have solved the dilemma of representation in Islamic art: his Quranic verses were swirled into human silhouettes, each in a pose of theatrical self-discovery – there was the dance of joy, the scream of anguish, and cross-legged meditation in the shade of a tree. Her review was restrained and respecting; the title was *Man Made* and appeared in large black letters at the top of the page. Sami was dumbfounded. His mother and sisters were quietly impressed. And Papu called her from Karachi and gave advice about paragraphing.

She was asked to sub the letters and the news pages. The material was exhausting: every morning she searched the incoming articles for mistakes, for excesses and slights against the generals. The newspapers had been warned, and had warned their staff in turn: she had to look out for references to the executed prime minister, to his daughter, who had inherited the party and was leading a muted campaign. She had to kill the adjectives and neutralize the verbs. Critiques of the Islamization programme ('Leave It to Allah:

God's Mandate to Ward Off the Threat of Democracy') were scrapped or converted into reports: 'New Legislation on Blasphemy Passed', 'Adultery Made Crime', 'Textbooks to be Revised in Accordance with Spirit of Islam', 'New Compulsory Subjects to be Taught in Schools'.

She was summoned to the editor's room. She was returning from her lunch break. The office was empty, lulled by the ongoing drone of the printer. A peon was waiting at her desk. She followed him past the abandoned cubicles, starting to dread the summons and expecting an additional assignment for the weekend.

The editor was on the telephone. He saw her and raised a finger. He was listening to the telephone, and saying only, 'Yes, she will, I will see to it personally, rest assured it will not happen again.'

She took a chair at the desk and waited. She saw that his face was sweating.

He hung up the phone.

'That was the governor,' he said.

She nodded.

'The governor of this province,' he said, in case she hadn't heard. Then he flung the Lahore edition across the desk and said, 'Page five.' His face was cobwebbed in the fingers of his hands.

She opened the page.

And he said, 'You let this pass?'

She had seen it. The Islamabad correspondent had sent it in the previous night, a story on the flow of weapons in the north, remainders from the war that was now being fought in Afghanistan. There was mention of CIA operatives, the Reagan administration and their unnamed liaisons in the Pakistani military. She had checked the spellings as well as the names of locations, and changed the heading from 'The Case of the Invisible Soldiers' to a tighter and more enjoyable 'Open Arms'.

'It came in late,' she said.

'I don't care.'

'But I fixed it.'

'You are warned.'

*

She went home and called Nargis. And Nargis converted the anxiety into outrage: Zakia had done the right thing. She was doing more than her job; she was doing a service. They went in Nargis's car to Hania Apa's house. And there the article was already a sensation, and Zakia was commended again and again for upholding the spirit of dissent in a time of censorship and for making what they were calling an intervention.

She had become an interventionist, a journalist who took risks and gave thrills.

She began to see the ways of intervening. She wrote a perplexed report on the country's banned sportswomen, expressing surprise at their desire to exhibit their sporting skills. That sustained note of surprise was ironic, an intervention. But it wasn't noticed. She had to take on a bigger subject. She commissioned a profile of the cleric who appeared on television in the evenings and advocated a ban on women in the workplace. The profile was unquestioning and even reverential, but came with a retrospective on the changing face of the professional woman: the beehived stewardess of the sixties with her short kameez and high heels; the bell-bottomed film star of the seventies; and the respectable and head-covering newsreader of today, who saved her smile and her hairstyle for her family. Home is Where the Heart is Indeed.

'Clever girl,' said the first-class portraitist.

And her friend with the eyebrows agreed.

In December she went with Nargis to attend a dinner party at the house of a socialite. It was a large, complicated house, with a long driveway and a small, enclosed garden, and had high pillars outside and old-fashioned windows fitted into the brick walls. It was a new style that aspired to oldness. The socialite was standing behind her door with an empty tray in her hands, a small woman with bright green eyes. 'He's here!' she whispered excitedly.

He was an intellectual who was visiting from America. He taught there now at a liberal arts college, but had lived for many years in Pakistan, and then in Algeria, where he had opposed the French, and later in America, where he was tried in court and acquitted for allegedly planning to kidnap the man who had caused the Vietnam War. But the man they met now was slim and wore a black polo and had thick white hair, and smiled and bowed slightly when Zakia was introduced to him.

She saw that one of his eyes was odd.

'How do you do?' he said.

She smiled.

'And what do you do?'

'I'm a journalist,' she said, without the old trepidation.

'Ah!' he cried, and held out his arms, as though it was providential.

They conversed.

'I was in the north recently,' he said.

'Really,' she said.

'Yes,' he said, and explained that he had gone there to research a paper he was writing. He had found the bazaars of Peshawar filled with Lee-Enfield rifles and AK-47s and American M1s that were selling openly at the stalls. The locals were like children with toys. But these were not toys, he said, these were dangerous, unprecedented in their quantities, and nothing was being done to stop their passage into the settled areas.

'Smuggled,' she said, because she recalled it from the report she had subbed.

'The agencies,' he said.

'They are seeing to it.'

'They are funding it, they are actively funding it, make no mistake.'

'Proxy war,' she said.

And he said, 'The blowback will be costly. Not just for us but for the whole world.'

She was nodding.

He shook his head and sipped his drink, and pressed his lips together until they vanished.

Zakia said, 'And for what are we doing all this? For what? For Uncle Sam?'

The man stepped back as if to shield himself from her. He was laughing. 'There are three A's for Pakistan,' he said. 'Army, Allah, America.'

'*And* avaam!' she cried indignantly.

'And avaam,' he conceded, humbled by her insistence on having it included, 'and avaam.'

Later in the night she was standing next to another man, a retired brigadier who was talking about the military.

'They are very proper people,' he was saying. 'People of *high* calibre.'

He was drinking whisky from his glass, and it was dark and undiluted. The men around him were listening.

'All these *rumours*,' he was saying, and he enjoyed the word, which made him smile and gave his short black moustache a shrewd lift, 'they are all rubbish.'

Zakia said, 'You should look at what's happening in Peshawar.'

He heard her but didn't look at her, and she knew that she had trespassed.

She said, 'Guns and grenades are selling openly.'

The men were looking at her.

She said, 'Lee-Enfield rifles.'

'What do you know,' said the brigadier, and looked at her face, 'about Lee-Enfield rifles?'

She said, 'I know where they're selling.'

There were smirks.

And she said, 'And I know that it is *wrong* that they are selling like that . . .'

She wished at that moment that she had been holding something. Her hands were unemployed and felt obtrusive.

The brigadier was looking at her face, his eyes thin and his lips parted; and then he was looking at her neck and at her collarbones, which were bare, and at her blouse, which was made of a shiny white material and was covered in sequins.

He said, 'Madam. I would advise women like yourself to stay at home and observe the proper injunctions.' He said it to her toes, with a courtesy that was owed to her sex and not to her, owed to the kind of woman she could never have been; and then he was smiling and saying to the men: 'I am all for Islamization. We are in need of some punishments.'

Sami came home at the end of the month. She had begun to show. She herself didn't feel it, but Nargis had said it was noticeable.

'What do you think?' she asked him.

He was looking at her perplexedly and trying to formulate an opinion.

She had a vision of him lying on top of her and panting. She no longer wanted to hear his answer.

'You are,' he said. He was smiling.

'Dinner is in the kitchen,' she said and went into the bathroom.

Later they were in their room again, and the lights were dim. He was lying on his back in the bed and gazing at the ceiling, his arms and legs spread out.

She was sitting in a chair on the other side of the room and clipping her toenails with a nail cutter. She enjoyed the snap, the way the hard nail was cut and then fell off.

He began to tell her about the new warplanes they had received from the Americans. 'Multi-role fighter jets,' he said, and made the sound and flew his hand around in the air. 'Bubble canopies. A sphere of glass. Nothing like it.'

He was one of them.

'What the hell are you so happy for!' she shouted.

He got up from the bed.

'Don't *fucking* shout at me, you *bitch*!'

She was going to be made to give birth to his child.

She threw the nail cutter on the glass table and it cracked.

He stared at her and then stared at the table. His mouth was clenched, his shoulders heaving up and down with his breathing. But his anger was going.

He went into the bathroom.

'Get out!' she shouted, and her own voice was deep and clear. 'Get out of my *sight*! Get out!'

Nargis got her the interview.

'She's at the office,' Nargis said. 'Tell them your name at the gate and they'll take you to her.'

She drove the car herself to Garden Town. She passed houses, slowing down to read the numbers written on the plaques outside. They were increasing. She was going in the right direction, and kept going.

She found the black building with the bougainvillea shower hanging over its gate. It had an unusual exterior for an office, but she saw too that it made no announcements and how there were advantages to that.

The security guard at the gate asked for her name, took it inside, came back and told her she couldn't bring the car in. She had to park it in the lane, and went with him into the building. It was cold inside: she was made to wait on a chair in a corridor. Then the lawyer came out of a door, and she was a short, stout woman in a black coat, wearing wide glasses on her small face. She said she had spoken to Nargis, and explained again about the case, things Zakia already knew, and led her through the air-conditioned corridor into a glass-panelled room.

'Shabnam?' said the lawyer.

The woman was sitting in a chair at the desk. Her back was to them. She turned her head slowly. She was wearing a shawl and it covered her head and her face.

'Shabnam, this is Zakia. She has come here to take your interview.'

Shabnam didn't speak.

The lawyer said, 'You must tell her everything, *achha*? Tell her all the things that happened to you. She is a very good journalist.'

An interventionist, she thought.

The lawyer left them.

Zakia sat in the other chair. She said, 'I will write down what you tell me and I will also record it in this.' She held up the small recorder. 'I won't give it to anyone.'

The woman looked at her, looked at the recorder. She was still holding the shawl over her mouth.

'What happened?'

The woman said her sister-in-law had drugged her and handed her over to a man who had kept her for three days.

'When were you drugged?'

The woman said, 'Thursday.'

'How were you drugged? Was it an injection?'

'Injection. Yes.'

She saw that she shouldn't have asked it like that.

'When did you come to your senses?'

'I don't remember.'

Zakia waited.

'On Friday morning.'

It was being recorded.

'What happened after that?'

'He misbehaved with me.'

'Who did?'

'Akhlaaq did.'

'Who is Akhlaaq?'

'I don't know.'

'Had you known him?'

The woman was silent. Her eyes had blurred.

'Did you know him from before?'

'I did not know him. He saw me, then she gave me to him. I don't know what happened.'

Zakia said, 'Where did he keep you?'

'In a room.'

'What happened there?'

The woman sobbed and said, 'I don't know. Do not ask me. Do not ask me.' Her voice had splintered, and she sniffled and dabbed her eyes with the shawl, which briefly exposed her face, the mouth stained purple and the nose with a stud in it. 'I won't go back,' she said and drew the shawl again over her face.

'Where?'

'Don't send me back to them.'

'Who?'

'My people. If I am sent back to them, I will die.'

'You don't want to go to your parents?'

'I will die.'

'What about the police?'

'I will not go back.'

'Have you been to the police?'

'They will kill me. I will kill myself.'

'When did you go?'

'They have taken me everywhere. I have gone everywhere. I can't go back now.'

Zakia stopped the recorder, pulled up her chair and said, 'Where will you stay? Have you thought about that?'

And the woman didn't look at her, and kept her shawl over her mouth, and said, without the tears and without the earlier expression in her voice, that her people were waiting and she couldn't be made to go back.

She went to see Nargis afterwards. And Nargis was in her room, the same room upstairs, with the air-conditioner now fitted into the wall and covered in plastic.

'So?' said Nargis. She was sitting on her bed with her legs folded beneath her as she always did.

Zakia said, 'Nothing. She wouldn't say anything.'

Nargis said, 'Did you ask questions?'

'I did.'

'What did she say?'

'The same thing again and again. She said she didn't want to go back.'

Nargis looked at her intently, then looked away and said, 'She's going to have an abortion. That's what they're trying to tell her. She's never been to a clinic. She says she'll kill herself.'

'That's what she said,' said Zakia.

She thought of the recorder in her handbag.

'Are you going to write about it?' said Nargis.

'I don't think I can.'

Nargis understood.

Zakia said, 'What do you do?'

'I don't know. You do something. I don't know what.'

Zakia thought of taking out the recorder and showing it to Nargis.

'Sometimes,' said Nargis, 'I feel like it's all in my head.' She was looking at the wall and not at Zakia. 'I see something, and I think I want to do something about it, and then I can't do it because nothing has happened and it's all been in my head.'

Zakia said, 'I know.'

'Talk of other things.'

'Like what?'

'How's Sami?' said Nargis. She closed her eyes and pinched the skin at her brow.

'We fought. He's gone back. He'll come back next month. How's Moeen?'

'The same,' said Nargis. 'Selling his father's carpets.'

A maidservant came into the room. She was carrying a tray. She settled it on the bedside table, removed the tea cosy from the teapot and went away. Nargis watched her perform the task, watched her go away and said, 'Did you see that? She doesn't see it like that. She thinks it's just the serving of tea, just something she does three or four times a day. I gave her money, I enrolled her children in a school, I told her to go home and make handicrafts. But she came back to me for more money. And the other servants in the house detest her for taking that money and they detest me for giving it to her.' Nargis was rocking herself on the bed.

Zakia saw that it was what she did in this room.

Nargis indicated the tea tray and said, 'This is what we should be doing. We should be drinking tea.'

They were able to laugh at that.

Then Nargis told her about another case: a blind girl had been raped by two men and had taken her case to a court of law, and was charged there with adultery because she had confessed to sexual intercourse while failing to provide the evidence that was required to prove a charge of rape. 'So the men who raped her are free. But she has confessed. So she has to fight another case.'

Zakia said, 'What can you do?'

And Nargis said, 'They want to protest. Some women will go out with banners and things and stand on the street. They won't show it on TV or anything. But it'll be out in the street.'

Zakia said, 'Are you going?'

'I am.'

'I'll come.'

But the pictures from that protest were printed in the newspaper. And Zakia was in the enlarged picture: she stood on the side of the street and held a stick in her hand, which was held on the other end by a policewoman, while another policewoman stood behind Zakia and held her collar and pulled her hair. Zakia's eyes were shut in the picture, and her mouth was open in a wail or a scream or what may even have passed for a loud laugh. The caption beneath her said: *Woman activist struggles with representatives of the state*.

Her sisters-in-law saw it and showed it to her mother-in-law. And she went into Zakia's room and shouted with her raised hand carving up the air. What kind of family did Zakia think she was from? What kind of mother was she going to make? Had she thought about the child she was carrying in her womb? Had she thought about her husband?

'What have we done?' cried the mother-in-law. 'To earn this shame? What have we done?'

She heard it for some minutes and then she shouted, 'I will do what I want! I will decide! Not you! Not your son! I will decide!'

When Sami came back the incident was already three weeks old. She was speaking to her mother-in-law again but in a new way, a way in which they understood and accepted and finally refused each other.

'Why did you do that?' he said.

'I'm sorry,' she said, because she had decided that it was easier that way, easier on her and on those who were attached now to her life. 'I should have told you. I will the next time.'

He said, 'What about the name?'

She said, 'Your mother's already decided. If it's a girl she wants to call her Samia.'

They were driving back from Nargis's house at night. It was late, and the Gulberg roads were empty.

He said, 'What if it's a boy?'

'I don't know,' she said. 'I like Imran. I like Imaad. I like names that begin with I. But your mother wants Moazzam.'

He said, 'We'll name him after you.'

'What?'

'Zaki,' he said. 'It's a nice name. Means "pure". I checked in a book.'

She took maternity leave because her doctor advised it. She was expected now to go and stay with her parents in Karachi for some months. But she didn't want to go there until the very end. So she stayed in Lahore and spent her mornings on the phone with Nargis: they discussed her sickness, the signs and the cures. A new room was required and had to be attached to the bedroom. An architect was summoned and drew up the plan for an appendage that would occupy the small space at the back of the house. It was a permanent attachment. And she was going to usher it into the world! The cot and the toys they had already bought, and Sami's mother had begun to preside over the wait with her silent, steady involvement: she paid for their things, paid for the doctor, the architect, the construction of the nursery – it was a strain, she said, but she had saved all along, had tended her property and leased it out and opened a bank account that earned interest. They were things Zakia still had to understand, earning five thousand rupees a month, an amount that paid only for the petrol in her van. The awareness of that dependence compounded the sense of responsibility, increased the panic and the preparation. She stood before the mirror and watched herself for changes. Her body was obviously distorted. But that was temporary. The aspect of estrangement persisted and fed the feeling of a lag between herself and the woman she was on her way to becoming. She stayed more and more in the house. Sami came to visit and put his ear to her mounding belly and was waiting for a kick, which came at last but left him disconcerted, like a rebuke.

He bought her a stereo. 'For company,' he said. 'It'll keep you cheered up.'

'I'm not depressed.'

'Even so.'

It was bought from an electronics shop on Hall Road, a second-hand Sanyo: the rounded netting of the speakers gave the impression of an insect. It stared all day and night from its place on the floor. Finally she bought an audio tape – *Evergreen Hits of Madam Noor Jehan* – and the device was roused: first she played it only in the mornings, then in the afternoons and evenings as well. The songs gave rise to a progression, a way of listening that was also a way of being: she played the tragic ones at dusk and the lively uplifting ones in the morning to start the day.

She missed the phone when it rang at first – she was in the bathroom and the stereo was playing – but then she caught the ring, muffled and pressing in the music, and she trundled out of the bathroom with a hand on her back, her belly high and humorous, her bare feet making flat slaps on the floor.

'Hello?'

They wanted to know if they were speaking to Mrs Shirazi.

It was odd to be addressed in this way, and on the telephone, which made it even more impersonal.

'Yes,' she said, and had the fleeting vision of a bank.

The voice wanted to confirm it was speaking to Mrs Shirazi.

'Yes, yes,' she said. 'I am Mrs Shirazi.'

They were calling from the air base. There had been an accident.

'What?' she said.

The plane had gone down with her husband.

She listened to the things the man was now saying about the funeral and her forthcoming pension, and she sat down on the bed.

'Are you sure?' When she said it her hand went to her mouth.

She left the phone in the room and went out to the veranda. She was walking. It was wrong that she could. She walked barefoot in the shadows and emerged out into the heat of the lawn, where everything was bright. She stepped across the grass, which was dry under her feet, the soil beneath it cool and moist.

She held the bark of the tree and spat.

Her spittle hung in a thread. She wasn't going to vomit and ran a sleeve across her mouth to dry it.

Her thoughts were distinct.

She wasn't crying.

She thought of the things she would have to tell her unborn child.

She was crying.

But she stopped herself. She had to go inside and tell his mother that he was dead. That was the first thing she had to do, bearing witness for the sake of another person, a thing for which she was unprepared.

She had to leave herself.

Two months later, in the curtained ward of a Karachi hospital she gave birth to me: I was born into a world of absences that became lacks in my childhood. My father was dead from the start and my mother seemed always to be going away, her feet in shoes on the veranda floor and the back of her van as it went out of the gate. There were hours to pass in the day, and days to spend, but always a wait for the promised return of what was mine to me.

'You are late,' said Daadi.

'I was working,' said my mother.

'I called the office. They said you had left.'

'I was working.'

'Don't lie to me.'

'I'm not lying to you. I don't need to lie to you.'

'Some sense, some consideration. I worried all day . . .'

'Well, you shouldn't.'

'You can take the driver, you can take the maid if you want.'

'But I don't see the need.'

'Every day there are stories, there are rapes and robberies . . .'

'I *don't* feel the need.'

'Then take the child, take the child if you don't see, if you don't want to see. Don't leave the child with me.'

And my mother did, to prove a point. But the outings were marred by other commitments, the responsibilities of a journalist: the smoke on roads and the traffic jams in the afternoon, the light red, orange, green and red again; the crescent on an ambulance, and the flashing red light of the cavalcades. The late sun bled and bled.

'I'm trying,' she said, 'be patient, please.'

At home, Daadi asked, 'So how was the day?' Her tone was armoured.

I said it was fine.

'We had a lot of fun,' said Samar Api, inserting her perspective to broaden the view, and later, to me, 'You're so selfish.'

After the protest, when the editor removed my mother from her job, she became briefly confined to the house. Her friends came over to condole, but then she tired of it and began to go out to see them. Her routine collapsed.

At once Daadi became conciliatory. She began to ask after my mother and initiated conversations that were unusual in their involvement and fervency. She was attuned now to the rigidities of journalism: the shortcomings and the endless risks and the futility – it didn't even pay well. And concurrently Daadi began to talk of her property in Anarkali. They could sell it and build a block of flats elsewhere and rent them out periodically. She had consulted Suri's husband, who knew about housing and said that now was just the time to invest. In fact they ought to seize the opportunity.

But my mother had made up her mind: she and Auntie Nargis were going to start their own magazine, a journal devoted to women's issues (but not confined to those issues). My mother was going to edit, and Auntie Nargis had agreed to run the Marketing Department. They were going to call it *Women's Journal*.

Daadi stared at my mother, said she should have known better and went to lie down on her bed.

Women's Journal was launched in the last week of October. Auntie Nargis went to see the chief minister and obtained a No Objection Certificate after showing him a dummy that was also a fraud: it had only four pages (they planned to have twenty) and showed women standing about in draperies. An actress agreed to attend the launch but called up on the morning of the event to cancel. My mother had to cut the ribbon. There was applause. A photographer took pictures, which appeared in the second issue of *Women's Journal*, in a section called 'Launch': there was a picture of Samar Api (*Young Samar*) and me (*and Young Zaki*), and one each of Barkat and Naseem, who were given free copies. The editorial was entitled 'Repeal the Black Laws!' Auntie Nargis drew a funny cartoon (she signed under a pseudonym) and provided a flattering sketch of Benazir to accompany a profile, attributed to someone called Sara Hasan, who was, like the other contributors, a fake: all the pieces were composed by the editor and publisher, who pretended nevertheless to have gathered a colourful staff from diverse ethnic backgrounds. (They came up with names like Tariq Bhatti, Aafia Khan, Mir Shadaab Baloch and Samuel Masih.) Some of the pages were joined at the edges and had to be torn. The price was twenty rupees.

The first real member of the staff was Miss, my English teacher at school. My mother recruited her at the parent–teacher conference. Miss had earned a master's degree in English from Punjab University and was sent out a few times to report on cultural events. But her writing style was choppy and unprofessional, and she was soon transferred to the Graphics and Layout Department. It was strange having her in the house with my mother, like a merger of separate realities in a dream, and her loss at school was mourned, because her replacement was an arthritic old lady who couldn't speak English, who carried a ruler for discipline and shouted 'Don't behave!' when the class was rowdy.

The circulation grew. Two hundred copies were printed and

dispatched in the first two weeks. In the third week no copies were returned, and a vet placed a black-and-white ad on the back page. A bumper issue appeared to mark the start of the new year. It said on the masthead: *The staff and management of* Women's Journal *wish you a happy and auspicious New Year!* The price was raised to twenty-five rupees. But the following week there were letters of protest, two from Lahore and one from Faisalabad, and the price retreated. In spring Auntie Nargis flew to Karachi to meet a businesswoman who had developed a liking for the magazine and wanted to support it in whatever way she could, and there was excited talk at the office of a full-page colour ad, estimated to fetch no less than forty thousand rupees.

One evening a woman went to Pioneer Store in Main Market and asked for a copy of *Women's Journal*.

The manager was sitting at his desk. He indicated the rack that held the newspapers and magazines and said, 'It is not there? Then it is not there.'

The woman looked at the publications hanging off the rack. 'It can't be,' she said. 'Everyone else has got it.'

'O JUNAID!' cried the manager.

'WHAT!' cried Junaid from the poultry section.

'DO WE HAVE WOMEN'S MAG?'

'*Women's Journal*,' corrected the woman.

'WHAT?' cried Junaid.

'WOMEN'S JOURNAL!' cried the manager. 'DO WE HAVE IT?'

'WOMEN'S JOURNAL?'

'YES, WOMEN'S JOURNAL!'

'NO!' cried Junaid from poultry. 'THERE IS NO SUCH THING AS WOMEN'S JOURNAL!'

'You are wrong,' said the woman and laughed disdainfully. 'It is the best new magazine. And if you haven't got it, you haven't got a thing. You have lost a customer in me today.' And she went out of the shop.

Then two children came in, younger boy and older girl, and asked for a copy of *Women's Journal*. The manager was distraught.

He picked up the telephone and dialled a number, and said, 'We don't have it here. But come tomorrow and you will find it.'

Outside the shop, in the van, my mother said, 'What did he say?'

'He said come tomorrow,' said Samar Api.

I said, 'He was calling someone on the phone.'

And my mother said, 'Good. Good. That's initiative.'

The next day Pioneer Store ordered twenty copies of *Women's Journal* and hung them on the rack.

Once a year my mother and I went to see Papu and Mabi in Karachi. They paid for our tickets, a detail that was mentioned again and again in Daadi's room and turned our trips into acts of privilege and privacy. Packing was discussed for days, and suitcases were stuffed and emptied and stuffed again. It was important to consider toys and clothes with honesty and to take only what was necessary.

'O God,' said Samar Api. 'Take something to read.'

She could say it because she had read many magazines.

I enjoyed the Beach Fantasy Hotel, though by now nothing resembling a beach fantasy could be found there. The water beyond the deck was black and swampy and stank of fish in the afternoons, and was surrounded by territorial seagulls that were always in a panic. The lifts inside the hotel were occupied by fat, fiddling men and made-up women, silent and habitual, as though they had dressed for a wedding that was perpetually round the corner.

But little had changed in the general manager's suite on the fourth floor of the tall, whitewashed building. My mother said Papu was like the man he used to be, pressed and cuff-linked in his suits, with only the thin new folds of skin on his face to show for his age. And Mabi was able to move around the suite with youthful ease in a sari, though she was shrivelled now and slightly stooped, like a chilli exposed to the sun. Sometimes our trips coincided with those of Auntie Shazreh, my mother's younger sister, who brought expensive chocolates from Canada but left her husband and children at home.

'Why does she do that?' I asked my mother.

'Because she still hasn't forgiven Papu and Mabi.'

'Why hasn't she forgiven them?'

'Because some people hold grudges.'

'What's grudges?'

'Look it up.'

I said, 'Does it mean something bad?'

'Not *bad* . . .'

'Then what?'

She thought about it and said, 'They're disciplinarians. And it's important to have some disciplinarians in your life.'

I said, 'Who's the disciplinarian in *your* life?'

'You're getting quite sharp, mister. Shall I leave you here with Mabi?'

'Sorry,' I said, because it was not something I could imagine, living with Papu and Mabi in the suite and having to eat all my meals at their small round table, where the napkins were starched and folded into triangles and placed on the smaller plates, and forks and knives were used in limited ways. It was not uncommon, while we were eating, for Papu to look up from his plate and say:

> Zaki Zaki Strong and Able
> Take Your Elbows off the Table
> This Is Not a Horse's Stable
> But a First-Class Dining Table

So I stayed away from the general manager's suite, and spent my time chasing cats in the courtyard by the lobby, or diving in the shallow end of the swimming pool. Sometimes I played with the children of hotel guests and drew them in with my knowledge of the hotel premises; I took them in the lift up to the conference room, and further up to see the Chinese restaurant with the revolving doors on the sixth floor, then down again to the lobby and back into the area by the pool. I led them from place to place until they began to understand their surroundings, and began to express their opinions and assert their independence; then I felt betrayed and fought with them and abandoned them and went back up in the lift to the suite on the fourth floor.

One day I went up to change out of my jeans, which were soaked after being in the pool and were starting to itch. The door to the suite was open.

'But I don't understand,' Mabi's voice was saying. 'You're young, you're attractive. What's stopping you?'

Auntie Shazreh said, 'You'll never understand her. You never understood *me*! Even then you were of the opinion –'

'Look,' said my mother. 'It's not what you think it is. I'm not stopping myself. And he's not the obstacle in my path.'

'Obstacle' was a mixture of 'obvious' and 'bicycle'.

'Then what is it?' said Mabi. 'You have to explain it to me.'

'I don't have to explain anything,' said my mother. She had stood up and was walking towards the door.

'Zaki!'

'Sorry,' I said, even before she had finished saying my name.

She was looking at me now, and looking as if for the first time, a boy in rolled-up jeans who had nowhere to go and was not the obstacle in her path.

'O God sorry!' I was crying now, bawling.

'Shhh,' said my mother, and lifted me up in her arms.

Her happiness was not in question. There was cause for thought, moments that belonged to a time when she was someone else, a girl in a Polaroid with the depths of mountains showing behind her. But even that was tainted by the incipient story of my life, as though I had been in her womb all along and was pushing her from the start towards the axial event of my birth. I couldn't ask her if she was unhappy because I couldn't ask her to say that I was not the cause of her unhappiness.

'Samar Api,' I asked one night, 'do you think she doesn't get married because of me?'

We were lying in wicker beds on the roof. It was August, the last month of the monsoon. All day the rain had been slashing and insistent; trees swayed and fell and lay like logs in the roads, which were swamped. The overhead wires had snapped; there was no electricity in the neighbourhood and the house was dark.

On the roof the night was clear. The clouds had left the moon in light.

'Not at all,' said Samar Api. 'She doesn't do it because she doesn't want to. There's nothing like your first love.' She closed her eyes and released a sigh. It merged with the breeze.

'Samar Api?'

She moaned.

'Make a wish.'

She cupped her hands, brought them to her mouth and whispered the wish, which was chosen without deliberation, without hesitation, then blew it away and watched as it went up into the night.

5

Morning assembly at an all-girls English-medium secondary school was usually rowdy: it took regimentation and surveillance and repeated warnings from the microphone on the headmistress's elevated podium to settle the hush. But this was the first day of the first term of the year, a new start by all accounts, and already the square was filling up with early arrivals: the girls stood in lines beneath the leaves of trees and were glad to find a flow in the atmosphere, the confused camaraderie that follows the relief of finding an altered sameness. Talk today was lively and encouraging and frequently involved a mention of Tara Tanvir, a new girl who had joined their school.

'I keep hearing her name,' said Samar Api.

'She's got a rep,' said Snober Tariq factually. She herself was plain and unremarkable, an ordinary girl who was not in the running for things.

'Have you seen her?' asked Samar Api. It was a way of furthering a conversation that had begun.

Snober Tariq said she hadn't, and added that, to the best of her knowledge, neither had anyone else.

The bell rang and the girls went to new classrooms. They were heightened, practised, discerning, alert to signs of progress, the way bodies had shed shapes and grown into new ones; and the voices were kinder, less jutting in their ownness, so that talking to one another felt easier and also surpassable. Samar Api took an empty desk at the back and settled her bag on the floor. She took out her new books and smelled the pages.

Mrs Waheed came in and said, 'First of all I would like to say that welcome back.'

Her hands held the topmost edge of the high teacher's chair at the fore of the classroom. She was wearing a green-and-yellow floral-print sari, a thing for which she was known, and her gaze sought to establish contact, then distance and order. 'I would also like to add,' she said, 'that we have a new addition to our class. She has just joined this institution and I have no doubt in my mind that you will make her feel at home in no time at all.' This kind of language was assumed to be an aspect of Mrs Waheed's specialization in English Literature. She enjoyed using words like *prudence* and *prurience* and enjoyed writing long sentences in her stylish handwriting on the blackboard.

'You may come in, Tara,' said Mrs Waheed and stood with her hands behind her back.

In the doorway there was no one and the pause that followed was charged with challenge. Mrs Waheed gave a smile that suggested her patience and experience as a teacher, then repeated her request without annoyance but also without the earlier note of invitation.

The girl came in. She stood against the wall with her schoolbag in her hands, her arms fair and rounded in the half-sleeved summer uniform and linked below her belly in a V as if against a chill in the room.

'Tara hasn't made any friends yet,' noted Mrs Waheed.

The girl was looking at the floor and at the fronts of desks.

'But I am sure she will make them.'

Other girls were smiling.

'You may sit down, please,' said Mrs Waheed withdrawingly and turned to the blackboard.

The girl began her walk along the column of desks, and was unfazed by the attentive silence. She seemed to live inside a wide-eyed imperviousness that caused a current of self-awareness to pass in her surroundings. Abruptly she chose an empty desk at the back of the room and let her schoolbag drop to the floor.

Samar Api saw that they were neighbours.

For some minutes they remained unacquainted.

Then the girl reached out a hand that left a ball of paper on her neighbour's desk.

Samar Api unrolled the ball and read it.

Hi I'm Tara! Wotsup?

Samar Api wrote, *Samar.*

The paper was crumpled and returned.

Nice name!

Samar Api wrote, *Thanks*

I hate my name!

Samar Api wrote, *Why*

I think its so dumb! But frankly I dont care!

Samar Api wrote, *I think its a nice name*

And Tara Tanvir wrote, *Thanks babe!!* And then: *So tell me something!!*

Like what??

Any thing!!

Like what??

Are you a virgin?

Later that day we met in Daadi's dressing room. I had tripped on the gravel path at school and had scraped my knee, and was looking for the bottle of Dettol in Daadi's cupboard.

'What are you doing?' said Samar Api. She was following the slow progress of a lipstick in the wardrobe mirror.

'Finding Dettol.'

'What happened?' Her interest was minimal.

'Fell.'

'Oh no.' She frowned at the mirror in a version of concern.

'What are you doing?' I said.

'My make-up.'

There was nothing more to say.

'Guess what?' said Samar Api.

'What?'

'Today I had the shock of my life.' She made a smack with her lips.

'What happened?'

'I met this new girl, Tara Tanvir. She's got a rep.'

I said, 'Wow.'

She screwed on the cap to the lipstick and returned it to the shelf, watching herself perform this function.

I said, 'What's your rep?'

And she said, 'I don't have a rep.' She altered her expression in the mirror to one of piety and innocence, then changed it abruptly to one of trauma and shock.

'What's mine?'

'Boys don't get reps. Only girls get reps. Like only girls get boobs.'

I said I understood.

'I'm going to her house in a while,' said Samar Api. 'She has a cinema in her basement. She invited me herself. You can come with me if you want.'

Tara Tanvir lived in Cantt. She gave directions to her house on the phone: it lay beyond the bridge in one of several small lanes, beyond a chowk that was popularly associated with a bakery. The gate was made of beige wood and the house number was engraved on a large brass plaque that was nailed to the outside wall. The rest was reassurance: the way was short; directions would suffice; the thing to remember was the bakery, beyond which everything was simple.

We left the house at sundown, when the roads were filled with vehicles returning from the day's destinations. Our driver Barkat was obliging and succumbed again and again to manipulations. Briefly, on the bridge, the traffic eased; then it thickened again. We emerged from the blockage into Cantt, where the roads were in night and the trees stood in pools of shadow, the houses large and lit behind high walls and gates. We passed the army school for boys, then the army school for girls, dark properties that were guarded by gates with the army emblem of two locked swords. We passed the famous bakery, where cars had gathered under bright neon lights. And then we were lost. The road was dark again and the lanes were unmarked and sprouted continually on either side.

'We will find it,' said Barkat.

'Oh yes,' said Naseem, imitating his manner and voice, 'we will find it.'

'O God!' cried Samar Api, because the time for our arrival had passed.

But we found the house: the lane led directly to the gate, which sat in a warm haze of lighting. Barkat corroborated the house number on the plaque and honked.

A guard appeared in a uniform. A rifle was slung in its casing behind his shoulder. He bent, placed his head in Barkat's window, took our names and went back inside.

There was a wait.

'They take precautions,' said Naseem. Her window was down and her elbow was settled on the felt. It was hard to tell from her tone if she thought this to be an affectation.

'Security,' said Samar Api.

Barkat nodded.

The gate opened and the car went in. It was another straight drive into a porch. The walls to either side were thick with ivy, high and obscuring, like walls in a maze. The car stopped behind two others, a jeep and its low relation, both parked in the shaded porch with their backs turned. The rest of the house rose above and behind.

'Let's go now,' said Samar Api and got out of the car.

'One hour,' said Naseem. 'No more. Other people have work to do at home.'

We went past the ivy and past the tinted windows of the jeep. The door to the house was dark and densely carved in wood, and could have been the door of a tribal chieftain, or the door to a temple, plucked and carted and fitted into the blank white wall of this house.

'Swati door,' said Samar Api and ran a finger along the carvings. They were real. She withdrew her hand and rang the bell. The sound was remote and pleasing.

I rang it again.

'Stop it,' said Samar Api.

A maid opened the door. She was like a dwarf, a foreigner with a small body and a large, swollen face, the eyes sleepy and lidless. She was wearing dungarees over a T-shirt. 'Yes, please,' she said in English and held the door guardedly.

The air inside was cold, and the floors were white and polished.

All about there was a smell of varnished wood, a severe smell that seemed to have been sprayed from a bottle. We went with the maid along a staircase, up into a drawing room where the sofas were empty and the walls were hung with paintings that lacked people or plants – they were just planes of colour with spots and streaks, like accidents, or jokes, but framed and lit from above for show.

The maid knocked on a door. It was one of several in the drawing room, all closed now.

'Maadaam?' cried the maid.

A girl's voice responded from inside, hassled and inquiring.

'You are guest!' cried the maid. 'They here!'

A pause; then thumping, the sounds of feet on a carpet.

'Oh, *hi!*' she cried, standing in the doorway with a hand on the doorknob, her head tilted to one side. Her eyes were naturally wide, and her face was washed and raw, the lashes thick and gleaming with moisture.

She said, 'That your younger brother?' She was pointing with her finger.

'Cousin,' said Samar Api.

Tara Tanvir held out a hand and said, 'Hi, I'm Tara.'

I held her hand.

She covered her mouth with the other hand and giggled.

'What's your name?' she said.

'Zaki.'

'Hi, I'm Tara.'

I knew.

'Come on,' said Samar Api and went inside.

The walls of the room were bare but for a large oval mirror and a mostly empty shelf, the few books on it slanting weightfully to one side. The curtains by the windowpane were gathered with rope at the waist, like curtains in a ballroom. Her bed had pillars, one atop each leg, and the bedding was thorough: there were pillows, sheets, a blanket, more sheets, and a final bedcover of dark, undulated fabric.

'So tell me, you guys,' she said, and scanned her own room now, like someone called in to give it a lift. She was dressed in a faded T-shirt and pyjamas that ended at her knees.

'You have a really nice house, Tara,' said Samar Api.

'You think so?' She sounded sceptical.

'It's really very nice,' said Samar Api.

'Ya, it's nice,' I said.

'Thanks, you guys,' she said with warmth, but belatedly, as though the remarks were false but touching. 'You guys are nice.'

We smiled.

'Oh, did you find the house?' she said.

It was not possible to say no.

'Ya, ya,' said Samar Api with a flapping motion of the hand and a frown to belittle our attempts, the long journey, the bickering in the car and the relief at the end.

'It was easy,' I said.

'Good!' said Tara Tanvir. She was glad and enlivened; she sat up on her bed and moved away towards the pillows, her movements tender and childlike, as if accustomed to physical assistance from a stronger person. Samar Api took off her shoes and sat with her friend, and I stood beside them at first, then sat on the edge of the bed and listened to their conversation, a continuation of what had started in the morning at school.

The Far Eastern maid came in with glasses of cold juice on a tray and placed them on round, white coasters on the bedside table.

'You guys want popcorn?' said Tara Tanvir.

The Far Eastern maid was waiting with the empty tray on her palm.

'Sure,' said Samar Api. She sat up and tucked a strand of hair behind her ear.

'Bring it to the basement,' said Tara Tanvir.

The maid went away.

'You guys want to go to the basement now or later?' said Tara Tanvir.

Samar Api thought about it and said, 'Whenever you want.'

Tara Tanvir continued to look at us, then shrugged her shoulders and threw up her hands and said, 'Why don't we go once and for all?'

*

It was a dark, flickering space with an atmosphere of submergence: the black leather seats were low and ran on in rows that led all the way to the back, where a projector cast its images in a beam onto the wall ahead, a simple trick of light and distance. The film was called *Indiana Jones*. It was about an American man of the same name who wore hats and enjoyed the company of blonde women. To pass the time he taught archaeology at a university; otherwise he had adventures. On this particular adventure he had travelled to India, first on a faulty aeroplane and then on a boat, and had found a grieving population who wanted him to rescue three egg-shaped rocks with magical properties from the hands of an evil man. We knew the evil man.

'O God Samar Api it's Amrish Puri!'

He was a famous Indian villain. He dressed flamboyantly and lived on addas in the wilderness, surrounded by assistants and dancing girls.

'O God,' said Samar Api and laughed.

In this film Amrish Puri had a side role, and was one of many Indian characters, including slaves, maharajas, children blinded by spells and wealthy Indian dinner guests who came to a palace and ate monkey brains at a long table. Amrish Puri was a part of this world. And, like everyone else in the world, he had to speak most of his dialogues in English.

The accent was odd, the consonants dull and thudding. And he wore a brown robe, which was like a sack. His head was shaved; he wore no hat to hide it. And his laughter was exaggerated.

'I didn't know he came in English films,' said Samar Api.

'Frankly I don't care,' said Tara Tanvir.

The film finished when Indiana Jones threw Amrish Puri into a swamp of crocodiles. Samar Api stood up and asked to go to the bathroom. Tara Tanvir said that the washroom – that was what they called it in her house – was at the end of the corridor outside. Samar Api said she would find it on her own and went away.

'So tell me,' said Tara Tanvir.

The cinema was still dark and we were alone in it.

'How do you like my house?'

I had already told her, and said again, 'It's very nice.'

'You're telling the truth, *na*?' Her voice had grown solemn.

'It's really very nice,' I said. 'I like your paintings, the ones on the walls.'

'See, that's what I like about you,' she said, and sat up in her seat. 'You're blunt. I like guys who are blunt. I'm *so* blunt.'

I looked at her.

She was waiting.

I said, 'Ya.'

'And it's *good* to be blunt.'

'Ya.'

'I always say that.'

'You should.'

'*Heina?*'

'Ya.'

She was pleased. She relaxed into her seat, pressing against the leather for her comfort. 'I'm glad we agree,' she said. 'It's always good when friends agree. I'm not saying you can't disagree, because sometimes you have to. I'm saying that there has to be trust.' Her sloping hands came together at the fingertips and formed a pyramid.

Samar Api returned from the washroom, her interest in the house revived: she wanted to see the rooms, the roof, the kitchen, the other washrooms, all of which she indicated in the puzzled and extracting questions she now asked Tara Tanvir, who answered the questions and also gave suggestions for things we could do: there was more popcorn in the kitchen, but we weren't hungry; a keyboard, a Casio, lying somewhere in the house; and there was a library, her father's, but it would have to be opened with a key.

'We can play something,' I said.

'Ignore him, Tara,' said Samar Api. 'He's always hyper.'

'You can be really mean sometimes,' said Tara Tanvir and laughed.

'I'm just joking,' said Samar Api. 'He's like my younger brother.' Her humour had subsided.

'You guys are lucky,' said Tara Tanvir. She was looking into her lap and stroking the side of her arm.

'You're lucky too,' I said, and wanted to cite the cinema, the popcorn, the cars parked outside in the porch.

But Tara Tanvir continued to look away and continued to stroke the side of her arm.

'Tara's an only child,' said Samar Api.

'So are we,' I said.

'You guys have each other,' said Tara Tanvir.

And we were humbled to find that it had made such a difference.

After that we returned to her room to play board games, which were kept in boxes under her bed. She owned *Monopoly*, *Scrabble*, a game called *Cowabunga*, and another called *Trivial Pursuit*, all of which were packed with care and whole, the quirky implements gathered and contained in their pockets. Tara Tanvir was tidy.

'Not at all,' she said with a guilty giggle, her shoulders shrugged in self-negation. 'The maid does it. I'm like not at all a tidy person. I don't even fold the boards.'

And board games were games with boards: *Monopoly*, *Scrabble*, *Cowabunga* and *Trivial Pursuit*, even the cracked *Ludo* set Naseem kept above the fridge at home, all were games with boards and belonged to the same family. It was an eye-opening journey, and threw a new light on the world of language, which shimmered momentarily with a profusion of journeys.

We played *Trivial Pursuit*, a quiz-like game in which correct answers led to the accumulation of colourful pies. The questions were phrased on the backs of coloured cards; they referred to events in faraway places, to crimes and discoveries and decisive baseball victories, to songs we hadn't heard, films we hadn't seen.

'It's not your fault,' said Tara Tanvir. 'I even know all the answers.'

We were sitting on the carpeted floor of her room.

'We can go outside,' I said.

'I think we should go home,' said Samar Api.

'You guys are bored,' said Tara Tanvir, in a way that acknowledged her own shortcomings but also implied a lack of consideration on our part. She began to withdraw the coloured cards and pies from their places.

'We *want* to stay,' said Samar Api. 'But we're already late and our family's conservative. We only had permission for one hour.'

'Shit, man . . .' said Tara Tanvir, whose own fear of conservative families was wide and vacant.

'We'll meet tomorrow, *na*,' said Samar Api.

'It's Friday,' said Tara Tanvir.

'So you can come to our house.'

She thought about it.

'Get permission, *na*.'

'Tomorrow?' It was possible.

'Ya.'

'Let's do that.'

'*Theek hai*, na?'

And Tara Tanvir closed her eyes and smiled and nodded and said, 'Definitely, definitely.'

It was announced that night that a friend of Samar Api's was coming to see the house.

'And I want orange juice,' she said.

'We have orange juice,' said Daadi.

Naseem said we had one unopened packet in the fridge that was going to expire.

'Won't expire in a day,' said Daadi.

'But I want freshly squeezed orange juice,' said Samar Api.

And oranges were added to the list of items to be brought the following day from the market.

They came with their leaves in transparent plastic bags, which were sent to the kitchen. Samar Api stood above the worktop and watched as the oranges were crushed on the slow rotating mound of the juicer. It was a lengthy process, requiring an effort and commitment disproportionate to the amount of juice it yielded: one by one the oranges were juiced, disembowelled, discarded; and the juice was only starting to collect.

'Go away from here,' said Naseem, 'or I'll drain it in the sink.'

*

There was work to do.

Samar Api decided to start with her own room.

She changed the bedsheets first, stripping the mattress of its polka-dot covering and replacing it with a plain white sheet, then a pale blue one. She spanked the pillows to get rid of the dust, patted their bellies and plucked their corners. The location of the two-hearted picture frame on the bedside table was altered from beside the lamp to behind the lamp, then directly in front of the lamp.

She went into the next room, where the curtains were drawn, the fan whirring in the shadows. Daadi was rigidly asleep on her bed and was covered in a taut sheet like a corpse. The cylinder of air-freshener stood among the medicines on the mantelpiece. Samar Api returned with it to her room and sprayed it around the bed. She paused to inhale the smell.

It was strong.

She opened the windows and switched on the fan.

She went into the kitchen and returned: the juice was complete.

She switched off the fan in her room and closed the windows. Once again, in the altered setting, she sought her vision: the bedding, the lamp, the picture frame, the posters of Amitabh on the wall.

'Looks nice,' I said.

But she wasn't satisfied. She went into my mother's room and looked in the wardrobe, looked in the drawers, then on the shelves, where she found a crystal ashtray and a brass bell that gave a tinkling noise when it shook. On her way out she took the telephone too, but without the wires, which wouldn't leave the room.

The items were arranged on the bedside table in her own room: the phone, the bell and the ashtray now joined the frame and the lamp.

'Looks nice.'

She agreed.

'What about the phone?'

'We'll say it's new.'

She went to inspect the veranda and found cobwebs on the upper walls. The lawn was not mown. In the heated sheen of the afternoon the driveway was parched and bare. The car had gone for servicing.

'I'll bring her inside,' she said, and went back inside.

She chose my clothes for me: a full-sleeved shirt, worn with a blazer and a pair of velvety corduroy trousers in brown.

'It's so hot, Samar Api.'

'Doesn't matter,' she said, and held up the shirt. 'You can do this for me once, can't you?'

And, having settled the rest, she retired to the dressing room, where she spent a long time, emerging at last in a dark shalwar kameez with short sleeves and a focused expression, her features sharp with added lines and colours. She went into the kitchen for one last look, then went into the veranda and sat in a chair under the fan, waiting for her friend to arrive.

The sounds came: a horn from outside, long and unhurried, the gate dragging, then the roar of a big car as it rolled up the driveway and came to a stop outside the veranda. The doors opened and slammed. Now silence, a long pause before the sounds returned, of shoes in the veranda, nearing, and voices fading in the distance.

'Go on,' said Naseem, who was standing with me in the kitchen and pouring the cold juice into two tall glasses to be taken away now on a tray. 'Your guest is here. Go and make her happy.'

'You go first,' I said.

Naseem sighed. She wrung her hands in the sink, lifted the tray and went away.

She returned with the tray, which was empty.

'She here?'

'Oh yes,' said Naseem.

'Did they drink the juice?'

'Must have.'

'You didn't stay.'

'No, no.'

'Should I go?'

'If you want.'

I went. I stood before the door and knocked.

'Who is it?' said Samar Api from inside.

'It's me,' I said. 'Your cousin.'

'You can come in.'

She was sitting cross-legged on the bed. And Tara Tanvir was standing, still immersed in the novelty of the room, a hand on her hip, a hand holding her glass of orange juice.

'I don't think he's that great,' she said.

Samar Api looked at me and looked away.

They were discussing Amitabh.

'He's tall dark handsome,' said Samar Api. Her juice was finished, the empty glass edged into the congestion on the bedside table.

'I like tall fair handsome,' said Tara Tanvir. She raised her glass to sip the juice but lowered it before it reached her lips.

'Hi, Tara,' I said from the doorway.

'Hi,' said Tara Tanvir but distractedly. Her back was turned; she was searching a poster on the wall for the alleged appeal of its subject. The back of her vest showed tight folds at the armpits.

'You don't have to stand,' said Samar Api.

'O ya,' said Tara Tanvir. She sought to settle her glass on the table, settled it on the floor instead, then settled herself on the bed. 'Zaki,' she said, seeing me now, 'you're dressed so well.'

'You can come in,' said Samar Api.

'Ya, come sit with us!' cried Tara Tanvir with the same enthusiasm, the same bright burst of an idea out of nothing that had marked the success of the previous night. I sat again on the edge of the bed, aware of the room now, the aspect of newness and the element of disguise.

'Who all lives here?' inquired Tara Tanvir.

Samar Api gave a surprisingly succinct account of the house and its inhabitants, their various roles and functions and their links to one another.

'Where's your mother?' said Tara Tanvir.

'My mother's in the village,' said Samar Api. 'His mother's at the office.'

'My mother never goes out,' said Tara Tanvir.

We were quiet.

'You guys!' she cried. 'Don't be formal!' She was friendly and rallying; she thrashed her foot in childish protest on the bed and laughed as if at the absurdity of her own remark, her shoulders shaking, her eyes small and thin with mirth.

'You're too much, Tara,' said Samar Api and laughed concedingly.

'I'm blunt,' said Tara Tanvir.

'Too blunt!' said Samar Api.

They laughed together.

'So what's the plan,' said Tara Tanvir when the laughing had ended.

Samar Api stretched forward and touched her toes with her fingertips. She said, 'Up to you.'

'I don't know,' said Tara Tanvir made a face. 'I'm here to hang out with you guys.' And this was said with self-exposure, with a frankness that was bold and then touching.

'Let's show her the house,' said Samar Api and climbed off the bed.

We went to the roof, which was bright and searing in the daylight; the aerial stood in an isolated corner like a rake. Tara Tanvir said she wanted to touch it, but Samar Api said it had the power to electrocute, and Tara Tanvir quickly withdrew her hand. She was led away then to the other side of the roof, where the trees and houses of the neighbourhood protruded in an endless view: clothes hung on clothes lines, still and sagging in the breezeless afternoon, the windows of the houses open and closed without purpose or consistency of design.

'You guys have neighbours?' said Tara Tanvir. She was squinting, her hand forming a saluting terrace at her forehead to keep out the sun.

And Samar Api told the stories of some of the houses in the neighbourhood, the eccentricities of former residents and the things they had left unexplained.

Downstairs again, in the uneven shade of eaves and ledges, we walked about in search of undiscovered meanings. The walkway, cracked for years, now acquired the menace of disrepair, a waiting air of doom: we kicked stones and stepped on fallen branches, which crunched. I ran a hand along the flaking wall, across the unmoving multitudes of mango bugs, grey and ripe: the wall was streaked with yellow juice.

Tara Tanvir squealed.

We passed the gutter. It was open and showed a steady gleam hurrying on in the darkness.

'No way,' said Tara Tanvir.

'It's just a gutter,' said Samar Api.

Tara Tanvir was enchanted. She knelt to lift a twig from the ground and dropped it in the hole. It went soundlessly.

'Now it'll come in someone's bathroom,' said Samar Api and laughed into her hand, not wishing to describe the process or to dwell upon the consequences.

We reached the lawn at last, and sat on the grass. The sun had left broad burns behind the day; birds flapped out of trees and fled in shifting shapes against the dark.

Tara Tanvir wanted a flower from the frangipani tree.

'He's really good at climbing,' said Samar Api.

They watched.

'Thanks so much, Zaki,' said Tara Tanvir, and twirled the white flower in her hand. She closed her eyes and smelled it, then secured it behind her ear. She leaned back on the grass against her palms. 'You guys, we're getting close,' she said. Then she said, 'You know I broke up with my boyfriend,' and laughed tragically. 'Ya. It was long distance. He lives in London. He's a family friend. He's older than me. I always go for older guys. My mistake, I guess. But he was such a good kisser.'

It was like a profession.

Samar Api reached out a hand.

'I'm over it now,' said Tara Tanvir. 'And frankly I don't care. Good riddance to bad rubbish.'

Samar Api continued to hold her hand.

'Let's change the subject,' said Tara Tanvir.

'What's better,' said Samar Api, 'London or America?'

Tara Tanvir said London was better because she knew people there. On Oxford Street, where she often went walking, there was always a chance of bumping into someone she knew. 'And London has Selfridges and Harrods,' she said. 'America only has malls.' She said 'mauls' and not 'maals', which was how we said it.

'You have a house there?' said Samar Api.

'We have a flat.'

'What do you do in London?' said Samar Api. She was leaning forward and trying to stretch a blade of glass between her fingers.

Tara Tanvir described a world of buses and taxis, squares where people gathered on Sundays and ate ice creams that were sold from portable counters on the street, a stick of chocolate in vanilla. 'It costs a pound and twenty pee,' she said, and explained that it was something she could afford since she kept all the change from other purchases in her handbag. 'In London all the change comes in coins,' she said.

'You're so lucky,' said Samar Api.

'Depends on how you look at it,' said Tara Tanvir. She said it quickly, without pause or inflection.

'You are,' said Samar Api. She tugged the blade of grass between her fingers, and it broke.

Tara Tanvir said, 'You know something?'

We waited.

She said, 'Forget it.'

'What?' said Samar Api.

'Nothing,' she said, and then told us about her father, who was having an affair. Her mother had tried to stop it, failed, and had an affair herself. Late at night, Tara Tanvir went with her mother in a car to a house in Defence, and waited in the lane outside to catch an incriminating glimpse of her father. And on other nights her father drank a lot of whisky and said unpleasant things about her mother that were difficult to hear. Tara Tanvir said she was unable to choose between her parents, and didn't know whose side to take or when to take it. And she said she didn't know when the fighting would end.

Samar Api held her friend's hand and told the story of her own family, in which her father was impassioned and unpredictable, her mother worried all the time and inconsolable. The extended family was worse because they lived in the village and had the ways of villagers.

'And Zaki doesn't even *have* a father,' Samar Api said.

'Isn't it amazing,' said Tara Tanvir after she had heard the stories, 'how we all come from broken homes?'

Samar Api went to Tara Tanvir's house the next day on her own, and on four days the following week. Thereafter it became a routine: she went in Tara Tanvir's jeep after school, which returned her to the house in the evening. She said they had formed a study group to distribute the homework. At home she rarely had time for playing, and preferred not to take dinner: she cited exhaustion and homework and withdrew with the telephone to her room.

I spent my afternoons with a boy called Mazri, who lived in a brick house with a barred gate at the end of the lane. Mazri's family didn't own the house; his father was employed there as a cook in the service of Mrs Zaidi, an abrasive widow who was suspicious of outsiders: she had the walls of her house lined with shards of broken glass to deter climbing, and watched contemptuously from her bedroom window when I came to call on Mazri. After that we played in the lane outside. No remarks were needed; ours was a friendship of activities: Mazri owned a bicycle, a bright red Sohrab Eagle his father had bought him from the stalls in Neela Ghumbat, and we took turns to ride it in the lane. Mazri was quick; he could speed up and down with his hands in the air, the tip of his tongue protruding in a knob of daring. He was generous too; he taught me to ride the bicycle and allowed me to ride it on my own. Together we flew kites on the roof. Mazri knew the natures of various kinds of string, and we cycled to Canal Park to purchase the supplies, taking turns on the bicycle, which had a second seat at the back, a flat hard rectangle that bumped and shuddered with the road. In the shop Mazri tested the string on his fingers – fine string always left a cut – and I paid for his selections with the money my mother had started giving me on the weekends for a sense of responsibility. Sometimes we stayed on in Canal Park to play video games in the arcade, a cement enclave between two permanently shuttered shops, a place that had no door and was exposed to the smell of the sewage directly outside. It contained four booths that were monitored intermittently by the owner, a fat, hairy man who sat on a plastic chair with one bare foot on the floor and the other up on the seat. We went to him repeatedly for tokens. I required more tokens than Mazri, who was better at playing the video game; he defeated me with ease and took on the game itself. He was better in real fights too; he fought without expression, using his hands and legs with calculation, and was unhurt by the pummelling and the furious threats of reprisal. He wasn't provoked when I called him a servant. He walked away with his bicycle and, reaching a secure distance, turned his head and shouted, *'Teri ma da phudda!'* I repeated it in front of Daadi, who touched her ears and cried, *'Astaghfaar!'* and sent me into the bathroom to rinse my mouth with water.

Up on the roof one day Mazri announced that he had made a discovery. He removed his shalwar and began to tug at his thing, which hardened. He said the same would happen to mine. I took off my shorts and Mazri tugged at my thing, tugged and tugged until it ticked and grew. I held his in my hand. It seemed to have grown a bone. His eyes were closed. When he opened his eyes he said I had gone too far, I was dirty and wanted to do dirty things. He said these things and went home. But the next day he returned, and the fight was forgotten; we did wheelies on the bicycle in the lane and went on it to play video games in Canal Park.

Then news came to the house of a breakthrough in technology. It was shaped like a dish and derived its name from this likeness. Samar Api said it would bring five new channels to our TV: a news channel, a channel with only English programming, an Indian channel, a sports channel and a channel for music only. She insisted it wasn't a hoax: she said Tara had it in her house, it worked all the time, and it wasn't a secret because the price was reasonable and people were queuing up outside shops to pay it.

Daadi agreed to give the money. A group of men with rolled-up sleeves came to the house in a van and dragged out a large white dish in plastic wrapping. They carried it noisily to the roof and began working, asking at intervals for tea and water, which were sent upstairs on a tray with Naseem. Downstairs Daadi paced her room because she feared that a fault in the set-up might, by some logic of extended betrayal, spread to the existing two channels and cause them to falter. One of the men was brought into her room to make the necessary adjustments: he placed a black device above the TV and knelt on the carpet, the soles of his feet black with filth, his fingers making calculated journeys in the darkness behind. He stood up and switched on the TV to check the channels, which were blank. He put on his sandals and went back upstairs.

At last he returned to conclude the procedure, and we assembled in Daadi's room. He stood before the TV with the bubble-wrapped remote control in his hand and produced the channels one by one: the news channel, where two aggravated foreigners were conversing behind a desk; the English channel, where two men were lying on a beach; then the music channel, where people were standing on a stage with guitars; a channel that showed poor people standing aimlessly in a bus – the forlorn music in the background was identified as flute and confirmed that it was the Indian channel; then cricket; then scratches; then nothing.

The man looked at the faces in the room and tapped his foot on the carpet.

He was paid and relieved.

Routines emerged. In the morning Naseem appeared with her perforated bowl of vegetables and settled cross-legged on the carpet. She watched the sports channel, cricket mostly, big matches between big teams, the one-day series and the World Cup, which Pakistan had won, but also county-level matches between unknown English teams. She peeled the vegetables and cut her hand repeatedly. Daadi turned to television in the afternoon, after waking from her nap, and was joined in her commentaries by Suri and Hukmi, who brought confectioneries from the bakery to show that they were contributing. After dinner my mother stayed on in Daadi's room to watch the news for an unbiased view on recent quagmires.

And late at night, after the others had gone to sleep, Samar Api took the TV and the telephone into her room, where she watched soap operas and discussed with the phone the significance of new realities, the kisses and confessions and the hanging sense they left of what was yet to come.

My favourite programme was *The Wonder Years*. It appeared on the English channel in the early evening, the ongoing story of a boy called Kevin who lived with his parents and domineering older brother in America. Every morning Kevin went to a junior high school, where the corridor was lined with lockers – Kevin's crush, Winnie, and his best friend, Paul, had one each. And inside his locker Kevin kept a file, a large, padded file with an external flap that he carried under his arm when walking in the dusk after school.

In the market the file was unavailable. The files at Anees Book Corner were hard and ugly, and contained grotesque metal rings inside. Others were slight, mere folders with pockets for holding papers, or large and unwieldy files that were used in offices and stored in the drawers of desks.

'Not for children,' said the salesman and withdrew his gaze concludingly.

The watching of the programme continued, and the need deepened for a file. It came at last from the *Women's Journal* office, an unremarkable black file with the one attractive feature of a magnetic latch: it snapped open and snapped shut.

'What's that you've got?' said Mazri.

I said it was a file.

Mazri was unimpressed.

'Holds papers,' I said, and revealed the empty flaps inside. 'See how it snaps.'

Mazri was amused.

'Hold it.'

Mazri held it in both his hands, like a tray. He turned it on its back and knocked a knuckle on the hard exterior.

'We can fill it up with papers.'

'And documents.'

'What about money?'

I said we could do that as well, though a wallet was better for storing money.

Mazri opened the file, fingered the lining, flapped the flaps. He closed it and produced the snap. The sound was appealing; he made it a few times and handed back the file. 'You can fill it up on your own,' he said and began to mount his bicycle.

'It's better than your bicycle,' I said.

Mazri was whistling.

'You don't even go to my high school.'

And Mazri, whistling, waving his hand from the bicycle, was trying to show that he was leaving me behind.

'Bloody Mazri,' I said when I went back inside. 'Doesn't even know a thing.'

'So?' said Samar Api. She was sitting in the one-seater with her legs dangling off the armrest, changing the channels on the TV with the bubble-wrapped remote control. 'You should make your own friends now.'

Yawar was a boy in my class. He became distinct the next morning in the classroom, listening to the things the Urdu teacher was saying about the importance of upholding a standard of cleanliness in society. He wasn't a bully but wasn't bullied either, lacking obvious vulnerabilities as well as the instinct that led more aggressive individuals to seek them out in others.

I approached him during lunch break. He was returning from the canteen with his lunch, an unopened sandwich that was held high in his hand like an item he wanted to store for later use or throw away. He didn't comment when I began to walk with him, and together we wove our way through the barren field at the back of the campus.

'You should come to my house,' I said. 'We'll make a time capsule.'

Yawar grunted.

I explained about time capsules.

'Sounds good, sounds good,' said Yawar, who was caustic by nature but amenable.

He came to the house on the weekend in starched white shorts and a colourful T-shirt, his shoelaces tied and settled like ribbons, his thick white socks pulled up to his knees. Daadi was pleased with his appearance and offered him food to eat, which Yawar declined, and a glass of juice from the fridge, which Yawar accepted and drank but left unfinished on the table. Of this too Daadi was approving; she said the lack of greed was a mark of good upbringing, and showed that Yawar's mother was devoted to the household, which was rare in these times, a blessing that hadn't been bestowed on other households.

We made our time capsule on the lawn. The capsule itself was a black plastic box we had found inside the house, strong enough to endure the eroding soil and the gnawing attempts of insects. It would surface after centuries, when man was estranged from the lives that preceded his re-emergence, and the excavation would lead to a discovery: some items from the past that offered proof of man's intelligence and his ability to find his way in a vanished world.

We looked first in the kitchen, where the knives and forks were locked in the cupboard; the key was with Naseem, who was sleeping in her quarters at the back of the house. We wanted items of instruction, items that would lead to conclusions about the past: we sought syringes, binoculars, lighters, none of which were found. We tried to contain the file within the box, tried to hold down its corners. But they snapped.

'It's boring,' said Yawar.

I went outside and brought what I found: a toothbrush, some pencils, a blue-nib pen, a compass, a lipstick and a hairbrush.

We drafted a letter. I wrote: *Dear citizen of the future, my name is Zaki Shirazi and I am a boy. I live in this house with my cuzzon.*

Yawar wrote *Yawar* and added the date and location.

'What if Americans find it?'

Yawar wrote *Asia* after *Pakistan*.

'What if aliens find it?'

Yawar wrote *Planet Earth*.

We sealed the box with masking tape, buried it in the ground and went inside. Yawar said he didn't think anyone would find it. He was restless now and wanted to go outside.

'There's nothing there,' I said.

But he went outside and found Mazri, who came up to the gate on his bicycle and did a wheelie. Yawar wanted to know about the bicycle; he said his older brother also had a Sohrab Eagle, but his was an older model. Mazri said his father had taken the bicycle to the petrol pump in the morning and had the tyres filled with air; they were good as new now; he allowed Yawar to mount the bicycle to test his claim. Yawar made a slow, wavering journey up and then down the lane.

'So then?' cried Mazri.

'Good as new, good as new!' cried Yawar.

When Mazri rode the bicycle he did it with flair. And Yawar stood patiently at the gate and watched him, grunting with pleasure at the showy turns.

'My turn now,' I said.

And Mazri laughed and said that I would have to pay him first.

At night I went out walking in the lane, which was deserted, and past the other houses in the dark. I climbed the barred gate of Mrs Zaidi's house and hopped. The knife I had brought was small and sharp. The windows in the house were all shut, the curtains drawn from inside. There were roses on the fringes of the garden, eerie in the stark white light that came from the porch, the buds meagre and shrivelled and the stems thorny, as if waiting to injure hopeful smellers. The bicycle had been leaned against a pillar in the porch. At first the knife had no effect; the rubber of the tyres was hard, and held. But stabbing in the same place proved worthwhile: the rubber popped, and the air began to hiss out.

'What did I do?'

'Get in,' said my mother and started her van. The school car park was not a place she visited regularly; she was angry already and aggravated by the unmoving cars ahead.

'But what did I do!'

'You know bloody well what you did,' she said, and swerved the van away from a car. 'All day long I work like a dog. And then I have to come home and listen to that old witch who lives in that house for twenty bloody minutes on the phone because she wants *new* tyres, she won't settle for repairs, she wants *new* tyres, and I have nothing to say because *you* are no better than riffraff.'

The traffic outside was worse. The road was blocked and the van was stuck.

'Sorry,' I said.

'Shut up.'

They had decided to send me away. I was to spend the Eid holiday with Suri and Hukmi and their children, away from the house and the television, away from negative influences. 'And it is good,' said Daadi, 'because Samar will be gone as well and there will be nothing to do in this house all by yourself.'

Samar Api was going with her mother to Barampur, where Uncle Fazal was hosting a lavish Eid lunch for his relatives and friends on the third day of the holiday. Families were driving in from other parts of the district, and Chhoti and her daughter were required to entertain the lady guests.

Samar Api didn't want to go. She fought with Daadi when it was mentioned, then fought with my mother when she went into her room for persuasion. Chhoti was arriving in a few days to take her daughter back to the village. Daadi said it was a matter of days – Eid was a family occasion that occurred only twice a year – and they weren't asking for more than that. But Samar Api refused to come out of her room. She said she wanted to stay in Lahore and go to Tara's house for Eid.

Chhoti arrived, unwarned, unprepared for resistance, and flew into a rage upon arrival; she cited hardships and sacrifices and cursed her own fate for giving her an ungrateful child. And she sulked, suggesting with her silence that her own family had done nothing to make it easier. Daadi was offended and withdrew her involvement, and my mother was left to mediate the correspondence between Chhoti and her child.

They left in the morning. Chhoti went to sit inside her car and instructed her driver to start the engine, which revved in the driveway. At last Samar Api emerged from her room, and her eyes were red and swollen with crying; she went outside with her schoolbag, in which she had her clothes, and sat beside Chhoti in the back of the car with the bag in her lap, refusing to look at her mother or at the assembled spectators outside, and stared ahead at nothing in defiance.

6

Suri and Hukmi lived with their families in the Gulistan housing colony. Their houses were separated by a low white wall and resembled the other houses in the lane, houses with brown iron gates and slanting, imbricating roofs, and strips of grass that fringed the outside walls and appeared to be of an equal length. It was a new way of living, a way out of the old joint-family system that hadn't done away with the better aspects of community life: there was a park in the heart of the colony, with slides and merry-go-rounds, a walking track, a cricket pitch and a badminton net held between two poles in the grass. A chowkidaar patrolled the lanes at night. The milkman had to report to the colony office for his salary and was punctual. There was no load-shedding at night, no problems with electricity, no water crisis at the last minute – problems, when they did arise, were addressed promptly and efficiently, owing to the built-in aspect of accountability. And still the houses continued to be available and continued to sell at reasonable prices.

At Hukmi's house today there was no one to answer the door. Her servants had left for the Eid holiday with advances on their salaries. Hukmi had to open the door herself. She was wearing a bathrobe and a towel in a turban around her head.

'They've all gone,' she said.

I followed her past the dining room, where the curtains were drawn and the light kept out, the chairs tucked into their places at the dining table, then past the paintings on the wall, paintings of fair-skinned babies and the robed, fair-skinned women tending to their needs. They were unlike the paintings my mother collected, which were childishly made and became interesting only after she had told a story about where they came from, or who had made them, or how they had been made.

'Shoes,' said Hukmi, indicating a wooden rack beside the bedroom door. It held several shoes at a raised angle, caught at the heels and held aloft.

'Take off, please,' said Hukmi and watched.

In the bedroom the lights were dim. Suri was sitting on the sofa under a golden clock and talking in tones of understanding on the telephone, though she now made a face at Hukmi that revealed her exhaustion. And on the bed were Uncle Saaji and Uncle Shafto, both lying on their backs with their heads propped up against pillows. They were watching a tennis match on the TV in the corner.

'He's finished,' said Uncle Saaji and puckered his lips. He was married to Suri and had once owned factories in Lyallpur. His soft, benign face gave his occasional bouts of anger the blunted quality of disappointment.

'Wait and see,' said Uncle Shafto, Hukmi's husband, a passionate man who had never owned anything of significance. 'The man will win. He will make a comeback. Born to win.' His upturned mouth was sealed in determination.

Uncle Saaji said, 'No, no,' and crossed his hands behind his head. The pose was uncomfortable; he returned his hands to his chest and settled and resettled them.

'Man's a player,' persisted Uncle Shafto.

'No, no.'

'Just see.'

They saw.

'Baakaap!' cried Uncle Shafto. His head lifted from the pillow. 'Baakaap!'

Uncle Saaji made a sputtering sound.

'Baakaap!'

'Finished,' said Uncle Saaji.

On the TV the audience were clapping, the two players walking to the net to shake hands and then walking apart, both looking humbled and dispassionate though one had just won the match and defeated the other.

'Actually it is bad luck,' said Uncle Shafto.

167

Hukmi came out of the bathroom in her clothes and sat on the sofa beside Suri. Her hair was wet and hung in braids.

Suri hung up the telephone and said, 'Marwa Madam wants to change the plan.'

Hukmi said, 'I'm not going.'

'Wants *us* to have it *here*,' said Suri.

'I am not going.'

'Always on the last minute –'

'I'm *not* going.'

It was settled.

'Zaki Shirazi,' said Uncle Saaji from the bed. He frowned in admonishment, then altered his expression and gurgled naughtily with a finger in his mouth.

'Oh yes,' said Uncle Shafto, taking note; he raised his neck and resettled the buffer of pillows behind his head. 'What a match, Zaki Shirazi. *What* a match.'

The TV was now showing golf: men in caps holding clubs, the people standing behind them in rows on the mown grass.

'It's a bore,' said Uncle Shafto.

Uncle Saaji changed the channel to the news. He said, 'Day-spending?'

'Night-spending,' I said.

'Why not,' said Uncle Saaji. 'Why not.'

Uncle Shafto said, 'Basically everything is allowed in this house. Everything I don't mind' – he began to count the things on his fingers – 'day-spend night-spend I don't mind, friends coming-going I don't mind, the car I don't mind, *every*thing I have allowed. But smoking?' He was flabbergasted. 'Smoking is *not* allowed, sorry.' He returned his attention to the TV but continued to shake his head.

Uncle Saaji sniffed.

And Hukmi stared.

Suri said, 'Zaki, *beta,* go upstairs. It is not good for children to sit around all the time with their elders. Go upstairs and find your cousins, go.'

The rooms upstairs were preceded by a passage, a dark place

where suitcases stood under shelves in angular poses, bellies rotting, some ruptured and damaged past the point of rescue, and where cricket bats and tennis rackets, once fresh and vital, now lay scattered about in the dust. One bat still leaned against the wall, displaying on its blade the autograph of a famous cricketer. It had torn at the handle and flattened out at the toe, flattened from striking and striking the ground in preparation, the blade bruised in all the places where it had struck. The pictures on the shelf above showed Uncle Shafto in white cricketing attire, posing with his bat at the wickets. They were like the other pictures on the shelves, no longer useful. And on the highest shelf sat a doll with a resilient expression in which one eye was blue and the other was missing, the mouth pink and parted in surprise: it had belonged to either Aasia or Maheen, whose voices now came from behind a door, and stopped, and started up again with the sounds of a televised cartoon.

The other door was open. Isa and Moosa were sitting on the carpet and playing a video game that was unfolding between two ninjas on the TV screen. Isa was absorbed in the game; his eyes were focused, his mouth open, his fingers waiting on the buttons of the joystick. Moosa saw that someone had come into the room but didn't look up. He said, 'Shit.'

His ninja fell. Above, in a corner of the screen, the bar that indicated its life reserves turned red and began to throb.

'Next time,' said Isa, 'duck and don't jump.'

'Duck don't jump,' said Moosa.

The new round was the same: Isa planned his movements and retreated, and Moosa was restless, hopping to and fro and squandering his movements. His ninja suffered, recovered and fell again.

He turned.

'Oi. What's your age?'

I said, 'Ten.'

'He's a frikkin' kid,' said Moosa.

Isa was selecting the options for a new round.

'Mama's boy,' said Moosa and laughed.

I said nothing in response.

Moosa turned around again and said, 'You go with your mama to your school in the morning?'

He had stopped laughing.

'You deaf?'

'No.'

'You take a lunchbox?'

'No.'

'I'll break your face.'

'No, you won't.' It was weakened by fear.

'No?' said Moosa. 'No?'

'No.'

He remained in his place. 'No? You only know one word?'

'Oi,' said Isa.

He was talking to me.

'You want to play?'

'Winner to stay,' said Moosa and edged away from his place on the carpet. 'It doesn't even matter if he wins. He's still a frikkin' kid.'

I played the round. And it was difficult but instructive: the moments of contact were brief at first, then developed into entanglements. Isa gave the codes for special movements, configurations on the buttons of the joystick that enabled flying, invisibility and the appearance of a rope that lassoed the opponent ninja and made him helpless. I lost the first two rounds but won the third, and Isa gave up his place for Moosa, who played the round blindly and frantically and was calm when he won.

'Next time,' he said, pointing to the TV screen, 'duck instead of jumping. You'll keep on losing if you don't listen to what I'm saying.'

In the evening we went downstairs for tea. We were going out for a drive and needed money. The elders were in the large and circular drawing room, which had a high ceiling and square windowpanes that looked out onto the lawn. Suri was bent over the tea trolley, assembling refreshments on plates and passing them round: there were lemon tarts on one plate, samosas and pakoras on another, biscuits in a jar, chicken patties and coils of jalebi in a heap on a platter. All these things were on the lower level of the trolley; the upper level held teacups and saucers, a sugar bowl, a jug of milk and a teapot in a tea cosy.

'It's hot,' said Suri and held out a cup on a saucer for Hukmi, who received it with both her hands.

'I want it!' cried Aasia. The idea had come abruptly: she was sitting on the floor with her legs poking out from beneath a puddled frock, playing with a pair of dolls that she now held threateningly apart.

'Me too!' cried Maheen from the floor. She was upset that Aasia had said it first.

'No,' said Suri.

Aasia resumed with the dolls.

Maheen saw that Aasia had recanted and looked weakly at her own mother.

Hukmi said, 'No,' and said it with severity to set a precedent.

'Dad,' said Isa. He was standing before his father with his hands in the pockets of his jeans.

Uncle Saaji looked up from the magazine in his hands.

'How much?' he said.

Isa made a calculation and said, 'Three hundred.'

Uncle Saaji saw how it added up.

'It's too much Saaji . . .' said Suri warningly.

Uncle Saaji counted the money and held it out. 'Bring my Alka-Seltzer.'

'Too much,' said Suri.

Isa took the money and tucked it into the folds of his wallet.

Moosa said, 'Dad?'

Uncle Shafto was leaning back on the sofa with his neck turned tensely to one side, his face stretched downwards and lengthened in a small round mirror that he held in his hand. The other hand held a pair of tweezers near the rim of his nostril.

Moosa was waiting.

And Hukmi was watching.

'My wallet,' said Uncle Shafto, 'where is my wallet?'

Hukmi said, 'Take it from me,' and abruptly opened the zip of her handbag.

Moosa went to stand before his mother.

Uncle Shafto resumed his tweezing.

'Taking the car,' said Isa and jangled the car keys in announcement.

'Bring my Alka-Seltzer,' said Uncle Saaji.

'And don't drive fast,' said Suri, 'because you don't have a licence and we won't come and find you at the police station in the middle of the night.'

We went to the next house, Isa's house, and took out the smaller car from the garage. It was a Suzuki Swift, a low car with an elongated snout and a flat back. Isa claimed it was promised as a present for his fifteenth birthday, which was still a year away, though he hoped by then to be driving an automatic. He said the Swift was good for practice; he drove it with a rough efficiency, the level of consideration that is owed a thing past its prime, past the time when it is singular and paramount. The houses of the colony travelled side by side until the car was out on the main road. There was noise in the streets, the sound of cars going past and of motorcycles revved in the night, a show of daring before the arrival of the holiday.

We stopped at the traffic light. An old hunched man was going from car to car with his palm held out. He knocked on windows and waited, knocked again, raised a finger to the sky and walked on, his hands dragging along the doors of the cars.

There was movement in the seat ahead; Isa shifted and seemed to be searching for something. Then the sound came, a chuck, and another: he rolled down his window and threw out the match.

Moosa watched him smoke the cigarette, waiting with fear and anticipation. It came to him at last, and he held it carefully between his fingers, smoking the cigarette with his eyes closed and pausing to inspect the ash, which hadn't formed. He puffed and puffed at it, the ember glowing.

He held it out.

Isa said, 'You want?' His eyes were in the rear-view mirror.

Moosa looked at Isa, then looked at me in the seat at the back.

'No, not now,' I said.

'Up to you,' said Isa.

He smoked the cigarette.

Moosa said, 'Don't tell everyone.'

But Isa said, 'He won't, he won't.'

We went to a white-lit utility store in Firdaus Market, where in the beverage aisle Isa selected three bottles of Malt 79, a non-alcoholic beverage that had the taste of beer. He paid at the counter for the bottles and for his father's Alka-Seltzer packet. Moosa paid for a new packet of cigarettes: the brand was Marlboro Lights and he wanted the soft pack, which didn't protrude in pockets. With the remaining money we went to a video shop, one in a row of lighted shops above a sunken car park. Isa went in by himself and left us to wait in the car.

I said, 'How long you been smoking?'

Moosa was fiddling with the glovebox in the front. He said, 'Not long. Roundabout one year.'

There was commotion in the street outside. The vendors and shopkeepers had come down from their stalls and shops and gathered on the pavement: they were looking expectantly at the sky, which burst now with lights, streaking flowers in violet and green and orange.

'Your dad know you smoke?'

'No, man,' said Moosa. 'Obviously not.' He gave a grunt and twirled the cigarette lighter in his hand. 'Even if he did, I don't see what he can do about it . . .'

'What if he found out?'

'He won't find out.'

'What if he did?'

'Why are you asking?'

It was a need to know how fathers fell into their roles, the rules they established and the positions they had to take when others had failed.

'Just asking,' I said.

Isa returned with the video and showed it to Moosa, who

confirmed that it was the one. They had a humorous exchange about the shopkeeper's comments – he was a pious man, an elder who was easily shocked and became curt and unresponsive when confronted with vice.

'But money talks,' said Isa and started the car.

And Moosa said we were going to have the best night of our lives.

It was slow to start. Suri and Saaji had left for the night and had gone through the shared door at the back to their own house. Isa had to go home and park the car in the garage, then go inside and deliver the car keys and the Alka-Seltzer packet to his father and ask for permission to stay the night at Moosa's. It was granted, but not without a complication: Aasia too wanted to stay the night with Maheen – she insisted that it was fair, relying on an established system of equivalence between the houses. Suri said she had to ask Hukmi first. Then phone calls were made from one house to the other and conditions were extracted: the children – the boys as well as the girls – were expected to bathe and dress on their own in time for Eid prayers in the morning.

Aasia went to Maheen's room. We went to Moosa's. Doors and windows were locked.

A voice, Hukmi's, was calling out for Moosa.

He went downstairs.

She wanted to know if the doors were locked.

He said they were.

And the windows?

And the windows.

He came upstairs but was summoned again. Aasia had changed her mind: she no longer wished to spend the night and was standing with her nightclothes in the doorway. Moosa had to escort her back to her own house, where Suri's reception of her was stern and unequivocal. In the other house Maheen was distraught, sobbing now for Aasia to come back, and succeeded only in drawing the attention of her own mother, who went upstairs and smacked her several times and put her to bed.

It was agreed that the girls had been unreasonable, Aasia more so than Maheen; but then Maheen was oversensitive and always made things difficult, and Aasia was scolded for not making her choices with a grown-up mind.

The matter was at rest, the houses closed for the night.

'Night is young,' said Moosa. He rubbed his hands and spanked them on his knees, then knelt on the carpet to attach the VCR wires to the TV. He was singing a song.

'Quiet,' said Isa. He was going downstairs to get the non-alcoholic beers, deposited earlier in the freezer for cooling.

'Oh sorry, sorry,' said Moosa.

He sang his song at a lower pitch:

> *O didi, o didi, o didi didi didiwa*
> *O didiwa, o didi, o didi didi di-yedi-yeh*

The beers came on a tray. Isa locked the door, then set about opening the bottles, his own neck tensing with the effort: one by one the bottles popped, the caps flew and the beer came seething up.

'Cheers.'

'Cheers.'

'Cheers.'

Moosa took a sip and hummed with pleasure and surprise. '*O didiwa!*' He looked amazedly at the bottle in his hand. '*O didi didi.*'

'Calm down,' said Isa.

Moosa hummed on for some moments and then drank his beer in silence.

Isa drank his own beer slowly and abstractedly.

Moosa finished his beer and brought it down on the table with a thwack.

Isa didn't tell him to calm down.

Moosa went across to the TV.

'Lights,' said Isa and switched them off. The room was dark, lit only by the scratches on the TV screen. Moosa placed the video in the jaws of the VCR and worked the buttons. Abruptly the screen was coloured, a bright day in a city with cars out on the streets and trees in the sunlight. Moosa reduced the volume; the music was faint, the picture warping with the slow silver lines that travelled again and again to the bottom of the screen.

Moosa went to sit cross-legged on his bed. He said, 'Ooh, baby.'

A golden-haired woman in a frock and an apron stood in her kitchen. She seemed to want to pass the hours; she swirled a spoon in a bowl, her head tilting to either side in distraction; she glanced sullenly at the clock on the wall, returned to the bowl and continued to swirl the spoon. She dipped her finger in the froth and tasted it. The taste was nice; she licked her fingernail, licked her finger, her thumb, sucking her knuckles, all covered now in the froth. She leaned over the worktop and sucked her forefinger again.

She heard the doorbell and turned.

Sucking her fingers and her knuckles, she walked out of the kitchen and into a lounge, taking her time, and fastening the apron anew so that it squeezed her waist and flared her above and below. She opened the door and hid behind it. She stuck out her neck and blinked at the visitor.

It was a man.

He followed her into the kitchen.

She motioned to the sink and shrugged her shoulders.

He unbuttoned the top two buttons of his shirt, rolled up his sleeves, ran a hand across his face, his nose and moustache and mouth and chin, and sank below the sink.

She waited.

He came back up.

She opened the tap to see if the water was coming.

It was.

He asked for payment.

She thought about it.

He was waiting.

She turned around, leaned across the worktop, hitched up the back of her frock.

'O God,' I said.

'Quiet,' said Isa, smiling.

176

'Ooh, baby,' said Moosa from the bed.

The woman was on her knees now and had the man's thing in her mouth. She sucked it and looked up at him in a questioning way, a way that asked if what she was doing was right and if he wanted more of it.

'Yeah . . .' said the man.

'O God!'

'Quiet,' said Isa.

'What's happening!'

'Shhh!' said Moosa, smiling and nodding, and fell back into the pillows on his bed. 'Just watch,' he said, closing his eyes momentarily, and bringing a forefinger to his lips to say that now was not the time to ask questions.

It was called having sex, a thing all people in the world had done in their lifetimes and were likely to do with regularity after marriage.

They had sex in bedrooms, sex in bathrooms, in the bathtub and against the wall, in kitchens and gardens and in garages. In hotels they did it in the swimming pool against the ledge.

'In the hot water,' said Moosa and made a face of dreamy contentment.

'Everyone?' I asked.

'Yup,' said Isa, and explained that it was the way to make babies. The white substance that emerged from the man in the end was the seed, distinct from urine because it came from the knees, as opposed to urine, which just came from drinking water.

'Orgasm,' he said.

Moosa said the sensation was unrivalled.

He got up from the bed and went into the bathroom to have it.

'He's going to use his hand,' said Isa, and moved his fist up and down. 'Mastipation.'

We waited.

Moosa returned with a scrap of tissue paper that was glistening at one end.

He had done it.

He ran a hand across his brow and gasped, and collapsed on the bedding.

'You can do it on your own until you get married?'

'You don't have to,' said Isa. 'Your babe can take the pill. Otherwise she'll get pregnant.'

'Condoms also . . .' said Moosa from the bed.

'Condoms suck,' said Isa.

Moosa made a squelching sound.

They laughed.

I said, 'Then do it with a boy.'

Isa and Moosa stared. They were repulsed. Isa said it was a sin for boys to do it with one another, a sin that was forbidden in the Quran much more than other sins: when two boys did it they caused the mountains to tremble, they sent tremors of lament to the highest heaven. 'Gays,' he said.

Moosa poked a finger in and out of his fist. He said girls were also not allowed to have sex with one another, though he wondered if it was a sin since nothing was going in.

It wasn't a sin when it wasn't going in.

'Obviously,' said Isa, 'because then you're not *doing* anything . . .'

Moosa said, 'Actions are judged by intentions. It's written in the Quran.' He looked at Isa for confirmation but worriedly, sensing the change in gravity his contribution had caused.

Isa said, 'It's not in the Quran. It's a saying. Of the Prophet.'

Moosa was reflective.

There was no retreat.

Moosa said, 'We shouldn't drink, man.'

'It's non-alcoholic,' said Isa. 'Use your brain.'

Moosa sank into exasperation. And Isa didn't respond to the suggestion of hostility, for he was not willing to concede that there had been the chance of a conflict. He stayed calm for the rest of the night and, once Moosa had gone to sleep, put on his shoes and went out to the balcony to smoke a cigarette.

'You don't have to come,' he said.

But I went with him.

He lit the cigarette and smoked it, a hand on his hip, considering the night, which was vast and total, the darkened houses of the colony protruding against the black in blacker ridges. He smoked the cigarette down to half and passed it to me.

'You don't have to inhale,' he said.

'I'm not.'

He watched.

'Your mother know you smoke?'

I told him I didn't smoke on my own.

He was impressed. 'Smart man,' he said, seeing considerations and calculations where there were none. 'Keep it up. Keep it up.' He puffed at the cigarette and released the smoke from the corner of his mouth. 'It's good you don't smoke on your own. Means you're not addicted.'

'You're addicted?'

He considered it. 'More or less.'

'Moosa also?'

Isa said Moosa had been smoking for a year now. And he was only twelve. Isa didn't stop him beyond a point – no one could stop anyone beyond a point. He mentioned it now only because I had asked; he wouldn't have otherwise; he wasn't one to comment on such things, which were personal. He smoked the remaining cigarette and smoked it to the very end, then flung the butt across the night. It landed somewhere and died.

Isa hadn't taught his younger cousin to smoke, but the blame always came on him. He was blamed for being older and for not telling the elders. He said he took the blame without complaint: he didn't hold these things, didn't hoard them in his heart, it was wrong and even pointless to hold grudges, especially against elders, who were concerned and imposed curfews and punishments that were necessary from their side. But from his own side Isa gave what he could: he gave help when there was need, advice if he was asked. Beyond that he kept his opinions to himself.

'People always do what they want,' he said. 'Even when they ask for your opinion they'll go and do what they want. Why should you stand in their way? It only makes *you* look bad.'

*

Woodpecker knocks came from behind the door in the morning. It was Suri. She was already dressed, and was saying that we were late for Eid prayers and had ten minutes in which to shower and change and appear for breakfast downstairs. We took turns. Isa went in first and was ready in a surprisingly short while. On his way to the bathroom he called out to Moosa, who was asleep in the brightened room on his side with his arm dangling off the edge of the mattress. Isa returned from the bathroom in his towel, shook Moosa awake and went back into the bathroom to make his hairstyle.

Moosa raised his head from the pillow. He looked around the room, frowning at the sudden light.

'What's the time?'

It was a little after seven.

'Fuck.' He scratched his head and tasted the taste in his mouth.

Isa came out of the bathroom with his hair slicked back and said that the water was cold.

Moosa said, 'Frickin' . . .' and fell back into the bed.

I offered to go first.

Moosa didn't object. 'Don't use my towel,' he said. 'And keep the water on for me. It'll get hot by then.'

Downstairs the atmosphere was one of frantic agreeability: queries were being swapped over the cutting sounds of plates and glasses, talk of lateness and the crowds at the colony park, where the prayers were going to be held. Uncle Shafto was issuing the warnings and Uncle Saaji was hunched attentively over a bowl of sawaiyya: he slurped the milk and leaned back in his chair for a brief rest, patting the sides of his mouth with a napkin. Both he and Uncle Shafto were dressed in white shalwar kameezes that were puffed and dented with starch. Uncle Saaji's cuffs were sealed with gold studs. Uncle Shafto's were rolled up to his elbows. Suri and Hukmi were wearing similar outfits, one in orange and the other in red, with bowl-shaped necklines and golden lace around the sleeves and hems, and Aasia and Maheen sat beside their mothers in matching pink ghararas. Both had been allowed on this occasion to wear make-up, Aasia exacting of all her features, Maheen still enthralled by the shock of her lipstick, a dark red one that belonged to her mother: she looked from one person at the table to another, hoping to elicit a remark or a glance that confirmed her newfound vividness to herself.

'Looking good on you,' said Suri, indicating my outfit with a surprised smile and a nod of acceptance. She looked to Hukmi for agreement.

Hukmi was not remembering.

'From Auriga,' said Suri.

Hukmi was blank.

'Oho,' said Suri. 'The fabric was for a reasonable price . . .'

Hukmi peered at the outfit.

'Remembering?'

'Oh,' said Hukmi. 'Of course.' She closed her eyes and nodded, relieved to have her memory.

Suri said, 'Not bad, *na*?'

'Not bad at all.'

They had selected the fabric together with Daadi on a recent trip to the clothes bazaar behind Main Market. Daadi had bought the cloth with her own money and had it tailored by her man in Liberty.

'All the things a mother does,' she had said, holding up the stitched kameez, 'all the things a mother *ought* to do for her child, I do them for you, in my old age, and still not a word of thanks, not a word.'

'Thank you,' I said.

She accepted and kissed me on the forehead, but not without adding that my mother had no taste in clothes because she had no feeling for such things.

Suri handed out the remaining bowls of sawaiyya. 'Eat quickly,' she said. Her tone was sharp and aimed at Isa, who was the eldest and her son, and therefore the most susceptible to blame. 'Up so late at night,' she said admonishingly. She may have known nothing of what had happened in the room upstairs at night. She may have known everything.

'Late for prayers,' said Uncle Saaji.

'We've missed it,' insisted Uncle Shafto.

Hukmi said it was our fault for waking up so late.

They all had sex.

We ate the sawaiyya in silence. Suri said, 'Buss ab chalo,' and plates were abandoned, outfits spanked for crumbs and tugged and straightened on the way out to the porch. We took Uncle Saaji's jeep from the neighbouring house. He drove it himself, Uncle Shafto sitting beside him in the front, Suri and Hukmi in the seats behind with Aasia and Maheen in their laps. We sat all the way at the back, next to a disused golfing kit and an old, veined map of the Margalla Hills. The drive was short since the park was inside the colony. But outings in cars were required here; the long, wavering lines of stagnant vehicles led up to the mud-and-grass compound of the park. It was covered in two separate tents: the men and boys were going into one, the women and girls into the other.

'We'll meet here,' said Suri.

The girls followed their mothers into the tent, looking over their shoulders at the other arriving families to ensure they were doing the same.

The men's tent was vast: sheets had been put out to cover the grass inside, and were also serving today as prayer mats; men left their shoes at the various slitted entrances and settled on the sheets barefoot. Some sat cross-legged, others with their knees drawn up and their arms enclosing the posture, still others with their legs folded beneath them in the posture of prayer. I sat beside Moosa, who sat beside Isa, who was sitting next to Uncles Saaji and Shafto in a line that continued to grow on either side.

Two boys in skullcaps were going around with a sack of cloth that was held between them like a hammock. There was money inside.

Isa said they were collecting chanda.

'Good cause,' said Uncle Saaji and took out his wallet. He held it for a moment without counting the bills.

Uncle Shafto didn't take out his wallet.

The boys came to Uncle Saaji, received his money, came to Uncle Shafto, waited for his money, waited another moment, and moved on without shedding or acquiring an expression. They seemed to know the ways of men, the things they held in their minds and hid in their hearts, the good as well as the bad, and the rewards and punishments that came their way as a consequence.

'Dad,' said Moosa after they had gone. He was embarrassed.

'Frauds,' said Uncle Shafto.

'Good cause,' suggested Uncle Saaji.

'Goes into their pockets.'

Uncle Saaji smiled in a kind of torment of faith. 'Who knows,' he said, opening one by one the bunched-up fingers of his hand and revealing a deeply lined palm. 'Only Allah knows. It is so – it is written. We must do our bit and leave the rest to Him.'

'Thieves,' said Uncle Shafto.

Uncle Saaji had done his bit.

Isa looked at Moosa, who continued to look at the backs of the men in the row ahead. His embarrassment had increased.

He said, 'You know how to say your prayers?'

I knew. Daadi had taught me and tested me in her room.

'Then where's your mosque?'

I didn't have a mosque.

'You say your prayers at home?'

'At home.'

'How many times a day you say them?'

I thought about it.

'Liar,' said Moosa. 'Lies about prayers.'

Isa intervened, indicating a podium that had now appeared on the ramp ahead. A boy was bent beside it and attaching the wires to a microphone; he tapped it twice and went away.

The maulvi emerged from a slit in the tent and walked up to the podium, his beard small and sharp, raised with his chin at an intelligent angle. He stopped at the podium, gripped the sides, looked up, down, up again.

The murmur of voices in the tent grew quick and loud before it was stilled.

'Bismillah Arrahman Irrahim,' said the maulvi. He paused to survey his audience. His breathing in the microphone was like a wind approaching.

He raised his chin and began to recite in Arabic.

The men stood up.

The prayer had begun.

I did what the others were doing.

When the prayer was finished the maulvi wiped his mouth with a handkerchief, recited another fragment in Arabic and said, 'Means what?'

The congregation was waiting.

'Means what?' The maulvi shifted from one side of the podium to the other, allowing his question to loom. 'Means,' he said at last, and stopped in the centre of the podium, 'that permission to fight is granted. Permission. To fight. Is granted. To *those*. Who are being attacked.'

There were nods.

'For they have been wronged.'

More nods.

'Is this true of today?'

The audience was thinking.

The maulvi smiled, nodding, his smile growing into a scowl. Our brothers and sisters in Bosnia, he said, were dying. They were being slaughtered in their homes, dragged out into the streets and shot, fathers forced to swallow the innards of their children and mothers raped and left to hang from ropes tied to trees. And what were we doing to stop it? We, the well-fed, well-clothed Muslims of Lahore, were coming from breakfasts of halwa and sawaiyya, and thinking ahead already to the lunches that awaited us at home: kebabs and chicken boti and matar pulao and biryani, and naan, and kheer for dessert, and glasses of sherbet to help us fall asleep in the afternoon.

The congregation listened in silence to the growing descriptions of bloodshed, which was prevalent in so much of the world. No land in the maulvi's telling was exempt; places that seemed far away from here, far too from one another, were revealed to have suffered similar fates. And still the Muslims hadn't learned. A logic of recurrence had emerged and was attributed to the Creator's design, the Creator who had given men the power to think for themselves, to reason and choose, a power not granted to beasts or angels. Time and again we had squandered that power, allowed our minds to go astray, choosing not to learn from the stories of our forefathers and repeatedly drawing His wrath upon us. Now, again, the signs of calamity were among us: usury and drinking were common, and gambling too, for what was the stock market but a gambling den? Men had become womanly and women had turned into men, wearing men's clothing and using men's language and leaving their homes at night to drive cars in the streets. A woman was now running the country, a Muslim country, and making the kind of mess she ought to have made inside her kitchen.

The Day of Judgement was approaching. The scrolls of the past were going to be unrolled, and every man was going to have to speak for himself. There would be no intercession, no appeal for forgiveness or another chance. The future was decided, closed.

The maulvi continued with his sermon. He was unable to end it, more involved now that he had disclosed an impending calamity. The murmur in the crowd returned, the roving restlessness that comes when things have stalled. At last the maulvi stopped, ending his speech on the prospect of redemption, a concept he had not had the time to develop; he twitched, swallowed, then stood back from the podium and cleared his throat. The congregation rose.

'*Allah-o-Akbar,*' intoned the maulvi, his hands clasped at his waist.

Outside the tent, the crowd of colony residents was dividing and subdividing. The men hugged three times each, said '*Eid Mubarak,*' and moved on to other acquaintances, a fractured dance of greeting in which groups formed and dissolved and formed without sequence or direction, so that some were finding themselves in the same places and finding that they were trapped. Away from the warmth and confusion, by a pair of benches, Uncle Saaji was conversing with two men, both bald and moustached and dressed in black sherwanis, with triangular red napkins tucked into their breast pockets. One of the men was slimmer than the other, and was listening to the shorter man, who was talking and making elaborate blooming gestures with his hands.

'Kureishi brothers,' said Isa. 'Family friends. Go back long way.'

Moosa said, 'Very long way.'

Uncle Shafto was standing with us near the tent. He was not conversing with anyone. 'Useless,' he said. 'Whole bloody place.'

Suri and Hukmi emerged from the women's tent, Aasia and Maheen behind them. They saw us and approached.

'Oho, Dad,' said Moosa. He was pointing across the grass to a group of men who had gathered in a circle under a tree.

'Oho!' said Uncle Shafto. He held his hips in preparation and smiled, recalling a prank or a joke, then cupped his hands around his mouth and shouted: 'Anjum Mian! You bastard!'

A man turned.

'Look here, bastard!'

The man saw. He gave a small smile, said something to his friends and began to walk across the grass.

Uncle Shafto brought his hands together in a slap. '*Caught* the bastard,' he said.

Moosa sniggered.

'My friend,' said Anjum Mian, approaching.

'Pardner,' said Uncle Shafto and tugged at his hand. '*Where* are you, pardner?'

Anjum Mian said he was right here and looked around him with bafflement.

'When's our promo pardy, pardner?'

'You know how it is,' said Anjum Mian. 'One day is planned for something, and some one thing or other will come up, right up to the last minute, and the plan is cancelled.' He enacted the cancellation with a dropping movement of his hands, one that was more suited to abandonment. 'So now we have postponed. Wife has said it, what to do. Her niece is getting married on the same day, chief minister's nephew, so their house we are going.' He brought his hands together in a clasp of resolution. 'Sorry, pardner. Next time.'

'Ah,' said Uncle Shafto, 'I see. I see I see. Well' – he offered his arms in an embrace – 'we will do it next time, pardner. Man must tend to wife – on that there can be no dispute. Give my best, *hanh*? Wife and kiddos.'

They embraced and shook hands. Uncle Shafto watched as Anjum Mian returned across the grass to his friends.

'Anjum Mian,' he said after a while. 'My colleague.'

'His wife,' said Hukmi, 'she's a *real* –'

'Such a –' said Suri.

'Total.'

'Complete.'

'So then?' said Suri in the car, in a tone prepared for amusement. 'What had the Kureishi brothers to say?' She spoke from behind Aasia, who was sitting in her lap with a reassured hand on the windowpane, watching the world go past. Her neck turned with the sights.

Uncle Saaji was driving with both hands on the steering wheel. He said, 'Oh, nothing,' and gave a sheepish little laugh.

'Still,' persisted Suri. 'Must've said *some*thing.' She removed Aasia from her lap and settled her in the seat.

Aasia didn't seem to mind.

Uncle Saaji said, 'They are setting up a mill. Were saying how difficult it has become to get loans. Have to go through ministries, you know. Not easy.' He tapped his fingers on the steering wheel.

Suri said nothing.

Hukmi said, 'Politics. It is *all* politics.' She had stopped bouncing Maheen on her knee.

Maheen screamed.

'*Shut* up,' said Hukmi.

Maheen was quiet.

'I am sure,' said Suri, 'that it is easier than they say it is. Every minister is their buddy. It is their government, their country. Why should they be worried?' She spoke in a sing-song parody of innocence.

From his seat in the front Uncle Shafto said, 'Actually they are all the same. All of them. Take Anjum Mian, my colleague. Man is a nincompoop. *Nin*-com-poop. But what is he getting? Promotions. Why? Connections. This is the game. He will be GM in a year or two, just wait and see. And mark my words: he will *take* this company *down* the drain.'

Hukmi reiterated her initial stance, maintaining that it was all politics, and Suri shook her head.

I asked if it was always like this.

'Always,' said Suri. 'From the very start. Democracy this and democracy that. Very well. But will you tell me, please, that is it democracy to steal people's lands? To take away the things they have lawfully earned? Land reform, they said. Land reform my foot. First the father came to steal, and now the daughter is stealing, and nobody can say a thing, because we are in democracy. Your Uncle Saaji used to have so much. Ask him, ask how much he used to have: he will tell you. The Kureishi brothers used to be his tag-alongs. But it goes – always it goes in the end – and like this the Kureishi brothers were gone, like this.' She snapped her fingers in the air. 'Now they go around in their cars like they have always owned the world. And why not? They are providing the commissions and getting the benefits. They have dinners and receptions.' Her tone of exaggerated innocence had returned. 'They are the business men. And she is the business woman.'

'Who?' said Aasia, alerted.

'The madam herself,' said Suri. 'The queen.'

Hukmi chuckled.

'Who's the queen?' said Aasia.

'Who!' cried Maheen, sensing a build-up and her own exclusion from the excitement. 'Who! Who!'

'A *bad* woman!' cried Hukmi, and it established the parallel between reprehensible women and the screaming little girls who demanded to know their names.

Maheen struggled free of her mother's lap and sank into the seat. She was frightened, and frightened of being frightened.

'Look,' said Suri, pointing, 'there she goes . . .'

It was a banner stretched taut between two electricity poles on the street. It thanked the people for electing the mohtarma a second time, and gave a prayer of thanks to God for sending angels to assist the people at the polls. Next to this was a portrait of the prime minister herself, watched over by a silhouette of her late father, and beneath it all the large, colourful letters that spelled out the name of the local politician who had paid for the banner.

I wanted to know if Benazir was a bad woman.

'God judges,' said Suri. 'God will judge.'

Hukmi said, 'I don't know why some people are *hell*-bent on supporting her . . .'

My mother was hell-bent on supporting her.

'It is not their fault,' said Suri charitably. 'They do not know. How can they, when they have not suffered?'

'Still,' said Hukmi. 'There should be some sense . . .'

'That *tau* I don't think there is,' said Suri.

'A sense of right and wrong . . .'

'No, no.'

'A sense of family . . .'

'None.'

The car was quiet.

Isa looked at me and looked away.

Moosa looked at me for a while.

Then, from the driver's seat, Uncle Saaji said, 'Leave it, *ji*. It is a blessed day, a noble day. A very noble day indeed.' He sighed extensively, releasing the anxious air he had carried with him all morning, and his mood was recovered. 'Zaki Shirazi,' he said. 'You may guess where we are going.' He drummed his fingers on the steering wheel for suspense.

'Where?'

'You may guess it.'

'Yes,' said Aasia, 'guess.'

'Guess!' cried Maheen.

We were going home – not to theirs, but to mine. Daadi's room was air-freshened and lamp-lit in anticipation, the bed made, the sofa plumped with new padding for the cushions. Daadi herself was waiting on the sofa and set about at once with instructions, presiding over the seating and admiring the outfits and departing in a hurry for the kitchen to see if lunch was ready. On her way out she said to tell my mother that we had come.

But it was better to stay in the room and enjoy the feeling of being in a family, which was, for once, complete, even if the family wasn't mine and the feeling belonged in reality to someone else.

7

In all I spent three nights and three days with the cousins. And towards the end it was established that I was welcome in their homes, newly integral to their lives, as they were to mine; we parted informally, not required to say goodbye or offer thanks. I was sent home in Hukmi's car with her driver, who had returned from his village after the Eid holiday and claimed in the car to have seen a jinn behind his neighbour's bushes – he told the story as if he'd told it many times, recounting the unreality at the heart of it in the same flat tones with which he described the fit his wife had thrown the following night (she wanted more than her usual share of his salary). 'Never marry,' he said, shaking his head dismally at his own faint reflection in the windscreen. 'You will forget the man you were, the man you wanted to be. Never marry.'

We drove past the houses of the colony, past the colony park, where the removal of the prayer tents had revealed patches of dug-up soil, demarcations for seed and fertilizer, for shrubs to snap from and bring forth flowers that in spring would bloom spectacularly.

At home there was excitement: Chhoti and Samar Api had returned from Barampur with stories of success. The lunch hosted for Uncle Fazal's relations and acquaintances had been well attended, and Chhoti had received many compliments, mostly praise for her young daughter, who had grown noticeably since anyone could last recall. Chhoti named a relative of her husband, a man who owned a considerable amount of land in Bahawalpur and whose wife had now indicated to Chhoti that they were interested for their eldest son, a lawyer.

'Lawyer!' said Daadi.

'Bar of London,' said Chhoti.

Daadi was impressed. 'So then?' she said to Samar Api with a look of probing complicity. 'What have you thought? Is it a yes or is it a no?'

Samar Api said, 'No, no,' and smiled indulgingly. She was dressed in clothes that revealed by suggestion, and rustled like wrapping when she moved in her chair.

Daadi approved of the changes and gave a complimenting nod to Chhoti, who was gratified beyond her ability to show it and began instead to list the virtues of village life, which had more to recommend it than she had initially allowed.

'Well, I have always said it,' said Daadi. She settled her hands in her lap and waited for the acknowledgement, if not the apology, that was her due.

'You have,' said Chhoti. 'You have.'

'So much to do *any*where,' said Daadi.

'So much.'

'Only a matter of finding it . . .'

'Only.'

'And of looking.'

'Of looking, no doubt.'

After tea Chhoti left. She said she wanted to reach Barampur before dark, or her sisters-in-law would complain. Daadi wanted her to stay but Chhoti insisted. And soon after she had left Samar Api announced that she was going to Tara Tanvir's house.

Daadi was surprised. 'But you have just come,' she said. 'Be patient. Wait a little.'

'But I have to go,' said Samar Api and went into the dressing room. She emerged after some minutes with her hair tied up. She was looking for a handbag; she held her dupatta behind her back while she bent to search in the wardrobe. She found it: she stood up, hung the strap on her shoulder, patted the bag with her hand and watched it settle, then adjusted the position of the strap, watched it settle once again and was ready to go.

'I'll come with you,' I said.

But she was in a hurry. 'You're not invited, Zaki. It's not polite to go to people's houses when you're not invited.'

*

Later in the week Daadi received a phone call from a woman who introduced herself as a schoolteacher and gave her name as Mrs Waheed.

'Shama,' she said. 'Shama Waheed.'

'Yes,' said Daadi.

The woman said she ran the Guidance and Counselling Department and taught English literature – that was her area of expertise, though she had also been the counsellor for almost a decade now –

'Yes,' said Daadi.

'Well,' said the woman, 'I am calling today in my capacity as the teacher of your niece, Samar.'

Daadi noted the style.

'She is a delightful child.'

The woman was kind.

'I have taught the girl for two years now. And I would like to tell you that she is a fair student – not to mention a pleasure – and I am pleased –'

'You are kind.'

'*You* are kind!'

They laughed.

'Yes,' said Daadi, sensing the ease, 'please tell me: is all well? I hope it is not the school fees that have gone up again . . .'

'Oh no,' said Mrs Waheed. 'Not at all. Though I would not be surprised if they did increase the fees one of these days. Profit, profit, all the time profit. That is the school's philosophy.'

'These schools,' said Daadi.

'Terrible,' said Mrs Waheed.

'You also feel?'

'Oh yes,' said Mrs Waheed. 'Oh, very much so. The fees are rising all the time, but teachers' salaries are staying the same, if you please.'

Daadi said, 'Terrible.'

'And we have children also, you know. We must also send our children to school. And if *their* fees are rising, and *our* salaries are staying the same, then *how* are we going to make up for the difference? It does not add up, you see.'

Daadi said, 'Terrible, terrible.'

'Well,' said Mrs Waheed and sighed, 'what a relief it is to let it out.'

'Yes,' said Daadi. 'Yes.'

'Well,' said Mrs Waheed, 'I hope you have felt as comfortable with me, Mrs Shirazi, as I have felt with you, or as you have *made* me feel, rather, in these few moments.'

'Yes, of course,' said Daadi, and placed her hand on the mantelpiece.

'Well,' said Mrs Waheed.

'Yes,' said Daadi.

'Well,' said Mrs Waheed again and blew out her breath. 'I wanted to say, Mrs Shirazi, that your niece has been absent for the whole of this past week from her school.'

Daadi said, 'No, no.'

'That is correct,' said Mrs Waheed.

'Cannot be,' said Daadi. 'There is a mistake. She goes every morning, Mrs Waheed, she has breakfast with me in this room, in this room where I am standing. How are you saying that she is not going?'

'Then I am right,' said Mrs Waheed.

'You are wrong,' said Daadi.

'No, no, Mrs Shirazi, that is not what I am saying. I have known for some time that something is going on . . .'

Daadi was stroking the mantelpiece.

'It is not your niece, actually, it is not these girls but the company they are keeping.'

Daadi said, 'Company.'

'Yes,' said Mrs Waheed. 'Tell me, Mrs Shirazi: are you dropping the girl to school yourself?'

'My maid goes. My maid and driver.'

'And are they picking her up as well?'

'No, she comes with her friend.'

'Tara Tanvir.'

'That is the one.'

'Well,' said Mrs Waheed, 'then I should tell you that Tara has also been absent from school on the very same days.'

Daadi was quiet.

'And her house you cannot even call,' continued Mrs Waheed, 'because there is no one to confront, no mother, no father, no one to take an interest, I don't know how many *hours* I have been *holding* on the line . . .'

Daadi was nodding. 'Thank you,' she said, 'for letting me know. The girl will go to school. She will go. I will see to it.'

They were summoned into Daadi's room. She turned first to Naseem.

'Where do you take her in the morning?'

'To her school,' said Naseem.

'To her school?'

'To her school – ask her, ask anyone –'

'Are you lying to me?'

Naseem said she was willing to take an oath on the Quran.

Daadi brought out the Quran and made her do it. Then she held the Quran before Samar Api. 'Swear,' she said. 'Swear on it.'

Samar Api was crying.

Daadi took her hand and placed it forcibly on the book.

Samar Api withdrew the hand.

'Let me . . .' said my mother.

'Swear!' said Daadi.

'Please,' said my mother, 'let me.'

They went into the next room and returned after some minutes. Samar Api was now sobbing into her hands. My mother stood beside her and explained: in the morning the girl went to school with the maid and the driver, was delivered to the school gates, where she waited for her friend, in whose car they then went to the friend's house. There they stayed all morning, and the friend's car returned the girl to her own house in the afternoon.

They were studying to prepare for their exams.

Daadi said she wasn't fooled.

'I will call my sister,' she said. 'And I will tell her what has happened. I will see to it that the matter is addressed, because *I* will not be held responsible, *I* will not be made to hear the taunts when tomorrow she goes and does something . . .'

Daadi continued to threaten and complain, and it was decided that her memory of the event had to fade. Until then no concession could be sought.

'Brought out the Quran,' said Naseem. 'Just think of it.'

Samar Api brought me into her room.

'Zaki, I have to tell you something.'

It was late at night. The light of her bedside lamp was the only one in the room, and sent its enlarged dim oval along the ceiling and down a wall. The door was locked.

She was sitting on her bed in her pyjamas, a pillow in her lap, her fingers spread out on the bedding.

'Zaki, I am in Ell Oh Vee Eee.'

She looked at me.

'Zaki, you can't tell anyone.'

'I won't.'

'You can't tell anyone, Zaki –'

'I won't.'

She accepted. She leaned back on her palms, then leaned forward and began to press her fingers into the mattress. She said his name was Jamal, he was the son of a politician from Multan; their family had gone to the lunch at Uncle Fazal's house in Barampur. That was where she had met him, though at the lunch itself they didn't speak, only saw each other from across the room. Later he sent her a letter through his cousin, a small piece of paper on which he'd scrawled a verse and signed his name. She called him at night on the phone and they talked. She had been to see him at his house in Lahore because Tara had taken her there. He spent most of his time in Lahore, she said, and he was older than her, twenty-four years old.

'Zaki, I need your help,' she said. 'I really need your help, Zaki.'

I said I would help her.

And it relieved her. She fell back into the bed and said she had

196

always known in her heart that she could trust Zaki. And she turned on her side, and hugged the pillow under her chin, and said that sometimes she had to hold herself to know that it was happening to her. 'Because sometimes,' she said, blinking in wonderment, in delighted disbelief, 'I can't believe that my Amitabh has arrived.'

8

The arrival of the dish antenna had coincided in the cities with the spread of hoardings. In Lahore they stood on all the main roads, in the newly licensed commercial areas as well as in the older neighbourhoods, ads for dentists and doctors near houses, for electronics on the busier thoroughfares, fridges and televisions and deep-freezers and split-level air-conditioners operated by remote control, causing happiness and enchantment among the women who stood by their appliances of choice with surprised expressions. One of these, the tallest of the hoardings on Sherpao Bridge, was taken down at the start of winter for readjustment. For days the site was veiled, obscured by a curtain made from many different sheets of cloth that stirred and lifted lightly in the wind and fell again into place.

And then it was there.

It showed a leggy blonde in an overcoat with her arm stretched out in stopping, one foot on the pavement and one in the air. The world around her was a haze of activities, of bodies passing in and out of buildings and of cars streaking past. But she was looking ahead and smiling, confident in her ability to cross the street.

Look at me! the hoarding cried. *I am Swiss Miss!*

A box of Swiss Miss cosmetics cost three hundred and ninety-five rupees.

'That much I have,' said Samar Api and emptied her savings onto her bed. She had more than four hundred rupees; she had one thousand, seven hundred and seventy rupees, her combined earnings from various gift-giving occasions, as well as savings from her pocket-money, which was no longer forthcoming since it was no longer considered necessary for Samar Api to go out of the house.

'We have to start going out,' she said. 'I think it's been long enough, Zaki.'

My mother appealed on her behalf: the grades were better, she said, and the teachers had no complaints. The girl went to school every morning and returned every afternoon and went straight into her room. 'Children make mistakes,' said my mother, 'and they should be forgiven. That's the way to set the example. To forgive and reward, not to punish all the time. How can there be improvements when there are no rewards?'

But Daadi was unwilling to end the confinement, and said that her decision to not inform Chhoti of her daughter's recent conduct was a big concession.

Samar Api went to school and returned from school. She came into Daadi's room at lunchtime, ate her meal and went back into her own room. She asked for the phone in the evenings but returned it before Daadi went to sleep. And she didn't ask for permission to go out.

Her essays and assignments, marked and graded approvingly by her teachers, were left around the house for others to see.

'This is remarkable,' said my mother. She was holding up a stapled exam sheet.

Daadi didn't ask to know the marks.

'Twenty-six out of thirty,' said my mother and looked around amazedly.

Naseem nodded.

And Daadi continued to wipe the bits of roti in her hand along the grease on her plate's rim.

One Thursday afternoon we went with Naseem and Barkat in the car to buy groceries from the market. And the following week we were allowed to go to Empire Centre to try a new dessert dish made of chocolate cake and vanilla ice cream that had drawn enthusiastic recommendations from Suri and Hukmi.

Samar Api said she wanted to go to Empire Centre with Tara Tanvir.

'No,' said Daadi.

'And why not?' said my mother.

'Not with that girl.'

'Why not?'

Daadi was shaking her head in sustained refusal.

'They are children,' said my mother. 'And children make mistakes. That is why they are children: they make mistakes and they learn from them. For God's sake.'

In the car Tara Tanvir said, 'Your grandmother doesn't like me, *na?*'

It was her way to ask a question, even a difficult one with a potentially hurtful answer, in a simple and carefree way that didn't leave room for elision.

I said, 'No, man, you're crazy, obviously not.'

We were parked in her jeep outside an audiocassette and CD shop in Fortress. More than an hour before we had delivered Samar Api to Jamal's house, which had a high white gate with sharply pointed spears along the top. Samar Api had said to collect her in an hour, though by that she usually meant longer.

'I know your grandmother doesn't like me,' said Tara Tanvir. 'I know she hates my guts.' She made guts sound especially horrible, but then laughed at the end into her hand. It implied big-heartedness on her part, or obliviousness, it didn't matter; she sat up now, brightened by her own high spirits. 'So tell me,' she said, 'what all have you been up to?'

I told her about my two cousins Isa and Moosa, with whom I had grown friendly over Eid.

She wanted to know their ages.

I said, 'Twelve and fourteen.'

'Too young, man!' she cried, and we both laughed loudly, reducing Isa and Moosa to a juvenile experiment, a leaping lesson in adulthood.

'I have these cousins,' she said, 'Tina and Sara. They're coming to visit from America. We'll all go out. You'll like them. Very your type. Tina more so than Sara. But Sara's out of her mind!' She touched her temples. 'Boozing-shoozing full time, and she's not like even thirteen! *Kassam se*. Tina's more down to earth, definitely more than Sara, older and more quiet-and-reserved-type.' She nodded understandingly. 'I guess when you have siblings you become like that. One's always more this than that.' The thought led to others. 'You and Samar are like that.' And she went on to explain the difference: Samar Api was more intelligent but in a grown-up way, a way in which girls grew up much faster than boys, who were generally more blunt, though Tara Tanvir herself was more like boys, then, because she liked to say what was on her mind.

'Tell me something,' she said. 'Does Samar ever bitch me out?'

I said, 'No, Tara . . .'

Her look was unrelenting.

'No way, man!'

'You're telling the truth, *na*?' She was solemn now.

'Of course, Tara . . .' There was no other way.

'I think,' she said, untying and then retying her hair into the ponytail with practised swiftness, 'that it's good to know what people think. Like even with your friends you should know. I don't know. I guess I like to find out beforehand, like I want to know before it's all over town, you know? Like I do *not* want to find out on the last minute.' She waved it away. 'Like I'm so *glad* to have you guys' – she hugged it to her heart – 'I'm so *grate*ful to have real friends. Like Samar and me are like this' – she held up two fingers in a knot – 'and I *thank* my lucky stars for that. I just don't ever want it to go wrong, you know?'

It had crossed over and gone beyond.

I said, 'Ya, man, you should, definitely you should.' And it had gone nowhere in the end, but still had the shape of a discovery that was agreed upon.

Samar Api climbed into the jeep and her perfume came in a gush.

She switched on the car light. Its dusty glow fell on her forehead, her cheeks and her chin, and brought them out as if for the first time. She was looking inside her handbag and frowning.

It was dark in the lane outside, the houses sharply outlined against the dusk. Somewhere a car roared.

Tara Tanvir looked at the time on her watch and said it was late.

'I know,' said Samar Api. 'Let's go.' She put away the small round mirror, zipped up her bag and sat back in the seat. She looked at her window and sent up a hand to hold the strap.

The jeep was roused, and moved away from the high white gate with the spears at the top.

Tara Tanvir started the music. It was a song about a lover, sung by a girl, the words rapped behind her by a boy to the fast beat.

'What's the latest?' said Tara Tanvir and turned in her seat at the front of the jeep.

Samar Api said, 'Nothing. We just talked.'

'About what?'

'Stupid things,' said Samar Api.

'Did he say I love you?'

'Not yet. But I haven't said it either.'

'That's good.'

The song had changed, and the same woman was singing about having sweet dreams at night.

Samar Api said, 'He's simple.'

'That's always good,' said Tara Tanvir. 'Simple guys are so much better at the end of the day.'

Samar Api was watching her window.

The jeep went past the houses and the lit windows, gathering speed as it climbed the bridge, and left the hoardings and the blinking clusters to the night.

'You know something?' she said.

I said, 'What?'

'When the car goes on the bridge?'

'Ya.'

'It's like everything becomes amazing. You know?'

I had no recollection of the experience.

She turned on her side in the bed and said, 'It's like you see everything at once, the houses and the sky and the trees and the long line where the sky meets the houses. Then you roll down the window and the wind is in your face, and the music is playing, and it's like you're so high. You know?'

I said, 'Ya, ya.'

She sat up, placed her palms on the mattress, then stood up on the bed. She lifted the hem of her T-shirt and placed her finger on a small round bruise.

'He hit you?'

'No, dumbo,' she said, giggling, and then came down to whisper it in my ear: 'It's a love bite.'

*

She went out a few times a week, and not always with Tara, whose name was still associated in the house with truancy and the other unnamed outcomes of excessive freedom. So she said she was going to have her threading done at the beauty salon, and required Barkat to fetch her in two hours. And she signed up for afternoon classes with a mathematics tutor who taught in the Lyceum building on the canal. Once she had to go out for a friend's birthday party at a restaurant, and there was no one in the house to take her; Daadi had sent Barkat in the car to find a plumber in Canal Park.

She called Tara's house but Tara had gone out with her mother. The Far Eastern maid gave no time for calling back.

There was no one now.

She was desperate.

I called Isa and asked him if he wanted to go out for a drive.

They came, Isa and Moosa, and waited in their Swift in the driveway.

'Thanks so much, you guys,' said Samar Api. She was dressed for the birthday party: she wore black jeans and a black jumper with no sleeves. Her hair was straightened and fell to her shoulders and from there curled upwards. She leaned in repeatedly from the back of the car to give directions to the restaurant, and Isa complied unquestioningly. Moosa was sitting beside him in the front and had the look of someone who is aware of being watched by many people.

'Smokes?' he said after she had gone. The drive was already a success, his role in it undisputed.

'She's a nice girl,' said Isa. 'We should all go out together, like in a group.'

The holy month of Ramzaan arrived that year in spring. Daadi went to the utility store in Main Market and bought a month's worth of supplies, tins of Daalda cooking oil and heavy plastic sacks of sugar and salt and ground black pepper and chaat masala powders that came in colourful cardboard packs. An afternoon was spent stocking and stacking the many tins and sacks and boxes in the kitchen cupboards. An electric water-boiler and a frying pan with a stainless-steel lid came from Al-Fatah; the pan was kept in a cupboard, but the boiler, which came with a one-year warranty agreement written out in many languages on a pamphlet, was stationed for convenience above the fridge, next to the tea bags and the jar of powdered milk.

At night there were sounds from the mosques, some nearer than others, indecipherable murmurings that overlapped continually, the work of an untiring nocturnal species.

At twilight Daadi awoke. She switched on a lamp. With her feet she felt for the slippers by her bed, found them and wore them, and went into the bathroom to perform the ablutions. She said her prayers in the dressing room, then made her way across the veranda to the kitchen, where she ate the sehri meal in silence with Naseem. They were the only ones fasting. (Barkat claimed to suffer wind-related pains in his stomach and believed that they exempted him in his old age from observing the injunctions.)

At school the canteen stayed open. But it was sparsely occupied: the eaters came in sprinklings and ate their lunches quietly, away from the hordes of fasters, who played fiercely and competitively in the grounds and then went back to their classrooms flushed with thirst, seeking to make impressions on their teachers, who were mostly female and took note.

Fasting – A Pillar of Islam.

It was a test we had to take in class. The higher marks went to those who had written from direct experience.

'This is absurd,' said my mother. 'I'm afraid I'm going to have to see the principal.'

'No!'

'Why!'

'You can't!'

'But why?'

'Just no, you can't, please you can't . . .'

The sun drowned for the day and Daadi went to stand in the driveway. She walked along it once, twice, then continuously and at a pace that gave the activity the appearance of sustained contemplation. She stopped now, looked up at the sky, and heard the climbing call of the siren that signalled the end of the day's fast.

The clattering kitchen cart brought food: samosas and pakoras and jalebis in plastic plates, fruit chaat and dahi ballay in bowls. But Daadi broke her fast in the old way: with a pinch of salt, a glass of water and a single shrivelled date.

The television was roused.

And the visitors arrived: Suri-Saaji, Hukmi-Shafto, Isa-Moosa, Aasia-Maheen. I came from my room and Samar Api emerged from hers. My mother was the last to arrive and brought descriptions of the traffic on the streets outside, oddly unfamiliar after years of driving in the city with the range of other people's endurances.

'Where are you going?' she said.

We were going out.

'But where?'

I said, 'To a restaurant.'

'But there's food here,' she said, and indicated the things laid out on the table. 'It's been made for you. It doesn't look nice when somebody goes out of their way to feed you and you say that you want to go out instead.'

'Leave them,' said Daadi.

We went to Pizza Hut. It was a famous American restaurant that had opened recently on a quiet road that had since become an exceedingly popular place to open restaurants. We were going to eat the iftar meal that consisted only of pizzas. At the restaurant Tara Tanvir was going to meet Isa and Moosa for the very first time. And she was bringing her cousins Tina and Sara, who had arrived from America and were staying with her until the end of Ramzaan.

The car park outside the restaurant was full; we had to park between two trees in a service lane. Isa locked the car and mentioned the possibility of a car-burglary, a thing that was on the rise these days, especially in residential areas.

But the restaurant had seated crowds at the tables and songs playing from hidden speakers and smoky frosted windows. The paintings on the walls showed men in rowing-boats with their mouths wide open, ostensibly in mid-song, though the artist had rendered them in a way that suggested they were going *Aaaaa* for a doctor.

Samar Api said we had seats in the smoking section, which Tara Tanvir and her cousins had already occupied.

'Nice . . .' said Moosa, looking around and nodding.

'Hi, you guys,' said Tara Tanvir and introduced her cousins. 'This is Tina and this is Sara. They're here from California.'

Isa and Moosa were nodding. The specificity was tantalizing.

'Hi,' said Tina.

'Hey,' said Sara.

They were quiet for most of the evening.

Tina, the older one, had bright brown hair that fell over her forehead in a fringe, and two conspicuous front teeth that appeared in a persistent glint between her lips, giving her a look of being constantly on the verge of comment, while Sara, the younger sister, was darkly pretty, and sat with her shoulders hunched and her hands tucked mysteriously under the table. She made no contribution to the conversation and seemed instead to watch it with amusement, as if making notes for a re-enactment. When the pizzas finally came each girl took one slice and kept it on her plate.

'You guys not hungry or something?' said Isa. It was the first time he had spoken directly to the sisters.

The question threw Tina into a turmoil. 'No,' she said, 'it's not, like, I'm not *hungry* or something' – she shuddered to resettle the fringe – 'even though like, I'm not *super*-hungry, like hungry-hungry, but more like: who knows what's in*side* that . . .'

'God knows,' said Sara and widened her eyes nightmarishly.

For most of the time Tara Tanvir talked out of a need to fill the newness, though she was also genuinely enlivened by the presences of Isa and Moosa, who were unaccustomed to her chaotic charm and were also, as she had earlier noted, too young for her liking; but they formed the kind of audience that by its very attentiveness makes room for a performance to take place, giving even the unintentional aspects a weight and meaning.

'We should go now,' said Samar Api. She had been waiting.

'Oh,' said Tara Tanvir, who wasn't finished.

'Tara and me,' said Samar Api, 'we have to go photocopy our notes.'

'Okay,' said Tina.

Sara said nothing.

'Ya,' said Tara Tanvir.

'Ya,' said Samar Api.

They sought their handbags.

'You guys?' said Tara Tanvir. 'Be nice to my cousins. Take them out or something. We'll meet you guys back here in a while.'

Tina wanted to know how long it would take them.

'Not long,' said Samar Api. 'We'll be back in an hour or so.'

We went for a drive. Isa drove the car and Moosa sat beside him in the front, and I was seated in the back between the sisters, both of whom sat facing their windows.

Isa lit a cigarette and passed it to Moosa.

Sara asked to use the lighter. She received it unthankingly and began to run her finger through the flame.

'Cut it out,' said Tina.

Sara didn't.

'*Cut. It. Out.*'

'Make me.'

We feared that this would now happen in the car.

After a while Sara said, 'Anyone have pot in this car?'

'Like what kind of a pot?' said Moosa. It was his turn to attempt optimistic contact with the aliens.

'No, dumbass,' said Sara. 'I mean *pot*, like *weed*, like *grass*. You understand?'

Moosa didn't.

'You got that?'

Moosa was overwhelmed.

'Yes? No? Yes-no-yes?'

'Ignore her,' said Tina. 'She can be a total bitch.'

'Hey!' Sara had felt this to be a distorted portrayal of the kind of person that she was.

'You so are,' said Tina.

'Whatever.'

'Bitch.'

'Freak.'

We drove to the Shadman housing colony and parked outside a dimly lit house that belonged to a boy who was famous among Isa's friends for his drugs. Isa and Sara went inside the house, and Moosa and I waited in the car with Tina, who said she didn't feel like answering questions about life in California. So we listened to music in the car until Isa and Sara returned with their eyes red and we drove all the way back to Pizza Hut, where Tara Tanvir and Samar Api were waiting without their photocopied notes.

'He's getting all possessive,' she said.

She was sitting on her bed. She had locked the door and switched on the bedside lamp.

'It's interesting,' she said, and began to tell the ceiling: 'Like today he goes I don't want you wearing jeans. First I didn't get it, I thought he was joking. But then he got all serious. He goes no, you can't, *buss*, I've said it now and you can't. I was like, O my God, Jamal, calm down! *Ek dum*, he's all quiet-type. He goes' – she couldn't help smiling – 'he goes you don't understand how I feel. I was like well well well, look who's talking!' She sat up and put the knuckles of one hand on her hip, and held out the palm of the other. 'I mean then he should tell me how he feels, you know?'

I agreed.

'I guess boys are like that,' she said and sank into the pillows behind her. 'Girls are just not made that way. Girls just talk and talk. Even when there's nothing to talk about they talk. I guess God has made them like that for a reason. It's written in the Quran, man! Look at nature: everything is there for a reason; birds and bees and flowers are all so different from each other . . .' Her hands were flying around in demonstration, as though nature with its abundance of miracles had come into her room.

Then she said, 'Zaki? Do you think it's wrong that I'm like all this in Ramzaan?' She motioned to herself and to the air around her.

I said, 'It's possible.'

She said, 'I don't think it's wrong if you're serious, like if you're thinking five years down the road . . .'

'That's true,' I said.

'You think so?'

'I think so.'

'*Heina?*'

'Ya, ya.'

'I also thought so.'

'Ya.'

'Ya,' she said, and continued: 'It's like everything depends, you know? Like a few days back I was thinking all these thoughts, like what if nothing happens in the end, what if something bad happens, *khudanakhasta*, and it doesn't work out' – it was difficult to face – 'between me and Jamal' – she had said it – 'and we *don't* get married and all. Then it's all wrong. Then it's always been wrong. And all of a sudden I was so scared, I was like Allah Mian, please, please let it work out' – she was rocking herself with her hands pressed together – 'and then sometimes, like right now, I just sit back, and I look at the situation' – she motioned frankly to the situation, which was here now – 'and I think: do I really want this? Is this how I want to do stuff? Like sneaking out and all. But then

I can't do anything else either. Like there's no way I could tell my mother. Jamal's parents have to go and propose properly and even then I can't tell my mother that I've been like all this. But then I think it's worth it, because it's me who has to make it work out in the end.'

I said, 'Do you love him?'

She was surprised. 'I mean obviously, Zaki . . .'

'Do you guys like . . .'

She couldn't see it coming, though she knew it was.

'Like . . .' I did a tumbling of the hands.

'Obviously *not*, Zaki! What kind of *question* is that? I mean he *wants* to, probably, I don't know, and in any case I wouldn't let him, no, Zaki, obviously not.'

*

The following week she was caught.

She and Tara were returning to the tuition centre in Tara's jeep, returning before the two hours allotted to her maths lesson had ended and it was time for her collection.

But Naseem was already parked in the lane outside the building.

They saw each other emerging from unexpected cars.

'Get in,' said Naseem. Her door slammed. She was breathing through her nostrils alone, back and forth with effort.

Barkat started the ignition.

'Tuition,' said Naseem. 'Going to my tuition. To study.'

Samar Api tried to speak.

'Not a word,' said Naseem. 'Not a word to me now. There is no need.'

From her own car Tara Tanvir was watching the scene with curtailed involvement.

'Naseem,' said Samar Api.

'No,' said Naseem. 'You will answer to those who wait for you at home, those who pay for your tuitions and pay us to drop you and fetch you and wait for you outside in the heat. No need to tell us anything – we are only servants.'

They came home and she followed Naseem into the kitchen.

'Don't talk to me,' said Naseem.

Barkat shut his eyes and shook his head despairingly, and raised a finger of silence to his lips.

But Samar Api lingered in the kitchen with explanations.

'Leave,' said Naseem. 'Leave now or I will go inside and tell on you.'

She returned to her room.

'Bloody Naseem.'

I asked to know what had happened.

She told me. 'I mean it's madness. She's a bloody servant, she should know her place, you know?' It was her turn to be indignant, her turn to be deceived.

'She saw you?'

'Ya, but so what!'

'I'm just asking . . .'

'Ya, but why are you taking her bloody side?'

'I'm not taking her bloody side!'

'Okay, fine then, fuck off, okay?'

And she went into the bathroom and unleashed the shower, and stayed inside for a long time in the hiss.

By evening she had decided to apologize.

She went to the servants' quarter at the back of the house. In the dank courtyard, in the spreading dark, Naseem was squatting by the tap above the drainage and clobbering a soaped shalwar in the water. The latrine door behind her was lit from within; there was a flushing sound, and Barkat emerged with his face wet. He stood by the door and wiped his face with the hem of his kameez.

Naseem looked up.

'Sorry, Naseem.'

Naseem didn't respond. She was no longer angry. She was washing and rinsing her clothes with resolve.

Barkat came forward with a chair. He settled its delicate legs on the floor, then settled himself carefully on the seat. He leaned back in it, then leaned forward and entwined his fingers.

He said it was not his place, being a servant, to speak on an occasion that did not involve him directly. But he would speak today in his capacity as an elder, an elder speaking to someone who was still a child.

'It is not good,' he said, 'for young girls to tell lies about where they are going. It can cast a doubt.' He nodded gravely at the word, at the very possibility of what it suggested, making doubt sound like a terrible thing, damaging and irreversible. 'And you are young,' he said. 'And the young do not always know what is good for them. They do not. And it is for us – your elders – to stop you when you do a wrong. Is it not?' He looked across the courtyard at Naseem, but she didn't lend herself to it, her back was still turned and she was rinsing and washing her shalwar in the spattering water.

Back in her room, her confidence restored, Samar Api asked to use the telephone and brought it into her room to call Jamal.

But he already knew. Tara had called him in the afternoon and told him about what had happened at the tuition centre. He said Tara was distraught too, and anxious to know what had happened when Samar Api went home.

'I don't know, Jamal,' she said. 'I just don't know any more.' The telephone cord was wound up around her finger.

She listened to what he was saying.

'But why are you saying it like it's my fault?'

'Ya, but why are you saying it like it's *my* fault?'

'But it's not my fault . . .'

'Ya, but you're saying it.'

Abruptly she was accusing him of saying things to upset her and of not saying enough when he should have; earlier occasions were recalled now and hurled collectively. And it lit up her features and her voice before it left her with the dread of having gone too far. 'Okay, Jamal, I'm sorry. Just forget it – please just forget it.'

She hung up the phone and stared at it.

'Samar Api . . .' I said.

But she looked away in time to hide the tears.

*

'Zaki, I think it's my fault.'

It was afternoon of the next day, and the gloom of the night had lifted. In its place now stood a spirit of self-examination, a hard new wish to identify the problems and an attendant belief in the powers of honesty and reason.

'I think I overreacted. But he should know I'm sensitive. But I should know he's sensitive too.' The reasoning had led to a dilemma.

She consulted the horoscope in the newspapers.

'See,' she said, 'he's a Cancer. He's like a crab. He's moody but he's also sensitive.'

And she looked for herself.

'And I'm a Capricorn! O God, it's so true. It says I'm stubborn and this week I should try not to be so stubborn. It says I should swallow my pride.' She was glad to know it. 'I can't be proud, Zaki. You can't be proud in a relationship. You have to learn to compromise.'

She had it confirmed on the phone by Tara Tanvir, who told her that it was true, she was stubborn and she could be proud. And she had been unfair to Jamal, who was simple and blunt by nature and could not be expected to attend to the needs of a Capricorn.

'O God,' she said afterwards. 'I'm like a total bitch!' She was considering it for the first time. It was exciting. 'Zaki, do you think I'm a bitch? Zaki, you have to be honest!'

It was turning into a joke.

I said, 'Sometimes.'

She gasped and threw a protesting pillow in my face, and I threw it back with twice the force, and we ended up having a pillow fight.

She laughed and I laughed.

'O God, Zaki!' She was laughing and grimacing at the same time, hugging her stomach with gaseous pain. 'O God, stop it . . .'

We laughed and gasped and blew whistles.

'Seriously,' she said, sitting up and placing the pillow in her lap, 'what do you think I should do?'

'About what?'

'This *thing*,' she said and waved at the wall. 'How do I fix it?'

I said she could call him.

'But no, *na*' – she slapped the pillow in her lap – 'I have to do something special that makes up for being such a bloody bitch.'

In the end she decided to buy him a present, a cologne and a selection of songs on an audiocassette that she would ask the man at Off Beat to record for her. She would have the items wrapped and delivered to him at his house. And then she would wait for him to call her.

We stood over her bed and counted her savings, depleted by recent outings to restaurants and cafés.

'I think we have enough,' she said and stacked up the notes in her hand.

But there was still the uncertainty of her confinement. Barkat and Naseem drove her to the tuition centre in the afternoon and waited now for her in the lane. Naseem hadn't told anyone in the house. But she had promised nothing, and the threat of disclosure remained. One day, watching Samar Api emerge with Tara Tanvir from the Lyceum building after the maths lesson had ended, Naseem said, 'From now on you will not be seen with that girl.'

'Why?' said Samar Api.

'*Buss*,' said Naseem.

'Listen to your elders,' said Barkat.

At home it was said that Naseem was turning into a nuisance. But Daadi said nuisances were necessary and only accumulated with age, starting with marriage itself, the mother-in-law and the sisters-in-law, and children too with their demands, and then daughters-in-law, until one was left with oneself and found that that was the biggest nuisance of all.

'Zaki,' she said. 'I need you to do me a favour.'

She wanted me to go to the market and buy the present, the

cologne as well as the selection of songs. 'And you can say you're getting them for yourself.'

But I didn't have the money.

'So you can say I got them for you.'

She explained that it was important for her to stay in the house for some time; she had to recover the earlier freedoms. She didn't think it would take her more than a month. And she was thinking ahead to the future: the subjects she was going to study for her A-Level exams, and her graduation, timed to coincide with her engagement; she was going to have his family solemnize the relationship in a hanh ceremony, an exchange of rings that was not binding but would enable her to meet him without these constraints.

I went to the market with her money. Isa and Moosa took me in their car, which was being driven today by Moosa. He was still too young to apply for a provisional licence. It didn't stop him from driving the car with confidence, with swift movements of the steering wheel, making a style even out of the mistakes.

Isa shouted.

'Chill,' said Moosa, and tittered.

We went first to Off Beat with the list of songs. The shop was located in the upper alcove of a small plaza on Main Boulevard. It was a hot day, and the shop's windows were tinted black against the sun. The air inside was suddenly cold. The stacks of CDs and audiocassettes went all around the walls, on shelves made of glass that were reflected in the narrow mirrors that stood at regular intervals and reached up to the ceiling.

The man behind the glass counter was sitting on a stool with his arms crossed over his chest.

I showed him the list of songs.

'Do you have all of them?' It was not unusual for songs on an Off Beat selection to end unfinished because the reel had ended, or to not be on the tape because the man behind the counter hadn't found them.

The man held up the list and angled his head and raised both his eyebrows and sighed.

'I Would Do Anything For Love'	Meat Loaf
'Dream Lover'	Mariah Carey
'Shy Guy'	Diana King
'Can't Help Falling in Love'	UB40
'Be My Lover'	La Bouche
'Lover Girl'	Alisha Chinai
'Kabhi Kabhie'	Kabhi Kabhie
'Roop Tera'	Bally Sagoo
'Chura Liya'	Bally Sagoo
'Sanu Ik Pal Chayn'	Nusrat Fateh

The man was nodding. It was possible.

I said. 'How long?'

He thought about it and said, 'Tuesday.'

But it was Wednesday.

'Sorry,' said the man, not in apology but in refusal.

'Sunday,' I said.

'Closed,' he said.

'You open it.'

He wasn't willing to consider it.

'Magazine,' I said. 'Long article about you and your shop.'

Now he was being stubborn because he had to.

I placed the money on the counter, on top of the list.

He sniggered contemptuously, an adult beholding a child.

'*Buss*,' said Isa and raised a palm in intervention. 'Saturday the shop is open. So five o'clock it is. You keep the money and we will come and pick it up. All set.'

And again at Al-Fatah, on the first floor, among the mirrors and the products and the swarming shoppers, we found our way to the cologne counter, where the bottles were kept in their cases on shelves behind a sliding glass pane. The salesman was a dark, balding man, and was presently writing up receipts in a notepad.

We waited before him with our hands on the counter.

He looked up inquiringly.

'Boss,' said Isa. 'And Cool Water. And what else?'

'Versace Blue Jeans,' I said.

'Blue Jeans,' said Isa.

The man turned to the shelves behind him and located the boxes from three different corners. One by one he placed them on the counter.

I wanted to open the boxes and take out the bottles and smell them.

'Cannot,' said the salesman. 'Sealed.' As if to eliminate any remaining doubts he pointed behind him to a sign on the wall that said FIXED PRICE PLEASE.

Isa asked for the prices; only Versace Blue Jeans was less than a thousand rupees. But Isa wanted me to get Cool Water – he was familiar with the smell and insisted that it was better than the smell of Versace Blue Jeans.

'You can come back with more money,' he said.

There was no more money to bring back.

I said, 'I'll take Blue Jeans. It looks much better.'

And the box was sent with a peon-boy in an Al-Fatah plastic bag to the front desk for payment and collection.

'Zaki, this is not right.'

She wasn't happy with the sheet of wrapping paper: there were too many lines in the pattern. She said she had wanted something simple, plain and elegant (she had said nothing of the sort at the time of designation). And she was dismayed to learn that the selection was going to take until the weekend to record. 'I wanted to send it all today or tomorrow,' she said. 'And now I'm going to have to wait until Sunday . . .'

She called Tara. And Tara told her that it was not necessary to send presents.

'Why are you even with him?' said Tara.

'I don't know, man . . .' She was trying now to feel sorry for herself.

'Seriously,' said Tara Tanvir, 'I'm only saying this because it'll be helpful to you. I don't have any problems with Jamal or anything. I think he's a nice guy, a great guy, I just don't see the point of this thing between you two, like I don't see where it's going.'

They talked about the relationship's strengths and weaknesses, the fact that it was perpetually long distance now, since it was difficult for her to see him without getting caught and he wasn't even trying to console her.

'And it's not like I don't understand,' said Samar Api. 'I know I overreacted, I know he's sensitive, it's a misunderstanding and people have them all the time, but it's like grow up, you know?'

'Frankly,' said Tara Tanvir, 'I don't think you overreacted.'

'You think so?'

'Completely. You just did not overreact. It's a fact. Why don't you face it?' And she gave the same reasoning: it was not that she disliked Jamal, but more a question of compatibility between two very different people.

'I guess opposites attract,' said Samar Api.

'I guess,' said Tara Tanvir.

They discussed it over the next few days on the phone, Tara Tanvir insisting that Samar Api and Jamal were two very different people, and implying that it was time to end the relationship. Samar Api listened to the justifications of her own behaviour, and found herself agreeing with Tara Tanvir. On Saturday the recorded selection arrived, was combined with the cologne and wrapped in the wrapping paper. And on Monday she took it in her bag to school and gave it to Tara Tanvir.

She returned from school.

'What happened?'

She said she had given Tara the present. 'And she took it and all. But she was all sad about it. She goes you don't listen to me, you don't care what I say. I was like what's wrong with you, just take the bloody present and give it to him, can't you do this for a friend? But she goes *you're* the one who's selfish. Can you believe that? She actually said that. I was like you've lost it, woman.'

She waited by the phone. She went into the next room to check the time on the clock. She tried calling Tara's house but no one was answering.

'Should I call Jamal?'

She decided against it.

She went again to check the clock and came back and said that it had now been more than an hour.

She dialled Tara's numbers, the upstairs number and the downstairs number, again and again, until someone picked up the phone.

It was the Far Eastern maid.

'Give the phone to Tara.'

'Maadaam in shower.'

But Samar Api insisted, and was made to hold on the line while the maid went looking, a scratchy orchestra recording keeping her unentertained in the meantime.

'I don't know why it's taking this long,' she said, holding the phone away from her mouth. 'I need to know his reaction and all.'

The music had stopped.

'Did you give it to him?'

Tara Tanvir said she had.

'What did he say?'

'He liked it, I guess. Why don't you ask him yourself?'

'Tara, why are you being such a bitch?'

Tara Tanvir laughed, released from the obligations of friendship. '*I'm* being a bitch? Well, excuse me.'

They were calm.

'Okay,' said Samar Api. 'So what did he say?'

Tara Tanvir was vague.

'I can call him myself, you know, Tara? I asked you because I thought you were my friend.'

'Oh, please,' said Tara Tanvir.

Samar Api said, 'What's wrong with you?'

'Nothing,' said Tara Tanvir.

'You think you can fuck up everyone's life because your own life is so fucked up? Just because you have your car and your driver all the time? You think you can play with people?'

And now Tara Tanvir laughed and said, 'You're so full of shit. Your family know it, your friends know it, and guess what: Jamal knows it too.'

'Don't take his fucking name, okay? Don't talk about my family, okay?' She was weakened and it was showing.

'Seriously,' said Tara Tanvir, 'you need to sort out your shit. Because I am so not dealing with it.'

'Fine. Don't.' She was dialling again.

I said, 'What are you doing?'

She was calling Jamal.

But it went directly to his answering machine. His voice was asking her to leave a message.

'Zaki,' she said, sobbing, holding up the phone.

'Samar Api,' I said. I placed the pillow in my lap, placed her head on it and took the phone away from her hand. 'You have to stop crying, Samar Api. You have to look at the bright side.'

There was no bright side.

'He'll call you, Samar Api. Just stop crying.'

'You think so?' And briefly the tears stopped.

'O God, Samar Api,' I said, and stared at the wall. 'Obviously.'

9

On the weekend Chhoti came to the house; she appeared at the door in a state of acute physical unease, her face sweating and inflamed and her cheeks puffing in and out. She fell on her back on the sofa, and the cushions nodded with the suddenness of her weight.

Daadi attempted to rise from the bed.

'Sit, sit,' said Chhoti and put up a palm.

Daadi was looking at her sister.

'The heat,' said Chhoti.

'It is not the heat,' said Daadi.

'Too hot over there.'

'It is not the heat.'

'What to tell you.'

'Look at your face.'

'It is the heat.'

'You never listen. You never have and you never will.'

The comment was also a sentence to the life it lamented.

'I am telling you,' said Chhoti, laughing now to show her recovery, 'I am fine. It is only the heat. Over there it is much worse than here, even in the car it can't be avoided.' And she told of the recent rounds of load-shedding in Barampur, where the sight of electrical wires was still a novelty.

Daadi wanted to know what the doctor had said.

'Sugar,' said Chhoti with a sigh, and with a habitual frown to suggest an insignificant ailment, 'and blood and heart. The same.' Her breaths were more deliberate.

Daadi asked to know the readings on the blood-pressure pump.

Chhoti told her.

Daadi said, 'You are not taking your medicines. It is on your face. Why do you do it?'

Chhoti said there was only one clinic in the village. And the nearest hospital was in Okara Town, which was an hour by road and required an effort Chhoti wasn't willing to make.

'It is your health,' said Daadi.

'I don't care,' said Chhoti.

'You are careless.'

'So I am.'

'You will die.'

'So I will.'

We went to Daadi's room in the evening. Naseem was sitting on the carpet and peeling raw vegetables into the perforated steel bowl. Daadi and Chhoti were sitting on the sofa and watching an Indian actress, now retired, who was presently being interviewed on the Indian channel in *Behind the Scenes*, a programme in which the reminiscences of showbiz personalities were interspersed with songs and dialogues from their films.

Daadi was repeating after the words of the song on TV.

Chhoti was watching her and slapping her knee.

'Oi hoi,' said Daadi, laughing.

'Too much,' said Chhoti, 'too much.'

Naseem was amused to see that it had caused such a sensation.

'At least you are young,' said Daadi. 'At my age these things are adventures.'

'Your age,' said Chhoti, 'is nothing.' And she gave the example of her three sisters-in-law. 'Their teeth are going,' she said. 'But their hearts are beating.'

Daadi was captivated.

Chhoti said, 'And with cooks and drivers.'

Daadi said, 'It cannot be.'

Chhoti closed her eyes and sealed her mouth, then opened them and said, 'Some women are like that. They cannot be contained by God or man.' And she touched her earlobes in the gesture for repentance.

Daadi said, 'Your life is full of glamour.'

Chhoti said, 'No, no.'

'Yes,' said Daadi. 'You cannot deny it. You are one of the movers and shakers.'

'No, no,' said Chhoti.

'Oh yes,' said Daadi, 'movers and shakers.' She swayed her head from side to side.

Naseem looked up from the television and grinned as though she had benefited personally from the moving and the shaking.

'Tell us,' said Daadi and looked at Samar Api, 'is your mother not living in the glamour?'

Samar Api smiled.

'You see?' said Daadi. 'Movers and shakers.'

Naseem hooted and clapped.

Chhoti sighed and said, 'This glamour is the work of the devil.' And she lamented the lack of plainness and simplicity in the world, which had succumbed to falsities. 'It is rare nowadays,' said Chhoti, 'to find a thing that is truly well intended. It is no longer the fashion.'

Naseem said it was a tragedy.

Daadi hummed.

Their attentions returned to the actress on TV.

'Look at her,' said Daadi. 'Look at her mouth.'

'Injections,' said Chhoti. 'They put rubber inside.'

A hand flew to Daadi's mouth.

'Yes,' said Chhoti, 'rubber and plastic.'

Naseem refused to believe in it.

'Oh yes,' said Chhoti. 'It is happening in America. You can change everything. You can change your nose, your mouth, anything you want now.'

Naseem watched the actress with renewed interest, the way her mouth was moving and talking, undeterred by rubber or plastic.

'How much is the cost?'

Chhoti said Naseem would have to sell her house and her clothes in order to reach the reception desk at one of the rubber clinics. 'And then you have to keep going back, because if you don't go back it all comes off. You could wake up in the morning and find your nose in your lap.'

Naseem was enchanted.

Daadi said, 'Drugs. They must be mixing in the rubber.' And she gave the example of Madhubala, the most famous actress of her time, who fell in love with Dilip Kumar on the set of *Mughal-e-Azam* and was then persuaded by her enemies to wear an ointment that poisoned her skin. 'The world,' said Daadi, 'does not spare those who want things. It is better to live with what you have. You don't have to like your nose. But you must live with it. You must learn to live with it.'

Naseem said, 'The wants never end.'

'Even for Madhubala,' said Daadi.

'Even for Madhubala,' said Chhoti.

The actress on TV was running down a hill and laughing.

Then Chhoti said she had seen a girl at a wedding in Multan, a girl whose beauty had caused a frenzy of speculation among the women. 'Every mother of every son is standing in the line,' said Chhoti. And she named the wife of the Multan politician who had attended the lunch at their house with his family. His daughters were engaged to their cousins, said Chhoti, but his son was unmarried. 'He lives here,' she said. 'And he does nothing. He sits in his father's house and is surviving on his father's money. Twenty-four years old and doing nothing. But his mother is looking for a bird of paradise.'

'Is she looking?' said Samar Api.

'Looking everywhere,' said Chhoti. 'Everywhere she goes. But who can stop her? She is one of those women.'

'I knew it,' said Samar Api afterwards. 'I always knew it.' She had recalled many incidents that at the time of their occurrence had been mysterious but were now explained.

She said she had known, for instance, that Jamal's two sisters were not on her side. 'They never came up to meet me. Not once. I went to their house many times. They knew I was there.' And she had never encountered Jamal's mother on her way into the house – a servant met her at the gate, led her though a back passage and along a staircase into Jamal's room. She had wondered then about the lack of a reception, though admittedly she had also wanted to avoid the awkwardness of meeting his family in their house without a way of introducing herself. 'But still, Zaki, you have a sense, you get a feeling when you go to someone's house, and the feeling I got just wasn't right.'

Now the feeling was explained: Jamal's mother wanted him to marry someone else. His sisters were expected to want the same. Only Jamal remained. And he wasn't taking her calls.

'Don't you see?' she said and flung her hands. 'They've brainwashed him!'

She was going to try everything. 'Anything and everything,' she said. 'That is my motto from now on.'

Shoes could no longer be left upturned. Whenever she saw one she stopped to set it right. 'You see?' she said, pointing to the sole. 'It's dirty. And it was pointing to Allah. That's disrespectful.'

At night she asked to use Daadi's prayer mat, which was spread out diagonally on the floor in her own room. It had to be pointing towards the Qibla, the direction of Mecca. Then she asked Daadi to teach her a special prayer for wishing. And Daadi instructed her to raise the number of nafals in proportion to the scale of her wish.

In the evening there were discussions on the principles of Islam, discussions that often fled from the particular and came to resemble, in their emphasis on yearning and intention, the higher logic of mysticism.

'The girl is maturing,' said Daadi.

Naseem said there was no doubt in it, and added that it was gratifying when strictness with children resulted in visible improvements.

The routines continued: Samar Api went to school in the morning and to her tuitions in the afternoon, where she saw Tara Tanvir from the distance that now stood between them. They were, said Samar Api, no longer on talking terms; she believed that it was Tara who had been unreasonable on the phone, and Tara who was now acting like a child. 'I don't think she has any reason,' said Samar Api. 'I'm not going to apologize.' And she made attempts at befriending the other girls at school, who had already formed groups that were difficult to join.

Gradually she succeeded in penetrating a group that came to her maths tuition. Two of the girls were at school with her; the other two had left to join a co-ed school in Johar Town. The group was undergoing alterations, expecting defections and looking to expand.

She came home and named the new friends.

It sounded sinister.

'Not at all,' she said. 'They're all delicate-type, all full-sleeves and all. They sing songs in class when the light goes.'

She walked with the two girls at school, and with the full group of four at the tuition centre. It was too early to exchange the information about themselves, so they talked of other things: the new friends were found to possess a fund of knowledge pertaining to the dark arts, to witchcraft and black magic and palmistry, and to old graveyards near R.A. Bazaar that were said to contain unusually long graves for the tall people who had once roamed the earth and were mentioned in the Quran. In return the new friends wanted to know about Tara Tanvir, whom they had noted like everyone else but never known.

'Do you think it's bad that I'm talking about her?'

I said it was.

'But then why is she being such a bitch?'

'You should talk to her.'

She thought about it. 'But *why* should I call her? *I'm* not the one who's acting all stuck up and I-don't-care-type. *She* should call me. She should call me and then she should wait.'

One evening she came home with a plan: she had learned about a woman, a palmist who lived in Tech Society and kept jinns that foretold the future. The woman was unrivalled; there was no palmist or sage or tarot-card reader in the city who could make predictions with her clarity and precision. And for proof Samar Api cited one of the new friends, a girl whose mother had been to see the woman and was warned of a medical crisis, which upon investigation was found to be a stage-one lump in the breast.

'Imagine,' said Samar Api. 'If it wasn't for her . . .'

'But how will we go?'

She said we could take a ricksha. 'We'll catch it on the street. It's very simple.'

'It's dangerous,' I said.

'Zaki?' She sat down on the bed, her palms placed patiently on her thighs. 'You know something? Let me tell you something. Girls? They never go for boys who act like sissies. Never. Girls like adventurous men, men who take *risks*.' At the emphasized parts she expanded the air around her chest. 'And I'm only saying this because it'll be helpful to you. One day you'll be all grown up, and you'll look back and you'll think of me and you'll remember these words.' And she said it with a literal certainty, envisioning a future where we weren't on talking terms but recalled each other's words with fondness and feeling.

*

The day of our departure was a Sunday. We waited until early in the afternoon for Daadi to take her sleeping pill and switch on the fan and shut the door to her room. I was then sent to inspect the kitchen: the cupboards were locked and the lights had been switched off. Naseem had stacked the dishes in the sink and left them in the unmoving water, and gone to her room at the back of the house.

I went into my mother's room. She was talking on the telephone.

'Yes, Zaki?'

'Nothing.'

I returned to Samar Api's room.

'She's on the phone.'

'What did you say?'

'Nothing.'

'Did she ask?'

'No.'

'Okay.' There was relief. 'Can you check outside now?'

I went beyond the gate and found Barkat and two of his friends in a shack built for the servants of a neighbouring house. They were playing *Ludo*. The heat had drained the men, drained their motivation and their luck; the die was yielding the same small progressions.

It was Barkat's turn. He shook the die in the small cylindrical container; it rattled promisingly; he released it with a flourish, and it rolled out and meandered and encircled its destination on the board and came to a stop.

It was a two.

'Fate,' said his friend. He was the closest to winning.

Barkat rubbed his knuckles into his eyes and looked out beyond the shade.

'Barkat,' I said.

'Yes, yes,' he said. On the weight of his palms he stood up. His ankles cracked; he winced with pleasure and then with pain.

'Going inside,' he said.

The friends said they were all going inside, each to his own house. They praised the Lord and rose.

Their houses were in villages.

The *Ludo* board was folded, the die and the other brightly coloured implements stored in pockets.

'Yes,' said Barkat, after the friends had gone. 'Where to now?' He was holding the car keys.

'It's all right,' I said.

'You don't want to go now?'

'We can go later.'

He was disappointed.

'Don't worry,' I said. 'We don't really need to go. We'll go in the evening. You should go to your room and have a rest.'

'Okay,' said Samar Api. 'I think we can go now.'

She locked her door from the outside and dropped the key in her handbag. It was plump with magazines. She was going to sell them at a second-hand bookshop in Main Market and take the money to the palmist in Tech Society.

We went through the veranda, our shoes making sounds.

But the gate was locked, and Barkat had taken the key with him to his quarter at the back of the house.

I offered to fetch him.

'No,' she said. 'He'll find out.'

A dilemma.

'We'll climb it,' she said, and made me do it first, watching my feet and hands go up the floral wrought-iron designs of the gate.

The upper ledge was narrow. Sitting on it was uncomfortable.

But the house was suddenly whole, like in the opening scene in *The Jungle Book*, when the jungle foliage parts obligingly to provide a semi-aerial view of India.

'Zaki, I can't do this.'

She was strangely feminine. Her body was foreshortened and her shoes with their heels were not made for physical exertion. The make-up was useless, and the handbag was a hindrance.

'At least try, Samar Api.'

'I can't.' She was shaking her head and looking away.

I took the bag and the shoes and instructed her to grip the tendrils.

'Now what?' She was nervous.

'Now raise your foot.'

She raised the foot cautiously and placed it on a flattened curve. She waited for the pain. It didn't come. She grew emboldened and rocked herself on one foot, rocked herself and then pulled up. At once the pain was sharp, and she was pulling the upper tendrils, scowling at the pain and trying to go up.

'Zaki, I can't!'

'You can!'

'Zaki, no, Zaki!'

'Come on!'

'O God!'

And she climbed the difficult gate. Her whole body was clenched, her hands pressed into the ledge and her legs stiff with fear. But she had succeeded. In the climbing of anything now there would be a repetition.

The house with its many windows was like a skull.

I jumped.

And she jumped.

And it was easier.

229

'Ouch,' she said, and held up the sole of a foot. It was starting to redden. She recovered the handbag and strapped on the shoes.

We walked along the lane and then drifted onto the narrow pedestrian track. Her heels left holes in the mud, a trail that broadened out with the growing confidence of her steps.

'Wait.'

She had stopped at the intersection of the lane and the road, and was waving her arm at the traffic. The cars didn't stop. The motor-cycles and bicycles were slower. A ricksha neared but continued on its way; it was occupied.

'It's hot,' I said.

'Doesn't matter, Zaki.'

We waited.

The traffic left behind its smoke.

No.

No.

No.

No.

'Zaki!'

She was running to catch a ricksha that had stopped. She spoke into the driver's window and nodded, motioned hurryingly and climbed in.

'Main Market first,' she said, and leaned back in her seat, which was hard like the rest of the ricksha, a bright tin box. The inside had been partitioned to create the illusion of room, for heads that touched the sagging plastic top and knees that folded forcibly against a metal buffer separating the driver at the front from the passengers at the back.

The ricksha sound was like a wail. It developed a consistency that broke only when the ricksha encountered a speed breaker and bumped.

'Where are you going?' said Samar Api. 'This is not the way to Main Market . . .'

The ricksha drove on.

'Excuse me!' She was knocking violently on the partition. 'Where are you going?'

The ricksha slowed down.

'Main Market,' said the driver, and he was a boy wearing a skull-cap on his small head, the few hairs on his chin recently grown.

'This is not the way to Main Market,' said Samar Api.

The driver looked out of his window and began to reverse the ricksha.

'Do you even have a licence?'

The driver was reversing.

'Are you listening to me?'

He was listening.

'This is *wrong*,' said Samar Api. 'We could be arrested. We could have an accident. Anything could happen. I am not going to give my money for this.'

The second-hand bookstore was located in the darkened basement of a small, crumbling plaza in Main Market. The shop adjacent to the bookshop was being rebuilt; the labourers were trying to demolish an uneven, already broken wall that had flaked down to brick.

The hammers rose and struck.

'This is wrong,' said Samar Api. She was arguing over the noise with the sales assistant for ascribing arbitrary values to the magazines she had placed before him on the counter

'Second-hand,' said the man.

'Look at this,' said Samar Api and held up a magazine, an anniversary edition of *Stardust* with a bathrobed Amitabh on the cover. The words *The King at Home* were blazing behind him in stark silver letters. 'This was for two ninety-five.'

The man considered the magazine and brought out his calculator. His finger was held above it.

He looked up at the ceiling.

The price came to him.

The finger struck.

He held up the calculator.

'No,' she said. 'I'm sorry.' She was shaking her head.

The man said, 'All right, all right.' He took hold of the piled magazines and brought them across the counter: he counted the number of spines with his finger and multiplied it by an average price.

He showed her the calculator.

'No,' said Samar Api.

'Last offer,' said the salesman.

'I'm sorry.'

'This is it.'

'No.'

'Take or leave.'

'But no . . .'

'The choice is yours.'

She sighed. She needed the money to take to the palmist and to pay the ricksha waiting outside. And she couldn't argue with all the sales assistants in all the shops. She stood before the counter for some moments, looking at her magazines, acquired over the years and read individually and stacked methodically on shelves, in wardrobes and shoeboxes. She watched as they were lifted now and dumped whole into a container that was swarming with dead magazines, the covers marked with big black crosses.

She was paid. And she didn't forget to thank the sales assistant.

The handbag, emptied, hung limply on her arm.

The steel steps shuddered on the way up.

'Tech Society,' she said to the ricksha driver, who roused the vehicle and drove on.

Tech Society was one of the housing colonies on the canal. And at this time of day the canal was deserted. The boys who came to dive in it had gone for the day, the mud-brown water undisturbed and wrinkling in the sun. The canal broadened on the way; the trees increased; it narrowed again and the trees thinned. We had been driving for some time when the sound of the zuhr azaan went up outside; the driver ejected the audiocassette at once, and Samar Api raised the dupatta from her shoulders and arranged it around her head.

The ricksha entered the high black gates of Tech Society, and the cars were instantly visible: they were parked in rows outside a small steel gate, which was open and led into a house: the men were standing in a circle in the garden; the women sat in benches on the patio. The house was moderately sized, the walls painted an unassuming beige and lined along the top with flower pots, which seemed to be the only attempt at decoration.

A slim girl in a black shalwar kameez was going around with a roster. She was tall and dark, had her hair in a small bun and wore a locket that touched her collarbones and slid from side to side when she moved.

'Forms,' she said, and held them out. She was chewing the gum in her mouth with indifference; her eyes looked away and her mouth made a bubble, which grew until it popped.

A name was called. Three women rose hurriedly from a bench and were led away by the tall girl.

Samar Api sat on the abandoned bench. We could hear the surrounding conversations, the expressions of curiosity and willing-ness. One woman was starting to tell another about her divorce, staring with frank, bloodshot eyes at her listener; another sat with her elbows on her knees and swayed herself on the bench, her face smothered in her hands. A man stood behind her and looked out onto the lawn; a woman sat next to her on the bench and stroked her back.

'Zaki? Do you think it's wrong?'

Her name was being called.

'You've come so far, Samar Api . . .'

'I know, I know.' She was conflicted.

The voice from inside was calling out.

'You don't have to,' I said. 'We can come back later.'

But she had already stood up.

The tall girl swept in through a door and then a hallway, lit weakly by white light, and now came to another door. She knocked. A voice spoke from inside. The girl opened the door and went in.

The woman was sitting at her desk. And it was littered with objects of organization: there were pens and pencils and coloured markers in a mug, a ruler and a paper-cutter, a device for punching holes in sheets of paper, a stapler settled next to a stack of staples, a round glass paperweight and a calendar opened onto a picture of sunflowers.

The woman was sitting behind her materials, beneath a large framed calligraphy of a Quranic ayat, and was lifting papers from a pile on her desk. She glanced at the papers, stacked them and returned them to the pile.

She smiled.

Her eyes were small and friendly behind her glasses.

'Hello, *beta*,' she said, and consulted the form in her hand. 'Samar.'

Samar Api smiled.

'A nice name,' said the woman.

Samar Api kept smiling.

The woman went on stacking her papers.

'Oh,' she said, noticing, 'please sit, please sit.'

We sat in the two chairs on the other side of the desk. The chairs were comfortable; the room was suddenly deep. The windows were small and located high up on the walls.

'What would you like to drink?' said the woman. 'We have Pepsi, we have 7UP. We have Fanta also. Would you like to have Fanta?'

Samar Api declined.

'Dieting?' said the woman.

'No, no,' said Samar Api, and laughed.

'You don't need to.'

'I'm not!'

'Promise?'

'Promise!'

'Good,' said the woman. 'I am trusting you.'

Samar Api licked her lips and folded her hands in her lap.

'So,' said the woman.

'Yes,' said Samar Api.

'You want to know your future.'

'Yes,' said Samar Api.

'Very well. Come here, please.' The woman was patting a stool by her side.

Samar Api left the chair and went to sit on the stool. It was high, and made her appear taller than the woman.

The woman asked for her hand.

Samar Api held it out.

'The other hand.'

'Oh . . .' Samar Api extended her right hand.

The woman received it in both of hers, and held it carefully, caressing the skin and folding and unfolding the fingers.

'Moisturizer.'

Samar Api laughed.

'Nivea?'

'Oil of Olay.'

'Oil of Olay,' said the woman, nodding. She was looking at the open palm. 'The lines are all good. Some curves here and there but overall you are on the right tracks. You don't want fame – am I right? Yes, you see: the line is fading. But that is all right. You don't desire fame. You are not that kind of person.' She was speaking with a mixture of certainty and doubt, making statements that were posed as propositions.

'What about my love line?'

'Yes,' said the woman, 'let me see.' She wasn't surprised by the question; she brought her face near the palm and trailed a finger along it, frowning and muttering to herself in concentration.

Samar Api looked at me.

The jinns were invisible.

'Yes,' said the woman, and sat up, removing her glasses and placing them on the desk. 'I see it. You are in a good place. You follow your heart. That is good, that is very good, though you should also listen to your mind. It is our greatest gift, after all, the mind. It is unbelievable.' She tapped the side of her skull. 'The mind is what directs us in life. I always tell this to my clients: Allah has said that man makes his own fate. That does not mean He doesn't know. Of course He knows; He is the one who has made us! But we are also given choices. At every turn in life. Oh yes. What is fate? It is the boundary. But within that boundary we have a lot of room for making choices.' The woman went on to explain the relationship between fate and choice, which were not, she insisted, the opposites they were held to be, but components in a larger system of reinforcements. Then she gave a prediction: Samar Api was going to make some choices in the next few weeks that were going to alter the course of her life. The important thing to remember was that the world was made of presences, and it was for us to find the right ones. 'Seeing is believing,' she said. 'What you see is what you know. The more you see, the more you know. As long as you remember that, and take it with you everywhere, nothing can harm you. But you must teach yourself to see.'

The consultation lasted less than hour. Afterwards we were shown out onto the patio, where the girl with the roster collected the consultation fee and gave us another set of papers to fill out, a form called Client Response. Samar Api checked all the 'Excellent' slots and wrote 'Bloody Amazing!!!' in the 'Any Other Comments You Might Have' section. The first words she spoke to me were in the ricksha. 'He will see,' she said. 'I will show him.' She flung aside the flap at her window and looked out at the warm, fading light.

'Zaki, I'm not going to call him.'

She had decided to withhold herself until Jamal came to his senses. He was going to have a realization, she believed, and accept that he had lost her to his own detriment. And then he was going to regret it.

It filled her up.

In the mornings she took her time to dress for school. She showered in the bathroom and stood before the mirror in the dressing room with the blow dryer screaming at her hair. She combed it and pinned it, then leaned into the mirror and carefully applied her lip-gloss to a tense, toothless smile.

At school, during lunch break, she walked with the new friends to the canteen and then across into the sports field. They talked and they laughed. Sometimes they walked past Tara Tanvir.

'You should see the look on her face. She's still acting all superior, all I'm-too-good-for-you-type. But it shows on her face. She's burning inside. It's so obvious. I don't even *feel* like talking to her now.'

Instead she talked at night on the phone to a boy called Sohail. He was a friend of Jamal, or an acquaintance, as she had put it – one of the older boys with whom he had a hello-hi relationship. They met on weekends at a farmhouse in Bedian, where they drank whisky and played cards. Sohail was in a good position: he was removed enough from Jamal to not know of the girl with whom he had had a misunderstanding, and near enough to know what Jamal was doing these days.

Samar Api took his number from one of her new friends and called him at night.

'So tell me,' she said. 'What have you been up to?'

Sohail had never met her. He said, 'How did you get my number?' She could hear the smile in his voice.

She said, 'I just got it, *na*. Why are you acting all offended-type?'

Sohail said, 'Okay.'

She said, 'So tell me, *na*. What are you doing?'

Sohail said he was lying in his bed at the moment, touching the hairs on his belly and staring at the ceiling.

She laughed. 'And?'

And he was drinking water.

'Why water?' It suggested a preference for alcohol.

Sohail said he drank water to drain his tension. He managed his father's gas plant in Sui and drove there once a week to carry out an inspection, a procedure he now described in unnecessary detail.

'What are your friends doing these days?' she asked, returning the conversation to her area of interest.

He said his friends were doing nothing these days.

'Nothing?' She was disappointed. 'Nothing whatsoever?'

'Nothing,' said Sohail, who didn't want to talk about his friends. 'What are you doing right now?'

From Sohail she learned about an upcoming ball at a mansion in the Old City, a benefit organized by a medical society for the blind. Sohail said he was going with his friends from the farmhouse. The ball was strictly guest list, he said, and the tickets were limited and expensive.

She influenced him with pleas and taunts into buying the tickets for her. And in return he asked her to meet him at a restaurant.

She called the ricksha driver. She had taken down his number on her palm on the day of the outing to Tech Society. (He had recited the digits in Urdu.) A man answered the phone; there was noise behind him, a chaos of people and cars on the street; there was a surprised pause when the ricksha boy was named, and then a distant shouting. The noise in the background continued until the ricksha boy came to the phone and shouted all his answers into it as though he were speaking to someone in another country. He came the next day to collect us from outside the gate, and we went to Polka Parlour on Main Boulevard, where Sohail turned out to be a very large person well past his boyhood, with rare strands of

238

hair combed carefully across the bald back of his head. He spoke in a breathy drawl, blinked sarcastically and laughed at his own jokes, and ate two banana splits for dessert. He told Samar Api she was prettier than she had sounded on the phone. Samar Api said Sohail was a pleasant surprise too and didn't finish her strawberry milkshake.

And when we left the restaurant we had two tickets to the ball.

*

Fifty Easy Ways to Lose the Flab and Gain the Abs!
You know the drill when it comes to losing weight – take in fewer calories, burn more calories. But you also know that most diets and quick weight-loss plans have about as much substance as a politician's campaign pledges. You're better off finding several simple things you can do on a daily basis – along with following the cardinal rules of eating more vegetables and less fat and getting more physical activity. Together, they should send the scale numbers in the right direction: down.

Start by stocking your fridge with the right ingredients. Here's a list of things any dieter will do well to grab at the grocery store:

Scottish Smoked Salmon: high in proteins and omega acids, this is a must for any diet. Apply generously over non-fat cream cheese and a toasted, whole-wheat bagel. There's breakfast.

Cooked Shrimp: you can find these little babies in the seafood section. But watch out for impostors! Shrimp in curry or cocktail sauce is a known friend of flab.

The list was long, and culminated in a colourful weekly schedule that included recipes and timings for meals. Samar Api tore it out of the magazine and attached it with Scotch tape to the wall.

She returned to the magazine. She was looking for the advice column. She slapped away the pages and they sent up a slew of sad, rich smells.

'Found it,' she said.

It was spread out over two pages, arranged around a hazy picture of a couple passing like ghosts through a bedroom. Below it was a picture of the Agony Aunt herself, a middle-aged woman in a black outfit, with black spectacles and short, spiky hair, and a wide and carefree smile.

'Listen to this.'

Hi,
I am a thirty-year-old receptionist. I had been dating this guy for some months. I felt we had a connection. We had the same taste in food, in movies, and we shared a sense of humour. The sex was great. Lately he stopped returning my calls. I can't think of anything I did wrong. I know I was needy sometimes, but that was my only flaw. My girlfriends say I should move on and start looking for other guys. Part of me wants to believe them. Part of me is lonely and misses him. I don't know what to do!
*   Torn,*
*   Dallas, TX*

'It's just like my situation,' said Samar Api, and read out the Agony Aunt's response.

Dear Torn,
*   Sounds to me like your guy has moved on to other (not greener) pastures. It's brutal, but it's the truth. How long has he been acting cold and distant? And, more importantly, how much longer do you want to put up with his behaviour? Your girlfriends are right: move on. And next time, don't act needy unless you really want something from your significant other. Remember: neediness is often an extension of your own anxieties. Give your self-esteem a boost, and start by disconnecting that phone!*

'O God, it's so true!' said Samar Api. She looked up from the magazine. 'Neediness is' – she sought the page – 'an extension of your own anxieties. O God! I'm just never going to act needy again. Never ever again.'

She spent some minutes reading the horoscope.

And then she was searching in the drawer.

'What are you doing?'

'Wait.'

She found the measuring tape, an old one of Daadi's that was coiled around a magnet and snapped violently when released. She stood on tiptoe and wound it round her waist. Her stomach was sucked in, and she was trembling with the effort; she read the measurement and let it go. The tape snapped.

'Twenty-seven inches,' she said. 'That is not acceptable, Zaki Shirazi. It has to be down to at least twenty-four in time for this ball.'

It was drastic.

'I'm going on a diet,' she said. 'I have to. Glass of orange juice in the morning, glass of milk at night. You lose a pound a day. I've tried it.'

The Liquids Diet began in the morning. Samar Api awoke and went into the kitchen and squeezed herself a glass of orange juice. It was more than a glass but she threw the rest away. And she refused the other items on the table – the porridge, the bread and the butter and the jam, even the tea – and said that she had eaten too much the previous night. Daadi was surprised but not to the point of concern, and failed to note it again in the afternoon, when Samar Api returned from school and didn't ask for the leftovers from lunch. At dinnertime she came into Daadi's room, piled a plate and took it back into her own room. And in the morning the empty plate was returned.

She borrowed an outfit from one of her new friends. She described it later as a halter-neck shalwar kameez, a semi-formal outfit that could be worn to a ball. The friend had said it was a revealing outfit and had expressed her concern.

'Which only shows you,' said Samar Api later, 'that you can't trust anyone these days. Imagine what they would say if I told them everything. Imagine.'

She said I had to wear a suit. 'Obviously, Zaki. It's a bloody ball!'

I stood before my mother in her room.

She was talking on the phone. 'Yes, Zaki?'

I told her I wanted money.

'What for?'

'For buying.'

'Buying what?'

'Things.'

'Sorry, Afraaz. Go on. How many senators?'

I went looking in her handbag.

'Afraaz, just one second. Stop it, Zaki! Stop it! What are you doing? *Give* it back to me. Doesn't grow on bloody trees you know? I want a receipt. I want a detailed account of how you spend it. And I want the change.'

Isa and Moosa took me in their car to Pace, the new shopping plaza on Main Boulevard. There were many in Lahore now, but Pace had grown famous for the escalators that connected its five levels. The news had caused waves of curiosity and excitement among the shopping populace. Little children treated it as a ride: they went up and down the moving stairs, holding on to the banisters and grinning at the people going in the opposite direction. But for others it was unexpectedly difficult; on the second-floor landing our path was blocked by a woman in a burqa who was unable to step on the stairs. Her family was standing behind her, urging her to take the step. She was trying: she held her daughter's hand and raised her foot, brought it forward and then down and then back again. She couldn't bring herself to do it. Behind her a queue was forming. Someone shouted and told her to get out of the way. Her husband now took her hand and stepped onto the escalator. And she went up with him, screaming, her hands at her ears.

The Suits 'n' Boots section was located on the fifth floor. The faceless mannequins had the stiff bent postures of break-dancers. One wore a suit made of a shiny black fabric. I touched it. The material was scratchy.

'Nylon,' said Isa.

'Why you buying a suit?' said Moosa.

I said I was going to a ball.

Moosa made a joke about it.

'So where is this ball?' he said.

I ignored him.

Later, in the car, he said, 'Why you acting all weird like that?

You shouldn't be so oversensitive.' It was an apology, and a prelude to asking again about the ball.

'Where is this ball?' said Isa.

'Somewhere,' I said. 'I was invited so I'm going.'

Moosa wanted to know who I was going with.

'You don't know her,' I said.

Moosa was defeated.

'You shouldn't keep secrets,' said Isa, and stayed quiet for the rest of the drive.

'Samar Api?'

She hummed.

'Who all knows?'

'About what?'

'You and Jamal.'

She was lying on her bed and looking at the invitation cards – squares of glossy paper with small black writing. She had written her name on one and mine on the other.

'Nobody,' she said. 'Just you. And Tara.' Her face soured at the memory. 'But other than that no one.'

'Do your new friends know?'

'Not at all. I can't tell them, Zaki. It'd be all over town in a day.'

She said it as though Lahore were a movie town with small cars on smooth roads and medium-sized houses that sat behind fences, with identical postboxes outside and small garages inside, and triangular wooden roofs with chimneys. The new friends went around this town in a car, stopping outside the houses to write Samar Api's name on the walls, and in the morning, when the residents awoke, they were shocked to see the writing, because in a movie town everyone knew everyone.

'Look,' she said, and held up the two cards in the lamplight. 'Nice, *na*?'

She tried on the outfit that night. She produced it from a box and carried into the bathroom. But the attempt was unsuccessful: the outfit was tight. She had not reached her ideal weight.

She decided to combine the Liquids Diet with exercise. The Jane

Fonda videos were excavated from my mother's room. Samar Api stood on a stool and retrieved the tapes from the uppermost shelf in the wardrobe, her face gently smothered by hanging nightgowns.

The video went into the VCR, and whined and grunted as old links were re-established. At first the image was absurd: three Jane Fondas appeared instead of one. They were frozen in a back-arching posture and shivering. Samar Api rewound the tape but it made a sound; she took it out and spat on the reel, then wiped her finger along it. The reel shone; the finger was black with filth. She returned the tape to the VCR, and now beheld the restored Jane Fonda with the burst of warmth that receives a long-departed relative.

Come on everybody! Can you feel it?

The results came quickly. Samar Api's jeans were suddenly loose. Her eyes were enlarged in their sockets, and a vein began to show at each of her temples. One morning she awoke to find a pink burning on the side of her stomach. When she returned from school it was red. And two days later it had turned into a settled silver streak, crawling upwards like a snake.

'It's a stretch mark,' she said. 'It'll fade with time.'

At night she wore the loosened jeans with a belt and stood before the mirror to enact mild variations on a scenario: a girl, ridiculed, retreated from the world. She stood before the mirror to identify her flaws and found that they were overcomeable. Her eyes became inspired; she removed her glasses and opened her hair. And time, so still and heavy in sadness, became light and quick in self-discovery, and passed in a rush of uplifting songs that were performed always, for some reason, by ecstatic black voices that were otherwise absent from the scenario. Time passed and the girl continued to change. And then time came to a momentous halt. The girl found the boy. Her legs went up to him. The legs became the body and the face. Heads turned. And in that charged moment, when he begged to have her back, she, who had changed, refused.

'Samar Api,' I said. 'What if he says sorry?'

'He will.' She was sure of it.

'I know but then what?'

And she produced it as if from a hat. 'Then I say it's okay. Obviously, Zaki. I love him.'

II

The day of the ball passed quickly. At school there had been lessons in the classroom and then games and fights in the grounds – things had happened at their usual paces, without the wayward pull of anomalies. At home in the afternoon our excitement, checked by secrecy, had developed an aspect of forced containment that had led in turn to restlessness. Samar Api went in and out of her room. She settled on the sofa and changed all the channels on the TV, then returned to her room and locked the door. There was music.

Daadi asked her to switch it off. She was going to say her prayers now.

'It's so irritating,' said Samar Api. To pass the time she brought the clock into her room and settled it on the bedside table.

I offered to try on the suit.

'Don't,' she said. 'They'll get all suspicious-type.'

She brought out her books and tried to read.

'Samar Api?'

'What?'

'When should we change?'

She looked at the clock. 'When they're going to sleep, Zaki. You'll have to wait until then.'

But the passage of those hours was slowed inevitably.

First the taking of tea was lengthened by a visit from Suri and Hukmi. They arrived at dusk and sat in Daadi's room through dinner, watched songs on the Indian channel and ate their food, then asked for green tea, which was prepared in the kitchen and brought to them on a tray. They consumed it unhurriedly; they were complaining about money, embittered by the results of a ladies' lottery that had failed to yield their names. It was a little after nine when they left.

'Thank God,' said Samar Api.

In her own room my mother was talking on the phone.

'See in the kitchen,' said Samar Api.

Naseem was clearing up.

'It won't take her long.'

And the prediction came true: Naseem stacked the dishes in the kitchen sink and left them there. She was tired and it was late; she would wash them in the morning; she locked the cupboards and switched off the lights.

'Good,' said Samar Api.

We waited in her room.

'It's almost ten,' she said. She was worried about the ricksha driver, who had been told to collect us from outside the gate at ten o'clock and had been told on the phone to desist from honking or ringing the bell in case there was a delay. 'If there's a problem,' Samar Api had said, 'one of us will come outside and tell you. But *you* shouldn't do anything on your own.'

Now she wanted me to go outside and lure Barkat away from the gate.

Barkat wasn't outside.

'Where is he?'

He was in his room.

'Oh, good,' she said. 'Very good.'

In Daadi's room the TV sounds had died. For some moments the light lingered; then it died too.

I went into my mother's room and found the book in her lap, its pages fanned out. Her eyes were shut and her mouth was open, her forehead still furrowed in concentration.

'Hurry up,' said Samar Api.

We changed our clothes separately and met again in the dressing room.

'How do I look?' She made a presenting gesture and twirled.

'Nice,' I said, and it was the only word that came then, one of many jammed superlatives that could have been held out and would still have failed to touch her beauty in that moment.

'Your tie,' she said. 'It's not tied properly.'

She began to tug at it frantically.

'O God, Zaki, *how* do you do this? Didn't anyone ever teach you?'

By saying it she had said that my father was dead.

'Look,' she said, and her hands were on my shoulders, 'we can tie it later. Please let's go.'

She went to the mirror and puffed out the perfume and grabbed her handbag and stopped.

'How do I smell?'

'Amazing.'

'And how do I look?'

'Amazing.'

'Why thank you,' she said, feigning courtly surprise, and slid her bare arm into mine.

The ricksha boy had not honked. And he had parked the ricksha intelligently: it stood two houses down the lightless street, under the shadow of a large tree. The driver was standing outside, leaning with his elbow on the tin exterior.

He saw us and became formal.

'*Salaam, baaji,*' he said.

Samar Api asked if he had rung the bell.

He placed a hand on his heart and said he hadn't.

Samar Api was sparing. 'What's your name?' she said. She had asked him earlier too.

The boy said his name was Altaf Shah.

His clothes were puffed with starch.

'Altaf Shah,' she said absently and climbed into the ricksha. It came alive now, chugging and trembling with revived energies. 'Old City,' she said. 'You know where that is?'

Altaf Shah thought about it.

'You don't know the Old City?'

He was thinking.

'Where the Fort is, where the Mosque is.'

And at once he understood. He nodded enthusiastically and looked sideways, and tilted the ricksha away from the empty street. He said they called it the Inner City.

'Same thing,' said Samar Api in English.

Altaf Shah said nothing.

Samar Api laughed.

And he laughed too, a self-mocking laugh propelled by new discoveries. His mood had changed. 'We will be there in twenty minutes, *baaji*. *Inshallah*, no problem.' And the English of these last two words was an act of daring.

'For some reason I *highly* doubt that!' said Samar Api in her own English, which was exclusive and impenetrable, and came with an exclusive and impenetrable English laugh.

The ricksha took us past the canal, its banks illumined at night, past the withdrawn foliage of GOR, the neighbourhood where the civil servants of Lahore lived in old whitewashed houses built by the British. And then we were on Mall Road. The traffic sped past the shops and the buildings with their lights, the neon signs and the food vendors standing on the roadside, a world kept busy this late at night by the electric efforts of its aspirants. We passed the old mansions and the old government buildings and came at last to the postmaster's clock. Here we turned right. And now the road was less defined, the world beyond was a haze, and the cars and buses were negotiating passage with wild lurching wagons and horse-drawn taangas and impulsive undaunted pedestrians who were continually crossing the road. We had left the new city behind, the place where we lived, a place whose newness had emerged only now, in relation to this, brought out with the loss of definition and the broadening out of the road's boundaries.

The ricksha drove on, one of many now; the walls of the Old City were nearing. We had turned and were tilting in a lane that led along the wall of the mosque, and then into smaller alleys; to our left and right were shops and balconies. Women stood in the upper windows and stared.

'Prostitutes,' said Samar Api. 'This is their area.'

I turned to see but the ride had gone on and left the women behind.

The ricksha slowed down and sputtered along on an incline. The cars here were parked in no particular order; guests in dark clothing were stepping out and walking on. Two women in shawls, with bare legs underneath, were walking ahead with two tall boys in jackets. The boys stopped at the large open entrance and spoke authoritatively to a man with a notepad. The man flapped away his pages and nodded. The boys gestured at the girls, who had been standing quietly behind them in the shawls and now became alert and went in.

'Stop it here,' said Samar Api.

She didn't want to show the ricksha.

'Here?' said Altaf Shah.

'Yes, just stop it. *Buss.*' She stepped out and spanked away the dust from the sides of her arms, spanked it off her knees, took my tie and rolled it up and dropped it in her bag. She stood me still and undid the topmost button on my shirt. She tweaked the collar ends, plucked them and pulled them down.

She turned this way and that.

'Very nice,' I said.

She took out the cards from her bag and handed them over. 'Walk ahead,' she said, and began to walk behind me.

The mansion doors led from an old brick pathway to empty elevations and then onto a vast open courtyard where, under the abrupt night sky, beneath the ivy that crawled out of old façades and wooden window frames and hung towards the end in little tendrils, was a sea of tables in white dressing, white tablecloths and white candles and white napkins tucked pointedly into glasses. People sat looking about in chairs and were chatting. There was here and there the movement of jewels, a recurrent flash in the night, and the shimmer of fabrics as women arrived and settled and rose and walked on behind their men and between the waiters, who were also wearing white uniforms and wove hurriedly between the tables with trays on their palms. There was a clearing in the centre of the courtyard, a polished wooden platform connected at each of its four corners to what looked like hanging string. And behind this was an elevated podium with a microphone attached to the top, the podium front bearing the colourful acronym for the charity organization that had arranged the ball.

Our chairs were at a table in a darkened corner. Two old

women were sitting in two of the chairs; the rest of the table was unoccupied.

The women looked at us and looked away.

One wore a scaly green sari with the skin at her belly exposed, and sat with her arms folded haplessly in her lap, her neck turned away towards the sounds and sights at the entrance. Her face was powdered a ghostly white. Her companion, who was also silent, wore a dark and spreading shalwar kameez and sat similarly but without the expression of aloofness.

Samar Api stopped a waiter and took a glass of pomegranate juice. 'Zaki?'

The waiter was waiting.

I didn't want it.

'No, thank you,' she said, and watched the waiter walk away.

'Samina,' said the woman in the sari to the woman in the shalwar kameez. She was referring to someone who had just arrived.

They rose with their outfits and went away.

'Do you think he's here?' said Samar Api. She was looking out at the sea of tables.

'Maybe. Should I go and look?'

'No, Zaki, please. Keep sitting.'

The chairs filled up. It was clear now that the podium had a purpose, and the guests knew this purpose and were prepared for it. A short, fat woman in a kaftan was floating around the wooden platform with the mobile microphone in her hand. She looked around and cleared her throat in it.

People sat and watched.

She turned and waved at the soundman behind her and tapped the top of the microphone.

'Hello, hello,' said the women into the microphone. It echoed.

She looked at the soundman and shook her head.

The soundman made adjustments.

'Hello. Hello, yes. Yes, this is better. Leave it here.' She turned to face the audience. 'Ladies and gentlemen,' she said, and proceeded to welcome her guests on behalf of the organization and its friends. 'At home and abroad,' she said, 'you have helped us over the years, to raise money for the blind.' At every pause in punctuation her head tilted to the other side. She went on to provide a history of the organization, described its fundraising procedures and some of the successful operations it had overseen. And she attributed the organization's continued success to the continued financial support of its friends. 'I am proud,' she said, 'to tell you today that you are living proof of the fact that Pakistanis are the most generous people in the world.'

There was applause.

The woman gave a short speech on the ethics of charity, using small pockets of opportunity to name the generous couples and individuals and families that had donated most generously to the organization. Then she gave a summary of the night's proceedings: there was dancing, dinner, an auction of paintings by some of the most promising young artists at home and abroad, and dancing again. As she said these last words the music started up behind her, and the lights dimmed down at the tables and became correspondingly brighter at the wooden platform, which rose now, generating a great mechanical noise, and revealed the wide wooden steps that led up to it.

Guests began to dance.

'You want to?' I said.

'Zaki, I have to know if he's here.'

'So we can look from there,' I said, and pointed to the raised dance floor, which had a central view of the tables.

She rose from her chair. She hadn't come to the ball with the intention of dancing. But, as the dance floor neared and the music grew loud, and the dancing people appeared, her resistance faded and fell away, until she was leading the way, her hand in mine, up the wide wooden steps and onto the floor.

We danced slowly, then freely and audaciously.

'O God, Zaki!' She was laughing. It was a new song with quick beats and frank sexual lyrics. The woman behind us was dancing alone, and with a strange intensity, her eyes closed and her shoulders shrugged and her hands pronged and shivering.

And the others:

A fat, balding man in a suit, dancing with his fists next to a tall, thin woman in heels.

A couple who were dancing together but looking around vacantly.

Four girls dancing in a circle that went round and fell back, and fell forward, and fell back again.

'He's here,' said Samar Api. 'Don't look.'

She fell into my arms.

'Now throw me up, throw me up.'

I threw her up.

'Don't look.' She was dancing, smiling and looking around and laughing too, but she was clenched with awareness.

'Where is he?'

'Behind me.'

I looked.

'Zaki, *don't* look.'

We went on dancing.

'How am I looking?'

'Good.'

'Just good?'

'Very good.'

'Okay, now look. Look behind me. Can you see him?'

I looked behind her at the tables, where a fresh wave of dancers rose with exclamations of surprise and delight at the change of song, and rushed forward from different directions, obstructing the view.

'Can you see him?'

I was trying. The people had blocked the steps; more and more were crowding on the platform.

'What's he wearing?' I said.

'A suit.'

All the men were wearing suits.

She said, 'He's sitting at the table behind me with his friends.' But she was dancing in front of me and had her back to the tables.

I danced on tiptoe and saw the men at the table, then the girl walking up to the table. It was Tara Tanvir. She saw me, looked away, hitched up her dress and sat in the lap of a man in a suit.

'Did you see yet?'

I said, 'No, not yet.'

The song was in Spanish. The dancers had decreased.

She said, 'Let's walk past the table.'

I said, 'Don't look, Samar Api.'

But she looked. And she turned around at once, her face not showing what she felt.

She said, 'Keep dancing.'

We were. The foreign words of the song gave no sign of abating.

She said, 'I can't, Zaki.'

I said, 'Let's go.' And I took her hand and began to break past the dancers. She was behind me, and I could feel her following closely, but I couldn't see her face.

We passed the table.

Samar Api laughed.

But they weren't looking.

'Samar Api . . .'

'Just walk.' She was walking very quickly now, past the tables and under the curving archways, then down the elevations and through the brick passage, and finally out of the big doors.

'Samar Api! Wait!'

She was running. She ran all the way to the ricksha, parked where we had left it, in an unnecessarily distant alley where it was most unlikely to be seen, and she climbed in and told the driver to take her home.

The ricksha started.

'Samar Api . . .'

But she snatched her hand away, and kept her face turned to the window, where she had begun at last to cry.

12

WOMEN'S JOURNAL, 21–7 OCTOBER 1993

EDITORIAL

Democracy and nationhood are not served on platters. History is a tumultuous, and often tragic, process. Ours has been especially so. But there are times to rejoice even in the long, hard march to freedom. That is why, as we stand on the brink of rediscovering our national soul, this is a moment to savour.

A toast to the caretaker government for overseeing the fairest election since 1970. It is a legacy we should cherish and fight for if necessary.

A toast to the leader of the opposition, who is no longer the stilted child of the military-business establishment. We now have a confident, popular leader who has finally come of age. This is no mean transformation. It augurs well for a meaningful two-party system in the country.

Finally, a toast to Ms Benazir Bhutto. Here is a courageous woman who has braved the odds time and again. She richly deserves being prime minister today, not least because she was unfairly ousted from power in 1990 and then hounded from pillar to post by her opponents. She has now been vindicated by the election results. We hope that with this second chance she will prove worthy of our trust.

And from there the editorial went on to impart advice: the prime minister must take 'concrete steps' now to ensure that the women of Pakistan were healthier and freer in the future, starting with the abolition of the anti-women laws instituted by the military under its so-called Islamization campaign. (There was a photo-feature in the middle pages on 'The Dark Laws', which showed women working in the countryside, women handcuffed, women holding their heads and looking out at the world from behind metallic bars.) Then the prime minister must turn her attention to healthcare and family planning, especially among women in the rural areas, where literacy levels were unacceptably low; then to education in general and to the secondary schools and universities in particular, which continued to rely on textbooks poisoned long ago by the anti-democratic forces. And finally the government must rescue the economy, which was sinking, and work to secure the assistance of foreign donors and development organizations to set it right.

Above the text, in place of the usually satirical cartoon, the cartoonist had composed a solemn picture: the restored prime minister was emerging from a crowd of her supporters, the dupatta worn high above her head, and was holding the green-and-white Pakistani flag, which gleamed incredibly with light and rippled like corrugated iron in the winds of change.

'Three years,' said Daadi, 'have gone by and none of it has happened, not one thing. But is anyone asking? Does anyone ask?' She held out her palm and shook it demandingly.

'Princess,' said Suri. 'She thinks she is a princess.'

'Oh yes,' said Hukmi gravely, as though this was a charge that ought to be investigated.

But *Women's Journal* continued to address its exhortations to the government, displaying a patience that in other publications (right-wing rags, partisan pamphlets) had already run out; another English weekly had published a two-page spread called 'The Million-Dollar Question', in which the mug-shot pictures of politicians were accompanied by the amounts they had allegedly earned in bribes, kickbacks and commissions.

A black-and-white photograph of the prime minister's husband was at the top of the page.

'Yes,' said my mother. 'We know there is corruption. There has always been corruption. But why do we look now? Why are we looking *only* at this government? Why don't we look at the corruption of those who rule with guns, and have ruled with guns for so many years and are even now waiting in the wings?'

Daadi said no one was waiting in the wings.

'You are sadly mistaken,' said my mother.

I said, 'Who are the guns?'

'The establishment,' said my mother.

'It is a word,' said Daadi, and held up a hollowed hand. 'A long, empty word.'

My mother said it was absurd and hypocritical, like pardoning a gang of known robbers who raided a house at regular intervals and then punishing a little girl for daring to steal an ashtray.

'Ashtray,' said Daadi one morning, and flung the newspaper across the table. The headline was UK COUNTRYSIDE PALACE SAID TO BELONG TO PM AND HUSBAND. There was a picture beside it of the discovered mansion, brown and withdrawn in the mossy English countryside, and an inset picture of the couple: she was sitting on a sofa with her hands in her lap and he was standing behind her in a black suit.

'Little girl,' said Daadi. 'And little boy. Jack and Jill.'

She laughed.

'Hand in hand,' said Suri. '*Hand* in hand.'

The *Women's Journal* editorials became subdued and conflicted, and readers began to seek explanations for the magazine's continued engagement with a discredited government. One reader, a resident of Karachi who was now pursuing a Ph.D. in political science at a university in Sydney, Australia, wrote to say that the magazine's silence was 'tantamount to quietism'. After that the news pages began to carry investigative reports on the alleged misconduct of sitting ministers, often with enlarged, damning quotes from members of the opposition. A highlighted rectangle at the bottom of the page insisted that the views expressed in these articles were those of the sources quoted, and did not necessarily reflect the editorial position of the magazine.

But the content spoke for itself.

*

Late one night the staffers converged in the veranda, and the chairs they sat on formed an elongated circle. The smoke from cigarettes rose silver in the dim light. A man and his companions had been killed in Karachi; the police had stopped their cars and opened fire, and were now saying that the victims had fired first. But no policemen had been killed in the encounter.

A man was saying, 'It is murder. It is state terrorism. And it is *her* government, *her* police.'

A woman said, 'It is her enemies who have done this. No sister can order the killing of her own brother.'

And another said, 'It is politics. They will do anything.'

'Daadi said you saw the light.'

We were sitting before the borrowed TV in my mother's room. She was watching the unbiased news channel, a discussion programme called *Debrief*.

'Daadi would say that,' she said.

The Indian journalist was now arguing with a politician on the panel, a fight over the fighting between Hindus and Muslims. The other two panellists – an elderly man and a corpulent, middle-aged woman in a golden sari – were both trying to look unsurprised, trying to stay unbiased for the viewers.

'Zaki, pack your bags. We're going away.'

'Where?'

'To Spain.'

'Who all?'

'Just us.'

'You and me?'

'Yes,' she said, and only now looked up from the programme, where the fighting between the panellists had peaked. 'Is that a problem?'

'Samar Api,' I said. 'We're going to Spain.'

It was early in the evening. She had returned from the tuition centre and, according to the pattern, had gone into her room and played sad songs on the stereo.

'Spain,' she said. 'Wow.'

Her eyes were lost.

I said, 'Will you be fine?'

'Of course I'll be fine.' She tried to make a surprised face, and failed; she looked confused instead. 'Of course I'll be fine, Zaki.' And now she sat up and nodded energetically, trying to show that she had been listening.

She thought of something and it made her want to cry.

She said, 'So when are you leaving?' It was posed with enthusiasm.

'Two weeks,' I said.

She appeared to make a calculation.

'And when are you coming back?'

'Two weeks after that.'

She made another calculation.

'So that's a month,' she said.

'A month from now.'

'You'll be back in a month.'

'No. We'll be back in two weeks. But we're leaving in two weeks too, so the total is a month.'

It was difficult and unnecessary.

'Will you be all right?' I said, and jokily, to make it light.

'Of course!' she said. 'I'll be fine, I'll be fine.'

But even in those two remaining weeks she was difficult to reach. She didn't talk of school, didn't talk of things she had done in the day or hoped to do in the next. She didn't talk of new friends or of old ones. She came home and did her assignments, then listened to the songs on the stereo. She had sold all the magazines, and the shoeboxes lay empty under her bed, the shelves on the wall carrying only books.

She went outside at dusk. And she was thinking the same thoughts, walking in the darkened driveway, alone with the sky and the black trees and the birds fleeing the night, and her thoughts had become the world.

She returned to her room and thought of improvement, rescue, miracles.

She was tempted by the phone and resisted it.

But sometimes she succumbed, and dialled his number and heard his voice on the answering machine, knowing that it would lead to the bathroom, to the shutting and locking of the door and the sound of running water to drown out the sound of her crying.

Afterwards she stood before the mirror and held the plump white bottle of eye-drop solution above her eyes, which were then less swollen.

She went into Daadi's room and made an effort.

'Eat,' said Daadi. 'Diets are good only for some of the time.'

And she was seen eating her food.

*

Our plane landed in the morning, a hot morning, a surprise in October; we waited in the empty blaze of the tarmac until a bus came and carried us to the inside of the airport. Our suitcase appeared on the conveyor belt ahead of others, and we took it through customs and out again into the sun. We took a taxi now, towards what my mother had described to the taxi driver as the Arab Quarter.

'Look,' she said, and motioned past her window at the dark, pointed trees, at the rushing hills and the dust. 'Granada.'

The taxi took us through winding towns, then up into a small neighbourhood in the hills. The houses here stood on a sloping stone street that narrowed at the turns and broadened out as it fell away to either side. The windows, painted blue or green or pink, were closed against the heat of the day and the terraces were decorated with flowers. Ours was the only house with a plain exterior.

'This is the one,' said my mother. She was trying to find the bell.

'We should just go in,' I said.

'Really? You think so? Isn't it rude?'

But she couldn't find the bell, and we pushed past the heavy door and went in.

And now plants, a garden, a winding thatch roof that led from the entrance all the way to the patio and carried vines with clusters of a dark little fruit.

'Grapes,' said my mother and plucked one.

'Ah yes,' said the woman. 'Welcome.'

She was tending to the plants at the edge of her garden, a wild, unplanned patch of fluff and fur and bright pods that stood unhatched on the ends of tall stems. She dropped her spade and began to wade through the uneven grass, at times brushing her knees, her kaftan hitched at her broad, loose waist. A large woman, she swayed as she moved.

'Astrid,' she said, and gave an august nod that seemed both to grant and accept a greeting.

'Hello, Astrid,' said my mother. She dropped the suitcase to the floor and shook the woman's hand.

'And this is young Zacky?'

'Zucky,' I said. 'Rhymes with Lucky.'

My mother was smiling nervously.

But Astrid was pleased; her laugh opened up her mouth and pushed back her head. 'Oh my,' she said, sighing and settling a hand on her heart. 'That's quite an introduction. I hope you like the company of adults?'

'He doesn't mind,' said my mother. 'He's very tolerant.'

'Do you?' said Astrid.

'Yes,' I said.

'Good,' she said, and clasped her hands jovially, 'because right now we only have adults in this house. In the summer we had two beautiful children, girl and boy, lovely kids, lovely parents, but they are gone now, back to America.' Her hand became a gliding aeroplane.

'Oh no,' said my mother.

'Yes,' said Astrid. 'But never mind. We will have our fun.' She frowned admonishingly and raised a rallying fist. 'Come inside. Let me show you the rooms.'

We had the honeymoon suite. The room contained two small beds, each swollen at one end with pillows, a table on the side, an awkward empty chair in a corner, a watercolour painting of the sea at high tide on one wall and a long, slim mirror on another. The curtains were thick and floral; my mother tugged at the rope and they lifted, revealing a wide view of the valley across.

'Astrid, this is lovely!'

'Yes,' said Astrid. 'The Alhambra is on the other side. One of the rooms has got a view but it's taken. American couple. Very charming. You will meet them.' It was assumed.

My mother was still standing at the window with a hand at her waist and another on her throat, and was taking in the view, which had altered the room, the narrow beds and the chair and the mirror, all swept up now in the charm.

'Oh,' said Astrid, remembering, 'let me show you the bathroom. There is a problem' – she stopped herself – 'actually it is not a problem, it's more of a trick.' She winked, opened the bathroom door and parted the shower curtain. 'You turn it like this, and then like this' – she had worked two separate knobs and brought them into alignment – 'and it is cold. Then like this, and like this, and it is hot. You have to mix and match. And don't leave it running for too long' – her eyes narrowed pleadingly – 'or the hot water will run out and the others will complain.' Her sheepish laugh was less embarrassed than explanatory.

'Okay now,' she said, busily smacking the sides of her thighs, 'I will go downstairs and work. You come down whenever. No hurries. We take supper around six.'

She closed the door with a practised click.

The room became ours.

'What's our plan?'

'There's no plan,' said my mother; she pressed her hands into the mattress. It was firm. She took off her shoes and drew aside the bedcover. 'I'm just going to lie down here for a little while.' She was testing the pillows behind her head. 'You can go downstairs and ask Astrid to guide you.'

'For what?'

'For doing things. You can ask her to show you a map of this place.' She was preparing to sleep. 'Or you can stay here and take a nap. It's up to you.'

Astrid didn't have a map. She said she used to have one but had lost it. 'Stay in,' she said, making it sound like a prospect; 'you can sit here and draw pictures.' She gestured upwards at the vines, crawling out in their intricate multitudes with the grapes hanging in tight, unripe bunches. 'You like to draw?'

I hadn't considered it.

'Wait,' she said, and went in, and returned with a writing pad. 'Here' – she smacked it on the table and placed a pen on top – 'draw. Make a still life. Or make a portrait of me if you like. I won't mind it.'

My mother came down in the evening. She was dressed in a cotton nightgown that touched the floor and followed her in a frothy trail. She came over to the table and settled languidly in a chair. The table was long and rough, and lacked a varnish, the working table of a carpenter.

'Rested?' said Astrid. She stood in the doorway with a large tray in her hands.

'Oh yes,' said my mother, who was pleased with everything, pleased to the point of self-saturation; the pleasure had become a process, a way of breathing the air and responding to inquiries. 'Very well rested, thank you.'

'Good,' said Astrid and landed the tray on the table. It displayed a long kind of bread, settled diagonally, and two different paste-like concoctions, one in beige and the other in a pale pink, inside large white bowls.

'Baguette!' cried my mother and broke the hard bread. She returned one half to the tray and broke the other half into three small pieces, dipped one piece into the beige paste, tore it off with her teeth and chewed. 'And hummus!'

'It's nothing,' said Astrid with a wave of the hand. 'There is leek soup after this; would you like me to bring it out or will you wait for the others?'

'Oh, we'll wait,' said my mother, chewing and nodding, 'we'll wait.'

Astrid went into the kitchen.

'Did you make this?' said my mother. She was looking at the drawing of the grapes. 'Zaki, this is wonderful. You really can draw.

You should draw more pictures. You really should. I should get you colouring books.' There were too many thoughts at once, and they opened up the chasm of parental knowledge, of how much she didn't know and should have but didn't.

Astrid returned with the china and cutlery. She placed a plate before every chair and a bowl in every plate. 'I wonder,' she said, arranging the knives. 'I wonder where they are.'

'Who?' said my mother.

'The Americans. I told them to come down at six.'

'We can wait.'

'Ah but they are here!' said Astrid and stepped aside like a presenter on a stage.

And there they were, the American couple: the husband wore jeans and a polo shirt, the shirt tight around the chest, which was like a wrestler's, part flesh and part rock; and the wife wore a frilly shirt and a wide ballooning skirt. Both were blonde-haired and fair-skinned, the wife slightly red around the face and neck.

They looked at us and smiled.

'Richard,' said the man and held out a hand.

'Louise,' said the wife. She almost curtsied.

My mother shook their hands and smiled and nodded. 'Pleasure, pleasure.'

'Okay,' said Astrid, and raised her fingertips like an orchestra conductor about to start, 'three soups coming up. We have leek today, is that okay for you?'

The Americans were amenable.

'And Zaki? Will you take soup as well?'

'He will,' said my mother.

'I will,' I said.

'Good,' said Astrid doggedly and went away.

'First time here?' said Richard. He spoke with a squint, the corner of his mouth curled upwards. He reached out a hand for the bread that remained.

'Yes,' said my mother, 'yes.'

'Ours too,' said Louise and smiled weakly.

'And what do you do?' said my mother.

She had asked Louise.

'Oh, me!' said Louise. 'Oh, I'm a teacher.' She giggled guiltily, finding it impulsive and irrelevant.

'But that's wonderful, Louise!' said my mother.

Louise flapped her hand.

'It really is! I think education is the way forward. It's the solution to every country's problems.'

Louise liked the idea, though she hadn't thought of it that way, coming from a country that didn't have as many problems.

'And you, Richard? What is it that you do?'

Richard said he worked at a bank in Chicago.

'Windy City,' said my mother with a melancholy smile.

'That's right,' said Richard with an owning smile. 'You been?'

'I haven't.'

'Oh,' said Louise and looked into her lap, as though what she'd had in mind to say no longer mattered.

'You live in Chicago?' said my mother.

'*We* do,' said Richard. 'Yes.'

'I'm from Nashville, originally,' said Louise in a breathy and sensuous drawl. 'I came to Chicago to teach, a lot of underprivileged kids over there, like you said' – and she gestured graciously at the source of this suggestion – 'in Chicago, you know, it's not like Nashville.' She laughed wildly. 'It's very' – she caressed the forthcoming word with her fingers – 'multicultural. Not like Nashville. Back then I used to work with Teach For America? I don't know if you know . . .'

'I don't,' said my mother. 'No.'

'Oh,' said Louise. 'Well.'

They ate the last of the bread.

'And you?' said Louise. 'Where are you from?'

'Pakistan!' cried Astrid, who had appeared with a wide and steaming bowl of the leek soup; she hurried over with it, wearing thick cloth gloves on her hands, and settled the bowl in the centre of the table. 'I thought,' she said, holding her hips, 'I thought why not just bring the whole bowl.'

'Why not,' said Richard.

'Good,' said Astrid and took the last empty chair at the table. She looked around and saw that the bread had finished. 'Should I bring some more?' She made to rise.

'No, no,' said Louise. 'I'll go.'

'We can wait,' said my mother.

They stayed in their chairs.

'So!' said Astrid. 'You've been talking?'

'Well,' said Louise, and gestured elegantly at her new acquaintance. 'We were just talking about where we *came* from.'

'Ah yes,' said Astrid, and settled her elbows on the table and looked frankly now at my mother. 'Pakistan.'

'Yeah,' said Richard and leaned in with interest.

Louise squinted her eyes attentively.

'Well,' said my mother and sighed, and began to twirl her empty glass on the table. She told of Pakistan's woes and troubles, the challenges it faced as a developing country, the cycles of military rule and the experiments with democracy; she spoke of poverty in the Third World and of women's rights, the life of an activist, the struggle and the constant testing of resolve; she described the protests and the marches she had organized, and she told of the let-downs, the many failures; she sighed again and dug her spoon into the hummus and confessed to having written a rather sharp editorial, nothing less than a condemnation of the present government and its policies. 'And it's depressing,' she said, 'because we were with her from the start, we had so much invested in her. But we've been let down. It's the truth. We'll have none of that, thank you very much. Astrid, will you pass me the soup?'

Astrid passed the bowl with both her hands and said, 'Amazing.' She was looking around at the other faces. 'Amazing.'

Louise was nodding.

'Huh,' said Richard, and grunted. He took a swig of his drink and held it up for examination. It was water.

'Wine?' said Astrid.

'Sure,' said Richard.

'You know,' said Louise, and inclined her head towards my mother, 'what you just said, about women and the workplace, it's just, it's so *true!*' She was shaking her head and blinking continuously. 'I just . . .' And she growled and held up her clenched fists.

Richard was looking at her. 'Well,' he said.

'No,' said Louise. 'It *is* true.'

Richard drank all the water in his glass and gasped.

'It is,' said my mother quietly.

'Yes,' said Louise. 'Yes, it is.'

'Voilà!' said Astrid, who had returned with the wine and the bread. She poured the wine, which was dark and shiny, into the glasses and paused tentatively at mine.

'A sip,' said my mother.

'A sip,' said Astrid and poured enough for many.

'To friendship!' said Astrid and raised her glass.

'To friendship,' said my mother.

'Friendship,' said Louise.

The glasses clanged.

'Wow,' said Astrid after dinner and dessert had been consumed. The bowls of pasta and salad had emptied; two slices of the charred-looking chocolate cake were left in the large plate.

Astrid leaned back in her chair and said, 'Isn't it incredible?'

'It is,' said Louise, and looked at my mother. 'You are.'

'Oh no, please,' said my mother.

But Louise said, 'You are,' and sipped her wine confidently, for she was feeling much better about it now. 'I think you're amazing.'

In the morning they went out with Astrid to buy the groceries. I stayed in the house with Richard, who sat outside on the patio wearing sunglasses and reading a book called *Harnessing the Power of Your Thought*. While he read the book he poked his mouth with a toothpick. I sat across from him and drew his portrait. Eventually he asked if he could go back inside, and suggested that we take up the drawing later, and I tore out a new page and began to draw the vines with the grapes.

'Hello there!' said Louise. She wore a broad hat and held a bulging wicker basket. Astrid and my mother came in behind her.

'You were right,' Astrid was saying. 'They overcharged us. I didn't notice but I should have.'

I waved the drawings.

'Oh, very nice,' said my mother and walked on into the house.

'She's tired,' said Louise to Astrid.

'I'm sure,' said Astrid.

They went inside.

'Your mother,' said Louise, who had returned with a tall clinking glass of ice in an opaque liquid, 'is quite a lady.' She sat down in the chair and removed her wide hat, and in the sunlight her hair was a blonde burning. 'How does she *do* all that? I mean, do you *see* her, for instance, at home, at night, at dinnertime . . .' She was drinking and gesturing.

'Sometimes,' I said.

'She's very strong,' said Louise.

I went on drawing.

Astrid emerged from the kitchen and sat down beside Louise. She said she had stuffed all their shopping in the fridge without worrying about who had bought what.

'Oh, it's fine,' said Louise. 'I was just telling Zaki how lucky he is to have a mom like that.'

'I'm sure he knows,' said Astrid.

And later at night I heard them again: they were sitting on the patio, out beneath the stars and the vines in the dark, drinking and talking. Astrid was saying, 'It must be difficult, living alone like that, in a place like that. My God, can you imagine? And then raising the child all by yourself. It can't be easy.'

'Do you think she'll find someone?' said Louise.

'Oh, I'm sure. She's young, she's attractive. She has time. I'm sure she will.'

'Oh, but I mean *here*,' said Louise.

'Ah,' said Astrid. 'Well, for that she will have to look a little. I don't mean she will have to seek it out, you know. But she has to keep her eyes open. She has to be more open to the idea. If your eyes are closed you can never see who's looking.'

*

'I hate this bloody bed-and-breakfast.'

My mother said, 'Then go outside and find something to do. You're old enough to do it.' She was standing before the bathroom mirror and trying on a hat she had bought from a stall in the Sunday market. It was small, made of dark wool and shaped like the top of a mushroom. She pulled it down below her ears and raised her chin. 'You don't need me to accompany you everywhere.'

'You *don't* accompany me everywhere.'

But it wasn't true. We had been together for most of every day, had gone out together to see the sights: we went to churches and cathedrals, to the empty bathhouses one afternoon, and frequently to the small outdoor restaurants, which they called cafés here, making no distinction between the two. Even then it had been difficult to go, difficult to watch the other people in groups of four and five and six and seven, talking and laughing and joining their tables in the cafés, while we sat alone at ours and ate the oily tapas in the bowls.

'When will we go home?'

'You know when.'

'Ya, but I want to go now.'

And she went on in the mirror with the hat.

'I'm going out,' I said. I was leaving the room.

'Wait,' she said. 'Where are you going?'

'I don't *know*.'

'Zaki, you have to tell me where you're going.' She had abandoned the hat. 'I can't let you go on your own.'

'You just said I could.'

She was trapped. 'Then take directions from Astrid. And don't go far. Stay in the street. I don't want you getting lost here.'

Astrid only gave directions to the main street below, where a few shops stood facing the stream. She said not to go beyond the shops; beyond there was only a neighbourhood, and then more alleys that led to houses. The bigger markets were on the other side and further up the hill.

'Wait for your mother,' she suggested. 'She will take you in the evening.'

But I had to leave the house, had to leave the odd confinement of the patio and the upstairs rooms, and I left now promising to return before long. Outside, in the sun, the cobblestone street shone; the walls of the houses were high and white and unknown, their painted windows shut. And at once the memory, brought on by the isolation, of home took root: the house appeared beyond the gate, and the car parked in the shade in the driveway, leading up to the cool of the veranda and then past into the rooms.

I took out the coins from my pocket and counted. They were enough. And there was time.

I ran down the street, the coins slashing.

It was a dark green box for storing jewellery. Samar Api had no jewellery to store, but she had drawers in which she kept things, pens and badges and lockets, and later she would also have jewels. The lid was domed, smooth to the touch, and lifted heavily; the inside was lined a deep red.

'How much?'

The girl at the till was sullen. She was punching the price into her machine and listening at the same time to a woman's voice that was shouting in the Spanish language from behind a curtain.

The girl pointed to the sum on the small rectangular screen.

I gave her my coins, and they added up. The machine coughed lengthily and opened. The girl stacked the coins inside their separate slots, tore out the receipt and went marching behind the curtain to address the shouts.

'Zaki!' It was my mother. 'Thank God, Zaki!' She had entered the shop. 'I've been looking all over and I told you not to go far.' She was standing here, wanting to have an argument.

I said, 'Sorry.' I wanted to leave the shop.

'But why did you do that?'

'Sorry.'

'You can't just say sorry, Zaki. You have to understand.'

'Sorry!'

And now she saw the box, saw that I had bought it, but it was too late to revive a mood she had destroyed.

'Where are you going?' she cried.

But I had already left the shop.

A church. She wanted to see a church.

'You can go.'

'You won't come?'

'No.'

She said, 'Zaki, please. Come with me.' And she had surrendered. But I said, 'I'm fine here. You can go.'

'Are you sure?'

'Yes.'

'Don't go anywhere.'

I watched her walk away down the pebbles, and into the dark mouth of the church. I was sitting on a bench under a tree in the courtyard. From here the hills seemed far; the Alhambra castle was a small clay object. A bare-chested man with a tattoo of the sun on his back was sitting ahead on the ledge and playing a guitar. The tune was romantic, anguished. He was playing it to the separated hills.

'Zaki, I want you to meet someone.'

She had returned from the church with a man, a tall, tanned man with Chinese eyes. His clothes were white, a translucent shirt rolled up to the elbows and white trousers rolled up to the knees.

'Zaki,' she said. 'Say hello to Karim.'

She was smiling terrifically.

'Hello,' said Karim.

I didn't shake his hand.

'Karim is from Malaysia,' said my mother, and then looked at Karim, who stood with his arms crossed at his chest, his white shirt trembling in the breeze. He was looking out into the sunlight like a man on the deck of a ship in a cigarette ad.

'I was telling Karim that you like to draw. Karim's an artist.'

Karim responded to this in no way at all. He was accustomed to having it said about him.

'You draw?' I said.

'I don't actually,' he said, and his hands went into the pockets of his trousers, 'I do other kinds of art. I make things, you know, with my hands.' And he looked at my mother and grinned.

We sat there in the sun, on the shadeless bench behind the on-going guitar music. Karim was telling my mother about his life in Malaysia, in a place called Kayel, where he knew many other artists and musicians; he said the arts were generally progressive but had suffered a break in a link: his hand sawed off a part of the air.

'We're colonized,' he said. 'In the end we're excluded from our histories.'

'Absolutely,' said my mother.

Karim was frowning at his fingernails.

'You know,' said my mother, and she was crossing and uncrossing her ankles, 'we're staying at a bed-and-breakfast here, in the Arab Quarter, and I was telling them, our hosts, or host rather, an Armenian woman, she has two other guests staying with her. But I was telling them the other day about the amount of red tape we have to deal with, just to get the small things done. And they wouldn't believe me! They would not believe me.'

'Oh, it's unparalleled,' said Karim.

'Still,' said my mother, 'I'm sure Malaysia is a good two steps ahead of where we are.'

'I wouldn't be too sure of that,' said Karim.

'Oh no,' she said. 'Believe me. Things are pretty bad there right now. We have every kind of crisis and a head of state who's buying up property in the West.'

'Look at it this way,' said Karim, and leaned in to explain, 'if it weren't for the system, if the system itself weren't as bad as it is right now, there would be no women like you to take it on.'

My mother thought about it.

'Frankly,' said Karim, 'I prefer it this way.' And he laughed and went on looking at her.

I stood up.

'What's the matter?' said my mother.

But I was running.

'Zaki, wait!'

I ran past the church and down and then up the winding streets, higher and higher until at last I reached the door and was past it.

'Are you okay?' said Louise.

'Where is your mother?' said Astrid.

I was kneeling, panting.

'Zaki!' She had come in after me.

'Are you all right?' said Louise, concerned now. She stood up from her chair at the patio table and reached out a hand.

I thrust it aside.

'Zaki!' said my mother.

I went into the house and up the stairs.

She came up after me.

'How dare you behave like that,' she said, and slammed the door behind her. 'She is *so* kind to you, and you were *so* rude to her just now.'

'Then why doesn't she find her own little children? Why does she have to be kind to *me*?'

'Because she can't *have* any! Do you understand that? Can you for once understand? It's not always about *you*, you know?'

'Then give me away!' And I collapsed on the bed with my fists, and was crying. 'Why don't you just give me away!'

She stayed standing near the door. 'Don't say that,' she said.

'I just want to go home now.' And the words, expressing so desperate a need, were clear in the sobs.

'We will,' she said, and sat beside me on the bed, her hand on my head.

It was our last day in Spain and we were going to see the Alhambra castle.

'Take a lot of water,' said Astrid. 'You will get thirsty after all the climbing.'

The castle was located at the top of a hill. And we had to climb that hill: we were carrying a picnic basket and swapped it as we went up. It was hot and bright, and the other climbers had come prepared in shorts and cotton T-shirts.

My mother was wearing a shalwar kameez.

I said, 'I'll take the basket.'

She said, 'Thanks, Zaki. You're so good.'

And we went up with effortful strides, our arms dangling like those of our primate ancestors.

At the top of the hill we had to wait in a queue. And, after paying for our tickets, we were allowed to go inside: the view was suddenly grand, a view of towering arches reflected in a long, still pool of green water. The tourists ahead of us were walking slowly, stunned by the altered atmosphere. There was a fountain with identical stone animals standing underneath it, and beehive-like formations that hung from the surrounding arches. My mother led me by the hand into a hall, where the ceiling was white and intricately carved with calligraphy, like thousands of snakes engaged in a celebratory dance. 'Look,' she said, cutting with her splayed palm an arc in demonstration, 'this is what Muslim culture used to be about: art, music, architecture. It used to be progressive.' And she made a small fist as she said the word.

'So what happened?' I said.

'To what?' she said.

'To the Muslims. What happened to them after all this?'

We were sitting in the palace café, which was for tourists to eat in, and hadn't been a part of the original design. We had ordered Cokes and were planning to consume them quietly with our picnic lunch, which my mother had hidden under the table.

'I don't know,' she said, looking around at the roaming tourists, who were mostly white. 'I suppose they forgot where they came from. They forgot their history, their culture. It happens to people sometimes.'

*

Lahore Airport was the same. The conveyor belt took its time to start and then, having started, stopped. There was confusion.

A young porter in the grey porters' uniform made a show of indignation and went in behind an unmanned door. After some minutes he returned, and stood confidently beside his assignee, an old, white-haired man in an off-white suit. The conveyor belt started up again. And the porter kept his look of indignation, not willing to overlook the lapse in the machine's function, aware of his victory in getting it started and aware too that his demand for a tip was now unassailable.

'Oho!' cried another porter, who was hurrying through the stranded crowd towards the bend in the moving belt. But the suitcase he lifted was not the one. He abandoned it and stood back, undaunted by failure or embarrassment.

He dusted his shoulders, first the right and then the left.

The man he had displaced said something from behind his back. It was ignored.

Our suitcase appeared and I caught it; we had no trolley and wouldn't need one – the suitcase had wheels and rolled. We rolled it across to customs, where it was stopped and opened and searched for illegal items, and then we rolled it out into the crowded haphazardness of International Arrivals.

My mother saw Naseem and extended an arm in a sideways embrace.

Naseem returned the embrace and took the suitcase by the handle, and led the way across the cracked airport floor. The night outside was suddenly cold, the sky blurred with smog.

'It's winter already,' said my mother.

We walked past the line of waiting taxi drivers, past two beggars settled against a pillar on the floor, an old man in a turban and an old woman, both thin and wrinkled and sitting on their haunches under the cover of a single shawl. Watching us go past, watching the people behind us go past, they were waiting for someone to stop.

'All is well?' said my mother. She was walking behind Naseem, following through the spaces between parked cars and buses.

Naseem was walking briskly now, and far ahead of us.

We reached the car, which was parked towards the end of the last row. Barkat emerged from the front and lifted the suitcase with Naseem and dumped it into the boot.

We sat at the back, Naseem beside Barkat in the seat ahead, and the car started.

My mother said our holiday had been enjoyable.

Naseem said nothing.

Barkat stopped the car to pay for the parking.

'What's happened?' said my mother.

Naseem was quiet for a moment, a moment in which the car passed through the check post and the airport gates and went out into the white-lit street. And then she spoke, but it was gravelly and splintered; she coughed, rolled down her window and spat out the phlegm, then rolled it up again. She said, 'The girl is gone. Her mother came and took her. We tried to stop her but we couldn't.'

'Sit,' said Daadi.

She was walking up and down her room.

Naseem said she was taking the suitcase to my mother's room.

'Go,' said Daadi.

Naseem left the room and closed the door behind her.

My mother sat on the sofa and said, 'Will someone tell me what has happened?' Her fists were pressed into her knees.

Daadi said Chhoti had arrived four days ago. She had sat with Daadi in her room, asked for a glass of cold water and drunk it slowly, pausing to consider her sips. Then she had gone into her daughter's room. Daadi hadn't suspected, and so she stayed where she was and didn't follow through the door. But then she heard the sounds, the thudding and the shrieks and then the crash – the lamp had tumbled and fallen – and when they opened the door they found Chhoti standing above her daughter with a shoe in her hand and bringing it down again and again.

Tell me, she said, *tell me what you did.*

The girl was screaming and sobbing.

Where did you take yourself? To whose house have you been? Is this what you give me? Tell me now.

Daadi tried to pull them apart.

She has soiled me, said Chhoti, *she has soiled me soiled me soiled me.*

It was known to the women of the village. The boy's mother had brought it to them. The girl, she said, had tried to seduce the boy. But the boy wasn't ready, and it was an unsuitable match, one they couldn't consider after knowing the ways in which the affair had been conducted.

Chhoti's sisters-in-law had been to see her at her house. They said they had heard disturbing things.

One bad egg ruins the batch.

We have our own children to think of.

This kind of thing is not tolerated in our family.

The girl must be brought back before her father is informed and acts in ways that are beyond your control.

'Tell me!' cried Chhoti. 'Tell me what you did!'

'We tried to stop her,' said Daadi. 'She was someone else. She was made of stone.'

Chhoti beat the girl and took her in the car. And there had been no word from her after that.

'I always said,' said Daadi. 'I always said send the girl away, send her back. But no, I was told, let her live, let her breathe, she is only a child. It was interference. She was not yours or mine to raise.'

My mother took me by the arm and went into her room. She didn't switch on the lights.

'You knew?'

I was looking at her face.

'Answer me!'

'Don't interfere,' I said.

'What did you say?'

'You like interfering in my business?'

'How dare you talk to me like that?'

'What happened to democracy? What happened to art music architecture? What happened to progressive?'

'How dare you?'

'Face it,' I said. 'You're nothing but a half-baked liberal.'

Her face was blank. Then her mouth twisted, and she raised her hand and struck my face with a force that swung her shoulder.

TWO

13

The difficulties of adolescence are the first of their kind. There is nothing like them in the chanciness of childhood, just as there is nothing, no resonance or meaning, in the sayings of those who have crossed the waters and speak now exhortingly as from the shore. Words are vacant, adrift, waiting for contact with life, for moments that will come to cause the unmistakable throb of recognition.

At home there was no recourse to hollow wisdoms. There was only the loss, and it took the place of life, of habitual arrivals and departures and of sounds from behind doors that now stayed shut. My mother woke late and slept early. On some days she didn't go to work; she stayed in bed and read, or watched TV and used the telephone. At night the only light in her room came from the bedside lamp, next to which she kept the packet of pills, small pink ones with a dose-maker's line running clearly across the middle. She had bought them without a prescription to ease the nights and had arrived at her own conclusions.

Daadi allowed the days to pass and then picked up the phone and dialled Chhoti's number in Barampur. She asked after her as if nothing had changed. Chhoti was not dramatic, and gave an unremarkable account of things. Daadi mentioned the remaining days of the school term and the fees that had to be paid, and Chhoti said she would speak to the administration herself.

'And the things?' said Daadi. 'The clothes and the things in the room . . .'

Chhoti said to pack them in boxes. She would collect them on the weekend.

Late on Friday afternoon the car came to the house. And the driver was alone. He stood by the open boot and counted the cardboard boxes, and watched as they were loaded.

Naseem was asked to clear the room. The bed was draped, the posters torn from the walls and rolled up and secured with rubber bands. The clothes had gone already; the picture frames and cosmetics and the few discovered magazines were packed into boxes and stowed away.

The lights were switched off.

And the door was locked.

'What's done is done,' said Daadi. 'No point dwelling on it now.'

But it was impossible to not dwell, to resist the pull of what had not been witnessed and survived only in the telling of others. Every version led to fresh imaginings. And to imagine was to enter alone, witnessing without witnesses, with some of the pain and none of the consolations allowed by actual experience.

I went driving with Isa and Moosa in their car. They were excited because they had tickets to a cricket match in Gaddafi Stadium. They struggled in the queue outside and struggled inside to reach the seats in the upper enclosure, and the whole match went by, the floodlights and the cheering and the tooting of horns in the crowded vastness, and again there was only the night, my bedroom and the shadows on its ceiling.

One afternoon Naseem went down the lane to Mrs Zaidi's house and returned with a thin, harassed-looking boy, who was made to wait in a chair by the gate. She came inside and said, 'An old friend has come to see you.'

But Mazri had come only out of obligation, and was too old now to play video games in arcades and to run after kites on roofs. He was awkward too, dressed in a loose grey shalwar kameez that was too big for his body, even after the sleeves had been rolled up and the shalwar hitched up at the ankles; his feet were in rubber sandals that extended well past the heels and flapped when he walked. He had little of interest to report: he was working now at a bicycle repair shop in Canal Park, fixing chains and pumping air into tyres; he had lost the old bicycle years ago (it was stolen from outside the arcade while Mazri was playing video games inside); he had not yet bought another, though he intended to – he had his eye on a Sohrab Eagle that had come into the workshop and needed only a little bit of work, it wouldn't cost him if he repaired it himself, and he had spoken to the workshop owner and the man was not opposed.

We sat in chairs by the gate and talked for some minutes. We agreed to meet again, perhaps at the workshop, perhaps even later in the week, and exchanged details about timing and location. Then we parted and I saw Mazri out of the gate, knowing already that the plan was cancelled.

Daadi said, 'You must make friends. This is no way to behave. Children your age are running around and doing every kind of thing, and look at you.'

Exams at school were left unattempted, the papers rolled up and compressed into balls and settled like decorations on the desk. Equations and unwanted sentences appeared instead on the sheets of drawing paper handed out in art class, the numbers and letters all carefully sculpted and shaded appropriately with darknesses. The art teacher snatched the sheet and took it to the blackboard and held it up for all to see. The class tittered and applauded.

One day, in the indoor gymnasium, the boys of the junior classes were learning to swim in a large inflated pool and a smashing sound sent them screaming and splashing; a window had burst – a stone had burst it. The boys went to stand by the supervisor and hugged their little bodies, naked and dripping, suddenly vulnerable and screaming with certainty. The incensed supervisor went outside to see and found the culprit standing at the site of the crime with his hands inside his pockets.

'Mrs Shirazi,' said the headmistress. She removed her glasses and sighed and brought a pressing fingertip to her temple. It stretched one eye felinely. 'I'm afraid this is getting out of hand. Homework we can handle. Active misbehaviour we cannot. You should take him to a child psychologist; it shouldn't be a problem in this day and age.'

'Child psychologist,' said my mother in the car. 'She should take her*self* to a child psychologist.' After a gathering pause she said, 'This school is no good, Zaki. I've felt it for a while, and now I know it. You're just not going back there. We'll find another school for you. There's no shortage of schools here. Child psychologist.'

And she gave a humourless laugh and shook her head, her eyes wide and alert and unaccepting.

It was agreed that Wilson Academy was the first choice.

'Most impressive,' said Suri boastfully, for she had been to the campus once. 'They have grounds and grounds wherever you look. They have stables for ponies, houses for teachers. Oh, they have everything, everything.' She looked away and dispelled the temptation with her hands.

Hukmi said, '*Uff vaisay . . .*' and smiled longingly.

But the brochure made no promises, and consisted of only two glossy pages, the first with a faded image of an old clock behind the text, which gave a summary of the school's history, its aims and objectives and the requirements for admission; and the second page provided a list of affiliated universities in Britain and America and Canada. A phone number and a fax number were given at the back for inquiries. There was no mention of stables or ponies.

'We'll just have to go and find out,' said my mother.

The next morning she called up the admissions office and was told that the school was closed to visitors. It was open only in the summer, in the two-week window between admission tests and the announcement of results.

'We'll wait,' said my mother. 'You can stay in this school until then.'

The wait was long and daunting. A tutor was hired and came to the house in the evening for lessons in maths and Urdu. My mother preferred to teach English herself; she divided the lessons according to the admissions criteria and anticipated the exam questions, which were unknown but fell broadly into the categories of spelling, grammar, vocabulary and composition. And, as the months passed and the efforts continued, a picture of Wilson Academy was assembled from what was generally known: the founding of the school in the nineteenth century by a British administrator, who had modelled it after the prestigious boarding schools of England; its passage into the hands of Irish missionaries, who ran it in the war years as if it were a circus, with public canings and whippings and colourful prize ceremonies; and then finally at Independence the school's transfer to a local administration, which had since overseen an illustrious roster of cricketers and gymnasts and lawyers and industrialists and diplomats and civil servants. Other aspects were recalled distantly: Uncle Saaji had played tennis with a group of Wilsonians in his youth and remembered them all by name. 'A fun bunch,' he noted nostalgically. 'But they had discipline. Oh yes, they had discipline.'

Uncle Shafto said, 'Fazl-e-Haq was my class fellow. His brother was Wilsonian.' He had made the connection. He looked around now and nodded clinchingly.

'It is difficult to get in,' said Uncle Saaji. He knew because he had tried for Isa many years ago.

'But you should try,' said Suri, for she trusted in the likelihood and was unafraid. 'There's no harm in trying. You might even get in. You never know with these things.'

The Wilson Academy campus occupied almost seventy acres in an otherwise congested part of the city. There was a logic to its seclusion: the school had been founded at a time of aridity, when the irrigation systems built by the British were still spreading and much of the present city was still barren, an emptiness recorded amply in watercolours and drawings and later even in photographs, some of the first of their kind, developed to an attractively high contrast of blacks and whites. From the start the school had drawn the sons of the very best families, who had seen to the improvement of its surroundings: the road outside and the avenues of old, high, spreading trees – these had come up around the school, because of the school, and were tied to its legacy of public service; many of the city's famous philanthropists had been Wilsonians, and had served on the school board, as well as on the boards of state schools and hospitals and public libraries. And so for more than a century the campus had resided in uncontested isolation, its noiseless acreage secure behind high brick walls and the tops of trees, only the crowning domes of its buildings visible to the outside world, the same domes that formed the school insignia, which was disseminated across a wide range of objects, including cutlery and wall hangings and a line of stationery that was recommended annually to alumni and made mandatory for enrolled students, who had to make their purchases at the school gift shop.

We waited in my mother's van outside the gate. It was the rear gate and faced a narrow two-way street behind the campus. The high iron bars were painted black and sharpened into spear-like tips at the top, and separated below by thin spaces, providing a view that was more obstructed than revealing.

'Why is it taking so long?' said my mother. She pressed the heel of her palm into the horn and held it.

A security guard appeared. He wore a beige uniform and a black cap, and walked up unhurriedly to the van.

'Admissions test,' said my mother.

The guard looked at her blankly, his hands on the exposed felt of the rolled-down window. He was a young man steeled to procedural silences; without a word he stepped back and brought out a notepad, wrote down the car number, then went back inside and opened the gate, and saluted as the van went in.

We followed a trail of sign boards, blue-and-white reproductions of THIS WAY TO PARKING that led along a winding path, broad enough to be a road. The evenly contoured hedges gapped abruptly and showed a ditch running on the other side. And the trees along the path were chalked up to the waist, with square tin signs nailed to the bark for identification: the names of the species were given in both Latin and Urdu, the scripts juxtaposed in showy equivalence.

We left the van among bicycles in the car park – there was no other car and still no sign of people; we went down a rutted old path and past the canteen, closed now, the stone benches outside unoccupied, then alongside a field that was smooth and vast, a hockey field or a football field – the rounds of competitive sporting activity were difficult to imagine on a day like this, with no cloud or breeze. We passed brick buildings that had gone over the years from what was still in places a soft pink to a hard hot grey, the colour of the granite path, which shimmered falsely in the distance with hints of wetness.

A bearer in white clothes stopped us at the entrance to a hallway for questioning. He checked the name on a printed list, then led us through the hallway and showed us into a room with upholstered chairs.

A woman was sitting in a chair with her hands on her knees. Her head was covered and her eyes were closed. She was swaying and muttering. My mother sat on a tattered red chair, folded her hands in her lap and looked around with feigned interest. The room had a high ceiling and no windows, and was lit faintly by the blaze from outside; the ceiling fan groaned lethargically and gave no relief. The walls carried paintings of flowers and fruits and vegetables, and were made by the students, signed and dated in the bottom-right-hand corners; in some the paint had come off, had chipped or had started to peel, or had formed bulging pustules that sat within the glass malevolently, like sores, constrained by slim black frames of the same size, so that some of the pictures had been decapitated in order to make them fit.

'Amma.'

A plump and sullen-looking boy stood in the doorway with a folded paper in his hands.

'Did you fail?' said the woman and rose from her chair.

The boy stared at his mother, stared at the paper in his hands.

'Did you fail? Tell me now: did you fail?' She was shaking him by the shoulders.

The boy was crying.

The woman snatched the paper from his hands, looked at it, took his hand and hurried out. Their voices receded down the hallway, the mother shouting and the boy bawling like a much younger child.

I looked at my mother.

She was looking at the pictures on the walls.

My name was called. The bearer reappeared in the doorway and was brisk now and energized; he went making musical sounds in the hallway, glancing importantly at the brick walls, at the pillars and the notices up on the boards. He knew we were following. At a door near the end of the hallway he stopped and gestured emphatically with his palms – we were to stop here and wait. He opened the door and parted the curtains, went inside and drew the curtains again. A man's voice was talking inside on a telephone, laughing and describing a hockey match the boys had won at a rival school. He mentioned the trophies, the team's impressions, the undeniably good reception given by the host school, and then said nothing for a while, only 'yes, yes' and 'God's grace' as he brought the conversation to an end.

He hung up the phone and said, 'Yes, please?'

The bearer parted the curtains and we went into a museum-like room, with framed English poems and sayings on one wall, and a collection of shields and trophies on two sagging shelves, one below the other. Another wall was devoted to the framed portraits of men, first a set of faded white men, made distinct by the sharp jutting darks of hairlines and beards and moustaches – they were the early administrators. The Irish missionaries, who were harsh-looking and wore black cloaks with small white squares in their collars, followed; then came the men who had served since Independence, men more at ease in these surroundings, gazing calmly and smiling occasionally. Their names and tenures were given on slim silver plaques below the frames. Only the last picture was undated, and showed a thin, balding man with lively eyes and lips sealed up in a smile, his expression one of childlike mischief or wonderment: he had the look of someone who has made a discovery and possesses it in the form of an unmade revelation. His name and title were given on the plaque: *Tabassum Ali Hassan, First Chief Coordinator, Wilson Academy.*

The man sitting at the desk beneath the picture was frail and completely bald; his shoulders were hunched behind him and his hands settled before him on the desk. But his eyes were still bright, and the smile, though twitching unconsciously at the corners, was still the presiding aspect of his expression, and promised both durability and resilience.

'Please,' he said, and waited for us to settle in the chairs.

My mother smiled and said, '*Slaamaleikum.*'

'Tabassum Ali Hassan,' he said, and touched his heart. The

gesture was perfunctory; it did nothing to the mask. He lifted a pair of spectacles from the desk and settled them on his face, and his eyes became magnified. 'Yes,' he said, and picked up a pen. 'Your name, please?'

'Zaki Shirazi,' said my mother.

'I asked him,' said the man.

'Zaki Shirazi,' I said.

'Zaki Shirazi, sir.'

'Sir.'

He waited as if for a retraction. Then his gaze relented and shifted to a notebook, and he located a page and took his finger to the bottom of it. 'Yes,' he said. 'And your age, please?'

My mother looked at me.

'Twelve,' I said.

'Are you lying?' It was asked in a disconcertingly tender tone.

'No, actually,' said my mother, and then remembered that she wasn't supposed to speak. 'Sorry,' she said, and covered her mouth with a hand. 'May I?'

He was nodding.

'Yes, well: he's actually still twelve, he'll be thirteen in August.' She smiled and nodded.

'That means,' said the coordinator, writing it down in his notebook, 'that he is thirteen. For our purposes. We select on the basis of age, you see. He will have to sit for the year-nine test.' He turned the page and continued to write.

'But he's only twelve,' said my mother.

'My sister,' said the coordinator and put away the notebook; his eyes were frank and uncomforting. 'There is always a complication. But we cannot always make an exception.' He looked at me, and his smile returned. 'He is a smart boy. That much I can see. In the end it is simple: if he is intelligent enough, he will pass the test. And if he passes the test, we will consider him intelligent enough to be in this school. It is the best philosophy.' And he laughed at the philosophy, a surprisingly robust laugh for a man of his proportions.

'Please wait,' said my mother. 'I have brought the documents with me.' She was looking for them in her handbag.

'But my sister,' said the coordinator and brought his palms together. 'Why search for a way when you have the destination? Please, I have told you. I cannot help you: my hands are tied.'

The test took place that afternoon in an upstairs room, in the presence of an elderly invigilator: he wore a beige safari suit and walked slowly up and down the room, his hands behind his back, and glanced repeatedly at the clock as though he had somewhere to go. I was unable to finish the maths section and was unfamiliar with the Urdu expressions, which had to be converted into sentences. At last I turned to the English test. I read the comprehension passage and answered the questions, then considered the last part, the composition, which asked for a story about human nature. I wrote about a pair, a boy and a girl, younger boy and older girl, who live happily in a house on a hill but are separated by fate and spend years trying to find one another. The boy becomes a forlorn judge; the girl becomes a mother of four in a village and lives a life of smothered respectability. But they are denied a reunion and eventually die tragic, unrelated deaths. 'The mourners gathered at their graves,' went the last sentence, 'and prayed for their departed souls, but who knows what lies ahead, beyond the ashes and the dust?'

The papers were tied with string and submitted. Two weeks later the package containing the results was delivered to the house: I had failed in maths, failed in Urdu and done badly on the comprehension passage, but the story had earned full marks. 'Superb,' was the comment, and beside it a mad swirl of a signature, attributed in typing to the principal of Wilson Academy, who had read the essay and approved my admission into the school.

Daadi said it was Allah's doing.

My mother said it was talent.

And Suri and Hukmi said it was all very well but stories alone couldn't get you through your life.

*

It was the first day of school and I was late.

'Naseem!' cried my mother. She went through the veranda to

the kitchen, then hurried back in her nightgown, looking around in delayed distress. We had emerged from the dressing room after having fussed over the tie and the shirt, which had not been ironed to Daadi's satisfaction.

'It doesn't matter,' my mother had said.

But Daadi had insisted and sent the shirt back to the kitchen.

'He is a growing boy,' she had said. 'And this is not that kind of school. It is not for your amusement.'

My mother said, 'Why don't you iron it, then? Why don't you pay the fees? Why don't you take over everything?'

And Daadi had said there was no need to have a fight in the morning.

Barkat drove me to the school. It took a while: the school-related traffic began on the canal and lasted all the way to the campus gates, two of which had already closed; it was late now, past the time for the first bell, and the few cars on the road were rushed. Barkat had to make an effort to reach the last gate before it was shut, and I ran after the other boys, who were marching far ahead in lines to the clanging of the bell.

The lines led through the hallway and out into a large circular field behind the main building. And here was the noise of so many voices speaking at once and the sight of hundreds of boys all dressed in the same clothes, the same blue shirts and green ties and pale khaki trousers. They were assembled in separate squares, each made up of five rows, the shorter boys ahead and the taller ones at the back. Beside every square stood a teacher: they were mostly men but there were some women too, and they were looking around and nodding and smiling at one another.

I joined the first square and stood at the end of the last row. It was a hot, damp morning, the sky low and overcast; I tried to loosen the knot of the tie but desisted when this began to draw attention. The other boys had starched shirts and neatly knotted ties, their hair combed and wet – they had showered in the morning, and some had even deodorized their armpits and now gave off the smell.

An older boy was going around with a register and a pen. He

wore a blue and yellow badge on his breast pocket, a mark of his separateness. There was an importance in the way he lingered and tapped the open register with his pen.

'Shoes,' he said.

'Sorry?'

He looked up from under a frown. 'Your shoes,' he said, and pointed the pen.

I looked at my shoes. They were black, like the ones shown in the brochure. 'What's wrong with these shoes?'

He began to blink. 'You have no respect?' He was suddenly close, his jaw jutting forward. 'What's your name?' His breath was sour and heated. 'What's your name?'

'Zaki Shirazi.'

He wrote it down. 'You come see me after this.' And he resumed his rounds with an attempt at preserving the initial pace.

'He's the monitor,' said the boy to my right.

I said, 'What's he going to do?'

'Nothing. He's new. He has to try.' This was a charitable assessment, not lacking in potential for humour or depth. I looked at the boy: he was narrow and of a medium height, his hair falling forward in thick slants and into his eyes, which were small and appeared to squint out as if at something bright.

I said, 'You're new too?'

But he wasn't. He had been at the school for a year but had developed an illness in the second term that had forced him to take leave and repeat the grade. 'Same class,' he said. 'Same teachers. Just different kids.' He smirked at this twist in his fate.

'I'm new,' I said.

'I could tell.'

We stood in the line and watched. A monitor was assigned to every gathering, which the boy, whose name was Saif, said were houses: first the monitors all walked out of their assigned houses and into centre of the field, where they stood in a line, their backs arched and their chests out and their palms stiff by their sides. They were waiting for a sign, which came now from a podium on the semicircular balcony that jutted out of the brick building: Coordinator Hassan was dressed in a dull grey suit with the buttons closed and the shoulders puffed out; he surveyed the assembly below and gave a single nod. And together the monitors cried:

'Attention!'

The silence was abrupt. The movement of a bird in a tree was painfully distinct: it flapped and tore inside the leaves and then fell away with a patter of its wings.

Coordinator Hassan leaned into the microphone and said, 'There will now be a recitation from the Holy Quran.' His voice echoed in the microphone; he held both sides of the podium, and his small body appeared to lift behind it.

A boy went up to the podium from behind the coordinator, took his place at the microphone and began to recite. His eyes were shut, and his body swayed to the drawn-out Arabic. Then he opened his eyes and said, 'Translation! In the name of Allah! The most Beneficent, the most Merciful! Praise be to Him! The Lord of the worlds! The Beneficent, the Merciful, the Master of the Day of Judgement! Thee alone we worship! And Thee alone we ask for help! Show us the straight path! The path of those whom Thou hast favoured! And not of those! Who earn Thine anger! And nor of those! Who go astray!'

The boy gave no bow or word of ending, and withdrew abruptly into the shadows behind Coordinator Hassan, who stepped up again to the podium and began a speech about the importance of fairness. Throughout the speech his head was bowed, so that he seemed to read it out from his notes, and when it was done he looked up brightly and said, 'And now for the principal, please.'

The applause was like a waterfall; the principal stood at the podium on the balcony and presided over the sound until, at a wave of his hand, it stopped.

He was a tall, regal-looking man with full white hair and a lush moustache. 'It was Eliot,' he said, his voice booming across the field, 'who asked the question, "Do I dare disturb the universe?" It is you, my sons, who must remove that final question mark' – he caught it in the air in his fist – 'and make of it a motto for yourselves. Disturb the universe. Disturb it by all means. Things will fall into place.'

The forceful applause returned.

'That was the principal, please,' said the coordinator over the noise, reclaiming his practical place at the podium.

The principal stood beside him with his chin raised.

The coordinator was looking at his notes and now spoke in a flatly cheerful tone: our hockey team had just returned from Bahawalpur; the boys had participated in the All-Pakistan Inter-School Hockey Tournament and gone as far as the semi-finals; they had brought back some trophies that were now going to be distributed; could the captain please come up and hand them out?

The assembly was dismissed after the national anthem. I waited in the house enclosure, which disintegrated as the boys headed out towards the hallway. There were five minutes between this bell and the next one, and I was waiting for the monitor to return, to resume the argument about the shoes and award the appropriate punishment.

'He's not coming,' said Saif, who was waiting with me. All around us the noise continued as the crowd slowly drained away.

'Then he'll come tomorrow,' I said. 'It's better to wait now.'

'He won't come tomorrow,' said Saif.

We began to walk away from the abandoned enclosure.

'What's wrong with these shoes?'

'Nothing wrong.'

'So? Why's he acting all worked up like that?'

'He has to. He's new.'

We walked through the field, then along the crowded hallway, where confident voices rose continually above the hum; boys embraced and shook hands and stood chatting in doorways; some were talking to teachers just inside the filling classrooms, and looking around as they talked, taking up their places again after the void of the summer holidays.

I asked Saif if he knew the monitor.

'Not yet,' he said.

We reached the building where the junior classrooms were situated, a low brick block with recessed corridors under a series of arches. The noise here was pronounced. Saif and I were in the same class (though he was repeating a year) but in different sections: every class was divided into seven sections, with no apparent method of differentiation; it was management, Saif explained, and it would undergo additional changes in the coming weeks, with boys being shifted from one section to another until the arrangements were defined.

'I can come to yours,' I said.

'You can't choose,' he said. 'The teachers will decide.'

The second bell had sounded and the commotion in the corridor had increased. Teachers were visible now, coming down the stone path from far-off buildings. Saif and I parted in the noise and went in opposite directions. I was in 9B, a room with a broken door, smashed in from long ago and left to hang at a slight angle in the doorway; the room itself had a high ceiling with grooves at the top and a single fan that dangled on a long cord; a dead fireplace sat to the side, a blackboard was hung at the front, and lots of chairs with thin legs were littered all round with slate-like surfaces attached to the arms. The room had filled up at the front and in the middle, and only some chairs at the back remained. I took the one near the window, which was made of a rusty old mesh and dented. A dead wasp lay on its back in a corner of the windowsill with its legs curled up. It had wandered in past the mesh and never found its way out.

The first period belonged to the English teacher, a woman. She came in with her books and walked up to the teacher's desk, landed the books, picked up a stick of chalk and began to write isolated words on the blackboard. The room was silent. The boys were copying the words. The English teacher wrote and wrote, moving width-wise along the board, then moving back and starting a new row of words, and onwards until the board was filled up. She twirled now and sat down in the teacher's chair. She was reading her own book, her head tilting in solitary involvement. When the bell rang she got up promptly with her pile of books and left the room. The noise started up again, and again stopped when the next teacher came in, a short young man who brought only one book. He wrote *Algebra* on the board and turned around to confront the class. 'In algebra,' he said, leaning against the blackboard, his legs crossed at the ankles, 'we use two variables, x and y.' He turned around and wrote x and y on the board. 'Algebra was invented by Arabs. Zero – you know zero – was also invented by Arabs.'

A voice said, 'Sir, will that be on the test?'

There were sniggers.

The teacher conceded a smile of amusement, and said, 'Maybe one question.'

The laughter was relieved.

'Arabs invented algebra,' he continued, 'and Arabs also invented the decimal – you know the decimal – which is widely used in mathematics today –'

'Sir, will that also be on the test?'

The maths teacher stared, his lips pressed out and his nostrils twitching. 'Stand up,' he said, and then in a shout: 'Stand up!'

The boy stood up.

'Get out.'

'Sir –'

'I say get out!'

The boy, a tall and clever one who looked older than the others, began to make his way past the chairs. When he had left the room the teacher turned again to the blackboard and wrote *Fixed Variables*. 'Write it down,' he said, his back to the class, the humour gone from his voice.

After the maths period there was the physics period, and after that chemistry, for which we had to go to the chemistry lab in a line led by the teacher, a quiet and dignified old man who performed an experiment with a test tube and tried towards the end to contain the chatter that had broken out in rebellion. The bell rang and a flood of bodies broke past the door. I managed to find my way back to the junior building, and then through the already empty corridor to 9D, which was the room allotted to Saif's section. It was deserted. I walked out again into the sun, and with my hands in my pockets, up along the hot path all the way to the canteen, which was located in a low white building. The queues inside were too long, and I waited outside by the benches and tried to find Saif among the groups. Then I started walking back towards the junior building, frowning in the sun, my hands secure inside my pockets, and the bell rang on the way and the noise and the rush swelled up, and the monitors appeared, shouting at the junior boys and stopping them to award punishments that were then carried out on the path.

At home that night my mother asked, 'And how was your day? Did you make any friends?'

'I'm sure he did,' said Daadi, but desisted from asking for proof.

I saw Saif in the mornings at the start of assembly. We no longer shared a house; I had only stood in his enclosure on the first day because I didn't then know that I had already been assigned a house, which was across from his on the other side of the field. It was a release from the monitor who had taken me up on the matter of my shoes. And my new monitor was kind and forgetful, a plump senior who had recently won recognition in the inter-school debating championships and was often late to assembly himself, lacking the time and the authority to conduct inspections. He stood at the back of the house enclosure and hurriedly marked the register with his pen, making comments that never led to punishments. The junior boys indulged him in the morning but considered him a failure because they saw the teasing way his contemporaries had with him, a way that was regretted and later ridiculed.

Saif was the one boy I knew. But he had a life from before, and had friends from before who accompanied him at lunch break to the canteen and sat with him on the benches, boys he had known last year and who were now one year ahead and brought with them the advantage of seniority. I sat with them a few times but felt alone; they had ways of talking to one another, ways of joking about other boys and teachers and the people they knew outside the school. And their methods were established: they knew where to meet and knew what they wanted from the canteen, and had a way of buying a collective lunch that was distributed equally. I listened when they talked, and laughed when they laughed, and gave them my money and ate the food they brought back from the canteen. But I felt alone.

The search continued in the classroom. All the chairs in the front were taken, and most of the chairs in the middle, but the chairs at the back retained a temporariness that was due to their proximity to the door. Here I had a series of vivid encounters, first with a boy called Daniyal, who was small and enjoyed making lewd jokes but was withdrawn and grudging when I asked to borrow his notes – he turned away at once and began to do his own work, as if to guard against a larger intention – and then with a boy called Saqlain Raza, a practising Shiia who gave solemn, lurid descriptions of the muharram ritual. He claimed to lash his own back with chains – he insisted that I touch the back of his shirt to feel the ridges, but the maths teacher saw us and told us to stand up and get out, a humiliating episode from which our friendship never recovered. Then Munawwar, who had moved from San Diego, and Ahmed, an aspiring scientist; and then, for a few days, a boy called Qaiser, whose father was a teacher in the Biology Department and whose views reflected the dilemmas and ambitions of schoolteachers. He enjoyed spending time outside the staff room and claimed to know the salaries of the heads of departments, and insisted that his father's was the highest, though at other times he said that the teachers weren't paid enough and were likely to go on strike.

When Daadi next asked about my friends, I told her I had none and told her also not to ask me again.

Naseem commented on the change in tone.

And Daadi said, 'The boy is maturing,' and closed her eyes serenely, drawing on her powers of persuasion.

*

The week consisted of five schooldays and every day (except Friday, a half-day) was divided into seven periods, four before the break and three after. Both English and maths were given a period a day; their importance was derived from the role they played in shaping the other subjects, such as physics, chemistry and biology, each occupying four periods a week. Urdu was allotted three periods a week; Pakistan Studies and Islamiyat one each, though they were taught by the same person, a hat-wearing, red-bearded man called Dr Qazi, who was rumoured to possess a Ph.D. and drew attention frequently to the lack of regard at this school for his subjects, which were the best subjects, since they alone determined our destinies in this world and the next; indeed Dr Qazi, with his dark trapezoid hat and fiery beard, wearing simple sandals and a plain white shalwar kameez with the shalwar raised an extra inch at the ankles, was conspicuous among the many shirts and trousers and, though ridiculed for his fervour, was singularly able to extract for his subjects an air of sanctity; the class was rowdy until he began to pace the room with his lecture, which was likely to appear on the test and had to be faithfully transcribed by each of us because there was no copy of it in the library.

'Women,' said Dr Qazi. 'What is the place of women in Islam?' He had stopped beside the blackboard; he hid his hands now and looked from one side of the room to the other.

Pens and pencils went to work.

Dr Qazi was pacing. 'The place of women in Islam is better than their place before the advent of Islam in Arabia.' He had delivered the sentence in a stretch; he turned now and began to pace in the other direction. 'The place of women' – his voice had slowed – 'in Islam' – he said it with imploring sweetness – 'is better than their place before the advent of Islam in Arabia.'

Hands moved quickly and efficiently. A few had finished with the writing and made a show of it; they went into hair, went to rest on cheeks, implying boredom and superiority. The boy at the desk across was still writing, but leisurely, his hand working in a continuous slanting motion. As he wrote he seemed to drift in and out of consciousness, leaning forward and back and then turning the angle of his face for perspective. He stopped now to examine the work, and his look was searching and then pleased, aware of his achievement, for while appearing to write he had begun to make a drawing.

He settled his hands on the desk and looked up at the teacher, his small dark face finely angled, culminating in a sharp chin that was raised slightly with interest. The hands were covering the sheet of paper to hide the drawing.

I looked away.

And he began to draw again, his hand moving with speed: the two eyes already made were darkened with lines above and below, and acquired lids and a sprinkling of lashes.

'Women in Islam,' said Dr Qazi, 'are to be regarded with tenderness. They are not to be inherited. They are not – it is forbidden – to be inherited, like slaves, as they once were. As they? Once were.'

The eyebrows determined the expression and made it artfully unaware.

Woman is given to man in the role of mother, sister, wife and daughter. The Prophet (Peace Be Upon Him) has gone as far as to say that 'Paradise lies at the feet of the mother.'

A line became a triangle, and grew into an M with two dots inside: a nose.

It is said in the Quran, in ayat four and verse thirty-two: 'To men is allotted what they earn, and to women what they earn.'

Two inward-slanting lines made the cheeks, then a plateau for the chin; a final M at the forehead was connected to a cascading hairstyle, and the face of the woman was complete. It now grew a neck and a body in a succession of quick lines and curves.

But there are differences. For while men and women are similar in the eyes of God, they are not made equal. They are not. Men have their place, and women have theirs. And they must know their place. In the Quran it says, surah twenty-four and ayat thirty: 'Say to the believing men that they should lower their gaze and guard their modesty.' And in the next line it says: 'And say to the believing women that they should lower their gaze and guard their modesty.'

The completed woman stood holding her hips, wearing gloves that came up to her elbows and boots that came up to her knees. There was a mirror beside her, containing a reflection, and an open window on the other side with the sky and the moon and the stars outside.

'Very nice.'

The hand had stopped moving. The drawing was almost finished.

'Beautiful,' said Dr Qazi, smiling.

The boy twirled his pencil slowly in his hand.

'We are learning,' said Dr Qazi to the class, 'about modesty. And this one here' – he thwacked the face with his hand – 'is making *this*' – he thwacked it again – 'in *my* class.' He squeezed the boy by the collar and hauled him up – he lifted limply – and threw him across the floor. The boy stumbled on a chair that was in the way, which the occupant then moved conscientiously to the side.

'Do it again,' said Dr Qazi, crumpling the paper in his fist and throwing it into the ashen fireplace, 'do it again and I will draw it on your smart little face and make you walk around this school in front of everyone, you understand?'

I followed him out of the classroom.

The bell had just rung and the corridor was rushed, but he found a way in it, walking beside the wall, his schoolbag strapped on both shoulders and his thumbs tucked in beneath the straps.

I said, 'That teacher's crazy.'

He was trying to walk ahead, his legs making precise, equal movements.

'You draw a lot?'

It was the wrong thing to ask.

'What's your name?' And this, at least, was not probing or pitying.

'Kazim,' he said in a way that was almost humouring, so that it sounded after a moment like a challenge.

'Zaki Shirazi.'

But he hadn't asked.

So I said, 'It's not right, what that teacher did. He shouldn't have hit you like that in front of the whole class.' But this had the sound of an added affront, so I said, 'Your drawing was really nice.' And then, to make it less meaningful, 'You're good at drawing, you should draw more. You should take art, you'll get good marks in it.'

We had reached the crowded car park, where the boys were waiting on benches and standing among the cars. And the stares were suddenly visible, daunting and stabbing and lustful and even surprised stares that now took on an aspect of reproach. It took a moment to recognize the intention.

'You have a lot of friends,' I said, and laughed without meaning to, hoping that he would understand the impulse and forgive it. But he was already moving ahead into the crowd. 'Bye,' he said, almost cheerfully, and walked on.

Kazim went home that afternoon in the school bus. And it brought him back in the morning: he emerged from the rear door, his hair combed back, his tie askew, a button missing from the middle of his shirt and his shoes polished and shining – an odd mixture of particularity and vagueness, a display of attention to a few chosen details within a larger negligence. He wore his schoolbag in the same way, tightly and protectively with his thumbs under the straps; and in that odd way, with legs that seemed to have only now learned to carry out the task, he stepped off the bus and began to walk.

He was absent at assembly and late to class. When he was present he appeared to listen and to work in his notebook, and was then found to have drawn inside the margins, below diagrams and on graphs. It was ignored by some teachers, but to others it gave a fresh chance for enactments of contempt and fury and revulsion that were later ascribed to the need for discipline, without which, they said, no schoolboy's character could be formed. In the first month alone Kazim Naseer was sent three times to the coordinator's office, twice for insulting a teacher (vulgarities were found at the back of his submitted homework) and once for failing to answer a simple question in class, which showed that he was elsewhere, mentally, even as he appeared to be involved.

He liked to spend the thirty-minute lunch break in the art room, which was located in an upstairs corridor of the senior building. It was here, in this large, many-windowed room, among the bottles of turpentine and linseed oil, the hardened brushes softening in the sink and the canvases recovering on easels and the paint tubes laid out on the windowsills, that he was free at last to do as he wished: he made his drawings on large, coloured sheets of chart-paper, using the crayons and markers he had got out of the supplies cupboard. He repeatedly changed his place, for he tired quickly of locations, and went to observe the progress of the few other boys who were allowed to work inside the room. (Entry was regulated by a slim, polite man who had once been a communist and was now an art teacher; he lived in a small brick house behind the campus, the nearness of which caused him to come and go at will, a habit that was noted by other teachers and had led to complaints.) The boys who came to the art room were not of a uniform disposition; they were athletes and debaters and academics, and some who had no professed interest or talent to mark them out; but here they wore aprons and worked with the same materials, and spoke to one another in the shared language of art. Some were better than others: a senior called Salman had a startling gift for rendering things exactly as they appeared in life; one of his paintings, the picture of an ordinary jar beside a window, was up in the principal's office and was displayed every year in the talent show. And there was a boy who had gone around with sticks of charcoal to the historic monuments of Lahore and produced sketches that were later shown in the youth section of an English-language newspaper. But the art teacher had told Kazim that he alone had expression, an ability to bring things out in novel ways. *Village Life* consisted of four murals that were up outside the art room and showed women, one from each province of the country, in traditional dress and setting, though even here they had staring eyes and sharply angled faces and developed postures that made them seem, among the even fields and matching trees and far-off bullock-carts, like transplanted entities.

One day he went upstairs and found that the murals had been defaced: someone had drawn a moustache on each of the women, the same black line in marker.

'Whores,' he said.

This was a habit: whenever he was called upon to give an account of something, to describe an event or explain a happening, he resorted to a language of types in which everyone was assigned a motive and a mission, and was made, in the end, a female. And so the principal and the coordinator were witches, with hidden lives in their offices, and had brooms and cats at home; the English teacher was 'Alto', named after a stout, economical car, while Dr Qazi with his henna-dyed beard was Ginger Spice. 'She's bursting,' said Kazim conspiratorially after enduring one of the beatings, which had reddened his ears and left a cut on his lip, a beating again observed in silence in the classroom, 'she's going to go home and suck on a carrot.'

We were walking towards the canteen, and passed the senior benches on the way. A monitor watched with surprised amusement as one of his friends stood up, placed a hand on his heart and began to sing a song about a girl with a tantalizing gait. The boys around him hooted and clapped.

I said, 'Don't you feel ashamed?'

And Kazim sighed, as if the only thing to feel here was exasperation, and said that they were dried-up women who went home to hidden lives, to armchairs and fridges and radios, and he carried on with this imagery all the way to the canteen, developing scenarios and laughing at comeuppances that hadn't been suffered and wouldn't be suffered, and kept it alive until we had entered the crowded area inside, where the real noise ate it up.

*

I was alone when Kazim withdrew to the art room. On those days I had to walk myself to the canteen, where I was not without options: Saif, my first friend, was still approachable. He had by now established his place at a bench behind the cypress trees, where he sat with two unchanging companions, friends from before. They were joined sometimes by others, who always brought their own food and left before the bell had rung, which was required of itinerants. Saif still offered to share his food with them but didn't insist when it was declined; restraint was a part of his personality.

'Shirazi!' he cried. He was sitting on the stone bench with his arms spread out and his feet lodged on the table.

I sat across from him on the adjacent bench, shook his hand, then shook the hands of his friends.

'Thirst,' said Mooji, one of the friends, a dark, muscular boy with a long face. He stood up and yawned.

'Coke?' said Saif.

Mooji thought about it and said, 'Coke.'

Saif took out the money from his wallet. The third boy, who sat slouching into himself with his elbows in his palms, was called EQ, which was short for something. He made no contribution to the funds, and didn't seem to think it was required.

'Shirazi?' said Saif – he was handing out the money. 'What do you want? Coke Fanta Sprite?'

'Fanta for him,' said Mooji.

EQ laughed.

Saif was looking at me and waiting for an answer.

'Coke,' I said.

'Coke,' said Saif. He passed the money to Mooji, who took it with him into the canteen.

'Where's your friend?' said EQ. He was looking at the tops of his fingernails. They were gnawed down and lined with filth.

'Oi,' said Saif.

EQ grunted and bit into his thumbnail. He tore it off and spat it out; the undernail was pink.

'Fucking animal,' said Saif, and his disgust was encouraging, a compliment EQ had earned. 'Fucking *rhino*.'

EQ was biting his other thumb.

Mooji returned with the Coke bottles held between the fingers of one hand. He placed them on the cracked stone table, and lowered himself slowly into the bench, looking around and frowning as if alerted to an ever-expanding threat in his surroundings.

'Cheers, mate,' he said in a jolly Australian accent; he laughed briefly and determinedly to fill the ensuing silence, and took quick, scowling gulps of the Coke. 'So,' he said, bouncing a knee in anticipation, wanting to hear some jokes since his own hadn't led to amusement, 'Shirazi's got a girlfriend?' He looked from me to Saif in puzzlement.

Saif shook his head disappointedly. 'Mooji, man,' he groaned, and then in a confidential whisper to me: 'Mooji's a homo. There's no cure for him.'

EQ was ecstatic.

'Oi!' cried Mooji, feigning offence, the kind that hasn't been felt: he made as if to strike Saif, then withdrew the hand and brought it down on EQ's back.

'Bastard!' cried EQ, whose hide was human after all.

Mooji chuckled, and EQ rubbed his own back to soothe the sting.

'Amazing,' said Saif, shaking his head and laughing in undisguised enjoyment, 'aren't they amazing? I tell you, Shirazi: stay with them and you'll never run out of entertainment.'

But Mooji said, 'He has entertainment,' and plugged the bottle firmly and frankly into his mouth.

'It's getting late,' I said.

'I know,' he said, with a knowingness he didn't have. 'It's time for the bats to fly.' He looked up at the sky, where the early dark was still a clear blue, undisturbed by bats or other beings in powered flight.

We were sitting on the pavement by the basketball courts and waiting for collection. I was waiting for my car, Kazim for the bus. We had just finished with a cross-country run, or I had, since Kazim had refused to participate on the pretext of an ailment; he got excused by showing a doctor's letter he had drafted himself at home but typed out and signed, the amount of fabrication on display outdone in the end by the amount of will. After the first few questions the coach had stopped arguing, then stopped staring and noticing as well.

'Why don't you play?' I said.

He said, 'My, my.'

'I'm serious.'

'So am I.'

'You're not.' I snatched the notebook from his hand.

'It's mine,' he said.

I flung it across the court. It flew a good distance and then fanned out and succumbed.

He got up archly and went across the court to fetch the fallen notebook. And I went to shoot hoops into the basket. But the ball wouldn't go in. I tried with patience and then in a blind fury of repetitions.

'Zaki!' he cried.

I ignored it.

'Hel-*lo*!'

The ball struck the rim, dithered, dropped.

'Miss Moodswing!'

'What!'

And I heard him say, 'Your car's here,' and then the sound of an abandoned ball continuing to bounce on its own doomed course behind me.

I was going to Kazim's house and my mother wanted to know for how long.

'A few hours,' I said.

'When should I send the car?'

'In the evening.'

'It's already evening, Zaki.'

Daadi said, 'Who is this Kazim?'

'A friend of his from school,' said my mother, and then, prompted by the question into another: 'What do his parents do?'

'I don't know.'

'Well, we should know where you're going, shouldn't we?' She stood with one hand on her hip and the other held out in a challenge of maternal concern.

But Daadi was glad to know that friends were being made. 'Don't worry about the car,' she said. 'It can stay with you. We don't need it here. Take Barkat. You can come back whenever you want.'

Barkat drove me to the house, which was located beyond the

bridge in a place called Township; the road here was cracked and undivided and appeared to function as one large thoroughfare. On the way we passed the site of an accident, the smaller car crushed into the mouth of a wagon. There were no lights on the road, which was littered with glass, and the vehicles continued to come and go at tilting speeds. We found the house behind an arching sign for the Law College, in a lane that had led directly from the main road but was surprisingly quiet, saved by its interiority from the noise outside.

Kazim appeared from behind the low gate. He was wearing socks and no shoes.

'You're here,' he said.

I went in through the gate.

He closed the gate and went on tiptoe into the house.

It was dim. The sofas were covered in plastic, the TV covered in cloth. A small crystal vase on a table had bright plastic flowers. On the way to his room we passed the kitchen, and it had a rich, meaty smell; the hiss of frying oil now confirmed that someone was cooking. Kazim went ahead into his room: there was a bed and a wardrobe, and three small cushions on the carpet.

'Sit,' he said, indicating a cushion. He went over to the bed and brought back his pen, his textbooks, his notebook, all dropped now on the carpet. We were going to study for the physics exam, which was scheduled for the following week, the start of the half-yearly examination period.

We spent the first hour attempting the multiple-choice questions in the physics topic book: it was made up of past exams, and provided the range of questions from which the examiner could choose.

'What do you think they did when they had no topic books?' he asked, closing the book.

'They must've studied from their notes.'

'How did they come up with the questions? If they didn't have any to repeat . . .'

'They probably made their own.'

He thought about it, crossed his legs and said, 'I can't imagine

Cobra coming up with her own.' Cobra was the physics teacher, fidgety and only slightly sibilant, a man.

I said, 'What question are you on?'

But he didn't want to study any more.

'No,' I said. 'I'm here to study, not to play with you.' And I reached for the larger book, the assigned textbook, and turned its diagrammed pages.

The door opened, and a woman entered with a tray: she smiled and nodded shyly and looked around for a place to put it.

Kazim tried to take it from her.

'Let me . . .' she said.

'It's fine,' he said.

She surrendered the tray and stood there another moment, wringing her hands. She said she had put the sandwiches in the lower compartment.

Kazim said, 'It's fine,' and stared into his lap until she had left the room.

'I'm sorry,' he said after she had gone. 'She's just' – he mimed an indescribable frustration – 'she's just like that.'

'Like what?'

'I can't explain it. You can't understand.'

'Why not?'

'You can't.'

'Why?'

It had led into a precarious excitement.

'Why?' I said, touching his arm, his foot. 'Why?'

'Stop it,' he said.

'You want me to stop it?'

We appeared then to fight, and it was the opposite of what we were doing, but there is a release in occupying an estrangement, and it gives weight to wishes and ways of arriving satisfactorily at what we already know. Afterwards it was possible to stay in that room without having to think about the smell of breath and the taste of spit, so like my own, and to see the linkless silence for what it was: a place waiting for words.

'Your house is nice,' I said. I was lying on the floor with my head on a pillow, gazing up at the ceiling now, appearing to think.

He was sitting across with his notebook and making something in it; he turned his head to one side, held up the pencil, closed one eye, then brought the pencil back to the page.

'What are you doing?'

'Nothing.'

'Show me.'

'Wait.'

I snatched it. And he tried to take it back but I had seen the drawing; and there were drawings on every page, profiles and frontal poses and drawings of the back of the head, still recognizable, and made with a knowledge that exceeded my own.

I said, 'When did you make these?' I was turning the pages to see how much there was of me.

'Different times,' he said. 'Mostly in class.'

There were drawings of the eyes alone, of other isolated features as well, of nose, mouth, hands.

'Can you make me from memory?'

'I can,' he said. 'You're simple.'

The next day there was no school, and I went with my mother to the office with my books. It was too late at night to get together for studying, and I called Kazim from the office and told him I wouldn't make it. We had planned to meet after the weekend, but the weekend came and went, and then the exams had started; we saw each other at school in the morning and exchanged notes before and after the exam, but then he had to go, relying on the school bus, which waited for no one, and I stayed on the campus with the other boys and took my time getting home.

14

Fresh elections were held in spring. The previous government, ousted on charges of corruption, lost at the polls; and the largest opposition party tore into power with an astounding two-thirds majority in the National Assembly.

'Well, it is expected,' said Suri, who claimed to have stood in the queue for almost an hour to cast her vote; 'the better party has won. And why not. The people are not fools all the time.' She sat looking sideways with the surviving indignation of a victor who has not forgotten the times of hardship.

'It is true,' said Daadi, who had also gone to cast her vote, and had later flaunted her inky thumb at home, 'these elections are the fairest I have seen.' Her mood was influenced by the news she had heard in the morning: Chhoti had called from Barampur to say that Uncle Fazal's favoured candidate had won the local elections and was going to become a minister in the next government. And although she had sounded merry on the phone, Chhoti had not allowed a longer conversation to take place.

'At least,' said Daadi afterwards, 'we now *know* someone in the government.'

'Oh yes,' said my mother, who had refused to vote, 'everyone we know is a minister, or knows a minister. We are the minister class. Ask Zaki: his friend's father is going to get a post.'

The implements of power were made available to Saif's father the week before he was sworn in: four security guards arrived with weapons and uniforms, to confirm publicly the possibility of a threat: two of the men went with Saif's father to Islamabad and the other two were given to Saif, along with a new jeep that displayed a small green flag on the bonnet and two green government number plates. The week after the jeep arrived Saif took me in it to Hall Road: he wanted new speakers. At the shop he sat in the driver's seat and reclined it all the way until he was almost supine, like someone on a beach. I stood outside, at the back of the jeep, and supervised the installation of the woofers, which we later tested in the car, playing the music at bursting volume. 'This is good shit,' said Saif, nodding his approval. 'Nice job, don.'

At school he applied for a house transfer and got it: I was to mark him present now at house events he no longer wanted to attend. (The only sport he enjoyed was tent-pegging, and his father encouraged it, and had bought him a thoroughbred from a stud farm in Jhang and kept it in the stables at the polo grounds behind the campus.) So I persuaded the coach on the sports field and spoke to the house monitor after assembly; I submitted his letters of absence to the coordinator's office on days when Saif was missing, when he wanted to stay at home and sleep. His nights were busy, and Mooji and EQ were expected to join him.

Later in the term he applied for a transfer to my section. Mooji and EQ sent in their applications too, but theirs were denied. Saif moved in one morning without a schoolbag, without a book: he sat in the desk next to mine and didn't acknowledge the invasion when the rightful occupant walked in.

'What's his name?' Saif asked in a prankish whisper.

'Kazim Naseer,' I said.

For exams we studied together at Saif's house. Mooji, EQ and I virtually lived for those days of preparation in the new 'portion', or wing, built in the upstairs part of that house: it was one bedroom attached to a large, formless space that had a winding oak bar, with mirrors behind the empty bottles, and sunken leather sofas that went along the walls and faced a large, flat TV screen. I studied for myself but didn't refuse to share my work with the others.

'Don!' said Mooji when the results came in. 'Cheetah-man!' He had passed all the subjects.

EQ gave a grudging grunt because he had failed in two subjects and barely passed the other six.

'Now we have to make you the monitor of the house,' said Saif, working it out uncertainly in the air, and finding to his amazement that it was entirely possible. 'That's it!' he cried. 'That's what we need!'

It was unrequired and also ultimately transparent, but was provided in the form of a promise, so that it enabled a distinct perception of myself, as a success sensed by others, to come into being.

Our acquaintances extended beyond the boundaries of the Wilson Academy campus. We functioned now as a group, and were friendly with other groups: we had alliances with boys at Beaconhouse Academy, Aitchison College and Ibn-e-Sina Foundation, and later with a group of boys who patrolled the grounds of the old campus of Punjab University. This last group was our most valued: the boys were known to us through Mooji, whose cousin was studying chemical engineering at the college and was also a member of the IJT, the student wing of the Jamaat-i-Islami. They had been in the news for demanding segregation between boys and girls in the campus canteen, and were known to threaten and beat the students who violated their edicts. We referred to them as Atif Bhai's boys (Atif Bhai was Mooji's cousin) and had met them only once, at the venue of a fight we had scheduled to take place outside a popular restaurant, where Atif Bhai and his boys had shown up on motorcycles, wearing shalwar kameezes and carrying chains. They spoke only Urdu, and attacked the other side with unexpected ferocity: two of the boys they attacked were taken to a hospital, and Saif's father called their parents and gave them money for their silence. Saif stayed at home for the next few days because he was advised to avoid being seen, and I went to his house with my homework and took his assignments to school in the mornings.

Mooji said, 'Don's in hiding.'

'Incognito,' said EQ, using a word he had learned recently.

But Saif was unconcerned; the incident with Atif Bhai's boys had entered the consciousness of his enemies and had increased his fame.

On weekends there were parties at Saif's house. Preparations began in the early evening: it was left to Mooji and EQ to fetch the alcohol, and they always went with the security guards, in whose presence the car was never stopped; the uniforms were recognized by the policemen who stood on street corners at night and waited to confiscate the bottles. Ours came from a man called Bhatti; it was the only name he gave, and he insisted on meeting in unlit residential areas, where he waited with a duffel bag strapped to the back of his motorcycle. He sold imported bottles of whisky and vodka, though Saif enjoyed wine too and had begun to stock it for the girls who came more and more to his house. But on most nights it was only the boys: they came from all over the city, boys our age and older, and sometimes grown men who possessed the spirit of a prolonged and carefree youth. These gatherings were called sessions: the alcohol was drunk above the music, which was played on a colourful new stereo that sat beside the wooden bar and made turbo swirls of blue and pink that grew and shrank and revived continually on the small black display screen. Good nights culminated in the smoking of hashish, which came from Billy Goodshit, an ambitious and talkative junior at school whose real name was Bilal. The first time he came to Saif's house he was wearing a baseball cap, and it was snatched and thrown around until we were steeped in the lull of the drug, and had to listen to Billy Goodshit's made-up monologue in silence, finding whatever observations we were having too arduous to articulate.

And there were other nights of action only, of loud, fast music and incessant chatter, the confidence of the boys derived from the confidence of the girls who came with them. Two girls were always present and came together. Their names were Uzma and Sparkle. Uzma was Saif's girlfriend, someone he had met in a popular chat room on the Internet: Saif was an SOP on the channel, a Super Operator, and had passed on his powers to Uzma, whom he had glimpsed only once in the darkened audience of a play at Gaddafi Stadium. He made her an OP, a position below that of the SOP but one that came with the power to ban selected users and change the topic of the channel. So on that first night Uzma had changed the topic to 'Thank You, Mister Blue!!!' (That was Saif's nickname.) And the next day she had set it to 'Sparkle's in Da House!' – a tribute to the girl who was her companion and best friend from school. They were a duo, Uzma and Sparkle: the first time they came to the house there had been some unease, a sense of expectancy that fed a mounting fear of failure: Uzma and Saif had never met, only chatted on the Internet, and he had gone now in his car to fetch her. (She lived with her aunt in Iqbal Town, in a house that didn't have an address plaque and was indistinguishable from the other small houses in the area. And she didn't have a car of her own, and was going in Sparkle's car to a restaurant, from where Saif was going to pick her up.) We waited in the upstairs wing, EQ and Mooji and I, and were relieved when they entered: Uzma was a lithe, kind girl with a withered beauty, like that of someone much older, and had quickly shown her devotion to Saif, of which he became stoically aware; and Sparkle was loud and frank and friendly, a chubby, chocolatey girl who asked many questions and became quickly scandalized, which was the impression she wished to create on that first night: it later emerged that she knew our history, the things we had done and even some of the things we had said to one another and could no longer recall, things she somehow knew and mentioned in conversations to create the effect of a deep, human knowledge. Towards the end of one of those nights she had taken me aside and made a proposition: there was a girl she knew, a girl called Farwa, she was pretty and came from Multan and lived in the all-girls hostel at Kinnaird College. Sparkle said she wanted me to try out the girl for her. 'She's from Multan,' said Sparkle, 'so she's a bit reserved. But I think she needs to be opened up. I think you're the one who has to open her up.' And she was speaking of suitability, of external symmetries she had sensed and now wanted to set in motion.

Sparkle made the introduction in a group window on the Internet. Then she withdrew for some days, supplying the things I had to say, lubricating things that had led by the end of the week to conversations on the phone. The week after that we went out to a restaurant, and Farwa and I were sitting there and starting to talk when Sparkle appeared – she had coordinated her arrival – and came and sat with us at the secluded table, talking loudly and picking compulsively at our portions, though she herself was on a diet and wasn't going to place an order. 'I'm not eating!' she cried. 'I'm just trying it out, okay?'

We settled on a weekend. Saif had gone with Uzma to the polo grounds, and had left me with the keys to his house and car. The car now had tinted windows, a security requirement insisted upon by Saif's father: the view from within was dark, but the view from outside was blocked – no one could see the driving. I drove it to the Kinnaird College hostel and waited in the row of parked cars outside. It had begun to rain, the start of a predicted shower; I switched on the radio and listened to it for some minutes. Then Farwa had appeared, she was sitting beside me in the front of the car, and I drove her to Saif's house and led her upstairs into the wing. And I returned her to the hostel at night, in the rain that hadn't stopped all evening, that had continued to gather weight and now hammered frantically; I watched her hurry out in the wetness, and pulled out of that car park, the car pushing on against the rain, hot and moist inside and wrapped in noise.

15

The sounds came from behind the door, and the wife heard them and awoke. They were tapping on the door; then they broke past it. There were many of them, policemen in uniforms and also in ordinary clothes, and they had rifles and guns with which they beat the editor, who was sitting up in his bed. The editor's wife asked to see an arrest warrant. One of the officers said he'd show her a death warrant instead.

They tied her arms and locked her in the bathroom, and they took the editor away.

It was reported in the newspapers. They were saying he had made a speech in India, an anti-Pakistan speech in which he'd criticized his own country; and the government was saying that it amounted to an act of treason, and could lead to a trial in a military court. Some had even written in to say that he was a spy for the Indian agencies and not really a Muslim.

'They are saying it,' said Daadi, who had read the columns in the Urdu newspapers. 'There must be some truth in what they are saying.'

My mother said, 'That's what they'll say when they come for me tomorrow.' It was morning and she was in a hurry; she was going with the editor's wife to the High Court to file a petition for the editor's release.

'God forbid,' said Daadi.

'You can't leave it to God,' said my mother.

'Don't say such things!'

'Can't leave it to anyone.'

'But why must you go?'

'I have to.'

Daadi went into the dressing room, returned with an amulet, hung it around my mother's neck and said that it would bring

317

bad luck if she took it off before the period of uncertainty had ended.

Daadi had voted in the last election for the leader of what was then the opposition party. She went with Suri and Hukmi to the voting booths in the FC College grounds, dabbed her thumb in purple ink, pressed it on the voting slip, oversaw the insertion of the slip into the green box, and came home and held up the stain on her thumb.

She was pleased when her man won the election. She wore her large glasses and sat before the TV, and heard his address to the nation, in which he talked about the well-known corruption of the last government, and promised to make improvements, to build roads and give electricity and gas to the villages. He spoke in a halting, roving way, repeating phrases and saying the words in different pitches, until he had landed like an airborne thing on the end of his original point.

Daadi watched his round, fair face, his large, fair hands, and said with a mixture of surprise and admiration that he looked like a foreigner.

'The wife is even fairer,' said Suri, who had seen her in a shop.

'The whole family,' said Hukmi.

But there were stories about him, and they had led to accusations that were being considered in the Supreme Court.

Daadi said, 'The judges are making a mistake.'

The Supreme Court building was attacked. A clip from the storming was shown again and again on the news channels: a minister from the present government was leading the mob of agitators towards the big white building in Islamabad. The judges were hearing the case inside.

Daadi said, 'Judges? They are the most corrupt.'

The president of the country resigned and a new one was appointed.

Daadi said, 'It happens.'

My mother said the new prime minister was trying to become the king of the country.

Daadi said it was a misunderstanding that had happened between two people. 'It happens all the time,' she said. 'People come and people go. Not everything is like your politics.'

Then, at the start of the summer, it was reported that India had tested a nuclear missile. The footage was shown on the channels, the beige uniforms of the marching Indian soldiers and the slogans of the crowds that cheered for them in the streets.

Daadi said, 'They are coming.'

My mother said, 'There will be sanctions.'

But Daadi said, 'They will come. Allah help us. They will come for us now.'

Pakistan responded to India's nuclear tests by conducting its own: the footage of the trembling desert, where the tests were conducted, was accompanied by the sound of a distant rumbling. There was dancing in the streets of Lahore. Naseem came home at night from the market and said that the world was ablaze with lights, there were firecrackers and fireworks everywhere, she had heard the firing and seen the men with the Kalashnikovs standing on rooftops.

Daadi said, 'He showed those Indians. Now they will not come, those little black Hindus.'

Naseem became emotional and said, *Vekho ji, bum da kamal.*

The government declared a state of emergency. A voice on Radio Pakistan announced in the morning that the right to convene any court, including a High Court or the Supreme Court, had been temporarily suspended.

My mother laughed and said, 'King of this country.'

He appeared on PTV, sitting at a desk with a portrait of the Founder of the Nation in its golden frame behind him on the wall, and said that the world was trying to punish Pakistan for declaring its independence. These were trying times, he said, but Pakistan had always emerged from its trials. He urged his fellow citizens, his brothers and his sisters, to stand with him in this time, to cut down on their daily spending and to pause and to think.

Hukmi said, 'Be a Pakistani and buy the Pakistani,' and it was a formal-sounding version of the slogan that was attached to the back of her car.

Suri said, 'If we don't, who will?'

So the air-conditioner settings were altered from High Cool to Low Cool and the number of dishes at lunchtime and dinnertime was reduced from four to three. The use of air-freshener, identified in this time of introspection as an unnecessary expense, was temporarily suspended; and there was no more buying of imported goods.

At night Naseem sat before the TV on the carpet, the lights in the room switched off, her face flickering in the TV darkness, and watched Pakistani songs, Pakistani ads for Pakistani goods, and cheered on the sports channel for Pakistani teams. Then she switched it off and went away, saying that she wanted to save the electricity for the country.

'It will not take long,' said Daadi, 'for things in our country to improve. Everyone is doing something. Everyone, from top to bottom, is making an effort. Everything will be all right.'

One day in late summer, a hot, windless day on which the clouds were dark and bulging but gave no rain, Suri and Hukmi came to the house and announced that there was going to be a new way of referring to the prime minister.

'Ameer-ul-Momineen,' said Hukmi, drawing it out.

Daadi was impressed. She said, 'What does it mean?'

'It means,' said Suri, 'that he will be' – she thought about it – 'from now on' – she was thinking – 'the *ameer*' – she was hesitant – 'of the' – but she was succeeding – 'of the *momins*. Yes, from *momin*, the word, comes *momineen*.' She looked at Hukmi and said, 'Is that right?'

Hukmi closed her eyes and said, 'Quite right, quite right.'

Daadi looked from one daughter to the other. 'I see,' she said, 'I see.'

'Yes, yes,' said Suri, and lifted one foot from the floor and brought it up to the table, and settled it there, just to show that she could.

'Oh very good,' said Hukmi, who couldn't have done the same with her own foot.

Daadi said, 'It is a good name.'

And Suri laughed wildly and said, 'It's not a name! It's a title!'

'A title,' said Daadi.

Suri looked at Hukmi and said, 'She thinks it's a name!'

Hukmi glowered and shook her head and said, 'Just look at her,' and reached with her hand for the crystal bowl on the table, a bowl that was empty. She looked around the room and said, 'Some peanuts, some cashews. There must be something.'

Suri said, 'Must be.'

Daadi raised her head from the pillow on her bed and cried, 'Naseem? O Naseem!'

In the morning the text of the proposed bill appeared in the newspapers. The prime minister wanted to amend the constitution, and the amendment included the clause that mentioned the change in his title:

A Bill further to amend the Constitution of the Islamic Republic of Pakistan:

WHEREAS sovereignty over the entire universe belongs to Almighty Allah alone and the authority which He has delegated to the State of Pakistan through its people for being exercised through their chosen representatives within the limits prescribed by Him is a sacred trust;

AND WHEREAS the Objectives Resolution has been made a substantive part of the Constitution;

AND WHEREAS Islam is the State religion of Pakistan and it is the obligation of the State to enable the Muslims of Pakistan, individually and collectively, to order their lives in accordance with the fundamental principles and basic concepts of Islam as set out in the Holy Quran and Sunnah;

AND WHEREAS Islam enjoins the establishment of a social order based on Islamic values, of prescribing what is right and forbidding what is wrong (*amr bil ma'roof wa nahi anil munkar*);

AND WHEREAS in order to achieve the aforesaid objective and goal, it is expedient further to amend the Constitution of the Islamic Republic of Pakistan;

NOW, THEREFORE, it is hereby enacted as follows . . .

My mother came into the room for breakfast and Daadi gave her the newspapers.

'Have you seen this?' said Daadi.

'Seen what?' said my mother. She had sat down in her chair and was making her tea on the tray.

'The bill.'

'What bill?'

'This one,' said Daadi, and indicated the newspapers. 'The one you are holding in your hand.'

My mother said, 'I will look at it.'

She read the pages and drank her tea.

Daadi said, 'So?'

'So what?'

'What does it say?'

'You have read it. It says what it says.'

'But what does it mean?'

My mother folded the newspaper and placed it in her lap, looked at Daadi, then at Naseem, and said, 'It means that you have voted for someone who wants to make himself a king of your country. That is the meaning of your bill. Your savings and your spendings, all of it has been for this.'

Naseem was amused.

Daadi said, 'It is all exaggerated,' and drew her hands into her lap, and made efforts to smooth out the wrinkles in the hem of her kameez, and continued to smile and sway her head from one side to the other.

A few months after the journalists were attacked, on an afternoon in October, Daadi was woken by a lilting steady sound that she knew to be the voice of a newsreader. At first she turned her head on the pillow in resistance. Then she sat up and saw that someone was in the room.

She left the bed and joined my mother on the sofa. The prime minister was attaching shiny medals to a man's shoulders, a smiling army man in the army uniform. The people around them were clapping.

'What is it?' said Daadi.

'New army chief,' said my mother.

'Where is the old one?'

'On a flight.'

They watched for developments.

Then Daadi said, 'To where is the flight?'

'To nowhere,' said my mother. 'He's been sacked and his plane is not allowed to land.'

Daadi thought about it and said, 'So where will he go, then?'

'I don't know.'

'What will they do?'

'I don't know.'

They watched the rest of the bulletin in an uncertain silence. Naseem came in, saw their expressions and sat down on the carpet.

The TV screen was black.

Daadi said, 'The wires.'

But the wires were in their places.

Now there were flowers on TV, an unmoving picture, and then an old recording of a singer with many mirrors behind her.

My mother went to the mantelpiece. She picked up the phone and dialled a number, waiting with her elbow in her palm, the phone in her other hand. 'Nargis?' she said, and listened. Her mouth opened, closed, and opened again, but her expression was the same. She nodded and said, 'Yes, yes, I will.' She hung up the phone and said, 'Change the channel, change it, change it.'

Naseem scrambled across to the TV.

'Stop,' said my mother. 'Leave it there.'

Soldiers were climbing a wall.

'Say something!' said Daadi.

My mother said, 'Four army jawaans and one major. Surrounded PTV headquarters. Prime minister under house arrest.'

'Allah!' cried Daadi and placed a hand on her mouth.

Naseem said, 'Should I change it?'

'PTV,' said my mother.

PTV was still showing songs.

'It's started,' said my mother.

They watched the foreign news channels and heard the discussions about the fragile situation in Pakistan, where ordinary people, it was being said, had not shown any signs of participation in the drama that was occurring in Islamabad. The footage was the same – soldiers climbing a wall – and was combined with pictures of the empty streets. They returned to PTV but it was still showing songs. And then, from different sources, the story was made to move: the army was everywhere; their trucks were going into the streets; PTV headquarters was surrounded; the prime minister was still under house arrest; the sacked army chief had finally landed, with very little fuel in his aircraft, and was going to change his clothes and appear on PTV to address the nation.

'Martial law,' said Daadi.

'Martial law,' said my mother.

They changed the channels and Naseem went into the kitchen.

*

At assembly the next morning there was no mention of the takeover, except for a suggestion that occurred when Coordinator Hassan, handing out medals to the wrestling team, said that brawn too was important in life. Later in the classrooms there was talk of arrests: they were going to take in the ministers and aides who were closest to the former government; and they were setting up an accountability bureau and had begun to make lists.

At lunch break, when we were walking to the canteen, Saif laughed and said, 'What a show. What a show.'

He didn't mention his father, and I didn't ask him.

*

Barkat went away that afternoon, taking the two-day leave he was allowed at the start of every month, and in the evening I took Naseem in the car to Main Market. We went first to Jalal Sons: she went into the stark white aisles inside and selected the insect-repelling Flit-dispensers, the small white phenyl balls that were placed above the drains of bathrooms and came in plastic packets, a stack of Capri soaps, three small jars of Dentonic dental powder and

324

three tubes of Medicam toothpaste; she dropped the items into the trolley and went into Feminine Care, selected Bio Amla shampoo and Kala Kola hair tonic, a tin of Touch Me talcum powder, a small blue bottle of Nivea face cream for Daadi and a tub of the cheaper Tibet Snow fairness cream for herself. I waited with the trolley at the till when she went upstairs to fetch the bread and eggs and milk. Then I drove her to the fruit-and-vegetable stalls outside Pioneer Store, where many cars and motorcycles were already parked, and where a slowed line of rickshas, and cars and wagons behind them, was trying to get to the other end of the street.

In the spreading dark, standing in the light of the bulbs that hung from wires above the stalls, Naseem examined the fruits and vegetables with her hand and made selections: apples, oranges, bananas, carrots, cabbages, cucumbers and a kilo of horseradish. They were weighed, placed in blue plastic bags and taken to the car. The vendor's assistant arranged the bags in the seats at the back and stood outside my window.

'Give him money,' said Naseem.

I paid him for the fruits and vegetables we had bought.

He was still there.

'Give a tip,' said Naseem.

I gave him ten rupees.

'Give more,' said Naseem.

I gave him another ten-rupee note, and he took it and went away.

'It is good to give,' said Naseem.

We drove with difficulty through the street, between the jutting bodies of parked vehicles, went along the roundabout and turned in towards the mosque. The azaan was sounding, and boys in skullcaps were going inside.

Naseem switched off the radio and drew her dupatta over her head. She looked outside at the boys in skullcaps and said, 'It is good to pray in the mosque. At your age it is very important.'

I said, 'I should.'

We left the mosque behind, and went past a butcher's shop where pink, headless torsos were hanging from strings.

'At every age,' said Naseem, 'there is a chance to repent.' She said that she had understood this only recently, at a time in her life when she no longer possessed the energies of youth. Still, she said, a man's youth was something else, a time of determinations and will. She said her own son was like that. He was intelligent but had fought with his schoolteachers and quit the school; then he had worked as a labourer and made buildings with his bare hands, but had quit that too when the contractor, joking around one day, had called his sister a name. Naseem said she had worried then for her son. But he had reassured her; he had taken Allah's name and said that there were many ways in the world.

He came home one day and told them that he was going to buy a car, a wagon, which he was going to fill with passengers, all paying the fare, and take them around the district. There was a route from Dipalpur to Haveli Lakha and then back to Dipalpur, and north from there to Kasur. The average ride was for fifty rupees. The total number of passengers a wagon could fit was fifteen (the one remaining seat in the front was for the driver) and there were at least ten journeys to make in a day. Adding it up, and subtracting the cost of petrol, and then multiplying it by the thirty days of the month gave a total of more than two lakh rupees. But from this he would have to pay the car dealer, who had agreed to receive the second half of the payment in monthly instalments.

'Even so,' he said, 'it will leave thirty thousand rupees.'

They were eating their evening meal in the courtyard of Naseem's house.

Her husband said, 'Allah will give,' and went on eating. He was unemployed, white-haired now, and had no money.

Naseem said, 'Who will buy the wagon? I will buy the wagon?'

Her son was chewing slowly. He finished the food in his plate, drank water from the steel cup and splashed the rest away.

She was filled with regret.

She said, 'How will you do it?'

Her husband went on chewing.

And her son said, 'Allah will give,' and got up from the low stool and went to wash his hands under the tap.

*

She thought of selling her land and giving him the money. She had three marlas behind a railway track, a small plot in a factory-workers' colony that was surrounded by sugarcane fields. She consulted her acquaintances and they advised her against it. The land, they said, was a place to hide her head in case she had to; it was a thing to keep, a thing to sell only when the price was high. She listened to them and agreed with them. But later, alone, she sank imperceptibly into her own thoughts. He was her son; and he would have a car of his own; and a car too was a place to hide one's head, a car had many uses, and could take them to different places. She saw herself sitting in the back seat.

He came home and she fed him, then sat them all down and made the announcement.

The wagon came. She heard about it first from Majida, her neighbour, who banged blatantly on the door and cried, 'Mubari-kaan! Mubarikaan!'

She hurried out to the door.

Majida stood in the doorway with her hand on the latch and said, 'You never told any of us.' Her tone was admiring and reproachful.

Naseem said, 'Is it here?'

'Leh,' said Majida, and took her by the hand, 'what a fool you are pretending to be.'

They went out into the street, and Naseem saw the people who had come out of their homes, saw the surprise and the excitement in their faces and the way they were looking at her.

She drew the dupatta over her head and tried to walk slowly.

'Come quick,' said Majida, leading her still by the hand, 'before the others start sitting on your seats.'

They went down the street and turned the corner. The wagon was standing on the main road, between the shops and the stalls, and was long and high and white and had two green stripes on its side and colourful stickers on the front and on the back.

Her son was sitting in the driver's seat, and was talking to a boy who stood outside his window and had his hands on the felt. Others had gathered around the wagon; they were waiting for a chance to touch it. On the way to the wagon Naseem was stopped by the washerwoman and then by the cobbler, and they were gracious and gave compliments.

Naseem smiled and nodded, adjusted her dupatta and said, '*Vekho ji, rab da kamal.*'

They went in the wagon to the shrine of Hazrat Karman Aley. It was the shrine closest to their village. The wagon was new and needed protection, and they wanted to have it blessed right away. Naseem sat at the back, next to Majida, who had come along, and with a crowd of children in the seats behind them, the little boys and girls who were attracted by the sound of the horn and had attached themselves to the doors.

Naseem said, 'There is no tape?' She meant the audiocassette player that was usually located in the front.

Her husband was sitting in the seat ahead and had his hand on the strap above his window. He said, 'No, no, there is none.'

Naseem's son said, 'There *is* a tape.' And with his one free hand he found the buttons, and abruptly the sound burst from behind, and it was Madam Noor Jehan and she was singing:

> O Bangle of Gold!
> The deal's the same
> Giving love, Taking love
> The deal's the same!

On the wide highway roads they went. It was early evening, and the sun hung low above the sugarcane fields. Their windows were down from before and wouldn't go up, but they were not complaining: the wind was coming in and was tickling their faces, trembling their hairstyles and making their clothes flap.

Majida turned to the children at the back and was harsh and scolding when she said, 'A mother's prayers, a mother's prayers, *that* is what gets you ahead in life.'

Naseem's face was in the wind.

'Mother!' cried Yakub, her son, from his seat in the front.

'Yes!' she cried.

'Are the cars coming?' He was about to turn the wagon, and they saw now that the mirrors were missing.

Naseem stuck her head out, and then drew it back inside and cried, 'There are no cars coming!'

Yakub cried, 'Very good!'

They waited.

And they cheered and whistled when the wagon turned the corner successfully.

The shrine was like a mosque but bigger, more spacious. Naseem knew from her visits to the courtyard inside that it could accommodate more people than almost any other place she had seen. There were no times for opening or closing the doors, and this laxity, while it was in keeping with the large-hearted persona of the dead saint, had also drawn the attention of wandering types, the beggars and drug-users and lunatics who came in and then rarely went away. Now their contingent passed a madwoman, dressed in her customary rags, sitting on a tattered old sheet in a corner of the white marble courtyard, and she looked at them and looked away. She had lost the urge to beg, it was said, because of the food that came here every day in pots from those whose wishes the saint had answered.

The children looked at the madwoman and prodded one another and laughed.

Majida slapped them and said, 'She will come here and eat your little faces.'

They went to the chamber that contained the saint's grave. Naseem's son had bought a chadar from a stall outside, a long, silken sheet that had prayers written on it and glowed differently in different kinds of light. He was going to place it as an offering on the saint's grave and say a prayer of thanks.

The men went inside the chamber. Naseem and Majida had to stay outside because of a new sign that was nailed to the door and said that women, by decree of the shrine's keepers and patrons, were not allowed in the chamber. They stood outside and said the prayer, not requiring the physical closeness.

Then they waited for the men to return.

Majida said, 'Our prayers are more effective than theirs. It is in nature.'

She wanted agreement. She had come here all the way to have Naseem's new wagon blessed and now she wanted some agreement.

Naseem said, 'In this there is no doubt that God listens to women.'

Majida nodded thoughtfully. The dusk had deepened and the lights in the courtyard had come alive, and they could see the mosquitoes above their heads.

Majida said, 'Keep praying, and Allah will keep giving.' It was a way of saying that she was happy for Naseem, and that she had not lost hope for herself.

And Naseem, who was privileged and could speak now from experience, said, 'I have always said it, always.'

It was Majida again who brought the news.

'Open this door!' she cried, banging on it violently.

Naseem came out of her room, went through her courtyard to the door and said, 'What is the matter? What has happened?' She wasn't expecting anything.

But Majida was panting and became anguished and held her temples when she saw Naseem in the doorway, and said that the wagon had been in an accident, the people in the other car were saying it had no mirrors and that was against the law, and the matter was quickly getting out of hand and they were going to take it to the police station.

Naseem stepped out of the house without her shoes. 'Where is it?'

'In the street,' said Majida, acting frail.

Naseem said, 'Who taught them the law? How do they know who has broken it?'

They reached the fray and found that it had finished: Naseem's son was standing on one side of the road with the wagon, which was full of passengers; and on the other side was a much bigger car, a white Cruiser jeep that started up now and began to drive away.

Around the wagon a crowd had gathered.

'*They* break the law,' Naseem's son was saying. 'And *they* blame it on us. It is because they think they have the authority.'

A boy was rubbing his back; another was leaning against the wagon and smoking a cigarette. The passengers inside were waiting for their journey to resume.

Naseem said, 'Where did they hit it?'

Her son showed her the dent on the door.

She said, 'From where are they coming? Why are they telling *us* to talk to them? Do they *want* to go to the police station? Do they want *us* to take them there?'

Majida said loudly, 'She drives a car in the city. She has bought this one with her own money.'

The faces in the crowd were watching.

Later she was told how it had happened: the wagon was emerging from the underpass and was hit from the side by the Cruiser jeep, which had turned in without warning, without so much as a honk. After the collision they stepped out of their cars: in the wagon it was only Yakub, who had been driving; the passengers were his customers and they stayed inside. And in the other car was an old man in a hat, a sweater, a shirt and trousers, sitting with his driver and with a uniformed security guard who stepped out with a gun. That was when the fighting started: people came from all sides to separate them, and it was being said, without consideration of right or wrong, that both sides were at fault and it was best to bury the matter and to go home with the damage.

'But there was one man,' said Yakub, his features dancing in the light of the fire around which they had gathered in the courtyard to listen, 'there was one man in that crowd who knew right from wrong.' And the man was described: he was a young man, not much older than Yakub himself, and he wore white clothes and a black turban on his head, and had a beard but without a moustache. 'He was the one,' said Yakub, 'who saw the dent on the door, who knew right from wrong, and asked to know what had happened, and took the guard's gun from his hand and told him to get in that car and go away.'

'A good man,' said Naseem, who had visualized him.

Her husband said, 'There are good men still in this world.' He was sitting on his haunches, enjoying the warmth from the fire on his palms, showing a ludicrous grin on his face. Naseem had learned after many years to ignore his moods, which went with the moods of those around him.

But her son said, 'I have thought about it. I will ask him to eat with us. When a good man comes along, it is good to be good to him.'

And Naseem said, 'It is a good thing you are thinking, son. I will cook for him with my own hands.'

Dr Shafeek agreed to the meal. Yakub escorted him from the mosque, where he was setting up a new programme, and brought him to the house in the early afternoon. It was a dry day, and the sun blazed above them; they went through the parched courtyard, the brick walls shining, past the kitchen (where Naseem, assisted by Majida, was cooking rotis on the fire) and into the cool room where they kept their belongings: the tin trunk was in the centre, visible below the table; the plastic plates and glasses were on a shelf hacked into the wall; the black-and-white TV (which hadn't worked for some months) was kept on a high shelf in a corner, and was covered with cloth to guard it against the dust. All around there were posters that showed the imagined features of dead saints, of Hazrat Ali with his black beard and green headdress and sword, and of the eccentric Lal Shahbaz Qalandar in a trance, and of the docile-looking Bhulleh Shah, whose shrine in Kasur they had visited in the spring.

Dr Shafeek was looking around the room and had a ready smile on his lips, which were oddly visible in the absence of a moustache and seemed to give his beard an added lift.

'Your wife's decorations?' he asked. He had used the formal word for wife.

Yakub grinned frankly and said, 'Not yet. No wife.'

Dr Shafeek's smile was the same as before.

He said, 'It is a tenet of our religion.'

Yakub nodded.

'You must do it young. And you may have more than one.'

It was said with seriousness.

Yakub said, 'Well, yes: please, eat.' And he raised the lids from the pots that were arranged in a line on the table and which they had brought out for the occasion.

Dr Shafeek expressed a desire to wash his hands.

Yakub led him outside, into the heated courtyard. Dr Shafeek crouched before the tap and washed his hands, his wrists, his elbows, then his mouth and his face. 'It is my habit,' he said afterwards, when they had gone back inside to eat their meal. 'When I was in Saudia, at every meal we washed in this way.' He said he had gone there first to study, and then, later, to obtain donations for the mosque and training centre he was setting up here in the village. 'Over there,' he said, 'it is all desert, all dry and hot.' His mouth was sour with severity, but his eyes were bright. 'It is scorching, scorching. The people are Bedouins.' He smiled wistfully. 'They are used to the heat. Oh yes. Thousands of years they have spent there. They are not like us, not used to this and that. Their lives are spare and simple.'

Yakub was smiling too, as if sharing in the recollection of the Bedouins, seeing the huts and camels and the customs that Dr Shafeek had not yet described.

'*Bismillah,*' said Dr Shafeek.

They ate.

The room was dank and decorated.

Majida came in with fresh rotis, dropped them into a plate and went away.

After she had gone, Dr Shafeek said, 'In Saudia women are separate. They have separate quarters, separate schools. Islam allows. But there are limits.'

Yakub took the hot roti from the plate, broke it in half and placed the other half in Dr Shafeek's plate.

'Your car,' said Dr Shafeek. 'It is new?'

'Very new,' said Yakub, who was assuming that Dr Shafeek had allowed for the manoeuvrings of a previous owner.

'It is a gift from Allah,' said Dr Shafeek.

And Yakub said, 'There is no doubt in it. We were saying yesterday how it was good to get it blessed. Otherwise there are many accidents, and many are fatal, destroying not just the car, which is made of metal, but also the flesh and blood inside, the men and women and the children.' He was talking like a schoolteacher now, which was another of the things he could have been.

Dr Shafeek said, 'Blessed?' His eyes were narrowed and his smile was incredulous and small.

'At the shrine,' said Yakub confidently. 'Hazrat Karman Aley Sharif.'

Dr Shafeek lifted his glass from the table and drank all the water in it. Then he brought it down on the table and gasped. 'My friend,' he said, and burped, 'it is all a fraud. These shrines' – he waved his hand about generally, and it very nearly missed the pictures on the walls – 'they are places of burial. Who is buried inside? A man is buried inside. You think that man is listening to your prayer? How can he listen when he is no more than bones? Who is listening to the wish that you make from your heart?' He was tapping Yakub's heart with his finger. 'Is it your fellow man, whose own heart is full of wishes, good *and* bad wishes, or is it God who knows the things you keep in your soul?'

Yakub had the sense to say, 'God.'

'So why,' said Dr Shafeek, 'are you praying to a man?'

Yakub was nodding.

'Tell me,' said Dr Shafeek and placed a morsel in his mouth, 'who bashed up your car that day?'

Yakub said, 'A man.'

'And who saved your car? Who saved *you* that day?'

Yakub was nodding, and said, 'You did, you did.'

'No,' said Dr Shafeek. 'Allah saved you.'

'Allah,' said Yakub.

'Allah,' said Dr Shafeek.

They continued to eat. They were men. It revealed the act of sitting together in a new light, made it mundane, and made them audacious and unafraid.

Dr Shafeek explained about the concept of *shirk*. It was when people ascribed godlike powers to entities other than God, to mere men (though in some parts of the world they were still worshipping stones and animals, and it was hard to say if that was better or worse), and thereby denied the oneness of God. 'There is only one place to go,' said Dr Shafeek, 'to receive a blessing. And that place is the House of God. You must go. It is your duty as a Muslim. And it is your duty to send your parents, to send your mother, who has no doubt made many sacrifices, and your father, whose blood is in your veins. Send them, and then go yourself, and see the blessings Allah will bestow.'

Dr Shafeek ate the rest of his meal, washed his hands once again in the courtyard and went away. And afterwards it was agreed that his visit to their house had been a visitation. They didn't immediately abandon the notion of shrines (though they saw now that it was a notion) and none of them dared at first to take down the posters from the walls. But on the matter of making the pilgrimage they were decided. Yakub said that he would start saving from the next day and promised to provide two aeroplane tickets for his parents to Saudi Arabia.

'But it is not enough,' said Naseem. 'We will need more than that. We will need for the time that we are there, for the things we will eat and the things we will buy.'

And she said, 'Allah gives. Allah will give. I will find.'

16

Daadi switched off the lights in her room and went to lie down on her bed. She allowed the descent into her thoughts. The day had passed; a government had ended, a new one had begun, and things were at rest. She thought of the soldiers climbing the walls. They were brave. But then she thought: it is duty, nothing more, and they all follow commands delivered by someone else, and their lives are for nothing, and their deaths are for nothing.

She thought it was a dream. And she thought she had forgotten it already, something she did often now, not like in childhood, when she remembered every single dream and what it was made of.

She sat up and swung her legs off the bed, put on her slippers and went into the bathroom.

But when she returned she was filled with dread. If she slept now she would dream again, and she knew that it would lead to mutations of the things she had seen in the day, which were mutations of the things she had seen in her life.

For some minutes she paced the room in the dark.

She went into the dressing room, found the small brass key under the carpet and opened her cupboard. It gave its customary creak, a sound of submission. She opened a drawer, took out an oval tin box and returned with it to the sofa in her room. She switched on a lamp. The pictures inside the box were the same. She saw now, in this half-slumber, that she had stopped collecting photographs at a particular point in time. She could name the year. And she could name the day. It was when her son died.

The crying had been a release until it became a habit, and she recalled the swollen eyes, the throbbing head and the squeezed ribs. She was glad it had stopped. But she wanted to know that she could do it still, and without having to revive a grieving self.

She took out a photograph and held it up like a shield. Her eyes were closed. When she opened them she found an old picture, one of her oldest, from the days when she was still a girl. The girl standing next to her with the hair parted in the middle was Amrita, her friend and neighbour, and they were standing behind the shrubs in Amrita's garden. It was the summer Amrita had left.

The Hindu family next door, the Parsi gentleman who lived in the secretive double-storey house and ran the laundry on Mall Road, and Amrita's family, a Sikh family – all of them had locked their houses and gone away.

The year before things were different. The word 'Pakistan' had been on people's tongues, a word they used mostly in slogans, and their lives in Lahore were unaffected by it. Daadi's father came home in the evenings and spoke about Gandhi going to jail, Nehru going to jail, Jinnah appearing in the newspapers and asking for concessions for the Muslims, and it was a part of his personality, his way of talking in English and smoking cigarettes on his own in the darkened veranda.

'Cripps Mission,' said Daadi in the morning.

'Cabinet Mission,' said Amrita.

The taanga was taking them to school. The horse's click-clock made them bump.

'My dear,' said Daadi, fifteen this summer and newly enamoured of the English language, 'it is all politics.' She said it and leaned back in her seat. The world around them was one of overhanging trees and dirt tracks paved recently for travellers.

'Politics,' said Amrita satisfactorily. Then she said, 'I don't think I look like her at all.' And she meant Noor Jehan, the young singer who had hijacked All-India Radio and was being praised for singing a difficult qawwali in the film *Zeenat*.

Daadi had told Amrita earlier that morning that she looked like Noor Jehan, who was marked by a cleft chin and sullen lips.

Daadi said, 'You look just like her.'

'You keep on saying it,' said Amrita.

'Because it is the truth, my dear.'

'I know why you say it.'

'Why is that?'

'It's because you don't look like anyone.'

'I look like myself.'

'Only yourself.'

'Thank you, my dear.'

'Damn you.' And Amrita said it and blushed, her sullen lips hanging uncertainly, and looked around as if for witnesses.

They were neighbours. Daadi lived in the small house with the terrace, and Amrita lived in the house with the telephone. It sat on a stool in their veranda and rang loudly in the evenings. A Muslim bearer hurried in, stooped to pick up the handle and passed it on to Amrita's father, a Sikh lawyer who wore his turban like a fabulous crown and reclined in his long veranda chair to discuss the amounts of money involved in his cases. People said Amrita's father was a show-off, and Daadi's mother had told her that people were jealous.

'In this neighbourhood,' she said, standing one morning with her sleeves rolled up by the kitchen window, 'everyone is one thing on top and another thing inside.'

She meant that they were unreliable, and she liked to give the example of her own husband, who spoke agitatedly of education and progress but had nothing to show for himself.

'If I didn't send him to work every morning,' Daadi's mother used to say, 'we would be paupers, we would be begging on these streets.'

It was true that Daadi's father was fond of sleeping. (He ran a pharmacy that doubled as a dispensary, and he claimed that nobody in Lahore required his services before noon.) She had to rouse him on her way to school. And she often had to go afterwards to bring Amrita out of her house. On the way she passed Amrita's mother, a round-faced, broad-boned lady with coal-black hair and a dark slit between her two front teeth. In the morning she sat on her burgundy rug and recited gravelly hymns from the Granth Sahib. She saw Daadi enter the house and nodded with her front-toothy smile. Then Daadi passed Amrita's older brother, Ajit, who took morning classes at the Law College. Ajit was a large fellow, high and hefty, with massive, sloping shoulders and a childish sulk. People said he sulked because he was struggling with his father's shadow; Daadi had heard their loud arguments, the ones that took place in the veranda and usually followed their legalistic discussions, culminating in the slamming of doors, which rang like gunshots. Amrita said her brother was like her father in every way.

'They should get along,' said Amrita.

'Not at all,' said Daadi.

'I think so,' said Amrita.

They had their opinions. Amrita wanted to have two children – a son and a daughter. 'Older son, younger daughter. It's always better.'

Daadi said she wanted two daughters and a son.

'Why not two sons and a daughter?' said Amrita.

'Because a girl needs company.'

Amrita said, 'Girls fight much more than boys.'

And Daadi said, 'What do you know? You're just making it up. You always make things up on your own.'

The arrival of the refugees was unexpected. Daadi heard it described in the house and informed Amrita.

'It's true,' Amrita said. 'My father has said they'll be coming to our house. My mother will make their beds.'

'How many are there?' said Daadi.

'I don't know,' said Amrita. 'It's all politics.' Then she said, 'Muslims are killing them for no good reason.' And she said the words like a lawyer, with her hands laying them out in the air.

Daadi said, 'Muslims were killed first.' It was what her mother had said in the morning with the rolling-pin in her hand.

'No, they weren't.'

'The truth is the truth.'

'Muslims lie all the time.'

'You don't wash your hair.'

'I do.'

'Your father doesn't. Your brother doesn't. They keep it all day in their turbans.'

And Amrita made a face and went home.

*

Earlier in the year there had been riots in Calcutta between Hindus and Muslims. Calcutta was very far away, a five-day journey on the train from Lahore. Rioting in Calcutta was as remote as the fighting (her father had called it a 'fiasco') that had happened between the countries of Europe. But the riots in Calcutta led to the killing of Muslims in Bihar, and then Hindus in East Bengal, and then, most recently, the killing of Sikhs and Hindus in the northern provinces. The northern provinces were not so far away, just a five-hour journey by train, and the attack on Hindus and Sikhs had sent them with their families to Lahore. Amrita's own house, in keeping with her prediction, was currently full of relatives who had fled the fighting.

Daadi's mother said, 'We should shut our windows. Who knows what they have brought in their hearts?'

Daadi's father was reclining on the diwan in the veranda. He raised his head from the pillow and said, 'Don't be so narrow-minded.'

Daadi's mother widened her eyes, opened the corner of her mouth and said, 'Yes, my dear,' and went away to shut the windows.

Later that night she said, 'These British. They are evil geniuses.'

But Daadi's father said not everything could be blamed on the British. He was lying still on his diwan, listening now to the gramophone that sat next to him on a high table and was possessed by the spirit of Noor Jehan.

'Whose fault is it?' asked Daadi.

'Our own,' said her father. 'Man is an animal. He must always curb his instincts. It is only under the influence of discipline and restraint that man is Man.'

The possessed gramophone sang a sad verse about moons and broken hearts.

By summer the madness was everywhere. The British were leaving and there would be two countries, India in the center and Pakistan on each side – a long strip to the left called West Pakistan, and then to the right, after one thousand miles of Indian territory, another Muslim land called East Pakistan. Hindus and Sikhs were going to India and Muslims were coming to Pakistan. The Parsis and Christians were unsure, and had been told to make up their minds.

Signs appeared on doors. THIS IS A PARSI HOUSE. THIS IS A CHRISTIAN HOUSE. Hindus and Muslims and Sikhs didn't put up signs because they feared identification. There were riots on Mall Road. The mostly Hindu neighbourhood of Shahalmi was torched. Thick clouds of smoke settled on the horizon and spread like the blackness that suggests a storm. The stories were fantastic: people had seen bodies piled up against walls, thrown into ditches, severed heads and hands and cut-off breasts. Refugee trains were arriving at their destinations with corpses inside. A woman who had made the journey across the new border said that she had climbed a pile of bodies in order to hop across a high wall. Daadi was trying to keep up with the stories, trying to picture Mall Road without the Parsi laundry, Shahalmi without Hindus, the River Ravi without its funeral pyres, a plain grey without its blaze of orange. Could there be Eid without Holi and Diwali, Noor Jehan without All-India Radio, Daadi without Amrita in the mornings?

She thought of an absence, and saw dark windows where the laundry had been, silence where there had been songs, a hollow house instead of a home. She would live to see the adjustments: how the shutters came down on an abandoned laundry and opened the next week on a bookshop; how Noor Jehan gave life to the microphones of Radio Pakistan; and how quickly that house, once Amrita's, came to belong to strangers. She would live to see it go into the blur of elapsed time. And she would learn difficult lessons: that ruins become relics; that a blankness is also a whitening, an opportunity for new inscriptions; that older losses become obscured by newer ones. And still the will to act remains.

It got worse. A Muslim shop in Mozang was burned by a mob of angry Sikhs. (Previously it was a hardware shop, because it sold locks and keys and hinges for doors, but now shops too were known by their religions.) There was a rumour in the neighbourhood: Amrita's brother Ajit had been in the Sikh mob. A woman said she had seen him that evening, sweaty and panicked in his damp shirt and trousers, hurrying in the darkness to the safety of his house.

Daadi's mother said, 'Lock your windows. Lock your doors and windows. You don't know who is going to do what.' She was going around with the rolling-pin.

Daadi's father didn't tell her to broaden her mind.

Late at night they were woken by a banging at the door.

Daadi stepped out of her bed.

'Who is it?' said Chhoti, her younger sister.

'Stay here,' said Daadi. She opened the door and went outside.

'Go in,' said her mother, who was going herself to the gate. Daadi's father was walking ahead of her. He was holding something.

'Go *in*!' said her mother, showing the lower row of her teeth.

Daadi saw that it was a gun.

She went back into her room but stood at the door.

'What is it?' said Chhoti.

'Nothing,' said Daadi.

She thought of a wide-eyed man with a gun and saw him open the gate. It shocked her to see that his face was her father's.

She opened the door a little and breathed slowly.

People were coming in.

'She will sleep here,' Daadi's mother was saying.

They knocked.

Daadi opened the door and found Amrita.

Daadi's mother said, 'They are staying with us for the night. Let her come in.'

Daadi stepped aside.

Amrita stepped into the room.

Daadi saw that Amrita's mother was crying but without the contortions of pain or sorrow on her face.

'Close your door,' said Daadi's mother. 'And don't open it for anyone.'

They went away.

Amrita was breathing like an asthmatic.

Daadi closed the door and said, 'What happened?'

'Nothing,' said Amrita between her deep, heavy breaths, her shoulders going up and down.

They went to lie down on Daadi's bed.

Chhoti's voice said, 'It's too dark.'

Daadi said, 'Go to sleep now.'

They lay together in the silence, two girls with their hands on their chests.

In a whisper Daadi said, 'What happened?'

Amrita said they were fleeing. Some Muslim men had tried to enter their house in the evening. But their Muslim bearer had taken an oath on the Quran and said that the owners weren't at home. The men said they knew it was a lie; and they said they would return in the morning, and would not accept another oath, even if it came from a Muslim.

Daadi said, 'It is all politics.'

Amrita said nothing.

Then Daadi said, 'Don't worry about anything.'

And Amrita said, 'I won't.'

They left before it was morning, when the world outside was still blue. A black car came to collect them. Daadi's mother had prepared a breakfast but they didn't want to eat; Amrita's father said they had to cross the border before the sun was out.

Daadi walked with Amrita to the car. Her sullen lips looked more sullen than ever. Daadi could tell it was because Amrita was feeling afraid and not sullen. She hoped no one would make the mistake and think otherwise.

Amrita's father was wearing his turban and his glasses and his black lawyer's coat. He said to the driver, 'Do we have oil?'

The driver said there were two spare boxes at the back of the car.

'Then we will be fine,' said Amrita's father, and knocked his knuckles on the shiny black bonnet of the car. He put his hands in his pockets, looked at his shoes, looked at the door of his house, looked at the sky.

'*Inshallah*,' said Daadi's father, who was frowning.

They embraced.

Amrita began to wave.

Daadi watched her recede with the jeep, which soon became an insect on the road, then a dot, and then nothing.

She went back inside.

*

The rains were fierce. Roads cracked by rioting and torching and the frantic movements of people were filled with water. The canal flooded; heavy trees came down and floated in the streets. By September the water had dried, and the shining sun revealed a new city. Shops reopened with the schools and colleges. At night the windows were yellow with light. It looked like any other summer, but it felt different: the shops had new owners, the schools and colleges new students. Evacuated houses had new residents. Some were demolished, their rubbled foundations sold for small amounts. The house next to Daadi's was repainted. A Muslim merchant moved in. He was alone – his wife and children were still in Amritsar – and he didn't have the money to buy furniture. He didn't own a telephone. In the evenings his veranda was silent.

Daadi finished school and was persuaded by her teachers to stay on for two years and obtain a bachelor's degree. But it was an uncertain time. The Hindu teachers had left, and the new ones had to learn the subjects in the syllabus as they went along. In that time Daadi made a new friend, a girl called Seema who belonged to the Ahmadi sect – her mother was a convert – and was related through her father's sister to people who now had land and were selling that land and building factories.

'Wajid Ali Shah,' said Seema one morning. She climbed into the taanga and placed her hand on the arm rail. She was tall and slim, had rounded, bony shoulders and wore glasses with elongated rims. 'He is the son of Maratib Ali Shah. Their family is coming up.' She meant that they were growing in importance.

Then she said, 'They are having a concert and Roshanara Begum is going to sing. She is like a big black cow. But when she starts to sing she becomes a beauty.' Briefly Seema closed her eyes, as if recalling the transformation, though it was evident that she had made it up and was now repeating for authority. 'Once she starts

344

singing she cannot stop it. She says it is no longer in her control!' Seema touched her collarbones and laughed.

Daadi was quiet.

The taanga was going towards Rattigan Road. The men walking on the footpath saw the taanga, and saw the two young women at the back of it, both wearing burqas with their faces uncovered.

Seema said, 'The concert will be in Lawrence Gardens. The gentry of Lahore is coming. We will have to wear saris.'

Daadi said, 'I am not going.'

Seema said, 'It is your decision. But I will be going.'

Daadi was unaffected.

And Seema sighed, looking out at the world and blinking from behind her glasses, her fingers continuing to clutch the bumping arm rail.

They went to Lawrence Gardens on a Saturday night. And it was chilly, the first intimation of winter; people came in shawls and were carrying cushions.

'To sit on,' said Seema, who had brought two embroidered velvet cushions and held them under each of her arms. She was going up the steps that led from the base of the small hill and into the amphitheatre. 'Keep following me,' she said.

Daadi lifted her sari from her ankles and went up the steps, one at a time.

A man and woman were behind them, the man in a stiff sherwani jacket and the woman wearing a blue sari.

Seema paused at the landing, smiling at the couple, allowing them to go first.

The couple went up quickly.

Seema said, 'They are Chiniotis. The wife is from here. Now she is one of the Chiniotis, so she is behaving like them. We know their whole family.'

She tripped.

She said, 'Sorry, sorry.'

People continued to go up the steps.

'Give them to me,' said Daadi, and took the cushions from Seema.

The amphitheatre had bare brick steps that led down to a moat-like partition, which contained no water, and behind which was the stage. The elevation of the hill, the shade of the trees, the glow of the lights and the movement of bodies gave the place a rich, removed feel. Seema and Daadi were sitting on the upper steps with Seema's father and mother on each side. Seema was naming the people in the audience, and her parents were listening attentively. 'Yes,' her father was saying. 'Yes, you are right, you are right.'

'That is Chughtai,' said Seema.

'Where?' said her mother.

'Over there,' said Seema, and indicated the steps below with her eyebrows. She looked at Daadi and said, 'He is the painter.'

Seema's father said, 'He is the very best.'

Seema said, 'He is friendly with my father. He offered to give him a painting but my father declined.'

Seema's mother opened her purse, brought out a small, embroidered pouch, opened the string and poured a powdery substance into the palm of her hand. She tossed it into her mouth, closed her eyes and chewed consideringly. She said, 'He is always declining offers.'

Seema said to her father in an urging, childlike way, 'Go to him and shake his hand.'

He said, 'I will, I will.'

Seema's mother laughed, crunching the mix in her mouth, and said, 'He won't do it. Just wait and see.'

'Ladies and gentlemen,' said a voice.

They looked at the stage. A man was standing before the microphone. He wore a cement-grey suit, tight at the waist and flaring below like a frock, and stood with his shoes joined at the heels. 'Ladies and gentlemen,' he said again, 'I have the honour tonight, of inviting to this stage, the Malika-e-Mauseeqi, the Queen of Music, in whose praise one can only say the following.' He held out the palm of his hand and, with lurching repetitions, recited a couplet in Farsi. Then he raised his voice and said, 'Please join me, in welcoming to this stage, the est*eemed* personage, of Roshan! Ara! Begum!'

The audience was clapping. The man was blinking and smiling. The Queen of Music was walking onto the stage with her musicians.

'Cow,' said Seema to Daadi.

The woman was short, dark, round, wrapped in yellow silk and glinting with diamonds. She could have been a washerwoman in someone else's clothing.

'Wait and see,' said Seema.

Daadi joined the tips of her forefingers and prepared herself.

The singer held out her hand. Her eyebrows went up, and her mouth released a single note. Her voice was nasal, importunate, and quavered uncertainly. The yawning strings of the taanpura floated with her. She went up and touched a place, fled from it and came back up. Now around that place she wove, higher and lower, and the place where she was heading, the place at the heart of it, the same as before, became a destination. But she touched it and went past it. And she was too high now, and fell; but she fell on the same place in a lower scale, so that her flight became a recovery she herself had predicted.

The audience clapped.

She opened her eyes and looked at her musicians, sniffed and dabbed her mouth with her shiny veil.

The tabla stumbled. The sarangi wept.

She was listening.

The sarangi gave a summary of what she had done.

She summarized it back.

The sarangi mimicked her and then took it higher, a challenge.

She copied it but brought it down.

They wrestled, and merged upon the moment when the tabla struck.

The audience clapped again.

She smiled at the audience and nodded agreeingly.

Daadi's fingers, joined previously at the tips, had joined fully now, and to someone watching she may have had the appearance of a devotee.

She inclined her head and said, 'What is she doing?'

347

Seema's father said, 'It is Shankara. It is the melody of Lord Shiva.' His hands enacted a flowering.

His wife said, 'People are listening.'

So they heard the rest of the song in silence. And it was the same after a while: the singer sought a ceiling, and sometimes she was able to touch it; but she always fell back and hung on the note that came before the last one. After the song had ended, when the Queen of Music was talking to her musicians and the people in the audience were talking to one another, Seema's father removed his glasses, wiped them with his shirt and said, 'It is a difficult melody, you see. She must bring out the quality of Shiva, who is *both* the creator *and* the destroyer.' His eyes were bright with emphasis, and his lips were smiling. 'There is a place between the two, you see. And she must bring it out. That is why she stays on that second-last note: it is where the yearning is the highest, the *highest*, but also the closest to ending.'

Seema's mother crunched disdainfully on her powders and said, 'He is always saying big-big things.'

At the end of the year Daadi was married, and moved with her husband into his three-bedroom house in Mughalpura. She was living there in one room with him; in another room lived his mother, a widow; and in the third room lived his younger brother. Within a year of their marriage Daadi's husband sold his shop (they made oil-based perfumes and sold them to retailers in the city) and became the manager of a rubber factory in Lyallpur. The factory was in debt; the rubber it produced was inferior. But the owners offered to make the manager a shareholder in the company, and the new manager, encouraged by his new wife, agreed to take the job.

He went away. Four months later he sent for his younger brother, who was to work with him in the factory. Daadi was alone in the new house with her mother-in-law. The woman awoke at dawn, said her prayers in her own room, then wandered out to the bathroom, washed her face in the sink, spat and gargled noisily and cleansed herself in other ways, and went to sit outside with her gramophone in the baithak room. She sat there in the light of the window, ate paans and listened to the gramophone, swaying to heartbreaking songs by K. L. Saigal and C. H. Atma. She expected her daughter-in-law to take her dirty clothes out to the washerman, dice the onions and tomatoes in the small kitchen, put the pot of water on the hob, and go into the bathroom with rags and a bucket and clean it up.

Daadi said, 'Anything else?'

'Not for now,' said the woman, swaying to the music.

Daadi went in and found a mound of soft, black shit in the squat-toilet with flies encircling its peak.

She came out and fainted.

Her mother-in-law said, 'She has insulted me!'

Her husband was gloomy.

Daadi said, 'I am not staying here,' and put her clothes in a bundle and went back to her parents' house.

It became a way of living. She fought with her mother-in-law, fought with her husband, fought with his brother's new wife, and came away always to her parents' house. She was likely to stay there a week. Then her husband was expected to appear with an apology, and she was expected to accept it; and they were expected to go back to Mughalpura in a hired taanga.

The same taanga brought her husband back to her parents' house. He said, 'She must come with me.' He was wearing a grey safari suit and pacing the veranda with his hands clasped importantly behind his back. His salary had increased, and was the source of his current confidence. In the safari suit his stomach hung like a sack.

She said, 'I will not take my daughter back to that little hole.'

The daughter was two years old. Her name was Musarrat. In the house they called her Suri.

Suri acquired a sister.

Seema came to see Daadi at her parents' house and said, 'She looks like a doll!'

Daadi told Seema that the child weighed nine and a half pounds.

Seema said, 'You must give her a strong name.'

They settled on Hikmat.

'Suri and Hukmi!' cried Daadi. 'Come here at once! We are going away from here!'

They were playing with the girls of the neighbourhood in the street. Daadi saw the stained faces of the children, their torn clothes and wild, lice-infested hair, and shouted, 'From now on you will not play with these urchins! You are from a *good* family! And they are from the *streets*!'

Offended mothers appeared, and came forward to claim their children.

In the taanga Suri said, 'They will never play with us now.'

Hukmi was crying.

Daadi said, 'And I am *glad* that they won't. I am *very* glad.'

Seema came to see her and said, 'You must build a house of your own.' She herself was living now in Rawalpindi with her husband, who was in the army. Seema had said that her house had six rooms, a garden, a driveway for keeping the car and a terrace with wicker chairs and a plastic table. 'All white,' said Seema, closing her eyes with satisfaction. 'Everything is white.'

Daadi said, 'We can't afford it.'

Seema leaned forward in her chair and said, 'Your husband is supporting his mother and his brother. The day he stops filling up their pockets you will have the money for your own house.'

Daadi smiled and said, 'It is not like that at all.'

And later, to her husband, she said, 'When will you stop filling up the pockets of your mother and brother? When will you do something for *us*?' She was standing in their shadowy room between the two beds, one for her husband and herself and the other for her daughters. She said, 'How long can we live here? How long?' She stretched out her arms on either side, and they almost touched the walls. 'Do you think I can bring up another child in this room?'

He sat on the bed, his elbows on his knees, his fingers on his temples. He said, 'We will see when you have another child.'

She said, 'Yes. We will see. We will see. That is what you always say.'

But it was a boy.

Seema said, 'Now is the time. *Now* is the time.'

And her wish was granted: her husband bought a two-canal plot in an area that had once been a mango orchard and faced the canal. She hired a contractor and took him to the site to discuss the possibilities.

Seema showed her the picture of a French house in a magazine: the corners curved, the lines sloped elegantly, and the windows were round like windows in the cabins of a ship. Seema said, 'It is a new style called Art Décor.'

Daadi summoned the contractor to her parents' house and said, 'Art Décor.'

He was an old man. He wore a checked blue-and-red lungi over his legs, which were covered in sores, a white turban on his head and misted-over glasses on his face. Most of his teeth were missing. He said, 'What?'

She said, 'Art Décor. It is a new style. In France.'

He didn't understand.

She took him to the site and said, 'Round, round, everything round.' And she showed him the picture of the house in the magazine.

He nodded thoughtfully and said, 'It will raise the cost.'

She said, 'You think we have sugar mills? You think we are sitting on a goldmine? What are you thinking in that head of yours?'

She went herself to the brick kiln to select the bricks. There was a cheaper variety of yellow brick.

'But I want the red bricks,' she said to her husband.

And she went to the office of a cement factory, bought the cement at a discounted rate and counted the number of bags that were loaded onto the taanga.

The contractor said they had to start building before the monsoon. 'Otherwise the walls will become soft,' he said.

She said, 'You have seven months.'

He said, 'The labourers will have to put in extra hours. It is not in my control. If it was a question of my hours you *know* I wouldn't ask you for more.' He was looking at her plaintively and licking his lips.

She said, 'I will see who is working overtime.' And she sat on a charpai in the shade of a mango tree and oversaw the construction. She noted the white insects on the bark of the tree; and she noted that with the approach of the summer their numbers increased.

Seema said, 'Mango bugs,' and shuddered theatrically.

Daadi told the contractor to take out the tree.

'You must have a tree,' said Seema. 'It brings good luck.'

Daadi said, 'I will plant it myself.'

And so began the project of the garden. She demarcated a patch at the front of the house, and planted a tree she had seen in other houses on the part of the lawn that abutted the gate. It grew slowly. She was tired of waiting for the small white flowers, and she dug out a line of soil around the lawn and planted it with marigolds. She had learned from the man at the nursery that it was a resilient flower, needing only water and light, and grew quickly.

She strung the orange flowers on strings and hung them around the house. They hung from the pillars in the veranda, from the handles of the cabinets in the kitchen and on the knobs of the bed. They looked pretty but gave no fragrance. On the third day they had shrivelled, and were brown and soggy. She thought it was deceptive.

Seema came to the house and said, 'But what is there to celebrate?'

She acquired a car. Her husband took it with him to the factory in Lyallpur but brought it back at the end of every month. And every morning she took the garden pipe and stood before the car, her shalwar raised to the knees, the sleeves of her kameez rolled up to the elbows, her dupatta tied into a knot at her waist, and shut her eyes and turned away her face and heard the water crashing against the windscreen.

Seema said, 'It is not a thing for the mistress of the house to do.' She was grave.

Daadi said, 'Who will do it?'

'A driver,' said Seema, and added that in Rawalpindi they had two. 'There are lines of them,' she said. 'You won't even have to look far. You just have to build a quarter at the back.'

One day, with the new driver, in the new car, they went out of the house. Seema and Daadi sat at the back and looked out of their windows at the world.

'Must say,' said Seema.

'Drive it slowly,' said Daadi to the driver.

They went first to Daadi's parents' house. Daadi and Seema went inside and came back with Daadi's younger sister, who was made to sit in the middle.

'I can sit in the front,' said Daadi.

'No, no,' said Seema. 'Not the mistress. Never.'

The car took them to Anarkali. They stepped out into the sun and shut their doors, and went into the cool shops, their dupattas taken over their heads. Inside the hosiery shop they saw a woman with her head uncovered. She was talking to the salesman without restraint. In the car Seema said, 'Did you see her? She was buying stockings! Next time she will appear in the shop wearing only those on her legs.'

Daadi laughed.

Chhoti was quiet.

They went to a restaurant in Neela Ghumbad and parked the car outside the bicycle stalls.

Seema said, 'It is a bakery. But the food it serves is very high quality. It is always serving the gentry.'

They pushed past the glass doors and went in like the gentry.

'Table for three,' said Seema to the waiter.

They didn't have to wait.

'I know what I am having,' said Seema. Still she raised the menu and frowned at it from behind her glasses.

Daadi said, 'I will have a black coffee.'

An actress had said it like that in a film and had settled her arms on the table.

Daadi returned her menu to the waiter and settled her arms on the table. It was sticky. She lifted her arms and settled her elbows on it instead.

Seema said, 'I will also have a coffee.' She told the waiter not to add milk or sugar. Then she said, 'There is another place here for coffee. But it is only for men. The big shots are there in the evenings.' She gave some examples.

'What do they do there?' said Daadi. She had unfolded the paper napkins and placed them under her elbows to combat the stickiness.

Seema said, 'To get away from their wives. To smoke lots of cigarettes.' She squinted and made a dying face and brought her trembling fingers to her mouth. 'They always smoke cigarettes when they are discussing politics. It is all they do. Sit together and talk of politics. What is political now? All of the politics has ended. One solid stick is all you need.' She meant the handling of the religious leaders who had taken out a demonstration against the Ahmadis. They had chanted slogans and smashed windows, and were beaten with sticks and arrested on the same day by the army.

Seema said, 'The army is efficient.' And she was speaking as an Ahmadi but also as the wife of a colonel.

The waiter was still standing beside their table.

'Chhoti?' said Seema.

Chhoti was silent.

Daadi said, 'Have something.'

Chhoti was looking at the menu, which was lying before her on the table, its pages closed.

Daadi said, 'She will have a coffee also.'

The waiter went away.

Chhoti said, 'I won't have it.'

'Then don't have it! Don't come here with me if you don't want to have it!'

Chhoti got up and went away towards the toilets. The women at the other tables were looking. It was not the way of the gentry.

Seema said, 'You don't have to say it like that.'

Daadi said, 'How else will I say it? What else will I say to her fat face?' She thought of the money she had brought in her handbag. She would part with it now for drinking black coffee, for placing her elbows on a sticky table and for behaving badly before the gentry.

Seema closed her eyes serenely and said, 'You must give her time.'

Daadi said, 'Give me that stick and I will set her right.'

And Seema said, 'You must be patient. The younger girls are not like we were. They are getting modern with the times. You have to be patient.'

Patience was what she had shown the matchmaker, the families that came to their house and went away, and the lamentations of her own parents, who were enfeebled by resistance and relied more and more on her interventions. Patience had drained her; and patience had led to this.

She said, 'I don't have the patience.' She was wiping her hands with a napkin.

Seema said, 'Your approach is wrong. You can't persuade anyone with ideas. You have to teach by your example. It is the first thing we learn.'

The Ahmadis were energetic proselytizers.

Daadi said, 'What example? I have nothing to show her.'

And Seema sealed her lips and sighed through her nostrils, and then said, 'This is the problem. It is *you* who can't see things. You are the one who has to change your approach, my dear.'

She went with Chhoti to the bazaars in the morning and took her to the children's schools in the afternoon. On holidays they chopped, cooked and cleaned in the kitchen, and sat afterwards in chairs in the veranda and wove patterns into quilts, scarves and sweaters. It was work; it took away the designations of age and made them equals, and brought on a knowledge of potentials, of what they could yet be. Then it was instructive to watch only their shadows on the veranda floor, enlarged diagonally and moving as if of their own volition.

Some evenings they went out in the car to the cinema, and Chhoti came back and sang the songs.

'I am thinking I should learn,' she said one day.

They had seen *Qaidi* in the cinema. Noor Jehan's voice had been used with Shamim Ara's long, forlorn face to picturize the main song, which showed the actress wandering by herself in an opulent garden.

'Learn,' said Daadi. 'It is a good thing to have in your life.'

But Chhoti said, 'I could sing for the radio.'

Daadi said, 'You are wrong in the head.'

'Why?'

'You know why.' She was feeling heavy inside, and it was making her smile sheepishly, as though she were suddenly to blame for this misplaced enthusiasm.

'Tell me why.'

'It is for young whores. You are too old.'

Chhoti stared at her and then took herself out of the room.

The sheepish smile stayed on Daadi's face.

That afternoon they went in the car to collect the children from their schools, and waited first for Sami in the corridor outside the classrooms, sitting on the white wicker chairs with the other aunts and mothers, and anxious for the flood of merry little boys to burst through the doors.

The war came, and Daadi opened her cupboard and brought out the knitwear. On the radio it was announced that all sizes were needed, so she packed the sweaters she didn't like – and then, because she felt watched, a few of the ones she did like too – into bundles and sent them with the driver to the collection tent that had been set up in Main Market.

At night there were blackouts. The siren rang and she yelled for the children. They went to stand in the L-shaped trench dug out in the lawn. Sometimes they heard the jets overhead, and one night Sami got out of the trench and went to stand by the gate.

'What are you doing!' she shouted.

'Just looking up,' he said.

'Get back here!'

He was laughing in the dark.

She took off her shoe and threw it at him. 'Get back here at *once*!'

It was announced that India's prime minister had asked to borrow soldiers from the Russian government.

'She is an evil genius,' said Daadi.

They were sitting by the light of the lamp in her room, preparing mufflers to send out. Noor Jehan was singing a newly recorded song on the radio:

> These sons of the soil aren't for sale
> Why do you search the bazaars for them?

Chhoti said, 'It is a blessing.'

Daadi said, 'What is?'

'Your children.'

'Yes,' said Daadi. 'Yes, they are a blessing for me.'

'For every mother,' said Chhoti.

Daadi looked at her.

Chhoti was knitting involvedly.

'Yes,' said Daadi. 'You are right.'

The voice on the radio continued to sing of irreplaceable sons, and their hands, trembling with mutuality and the new-found emotion, went on interlocking the colourful loops.

Seema arrived with a box of jams and squashes. 'Not much else to buy in Rawalpindi,' she declared. Then she said, 'This army takeover has transformed the country. That area used to be a village. Now it has roads and buildings. They say in five years the new capital will be like Europe.'

'How long by train?' said Daadi.

'A few hours,' said Seema. 'But you must come. I have been there for so long now and still you haven't been.'

Daadi said, 'I will, I will.'

They had brought out the chairs onto the lawn and were squinting in the sunny stillness.

Daadi said, 'At least this war is finished.'

And Seema sighed and said, 'You never know with them. It could start again tomorrow. Of one thing I am sure: if it weren't for the army we would be in the hands of the Indians right now.'

Daadi said, 'You are right.'

Seema said, 'There is no other way for us.'

Daadi said, 'Yes, yes.'

'Force is what we need.'

'Force.'

'Always.'

'Yes.'

The spirit of reinforcement was expiring.

Seema said, 'I have brought you marmalade.'

'There was no need,' said Daadi.

'But you must try it.'

'I will.'

Then Seema said, 'The children?'

And Daadi was relieved. She told Seema that Suri and Hukmi were both speaking like the nuns who taught them at the convent school. 'They say "May-ray" and not "Mary" like we say it over here.'

Seema was impressed.

'But Sami runs away from his books.'

Seema was dismayed.

'He runs after aeroplanes.'

'Aeroplanes!' said Seema.

'That is all he wants,' said Daadi. 'He says, "I want to be *in*-fallible, *in*-vincible, *out*-standing!"'

Seema tittered.

And Daadi smiled. There was another word he had taken to writing again and again in his notebooks: it was *reconnaissance*. But she feared the pronunciation.

Seema said, 'If it is aeroplanes he is after, you should send him to the academy.'

'Academy,' said Daadi.

'Air force,' said Seema. 'It is top-class. They are giving so many benefits now.'

Daadi was struck by Seema's confidence.

She said, 'Benefits?'

'So many benefits,' said Seema. 'I think everybody should have them. If we keep going like this, one day we will have a country in which everyone has benefits.'

Daadi was listening and nodding. She said, 'Seema, you have become so confident.'

Seema flapped her hand and said, 'Oh let it go!'

Daadi said, 'You have.'

'It is nothing,' said Seema.

'It is everything.'

'Well,' said Seema, whose confidence had now peaked, 'if it is good for helping others, then so be it.' And she told Daadi about an idea she had been having: there was a family in a village called Barampur, a landed family with ties to a well-known landowning family in Mutlan. Seema said she had learned that their son had divorced his wife and was now in need of another. 'No children from this marriage,' she said, 'so there is no problem.'

They owned four hundred acres in the countryside, and they lived in a big house. The money that came in from the lands was good. The boy's sisters had been to see Seema, and she had thought at once of Chhoti.

'Many benefits,' said Seema. 'And not many worries. They are old money. But they have values: their women cannot go about in the open like this. I think you should think about it.'

Daadi said, 'Let me tell the girl.'

And Seema said, 'Tell her and tell me.'

Less than a year after that Daadi went for the first time to the big house in Barampur. Chhoti was living there now, and had suffered an early miscarriage. Daadi went in the car with her mother. It took them two hours on the road that led onwards to Multan. There was a sharp turning in the road they had been asked to follow, and it led them past saffron fields, yellow in daylight, and then past a buffalo pond to the house. They were shown into a high room where all the windows were shut. And the dust was what she would recall: the dust on the tables, the dust that had coloured the white sofas, the dust on the frames of the two pictures of flowers against a black background that were on the wall for decoration. She touched one of the frames, and the darkness came away on her fingertip.

The house was old. And oldness was unassailable, a benefit unto itself.

She brought the fingertip near her mouth and blew the trace of dust away.

*

Daadi returned the photographs to the oval box and switched off the lamp. It was dawn. She could see the light beyond the curtains, and could hear the birds outside, shrill and panicked. She went across to the TV and switched it on. The *Good Morning India* hosts were setting out their agenda for the day. She switched it off and went outside, walking up and down the driveway, her sandals making the slow and steady smack of someone chewing. There was dew on the grass.

She went back inside and lay on her back on the bed. She watched the ceiling, and heard the sounds outside: the car was going; then the van was going. She could sleep. And if she slept now she would still be up before it was dark. She got up once again, drew the curtains, closed the doors, and returned to the bed and gave in.

When she awoke it was afternoon. She went to her door and saw that the cars were parked in the brightened driveway. Her eyes were swollen, and stung. She rinsed her mouth in the bathroom, then washed her face, her wrists and elbows, her feet and ankles, and returned to her room with the prayer mat. The curtains were still drawn, and to this partial light her eyes were accustomed. She sat on the mat, her legs folding with some difficulty beneath her, and said her prayers to make up for the ones she had missed in the morning.

She folded the prayer mat and went into the kitchen.

Naseem was washing the dishes in the fizzing sink.

'Everyone has eaten?' said Daadi.

'I haven't,' said Naseem. Her sleeves were rolled up. She was scrubbing a yellow enamel pot with the Scotch-Brite rag.

'Then eat,' said Daadi. 'Leave these for later.'

Naseem said, 'What about you?'

'I am fine,' said Daadi.

She went back into her room.

In the evening she had a visitor. She was watching the songs on the Indian channel when Barkat came in and said that a woman was waiting at the gate.

'Which woman?' said Daadi.

He said she was in a car.

'For me?'

He said the woman had asked to see the mistress of the house.

'Did she ask for Zakia?'

'For you,' said Barkat.

'Let her in.'

She went to stand in the doorway and watched Barkat open the gate. The car was small, red, and dented in places. A driver was driving and the woman was sitting alone at the back.

Daadi kept her hand on the doorknob.

The driver stepped out and held the door open, and the woman reached out a hand, settled it on the edge of her door, brought out her feet and hauled herself up. She was tall, frail, wore glasses, and was smiling in preparation.

Daadi squinted.

The woman said, 'You haven't recognized.' She was approaching.

Daadi was squinting and smiling.

The woman said, 'Seema.'

Daadi said, 'Seema?' Then she clapped her hands and said, 'Seema!'

Seema said, 'Yes, yes, still the same.'

She came in and they were able to embrace.

'I didn't even recognize,' said Daadi, leading her into the room. She switched on the lamp, switched on the fan. She was smiling uncertainly.

Seema sat on the sofa and said, 'How many years?'

'Oh who knows!' said Daadi. She was aware of her belated enthusiasm. She turned around and said, 'You will have tea, Seema?' Saying her name again and again made her presence real.

Seema looked around the room and said, 'Why not, why not.'

Daadi opened the other door and cried, 'Naseem? O Naseem!' She returned with her smile to the sofa. 'How many years?'

Seema slapped her hands on her thighs and said, 'Too many years, too many.'

They laughed and panted.

'Everyone is well?' said Daadi.

'Everyone,' said Seema. Her grin showed her teeth, which had eroded and gleamed wetly.

Daadi held her hand and said, 'In Canada?'

Seema closed her eyes and said, 'In Canada.'

Daadi said, 'The name of the place –'

'Mississauga.'

'That is right,' said Daadi.

'Yes,' said Seema. 'Yes.'

'Your children?' said Daadi.

'Very well,' said Seema, and looked away briefly to prepare the order of the details: 'Salim is in Toronto. And Rukayya and Rehana are in America. Rukayya is in Maryland. And Rehana is in Boston. I have seven grandchildren now, *mashallah*, so all has turned out quite well.'

Daadi was nodding, and was looking at Seema's hair, which she had dyed a stark, alarm-raising red. Daadi attributed it mentally to the influence of Canada and said, 'Your husband is well?'

Seema said, 'The same, the same. He is in a wheelchair now.'

Daadi was sympathetic.

'It is fine,' said Seema. 'He watches the snow and curses it.' She laughed sadly. 'He has not forgotten Pakistan.' And she had stopped laughing.

Daadi was smiling in compensation. She said, 'Yes, but I am sure he is able to visit.'

Seema said, 'He doesn't want to visit.'

Daadi was nodding.

'I come and go. But he says it is too much for him. Old times, you know. How can you forget? He says it is better to be in exile. It is a test, in a way. But our community is strong there. In Canada they have no restrictions.'

Daadi said, 'Over here: what is it now?'

'It is not very bad,' said Seema reasonably. 'But there are problems for the mosques, and problems for promotions. You cannot be in government. They will promote you to a point and then they will retire you.' She spoke without bitterness, though it had happened to her husband in the same way.

Daadi said, 'My daughter-in-law is always writing about these things. You should tell her. She has a magazine now.'

Seema said, '*Mashallah, mashallah.*'

Then Seema said, 'And Zaki is well?'

'Very well,' said Daadi. 'He is going to the best school.'

'Then all is well,' said Seema and squeezed Daadi's hand.

Daadi closed her eyes and allowed the hand to be squeezed. She said, 'By the grace of God.'

Naseem came in with tea, stooped above the tray and made their cups according to their requirements. Waiting for the procedure to end, and waiting to perform an act they had consigned now to habit, Daadi found that her enthusiasm, brought on by the sense of renewal, had begun to leave her. Seema's religious affiliations had eventually sent her out of the country; and Daadi had lost a child, fought with her sister and been living on the one piece of land her husband had left her.

She raised the cup to her lips and said, 'So much has changed, Seema.'

And Seema said, 'I think nothing has changed.'

They were looking at each other.

Seema said, 'The army is back.'

Daadi said, 'Again.'

Seema said, 'And where have elections led?'

Daadi said, 'To the same place.'

'So what has changed?'

'You are right, you are right.'

They drank their tea.

Seema settled her cup on the table and brought her hands into her lap. She said, 'Are you speaking to Chhoti?'

Daadi began to look around her. She said, 'Yes. We speak. She calls me from there. We talk. She has not visited in some time. But she calls me on the phone.' Daadi was looking at the white silk cushion beneath her arm and was stroking it.

Seema said, 'I saw her.'

Daadi said, 'Just now?'

'Two days ago.'

'Where did you meet her?'

'In Multan,' said Seema. 'I had gone there for a wedding. Many people were there. Singing and dancing, this and that. It has become so vulgar.'

'Yes,' said Daadi, and gave a sigh. But then she said, 'Was Chhoti well?'

'She is well,' said Seema. 'She is well.'

'I am glad,' said Daadi. 'I am glad.'

Seema took Daadi's hand and said, 'You have to help her.'

'What has happened, Seema? You must tell me, Seema.'

Seema said Chhoti's husband had married again. The new wife was young, the daughter of a politician. Fazal's sisters had arranged the marriage. And Chhoti and her daughter were living in two upstairs rooms in a separate section of the house. 'The new wife lives in the old house,' said Seema. 'And she lives there like it has always been hers. She expects it to be hers very soon. She is expected to provide children.'

Seema said Chhoti had looked ill from afar. When Seema asked after her health she gave no answer. But she had hollows under her eyes, her face was jutting with bones, and there was no one there to take her to a hospital and show her face to a doctor.

'She said to me,' said Seema, 'to look for a place for her daughter. I said, "Come with me to Lahore. We will go to see your sister, we will find a solution." But she said, "No, I must stay here, and you must help me, Seema. You must help me." After that I stopped trying to persuade her. I sat in my car and I came back. But the look on her face I cannot erase from my mind.'

Daadi called Chhoti in the evening.

A woman picked up the phone.

Daadi said, 'Where is my sister?' She heard her own voice; it was uneven. She placed a steadying hand on the mantelpiece and said, 'I want to speak to my sister.'

The woman went away.

She came back to the phone and said, 'She will call you.'

Daadi said, 'Who are you? Who are you?'

The woman said it was her house.

'It is not your house. We will do a court case. Do you have any shame? Where have you kept my sister?'

The woman had hung up the phone.

Daadi dialled the number again. Her hands were trembling. But no one was picking up the phone.

She thought of calling the police. But there was nothing she could say to the police. She thought of going in the car to Barampur. But it was night already.

The phone rang.

'Who is it?' said Daadi.

It was Chhoti.

Daadi said, 'Where were you? Why won't they let you come to the phone?' She was holding the phone with both of her hands.

Chhoti said, 'What did you say to them?'

Daadi said, 'We will do a court case.'

'You will do nothing.'

'Where are they keeping you? Where have they kept you all this time?'

Chhoti said, 'You are not needed here.' And then she said, 'There is nothing we want from you.'

Daadi said, 'I have done everything for you –'

'You have done nothing!'

And Daadi said, 'I have done everything! I am the one! If I don't call for you –'

Chhoti said, 'Don't call for me.'

'I won't.'

It had ended.

Daadi went to sit down on the sofa. Her chin was in her hand.

Naseem came into the room and began to arrange the empty

plates and teacups on the tray. Then she stood back and said, 'I wanted to ask you something.' She was looking at her feet, the toe of one foot making arcs on the carpet.

Daadi was watching her.

Naseem said, 'I want to go on the pilgrimage.'

Daadi was quiet.

Naseem said, 'My son is buying my ticket. But I will need more for the time I spend there. I will need to –'

'I don't have time for your needs.'

'You must help me,' said Naseem.

'I must do nothing,' said Daadi. 'Go away from here.'

'I have worked for you my whole life.'

'Go now or I will throw you out.'

Naseem said, 'I have never asked you for anything.'

'I pay you,' said Daadi. 'I feed you. I keep you in my house. If it weren't for me you would starve on the street. Now get out of my room.'

Naseem said, 'This is what you are giving me?'

'Get out!' said Daadi. 'Get out of my house!'

And Naseem did.

17

Grime gathered in the kitchen, grease on the plates, grease on the pots. It clung to the metal and hardened. The sink was clogged. The food came every morning from a housewife who was advertising her home delivery programme in *Women's Journal*, and was stored in the fridge and heated in the oven at mealtimes. It amassed in the rubbish bins and stayed. There was no one to take it out now, and no one to point it out in the bins.

Naseem's room at the back of the house was empty. She had moved into Mrs Zaidi's house at the end of the lane. Her job was to sweep the bathrooms, sweep the floors and to look after Mrs Zaidi, who had angina and considered herself vulnerable.

Barkat brought the news to Daadi.

'I don't want to hear it,' said Daadi after hearing it. 'And if you want to leave too you are welcome to do it.'

Barkat didn't bring it up again.

'We don't need a cook,' said Daadi. 'We don't need a driver. We don't need anybody in this house. I will look after myself and so will Zakia, and so will Zaki.'

I was spending my afternoons at school. The monitor appointments were going to be announced at the end of the term, and I was working to compile a portfolio. There was much to do: I signed up with the debating team and went with them in the school van to participate in a declamation contest at another school, and signed up for charity work at a children's centre, a two-week project, evenings and weekends only, which would earn me their certificate. On some nights I went back to the campus to use the swimming pool; I had decided to sign up for the swimming gala, and had settled on the idea of the twenty-metre backstroke.

My nights were full.

And my friends complained.

'What's happening?' said Mooji. 'Haven't seen you in a long time.'

Sparkle said, 'Where the *hell* are you, man?'

I told them about the work I was doing.

'Who's your competition in the house?' Sparkle wanted to know on the phone.

I said, 'No one.'

She said, 'Who's the competition in Saif's house?'

'Saif's in my house.'

Sparkle thought about it and said, 'So he's okay with you going ahead for it? Like have you guys agreed on it?'

I said, 'There's no agreement.'

Saif's answer was the same. 'He said the exact same thing,' said Sparkle urgently. 'There's no agreement. What are you guys going to do?'

'I think Saif knows I'm going to be the monitor,' I said.

'Zaki, how can you say that . . .' Her tone implied that I had said something inappropriately wilful.

I said, 'It's not like that. This is between me and Saif.'

The next morning I saw him at assembly. He was dressed carefully, wearing a starched shirt and trousers, his shoes polished and his hair combed to the side. It wasn't his style. He was handing a large beige folder to the housemaster when I walked in.

'Don!' he said.

We embraced.

I said, 'I thought you weren't coming today. I was going to mark you present.'

But he said, 'No, no, not necessary. From now on I'll do it myself. I thought: my attendance is pretty good, why ruin it now.' And he winked and grinned.

I filled out the monitor application and arranged the forms in a file. I went up to the housemaster at morning assembly, presented him with the file and only then saw that Saif had done it before me.

The housemaster said, 'Your name?'

He didn't know my name.

'Zaki Shirazi,' I said.

He wrote it down on the file.

'Father's name?'

'Sami Shirazi.'

'Profession?'

'Pilot.'

'PIA?' He was interested.

'No, sir,' I said. 'PAF.'

There was no way of bringing it up. I sat with Saif and Mooji and EQ on the stone benches outside the canteen, and talked with them in the old way of other things; and at night I talked to Uzma and Sparkle on the phone and sensed in their unconcern a troubling assumption, the feeling that they knew who was going to win and were resigned to it. Then I thought they expected that resignation from me as well.

One day, on the phone, Sparkle said, 'No, it's true: you're very lucky to have a friend like Saif.'

I said, 'Why am I lucky? Why isn't he lucky? Why aren't you lucky, man? Why aren't Uzma and EQ and Mooji lucky? Why is it about me all of a sudden?'

Sparkle said, 'O God, Zaki. What's happened to you?'

I said, 'Nothing.'

But I knew she was going to report it.

The next morning Saif moved his desk to the front of the classroom. He sat there through the first two periods in a state of absorption, wearing his ironed shirt and trousers, listening and writing and raising his hand repeatedly to ask questions. And at the start of the third period I moved my desk too, back to its initial position, which was to the right of the blackboard and further behind, and found myself sitting beside a neighbour I already knew.

*

The monitors were appointed every year at the end of the spring term. A list of names went with the housemasters to the co-ordinator's office and from there to the principal's office. The principal then called a meeting of the staff. And in that meeting the

369

merits and demerits of the candidates were discussed and compared until they led to a selection of ten monitors, one from every house.

'But you have to do more things,' said Kazim. 'You don't have enough things.'

He had brought me into the art room to have this discussion. The door was locked from inside.

I said, 'Like what?'

He thought about it. 'Art,' he said. 'Make paintings. Things to show the world. We'll do them together. I'll show you.'

He went with me in the school van to debating competitions, took me to the art room at lunch break for the rehearsal of my speeches, and followed me to the grounds for sports after school. He said we were going to make an 'all-rounder' out of my personality, develop it in the main areas so that in the end, when it came to the selection process, my name would stand out.

Enthusiasm led to frustration: he was quickly disappointed and embittered; he was sullen if I didn't ask his opinion, betrayed if I failed to keep a promise or failed to show up on time. He wore glasses now, and the effect was comical, like something out of one of his own drawings.

Abruptly he revived, full of faith in the ideas he had thought up: he wanted me to go every morning for a few minutes into the coordinator's office ('You have to keep up appearances') and he wanted me to separately introduce myself to all the housemasters, whose opinions in the final meeting were given more weight than those of the other teachers. 'No stone unturned,' he said. 'That has to be your motto.'

He stood outside the swimming pool in the failing light and timed my lengths with a stopwatch. Afterwards he shared his observations: the speed was good but there was a deviation in the line, it was noticeable and would need correction. Carefully he touched my arm, which was swollen from the effort, and withdrew his hand and said, 'Impressive.' When I won the bronze medal in the swimming gala he bought me a card and a large book of photographs on the greatest swimmers in the world. 'You can take it up,' he said. 'It can be your profession. Nothing is impossible.'

But I left the book in the art room, and in the morning he was sullen.

He noted and reported every sighting or rumour of consequence. He said he had seen Saif in the coordinator's office, and had seen him on another occasion, talking to an influential housemaster outside the junior building. 'Very clever,' said Kazim, in a proud detection of cunning. 'You have to be very careful with that one.'

When we appeared to walk together in the corridors, or on the stone path, he was full of a sense of himself. He said, 'They will see!' It was enough for him to experience the sensations, even if the experience itself was deferred. In those moments he seemed to grow outwards, to leave his limitations behind and become his potential.

We went to the Lahore Museum. He said he wanted me to get inspired. We went first into the painting gallery, a long room with unrelated pictures hung in two adjacent rows on the walls. Kazim explained that it was chronological. 'Chughtai,' he said, pointing to a picture of a woman with elongated eyes. She was sitting in a pool of darkness and held a lighted lamp in her small, fine hands. 'This is Ustaad Allah Bux,' he said when we passed a blurry painting that showed a shepherd with his flock of sheep. 'Now things get political,' he said excitedly, and led me to a painting of brick kilns puffing out dark smoke. 'He was a Marxist,' said Kazim.

And he said, 'This man is a Christian.'

We were standing before the picture of a wine bottle. It stood on a striped sheet of cloth. There were two gleamless oranges beside it.

'Why is this great?' I said.

He threw up his hands and said, 'Isolation. Loneliness. Don't you get it?' And his voice echoed in the empty gallery.

We went in after that to see the statue of the starving Buddha. It was broken. Around it, in the other glass display cases, were more broken things from the past.

A cockroach crawled out from under the display case, chased itself in a circle and went back into the darkness.

'I'm inspired,' I said. 'Let's go.'

*

The next day he said, 'You have to meet the important house-masters.'

'I've met them,' I said. 'I say salaam to them every morning.'

He said, 'No, no. That's not enough. They're hard old hags. They need to see your love.'

We were walking to the car park. The last bell had rung and the corridors were empty.

He said, 'We'll go tonight. I've made the appointments. Just come to my house at seven o'clock.'

I said, 'Your house is too far.'

But I was at his house a little after seven. He was standing outside the small, scratched gate. He wore a long black polo neck and tight jeans that had collected in wrinkles near his ankles.

He climbed into the car and his eyes were green.

I said, 'What's *wrong* with you!'

He sighed, his hand on the window, and moved around in his seat. 'They're lenses,' he said.

I made him take them off before we reached the housemaster's house. (He performed the action quickly and effortlessly in the rear-view mirror.) We had come to see the housemaster of the biggest house, a teacher who had been in the school for more than twenty years and was presently the head of the Maths Department. He lived in Sant Nagar, an area of many narrow lanes and small, unpainted houses. On the way we passed one marble engraving of a defaced elephant, then another.

'The Hindus used to live here,' said Kazim.

We parked the car in the lane outside the house.

Kazim said, 'Five minutes.'

We went inside. There was a room with sofas pushed against all of its walls. The sofas and the carpet were brown, and the walls were bare except for a large framed photograph of the Kaabah, a sea of white-clothed pilgrims surrounding it.

We sat on the sofa and waited.

A door opened and the teacher came in.

We stood up.

'Salaam, sir,' said Kazim.

'Salaam, sir,' I said.

Sir nodded. He was a short man, and sat on the adjacent sofa with the ankle of one leg balanced on the knee of the other. His feet were bare, and he was caressing the raised foot with his hand.

He said, 'How is your mathematics?'

Kazim looked at me.

I said, 'Sir, it's not bad, sir.'

He was poking his mouth with a finger; he brought it out and frowned at it, then placed it again into his mouth. The other hand was still caressing his foot.

Kazim said, 'He is very good, sir.'

Sir said, 'You are looking to improve?'

Kazim said, 'Yes, sir.'

He said, 'I have too many pupils here in the evening. Maybe there will be an opening next week. Maybe. You can come again next week. The rate is one thousand rupees.'

Kazim said, 'Thank you, sir.'

In the car I said, 'I'm not taking tuitions from him.'

Kazim said, 'You don't have to. I'll take the tuition. You just have to make sure you keep up the connection.'

On the weekend he came to my house with a poem he wanted me to recite. The inter-house recitation competition was scheduled for the following week, and Kazim wanted me to win it. The staff meeting was scheduled for the week after that; Kazim said it was psychologically important to win something now in order to stay fresh in their minds. And he brought good news: he had gone to the principal's house with a painting, had shown it to him and told him that it was mine. (He had made an abstract picture, he said, in a style deliberately unlike his own.) The principal was impressed. 'They won't forget you now,' said Kazim. 'Whenever they mention your name some little thing will come up.'

'What about Saif?' I said.

He made a face, then gave a shudder; he had gone too far in anticipating my feelings.

'Saif's still my friend,' I said.

He sighed.

I said, 'What did I say?'

'Read it on your own,' he said, and sat sullenly in one of the veranda chairs.

I walked up and down the veranda and recited the poem, which was about barren landscapes and fresh flowers, a poem he said he had found in *Palgrave's Golden Treasury*.

Later we sat in the darkened veranda and went over my pronunciations of the words. A bat came in and then couldn't get out, and spun and spun until it crashed against a door.

'Who lives there?' asked Kazim.

I said, 'My cousin used to live there.'

'Who lives there now?'

'No one,' I said.

I didn't win the recitation contest. But I won an honourable mention and was given a certificate of merit. I took it before lunch break to the coordinator's office for submission.

The coordinator said, 'What is this?'

'Certificate, sir.'

He considered my standing form, then turned the certificate around in his hand as if assessing its weight. 'You've got the spirit,' he said.

'Sir.'

'You don't think you'll fail.'

'No, sir.'

He said, 'Good, good. Keep it up.'

*

The list went up in the morning. First the boys went to see if it had been put up on the bulletin boards in the hallway; after assembly they checked again. And then, after the first-period bell, the names began to come in: Saqlain Raza had made it because he had won the tent-pegging trophy; a boy called Babar Rahim had made it because of his grades. My name hadn't been mentioned when I left the classroom.

Kazim was standing in the hallway. He said, 'I don't know what happened.'

The boys were crowding around the bulletin board.

They weren't looking at me.

I said, 'It's fine.'

'You deserved it,' he said.

But I kept saying, 'It's fine. It's fine.'

At lunch break I went to the canteen to congratulate Saif. And he was gracious; he neither condescended nor acknowledged the rivalry. He was buying and handing out drinks to his well-wishers, and he met me as only one of the crowd.

'Don,' said EQ.

'Don,' said Mooji.

We embraced and sat on the bench, waiting for Saif.

There was a party for him that night. Uzma had reserved a table at an expensive restaurant. 'It's just his very close friends,' she had called to say. 'I'm baking him a cake. He asked me to invite you.'

And, after Uzma had called, the phone rang again. It was Kazim. He said he had been to see the principal, who had told him what had happened at the meeting: my name was discussed. But the housemasters said there had been discipline problems in the past, and someone had cited a fight from two years ago, a fight that had taken place outside the campus. The principal had crossed out my name and asked for the name of the next contender. And the housemasters had recommended Saif.

'It's sabotage,' said Kazim.

I said, 'You use really big words, man.'

He said, 'They deliberately sabotaged your name.' He was breathless.

But I said, 'It's not a big deal. Saif deserves it. You shouldn't say all these things about him. It's really not good to get involved in someone else's life like that.'

At the restaurant there was a commotion. Saif was standing with EQ and Mooji beyond the door and talking loudly on his mobile phone; and inside, under the dim lights, Uzma and Sparkle were leaning across the table towards each other and talking.

I said, 'What's going on?' and sat down on the chair next to Sparkle's.

Uzma looked at me and looked at Sparkle.

Sparkle said, 'We don't know what's going on.' She looked briefly at Uzma and went on: 'Saif got a call from his school. There's been a complication. I think he's talking to his teacher right now.'

Uzma dropped the menu and said, 'He's been suspended. His name has been taken off the list and he's been suspended.' Her look was thinly accusing and broadly demanding.

Sparkle said, 'Someone went to see the principal and said all kinds of nasty things about Saif.'

Uzma didn't look at me.

Sparkle said, 'You should talk to him when he comes in.' Her tone was understanding; it contained an assumption and a warning.

I said, 'This is crazy.'

Uzma said, 'We trusted you! *He* trusted you! How could you *do* something like that to your *friend*?'

I said, 'I didn't do it.' I wanted to say more.

Sparkle put a final hand on my arm and said, 'I guess he's angry that you tried to get back at him like that.' Her head was tilted into her shoulder. She was blinking reasonably. 'Just stay here,' she said. 'He'll come in just now and you can sort it out.'

But I went outside with the intention of seeking a fight. And the traffic sounds ate up the things I said, first in panic and then in anger and then finally in the clarity of rage: their knuckles hit my face, and then my own hands and feet were moving and I was on the floor, and the taste of blood was strange but unstartling in the way that something delayed for so long will dissolve in the last light of waiting.

*

I awoke in my bed at home. I saw the light beyond the curtains and tried to raise my head but couldn't.

My mother came in. She sat on the bed and said, 'Go to sleep.'

She touched my forehead, and I felt the gauzy wrap of the bandage.

Daadi came in and said, 'You are not going back to that school.'

In the morning my mother called the admissions office and asked to speak to the coordinator. She said she wanted to lodge a complaint.

The telephone operator said that the coordinator was busy. She could try calling again in the afternoon.

'This is unacceptable,' said my mother. 'I am going to withdraw my child from your school right away.'

The operator said that removals didn't require a conversation with the coordinator. The operator himself could strike the name off the list.

'Yes,' said my mother. 'Please do that. Thank you so very much.'

I went back to Wilson Academy on an early summer's day, to withdraw a copy of my transcripts. It was a hot, dry day, and the fourth period was in progress; the stone path was parched and deserted. I went into the senior building to collect the papers, waited in the registrar's office, obtained the papers and paid the money and then went upstairs to use the toilet. I passed the art room on the way, but there was no one inside.

Two years of secondary school remained, and my mother had found a tuition centre in Johar Town that provided coaching for the SATs and A-Levels. It also offered a Guidance and Counselling Department; the tuition centre was affiliated with many good universities abroad. My mother and I went to see the campus. It was a converted house, a brick building with dark-tiled floors. The administrator, a round young lady with a brisk, businesslike demeanour, gave us a tour of the place, which was surprisingly well furnished: the rooms had new chairs and blackboards, new split-level air-conditioners; in one room the administrator switched on the machine by pressing a button on a kidney-shaped remote control. Then she switched it off. We followed her out of the classroom and into the canteen, which had high glass windows, a coffee-maker and a squadron of terracotta pots with bristling plants. The computer lab was in the basement, a white room divided into thirty cubicles, each with a computer and a keyboard covered in a sheet of plastic.

The administrator took us back into her office and described the programme: students came for three hours in the afternoon to pursue independent courses of study. The faculty was highly accomplished; the student-to-teacher ratio was tight; textbooks were optional; a uniform was not required. The administrator showed us a list of students from the last two years who had won admission to the top national colleges, plus two in the UK, one in Canada and one in America. The monthly fees were high but not higher than usual.

'Good enough,' said my mother, and signed the forms.

In the morning I went into the kitchen to make tea. It was in a round plastic container by the stove. I waited for the water to boil, poured in the tea, then waited for it come to a second boil. The water bled and bubbled. I found the teapot in a cupboard above the stove and found a family of dead insects inside. I washed it in the sink, scrubbing it with a green Scotch-Brite rag I found by the tap. It was stiff with filth but thawed in the water. The milk in the fridge was sour; I threw it into the rubbish bin, and saw that this was piled high with wrappers and bones from last night's meal. I found the sachet of powdered milk on the condiments shelf, which was, like the rest of the kitchen, in need of reorganization.

I carried the tray into Daadi's room. She was surprised. She lowered her newspaper and watched curiously as I settled the materials on the table, made her a dark brown cup with just a splash of milk, no sugar, and placed the teaspoon in a gleaming diagonal on the saucer. I passed it to her.

She took a dainty first sip.

She nodded.

I drove her to Pioneer Store to buy the groceries. She didn't object to my driving, and sat in the back with her handbag. We passed Mrs Zaidi's house, and Naseem was outside, crouched by

378

the gate, wiping its bars with a rag. She saw the car and stood up.

I lifted my hand from the steering wheel in greeting.

Naseem waved, smiled, then looked around as if she had misplaced something.

I washed the car, read its manuals and learned to recognize its sounds. I took it with Barkat to the Caltex petrol pump and had it serviced. I spent the morning showing the sooty mechanic the faults I had identified: the handbrake was loose; the car veered to the left when I abandoned the steering wheel; the lock in one of the doors at the back was jammed; and there was a scraping sound that came from beneath the car when it went over a speed-hump.

The mechanic lowered himself to the ground and crawled into the darkness.

There was scraping.

'Yes!' I said. 'That's the sound.'

He came back up and said, 'Silencer.'

'Silencer,' I said.

'Yes,' he said. 'Silencer.'

He kept the car for the day, and I had to pay him two thousand rupees. I persuaded Daadi to buy a lawnmower and dragged it along the grass on Sundays. It was noisy but did the work: all morning it sent up sparks of green, which I later cleared with a rake. One day the lawnmower bumped, and I knelt to inspect the obstacle it had uncovered. It was a bulge in the ground. I dug it out with my hands and found a box that contained a toothbrush, some pencils, a blue-nib pen, a compass, a lipstick and a hairbrush.

And there was a letter that said:

Dear citizen of the future. My name is Zaki Shirazi and I am a boy. I live in this house with my cuzzon.

Yawar

Lahore

Pakistan

Asia

Planet Earth

Thrilled with the rush of memory, I ran with the box into the house, into my room, pacing and remembering. I thought of taking it outside again and showing it to someone. But there was no one outside, and I stayed in my room and went over the contents again and again.

Winter came and the water from Daadi's shower was still cold. I brought a plumber from Canal Park who claimed to know all about bathrooms. He fixed the shower in a few minutes but embarked on a lengthy inspection of the toilet and the drain. He rolled up his sleeves and rummaged in dark holes, groaning and muttering when he found things, groaning and muttering when he didn't. In the end he demanded more than the promised amount, and Daadi parted grudgingly with the money. But in the morning it emerged that he had solved one problem and created another: the drain was clogged. Daadi's bathroom was a swamp after she showered and took the day to dry up.

I offered to fetch the plumber.

'No!' said Daadi. 'That's just what he wants!'

One evening, while she was conducting the ablutions that preceded her ishaa prayers, she slipped on a wet patch and fell on her hip. She cried for help but no one came; her shouts were swallowed by the deaf hollows of the veranda. She sent up a hand, managed to clutch the rim of the sink and raised herself with a limping effort. That night she made the announcement: I was to move in with her, because if tomorrow she died . . .

'O God,' said my mother.

'At my age . . .' said Daadi.

And so, after years of denial and disuse, the room next to Daadi's was reopened, aired and fumed. A group of professional cleaners came to the house and swept through the downy cobwebs. The bed was taken out into the driveway and left to sit under the sun. A patch of dust, exactly the size of the bed, was discovered underneath, and also a cardboard box, sagging at the top as if from the weight of an invisible burden. It contained one or two magazines, three video tapes of *Jane Fonda's Complete Workout* and a picture frame comprised of two small hearts that touched when they folded.

I sealed the box with masking tape and left it under the bed.

And the next day I moved in with my things, aware of the intrusion, the presence of ghosts, but determined not to disturb the ether in which they roamed.

*

The Guidance and Counselling Department advised me to apply to a liberal arts college in America. There were some that gave financial aid to international students.

'I don't see why not,' said my mother. She appeared to be thinking it through. 'But the cost, Zaki . . .'

'They give financial aid.'

My mother was looking at Daadi.

'Too far,' said Daadi.

I said, 'It's not.'

'Apply,' said my mother.

'And what if I get in?'

'Then we'll see,' she said.

I arranged the computer in a corner of the room. The desk was black and shiny, wood that didn't feel like wood, and came with two drawers that I resolved to devote to the application materials. At night I sat before the glowing screen, looking into a world of white yards and black trees that twisted like arteries. The state was called Massachusetts, and sounded like twigs snapping. *Indiana Jones and the Curse of Massachusetts*. The picture showed a white girl, a black boy, a Chinese girl, and another boy who was brown but appeared to be a foreigner. They were struggling and squealing, engulfed in the raptures of a snow fight.

I clicked on the link for prospective students.

Write an essay about a person who changed your life.

I read the topic a few times and looked at the walls of the room in which I sat.

Samar Api and I grew up together in the house.

*

I spent my afternoons at the tuition centre, three hours of books and murmurs, the hum of the air-conditioner, an immersion in the slowly clearing mist of test-taking techniques and strategies. After class I went with a boy called Amaan in his car. Amaan had withdrawn from his school earlier in the year because he had failed the half-yearly exams, and claimed with casual contempt that it was the system's fault and not his. For him everything was a part of the system. The practice tests were designed by the system; the system would bar us entry into good universities; the broken roads of Johar Town that caused Amaan's haunchy Volkswagen to bump and shudder were the proof of the presence of the system. He was a buggish boy with large, lidless eyes, and in the morning his porcupine hair was sharp. In the evenings Amaan and I went to the grounds at FC College, where boys from other schools (and some who went to no schools) gathered to play fierce rounds of football. The teams changed only when a member withdrew, and Amaan and I resolved to play together. But Amaan was a chain-smoker and had no stamina, and after the first few rounds he announced that he was going to umpire the matches. Thereafter he jogged alongside the players with a whistle hanging from a string around his neck, his body only mildly exerted and his face contorted with involvement. And in the car he gave critiques of my performance, and said one day that I had the speed but not the flair that was necessary for greatness.

I was home in time for dinner, which still came in soft cardboard boxes on a Home Delivery motorbike. I entered Daadi's room one night and found the unopened boxes waiting on the table. Daadi and my mother were sitting before the TV. An American newsreader was frowning into her microphone, her shoulders sagging, her hair stirring in a dusty breeze. Behind her was a thick cloud of smoke. And then came the image of two tall buildings, sparkling in daylight until they were hit, one after the other, by apparently blind aeroplanes.

'Sit,' said Daadi.

I sat.

My mother looked at me.

Daadi placed a hand on mine and said, 'You are not going to that country.'

My mother's editorial that week was titled 'The Blowback'. It was passionate and complicated, and exceeded the usual length. And the talk at the tuition centre was grim. Amaan said there was no point applying now to American universities because no one would get in. 'The system,' he said, tapping his temple, and nodded gravely.

It came on a Tuesday morning in April. One new e-mail. *Admissions Decision.* I watched it briefly, the fresh, suspenseful blue. *Admissions Decision.* The title said no more.

I waited for the page to load.

Dear Zaki,
The admissions committee is pleased to tell you . . .

'I'm in I'm in!'

My mother came into the room. 'O God, he's in!'

Daadi went to the mantelpiece and called her daughters. She told Suri, she told Hukmi, she hung up the phone and dialled again.

'Zaki has got in,' said Daadi. She listened. She said, 'You should come, just for a day you should, these children, you know how it is, they go and then they are gone, if only for a few hours you should come.'

And Chhoti said that she would.

She came alone. She was frail, a small woman made smaller and weaker. Her eyes were enlarged and had welts underneath that seemed to have been pressed in by hard fingers. She brought a crate of mangoes that her driver carried into the kitchen.

The conversation was cordial. She didn't mention her husband, or his sisters, or his new wife. And she didn't mention her daughter. She said that in Barampur the heat of summer had begun to take its toll.

Daadi said, 'You are looking weak.'

'The heat,' said Chhoti.

'You should stay –' began Daadi.

But Chhoti said, 'I can't. I must return by tonight. You know how it is over there.'

18

'Zacky Shirazzy?'

An officer in a dark blue uniform inclined his head. His golden hair was short, recently shaved, and had grown back like grass. He led me into a room that had two chairs, a desk and a computer.

'Okay,' he said, and settled into his chair. It gave a hingey caw. He flipped through the rigid pages of my passport and tapped the keyboard. 'Come on . . .'

It came on.

He raised the passport, turned to the first page and typed PAKISTAN into the machine.

'Put your right index finger on the red screen, please?'

I placed my finger on the small box he had indicated. The screen was red with laser.

'Left index finger?'

I placed it on the box.

'Look into the camera.'

A robotic snake with a slim, flexible neck appeared. Its one blind eye was also red.

I looked into it and smiled.

'Stay still . . .'

I did.

'All set,' said the officer. He stamped and stapled my passport and held it out like a gift. 'Welcome to the United States,' he said, addressing the wall behind me.

My room was on the fourth floor. Climbing the stairs with my suitcase was difficult, and I paused at the landings. Finally I reached the door. It said E52 on a rectangular white card.

I knocked.

'Hey!'

It was a boy in a T-shirt. And he was Chinese. The letter had said his name was Benny.

I said, 'Benny?'

He nodded and said, 'You got it.'

'Hi. Zaki.' I offered him my hand.

He smacked it with his and pointed to my suitcase. 'Need help with that?'

'It's fine,' I said, and carried it into the room.

'So,' said Benny, holding his hips and scanning the room as if for flaws, 'this is the common room. This is your desk. That's mine there. Yeah, I went ahead and threw my stuff on it. Sorry about that.'

'It's fine,' I said.

'You don't care?'

'About what?'

'The desks.'

I said, 'Oh! No, it's not a problem, it's not a problem.'

We laughed.

'Oh, and the bathroom?' he said, leading me to it. 'It's pretty big, so like, we're all set.'

'Great!'

'You wanna see the room?'

I followed him past the bathroom, into a dark, dusty space with just a window and a bunk bed.

'Top, bottom, whatever,' said Benny, 'your call.'

Our proctor's name was Peggy. She lived with her partner, Jo, in a two-bedroom suite at the foot of the stairs. Peggy and Jo were hosting the first house meeting in an hour. I showered using Benny's toiletries (he owned a bottle of shampoo and a bar of unscented soap), changed into the suit I had brought with me and sprayed cologne around its lapels. Benny said he wasn't going to change his clothes. He was typing very quickly at his computer. When it was time to go downstairs he got up from his desk and put on a pair of rubber sandals.

I said, 'You ready?'
'I guess,' he said.

A woman opened the door. She was small, wore black clothes and no make-up, and had very black eyebrows. Her smile was toothy and expectant. 'Zaaki!' she said, pointing to me, and shifted the finger of identification to my companion. 'And . . . *Benny!*'

We nodded.

'You must be Peggy,' I said.

'Oh no!' – a hand went to her throat – 'I'm Jo. That's Peggy there.' She pointed behind her to a tall blonde woman who was talking with emphatic movements of her hand to a circle of nodding students.

'Come on in!' cried Jo, frowning in humorous annoyance.

We sat on the carpet with our backs against the walls. The small square table in the corner was stacked with cans of Coke, Diet Coke and Cherry Coke; nachos and salsa; white plastic plates; and red plastic cups with white rims. Peggy sat cross-legged in the centre, her feet joined at the soles and her hands around her ankles. (Jo had fled to some undisclosed destination.)

'Well?' said Peggy, surveying the room with a stable smile. 'Welcome? Let me say, before we start: this is your first time, I know, you're all nervous, but let me tell ya' – here she made a frazzled face – 'you'll be doing this a *lot*. Name, hometown, interests, all of that stuff' – she waved it aside – 'it's gonna get boring pretty soon. So don't be shy. Okay?'

There were nods and blinks.

'Okay,' said Peggy, and placed her honest palms on the floor, 'we'll start with me.'

Peggy Grant was from Delaware, Ohio. One of three siblings (a younger brother and sister, both still in Ohio), Peggy moved here for college in the late sixties, studied psychology, which was *the* major back then, oh yeah, everybody was into psychoanalysis, a crazy time, and hey, fun too (one word: Woodstock), and she did fun things, whacky things, but then she went home for a while, to figure things out, she worked there in a library, four years of her life, when she realized that her heart was still in Massachusetts. So she returned to the best state in the country ('Go Red Sox!') and started teaching at a school. Twelve years ago she met Jo, and that changed her life, and they'd been living together since, first in a run-down apartment in Somerville, and now here, on campus, where Peggy was currently pursuing a master's in education while Jo worked as a chef in a restaurant that specialized in fusion vegan. 'I'm biased, I know,' said Peggy, raising one confessional palm, 'but I gotta say: the food is great.'

Hooting and clapping.

'Now,' said Peggy, searching the room, 'I'm gonna pick a random person . . . You!'

A fragile, sun-browned girl with gleaming legs had been identified. She pointed a finger to her collarbones.

'Ahaan,' said Peggy, firm with her grin.

The girl swallowed, sat up, tucked a strand of hair behind her ear. Her name was Alexandra but she went by Alex; she was from San Diego, California; she was interested in history but also in culture (a dilemma she enacted through a see-sawing motion of her hands) and was thinking about a double major, maybe, she wasn't sure yet, for now she was really happy that she had an awesome roommate.

'Aww . . .' said the roommate, a much larger girl with glasses and a shy voice.

'Good!' said Peggy. 'Next person.'

Sebastian said he was from New Jersey.

'Whereabouts?' said a hoarse little girl from across the room.

'Hoboken?' said Sebastian, whose limbs were very long.

'Ho-Ho-Kus,' said the girl.

'Cool,' said Sebastian, and puckered his mouth into a silent whistle of consideration.

Peggy said, 'And what do you do, Sebastian?'

'Ah . . .' said Sebastian, and rammed a fist into the palm of his other hand, 'let's see: basketball, basketball and basketball.'

There was won-over laughter at this.

'Will you be playing for us?' asked Peggy.

'Most certainly will,' answered Sebastian.

'Great! Next person?'

In this way we went around the room. Names and places emerged, spun their arcs of particularity and dissolved into the soupy atlas that was now in motion: Dallas, Kansas, Pittsburg, two Mikes, three Jennifers, Mary from Manila (the only other international student), a Kevin from Columbus-Ohio who shared brief notes with Peggy. Benny, my roommate, was from Bethesda-Maryland, and had one older sister who had also attended this college, class of '98. And then it was my turn.

'So!' said Peggy with a startled smile.

'Hi. I'm Zaki. From Lahore, Pakistan . . .' I was aware of the suit and the cologne.

Peggy said, 'You know we had someone from India last year . . .'

'Oh?'

'Yeah!'

'Wow!'

'Mmm . . .'

Silence.

'Interests?' offered Peggy.

'Oh, ya . . . well, lots of stuff . . .'

Peggy saw and said, 'What do your folks do?'

(Someone opened a can of Coke with a *pssst-crock!*)

'My mother's a journalist,' I said.

'Oh, very nice!' said Peggy. 'And your dad?'

'He's dead.'

Peggy nodded. 'Siblings?'

'None,' I said, and sealed it with a quick smile.

I bought a phone card from a 24-hour pharmacy that sat just behind the dormitories and was the first in a long row of shops, most of them now closed for the night. I asked to borrow Benny's mobile phone, and added quickly that it wouldn't cost him because I had a card.

'Chill out, man,' said Benny.

I took the phone into the hallway. It was a toll-free number. I entered the pin, dialed the country code, the city code, the area code and then the number.

You have! Two! Hundred! Minutes! To-make-this-call!

I waited.

'Hullo?' It was Daadi.

I told her I was speaking from America.

'Zaki! It's Zaki!' cried Daadi.

My mother took the phone. 'Have you reached?'

'Yes.'

Daadi said, 'Is everything all right?'

I said it was.

'Have you eaten?'

'We had this meeting,' I said, 'and they had snacks –'

'He hasn't eaten,' said Daadi.

Again my mother came to the phone and said, 'Zaki? Zaki, why aren't you eating?'

'I'm eating, I'm eating.'

'What have you eaten?'

'Pizza.'

'Pizza,' she said, and away from the phone, 'They are giving them pizza.'

'Zaki?' Daadi again. 'Zaki, is it cold over there?'

I said, 'No, it's warm.'

'You have bedsheets?'

'Yes. You packed them into the suitcase.'

'Have you taken them out?'

'Yes.'

There was a pause. Daadi said, 'Was the flight all right?'

'It was fine.'

'He says it was fine . . .'

My mother took the phone. 'How is the college?'

'It's very nice. My roommate is very nice. This is his phone I'm using.'

'Good. Good.'

'And you?' I said. 'Everything is fine?'

'Yes, yes,' said my mother, and I could tell she was looking around the room, 'we are fine.'

In the common room Benny was decorating his desk. He had some books, a coffee mug with pens and pencils, a planner with the college insignia on its cover and a framed photograph of his family. Benny's mother and sister were seated. His sister wore a white dress and held a bouquet of white roses. His mother sat next to her, less luminous, her worn hands folded demurely in her lap. Benny and his father stood behind them in black tuxedos. Everyone was smiling.

'You bring pictures?' said Benny.

I told him they were with me and went into my room.

*

Happy families are all alike. Every unhappy family is unhappy in its own way.

It was the first line of the first book I read on a course called 'Reading the Russians'. Every lecture lasted an hour, and took place in a deep, wood-smelling room on the second floor of the English Department building. The one-page syllabus was heavy with names: Tolstoy, Dostoevsky, Gorky, Chekhov, Turgenev, Pasternak, and also Nabokov, who was a favourite with the lecturer – a flamboyant young man who wore dark polo necks to class and posed passionate questions that were answered gradually by squeezing invisible udders that appeared to hang before him in the air. I made friends in his class, two Croats who introduced me to the larger community of international students. I ate lunch with them in the dining hall, studied with them in the library, and accompanied them on the weekend to the jazz bars in Cambridge and Somerville. They were adventurous and cynical, warm and disdainful, and talked about their classes, world events and the weather with a rapidly de-veloping vocabulary that was culled carefully from their readings. Their clothes came from obscure and alluring parts of the world. Many of them were smokers.

On weekends I ventured into the Greater Boston area on my own. I went into the pricey shops on Newbury Street and fingered the merchandise, then went to sit by the pond in Boston Commons, which was ablaze and crackling with autumn. I learned to time my journeys on the Red Line in accordance with the five-minute interval between each of its stops: the cello-playing madman at Porter; the chiming bells at the Kendall stop, designed by MIT students; and then the flash of sun as the train swept over the shattered shimmer of the Charles. Once I took a sunny tour of Harvard Square with a gang of Japanese tourists who were determined to photograph everything they passed. Our tour guide was a Harvard student. He told funny stories about the college and its history; he pointed to the rooms we passed and told stories about their former residents. At Eliot House he pointed to a room on the second floor and said it had been the room of Benazir Bhutto, the former prime minister of Pakistan. And he looked at me while imparting this information, as though he expected me to know what had followed.

I spent my weeknights in the local bookshop. It had two floors, with new books on the first floor and bargains and remainders in the basement. I couldn't afford to buy the books (I had just bought a mobile phone) and sat cross-legged on the carpeted floor of the basement, searching the earmarked pages for inscriptions made by intimate strangers. Once a month the bookshop hosted a talk by a visiting author, and a flock of people, mostly graduate students, settled eagerly into the plastic chairs with their pens and notepads.

One evening I was passing the bookshop and saw a poster in the window and stopped to confirm that it was him.

It was a still from an old Indian film, and his form was lifted from the original context and planted weightlessly on a white background. His fists were up like a boxer's, his eyes were bloodshot, and his mouth was twisted in a grimace. He was wearing his white vest. The poster didn't give his name. It said:

THE POSTCOLONIAL PREDICAMENT: A DISCUSSION

The discussion had started. I opened the door and went to stand behind the people in the last row. They were listening to the lecturer, a small woman obscured by the podium, only her face visible above the wood, a firm, ironic face, the eyes darting and watchful, the hair short and white. Her words were strange and difficult, and she delivered them with emphatic carving motions of her hand, dividing the air into fissures and fractures, ruptures, currents, layers. I listened to her for a while. Then she lost me, and I slipped out.

*

My mother called in the mornings. It was night for her, and the long-distance call was cheaper. She caught me on the way to class, or eating breakfast in the dining hall, and our conversations were brief. She called to check if I was fine, to ask if I needed anything. I told her I was fine and needed nothing. I had started working part time at the Faculty Club and my wages were enough.

The call was unexpected because it came late on a Friday night. I was in a room, not mine, and hurried out into the hallway with my shirt only half on. The effect of the wine had started; I buttoned the buttons in confusion, and the phone fell from my hand. I knelt to grab it. 'Yes?' I said.

She said, 'Where are you, Zaki?'

'What's wrong?' I said, and settled on the floor against a closed door. A girl hurried up the stairs and gave a vaguely disapproving look.

My mother said she had been in Barampur.

'Why were you in Barampur?'

She began to cry, and I knew that she had been crying earlier too.

I held my head and waited for her to speak.

19

Daadi was in her room when the phone rang. It was late morning. She folded her newspaper and walked over to the mantelpiece.

It was a woman's voice. And it was unfamilar. She said she wanted to speak to the mistress of the house.

'Yes,' said Daadi.

The woman said she was calling from Barampur. There had been an accident, a case of mismanagement at the hospital, some nurses hadn't checked the medical records.

'Whose records?'

Chhoti's. She had fainted last night, and they took her to the nearest hospital and left her there in the emergency ward. But the nurses had put her on a glucose drip without checking her medical records, and had kept her there all night.

Daadi said, 'Where is she?'

The voice said it had called for that reason. It said that a funeral was being held in a few hours, and that if they wanted to bathe the body they ought to leave for Barampur right away.

'What are you saying?' said Daadi.

She held on to the phone. Then she put it down and walked out of her room. She went into the driveway, past the lawn, past the gate, all the way out to the lane. She stood there, waiting for someone to come. When no one came, she turned back.

She went into Barkat's room and said, 'My sister has died. I must go to Barampur for the funeral.'

She didn't cry in the car. Barkat drove, and my mother sat next to Daadi in the back. Daadi gave directions, the turnings on that road that she recalled, past the rusting shanty towns, where the shrill sirens of buses had converged, and then past the vast empty stretches of land, things she recalled from a journey she had made many years before.

It was afternoon when they arrived. Men were sitting on charpais in the courtyard, and Uncle Fazal was standing at the entrance to the house. He was wearing a black shalwar kameez. His hair was white. He embraced the men who came towards him and ushered the women into a doorway. There was a murmur around him of greetings and condolences.

'Where is my sister?'

Uncle Fazal gestured to the doorway. He said nothing else. He stood there for some moments and then saw that a black car had come in through the open gate. He went away.

The body was laid out on a charpai in the drawing room, which had been cleared of furniture. Around the charpai sat a mob of wailing women. They howled and beat their chests and recited lines:

A princess has died.

A queen has died.

They were professional mourners and had been hired to grieve.

The three sisters-in-law were sitting on a white sofa that was stained with grease. They appeared to preside over the mourning and didn't stand up for Daadi when she entered.

Another woman was going in and out of the room, and from her manner and appearance they could tell she was the new wife. She was a girl. She was showing the empty places that remained on the white sheets that had been spread out to cover the floor. She wore a flowing, robe-like outfit, and even with the obscuring folds they could tell that she was going to have a child.

Daadi stood over the body. It was draped in a white shroud. The face was exposed. The eyes were closed, but a sliver showed in each eye, and it was a sliver of light.

She saw that it was a reflected light.

She stooped, removed the wads of cotton very carefully from the nostrils and took the face in her hands. 'Wake up,' she said, and patted the face. 'Chhoti, wake up.'

The wailing had stopped. The mourners were looking around for signs.

The new wife wove her way through the seated bodies and tried to take Daadi by the shoulders.

Daadi didn't let her. 'Wake up, Chhoti. Chhoti, wake up.'

The new wife went away.

My mother took Daadi's arm, and two unknown women came forward and succeeded in leading her away.

Daadi was crying but her eyes were closed.

The mourning started up again. The room filled with howls and with the thudding of hands on chests, the shuffle of cloth and the footsteps of people who were still coming in and going out.

They didn't recognize her at first. She sat beside the body with her forehead pressed into the leg of the charpai, a silent mourner in a room full of sounds. Her feet were bare.

'Samar!' cried my mother.

But she didn't look up.

They had to bury the body before dusk. Four male relatives were required to carry the janaza to the graveyard. They were the husband of the deceased and his nephews. They lifted the janaza on their shoulders and carried it out of the house, past the mourners, and then out into the street, reciting the kalima shahadat as they went.

The body shuddered with their steps.

The women watched from windows and doorways and stayed in the house.

By night the mourning had stopped. The professional mourners had been sent outside and were sitting on their haunches in the courtyard. They had been fed, and were waiting to be paid. A servant brought them tea in steel cups. Their voices were heard inside, the low voices in which they spoke to one another and mourned other things.

Inside, the men and women were sitting in separate rooms. Daadi was slumped behind the door in the women's room and was no longer crying. Her eyes moved along the walls of the room, and she seemed to want to say things. But she said nothing and only moved her eyes.

The women came and went. The new wife was giving instructions to a tired maidservant who was visible only when she carried the tray of pastries back into the room. The sisters-in-law were watching her.

And the other girl was not in the room.

They were not asked to stay the night. They had done what was required of them and were expected to leave. The tired maidservant showed them out.

'The girl,' said my mother. 'Where is she?'

Daadi was held between the maidservant and my mother, and was lurching.

The maidservant pointed to a door they were passing and said, 'She is inside.'

'Petrol,' said Barkat in the car. He was pointing to the needle, which was red.

My mother told him to stop at a station on the way.

They left the house, the lights still on inside, some cars still parked outside. On their way out they passed a family who were now heading back to their car. They were not recognized, and the looks were searching but brief.

The PSO station came after the first toll-booth. Barkat took the money from my mother and got out of the car to monitor the infusion. Daadi and my mother were alone in the back. Daadi had her face turned to her window. The silence ended when Barkat returned to his seat and revived the engine. He took the receipt from a boy in a grey PSO uniform and a green cap, and held it out for Daadi to put in her bag.

'I'll take it,' said my mother.

The road was empty. The occasional lorry came and went at a swaying speed, its lights dimmed. Otherwise the view was dark and unmediated. They drove for some minutes, their windows rolled up. At the first kerb my mother told Barkat to reverse the car. 'Turn it around,' she said. 'We have to go back.'

'What have you left?' said Daadi. Her voice was dry.

'We have to go back,' said my mother. 'Turn it around.'

The car turned at the kerb.

They were sitting in the drawing room, Uncle Fazal, his wife, his three sisters and their sons. They stopped talking when my mother came in. They had parted with their last guests, and the mood of reception was still in the room.

Uncle Fazal placed his palms on his knees.

My mother said, 'We have come back to take the girl.'

Uncle Fazal continued to look at her and moved his palms back and forth along his knees.

My mother said, 'Where is she? Where have you kept her?'

One of the sisters said, 'The girl is ours. She was taken away once and it was against our wishes.'

Another sister said, 'We have learned from our mistake.'

'Where is she?' said my mother.

And the third sister said, 'If you think we will part with our children you are mistaken.'

'I have raised her,' said Daadi.

She was in the room, and was standing by herself in the darkened doorway.

One of the women laughed and said, 'But who will feed her? Who will clothe her? Who has paid for her all these years? We have. Our brother has.'

Another sister said, 'They think they can take what is ours.'

But Daadi said, 'I will feed her.' And then she said, 'I will pay for her. I will clothe her. I will take what is mine. I don't want what is yours. I want what is mine.'

My mother said, 'We will do a court case. We will send the police here and have this house raided.'

The women were looking at Uncle Fazal.

My mother said, 'We will put it in every newspaper in the country.'

Daadi said, 'Allah has taken from us. Now He will give.'

One of the women said, 'Don't come here when it all runs out, because we will not be giving.'

Her brother said nothing.

Daadi said, 'Where is the girl?'

And my mother said, 'Come with me.'

They went out of the room and through the hallway, which was emptied now of voices, and to the door they had passed earlier in the night. And they opened that door and went in.

It was a small room, bare unlike the room in which she had grown up. The floor was tiled and uncarpeted. The thick curtains were drawn. A small brass lamp was kept alive on a table by the bed. She was sitting on the bed, wearing the same black clothes she had worn in the day, her arms folded around her knees, which were drawn up and pressed into her chest. Below the bed, next to her sandals, was an opened suitcase; and it showed the clothes she had folded and kept inside as though, on the basis of what she recalled, she had led herself to believe that they would come.

20

News from home makes you aware that the flow of memory has stopped. A life you no longer live is a life you no longer know. But you rely on memory to inhabit, however falsely, what now lies outside your experience; and every homecoming involves the puncture of memory's airy bubbles.

News came in e-mails from my mother. They had headings and indentations, and contained mildly musical paragraphs that were marked by a novice-like formality of tone.

My Dear Zaki,

How wonderful to hear from you! Samar sits beside me as I write this, so this is, in all seriousness, a joint enterprise. Let me therefore begin anew. We are well. The house is alive again, and it is almost strange to hear sounds in the morning, sounds at night, though of course it does not begin to make up for your absence. We miss you so.

Naseem is back. Mrs Zaidi was unhappy but Daadi spoke to her on the phone. Naseem has applied to the Hajj branch of the Zakat Ministry and wants to perform the pilgrimage. It is difficult to get but I have asked Nargis to intervene. She knows the man at the Zakat Ministry, and he has said he will see what he can do. I have prepared Naseem's application forms and will post them tomorrow from the office.

Samar has joined the office! Isn't that wonderful? She is working on the features pages, and her first article will appear next week. It is a review of a fashion show. I will send you a clipping as soon as the issue is out.

That is all for now. We will write later.

But first you must write with your news.

Lots and lots of love

I didn't go home for the winter holidays. The ticket was expensive and I didn't want to ask my mother for the money. It was a two-week recess anyway, so it made sense to take the Grey-hound bus to New York. We went in a group of eight people, and slept three to a bed in a tiny sublet in the East Village. (The owner had gone on holiday to the Caribbean.) I took pictures with my new camera and sent them as attachments to my mother from the Internet café downstairs. And she wrote back with more news.

My Dear Zaki,
Barkat was retired today. He was in need of a cataract operation and I sent him to the people who run the trust for the blind. The operation was successful. But they have said he should not drive. So today Daadi gave him his salary and saw him off. He will live now with his son in his village. Samar will not consider the possibility of marriage. I have told her to look around, to keep her eyes open at least. I have asked her if she would like me to look. And she keeps saying her Amitabh will come for her, as if he's going to appear on some white horse out of the blue!

In May, Daadi wrote her will. And she agreed to pay for Naseem's accommodation in Jeddah, because the return tickets from the Zakat Ministry had arrived.

Naseem and her husband left for the Holy Land on the PIA flight from Lahore, and returned with two Samsonite suitcases that opened and closed with buckles. Later Naseem claimed that the weight of her suitcases had made the porters stumble, and attributed this weight to the cartons of the Aab-e-Zamzam, the holy water, which she had brought with her from the Holy Land and stored in Daadi's fridge, and served in glasses to her acquaintances when they came to congratulate her.

My Dear Zaki,
Will you be coming home for the summer holidays?

I wasn't going home because I had won a grant to conduct research in New York City for my sophomore tutorial. (I had said in the essay that I wanted to explore the discursive space allotted to Other cultures in the American media.) The grant paid for housing and airfare, and I saved some money by sharing a room.

My Dear Zaki,
So glad to know that your summer was a success! I am quite envious of your travels.

At the start of the autumn term I became a subscriber to *Women's Journal*. My copy arrived by post and was always two weeks late. But I read the editorials and wrote to my mother:

Read 'Supremacy of Parliament' (*WJ*, 20–27 Sept.) and disagreed completely. How can you ask the same people – the very same people – to come back and run the show? Can you give me a better example of a compromise?

And she replied:

My Dear Zaki,
These are processes. At the end of the day we must look beyond the limitations of individuals. And we have to work with what we have. But I am glad you disagree. It would be so boring if you didn't!

In October I joined the editorial board of a magazine called *Peace and Justice*. The day after I joined it the editors participated in a sit-in with the janitors who were working on the campus. And the week after that we led a protest march from Kendall Square to Downtown Crossing, waving flags and chanting slogans to condemn the occupation of a country with which I had no connection but which I found, in this time of new kinships, similar to my own. I was in charge of magazine publicity, and took their flyers everywhere: I went to the Nineties Dance; to the Queer Dance; to the South Asian Dance; and to the Islamic Society Banquet, all points on the compass that was now in my life.

Subject: Great News!

Samar Api had met someone. His name was Imran. He had an LL B from London and had returned to join his father's law practice in Lahore. The engagement had taken place, and my mother had waited to tell me until she could accompany the news with a picture.

788 KB file. No Virus Detected. Download Now.

The image appeared in small, evenly spaced bursts of colour, and I closed my eyes until it was complete. When I opened them I smiled.

He was clean-shaven, a cutout in his outfit – black suit, white shirt with broad collar, bright red tie – and his cufflinks were sharp white dots in the camera's flash. His arm was curled confidently around his fiancée, who wore a green shalwar kameez that had the broad gleam of silk. She was slimmer now, blossomed with blush, and wore rings on the hands that she had folded in her lap. Her expression reminded me of the *Mona Lisa*'s: I couldn't tell if she was smiling.

My Dear Zaki,

I cannot begin to tell you just how delighted we are to hear of your decision. You will reach just in time for the wedding. Will you send me your flight details? I will make arrangements.

I returned to Lahore in late December, to unshed leaves that were silver in the daytime and thickened with shadow as the light withdrew into evening. Bombs had begun to go off in the north of the country. And they said that it would come to the roads of Lahore, where there were more bicycles now, more rickshas, more cars hastened by bridges and underpasses where once walls had stood.

The house had aged. The tree was stooping in the garden, the walls bulging behind the paint. My mother's hair was threaded white, and Daadi descended the steps of the veranda with caution, lifting her shalwar at the ankles as if preparing to step into water.

Samar Api was in her room. I was told to knock on the door. She was covered in uptan and didn't wish to be seen until the paste had come off.

I knocked.

'Who is it?'

'It's me. Your cousin.'

I waited.

'You can come in.'

She was talking on the phone. The turmeric in the *uptan* had rendered her complexion a flat beige, conceptual like a cartoon character's. The bed was a mess of magazines, bridal specials with flashing covers. The walls were blank.

She indicated a place by her side on the bed. With one hand she passed me the two-hearted picture frame that was again on her bedside table: she was new in it, withdrawn and watchful, posing on the night of her engagement.

I pointed at the grinning boy in the picture and pointed to the phone in her hand.

She nodded.

I read a magazine.

Then she had hung up the phone.

'That's him?' I said.

'Ya,' she said.

'You love him?'

She thought about it. She watched the words form on the ceiling, then watched them form in her hands. She spread out her fingers on her knees as if to make sure there were ten. 'He loves me,' she said, 'and I'm happy.'

I said, 'Good. As long as you're happy.'

'I am,' she said.

'Good.'

It was over, and we were quiet.

*

She had started going to a new gym with my mother, and she had a trainer who had caused her to lose weight. She said she was on a diet now that was designed for women like her, women who had little time.

But I said, 'There's time. There's time.'

They were thinking of going to London for their honeymoon. She had suggested it, and he had agreed. She said they were thinking of stopping in Boston on the way back.

'Boston's on the other side,' I said. I indicated the otherness with my head. I had no way of describing it.

'What's better?' she said. 'London or America?'

I said I hadn't been to London.

'We'll come to Boston,' she said.

But I told her it was a bad idea. The wind, the snow, now was not the time.

Then she asked about college, and I told her that I liked it, and that it had been good for me in many ways.

She said, 'Is it nice?'

I said, 'Very nice.'

She said, 'I know you're having fun.'

'How do you know?'

'I can see it in your face!'

And she told me about the wedding, which she had planned herself. There were going to be flowers on the walls, flowers on the gate and around the tree, flowers around the pillars in the veranda, and flowers on the car that would take her away. 'I want marigolds,' she said. And then she said, 'I want you to hold the Quran when I'm walking to his car.'

I said I would.

And she said, 'Good. Good. That's how I want it.'

*

I took the flask from her hand and put it to my mouth. It was empty. I peered into the black hole. '*Khatam*,' I said, making a smacking sound to mimic the suction, 'finito.'

'Don't tell me,' she said, and hiccupped. The bridal necklace jangled.

The chatter of the guests outside had stopped. The opening gate made its dragging drum-roll noise. Now there were trumpets. I rushed to the window to see.

'Who is it?' she said from the bed.

A car, decorated with tuberoses and marigolds, was entering the house at the pace ordained by the band. The women of my family stood to either side of it, showering the bonnet with rose petals. A man in white clothes and white shoes stepped out, his face hidden behind strings of jasmine, and my mother came out of the marquee with her arms stretched out to receive him.

'Samar Api,' I said, drawing the curtains, 'your Amitabh has arrived.'

Acknowledgements

The author would like to thank the following:

Farzana Munawar, Aliya Iqbal Naqvi, Jay Butler, Huma Farid and Amitav Ghosh for early encouragement and support; Salman Toor and Komail Aijazuddin for peace and quiet; Sajjad Haider and the late Khalid Hasan for their help; Zahoor and Parveen Noon, Moni Mohsin and Shazad Ghaffar, Omar and Latifa Noman for providing rooms when they were needed; Sitwat Mohsin for sharing stories; Megan Lynch and Simon Prosser for their patience; and Donna Poppy for her timely intervention.

The author is grateful to his parents and sister for putting up with him; and to Barney Karpfinger, who has enabled this book in every way.